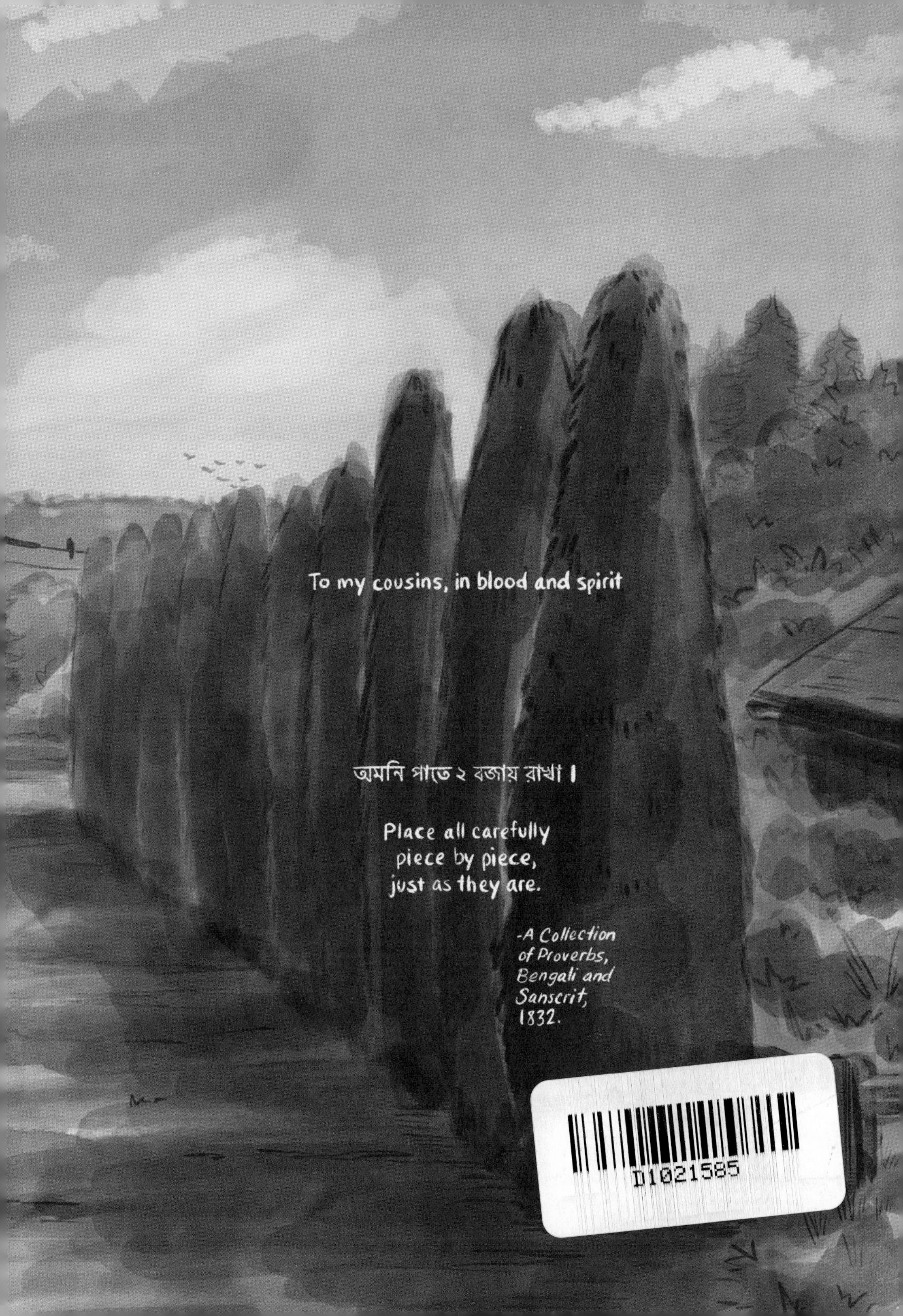

To my cousins, in blood and spirit

অমনি পাতে ২ বজায় রাখা ।

Place all carefully
piece by piece,
just as they are.

-A Collection
of Proverbs,
Bengali and
Sanscrit,
1832.

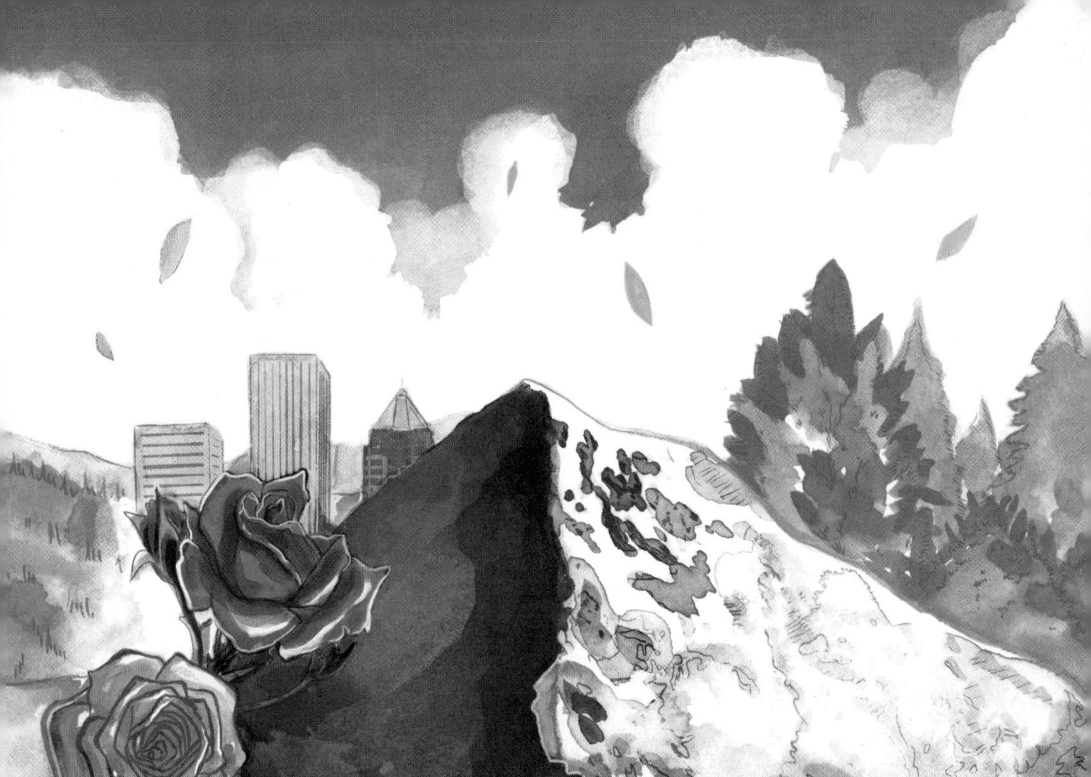
Portland, Oregon. 2002

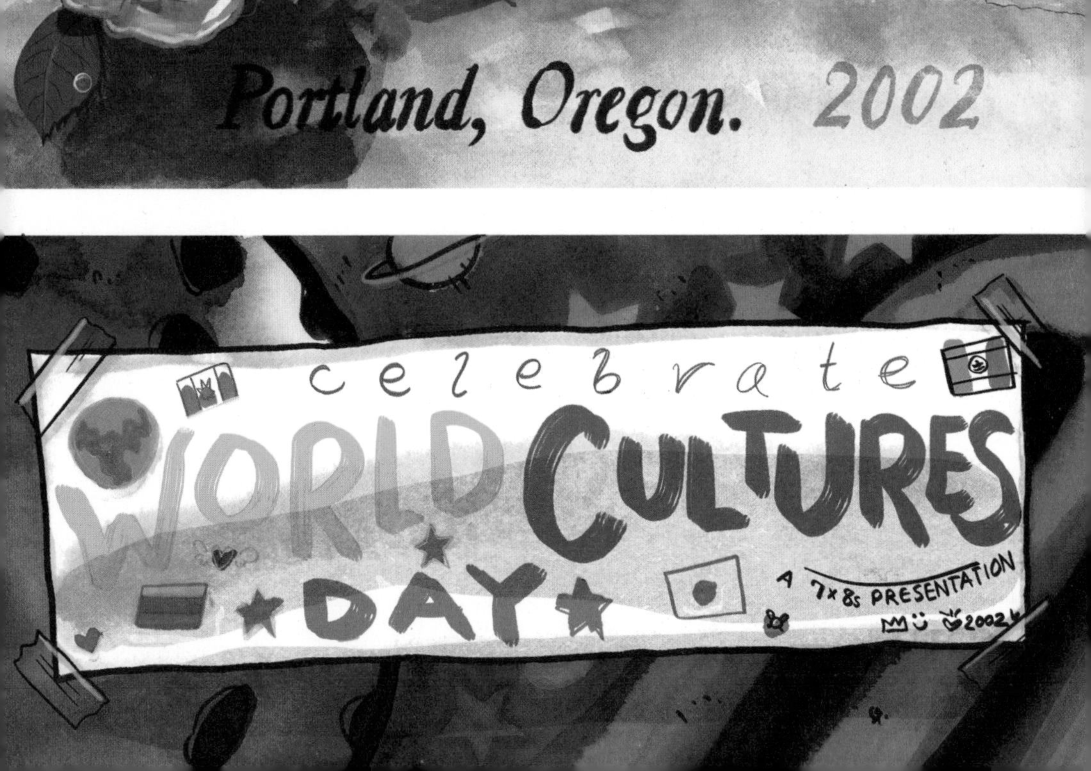
celebrate
WORLD CULTURES
DAY
A 7x8s PRESENTATION
2002

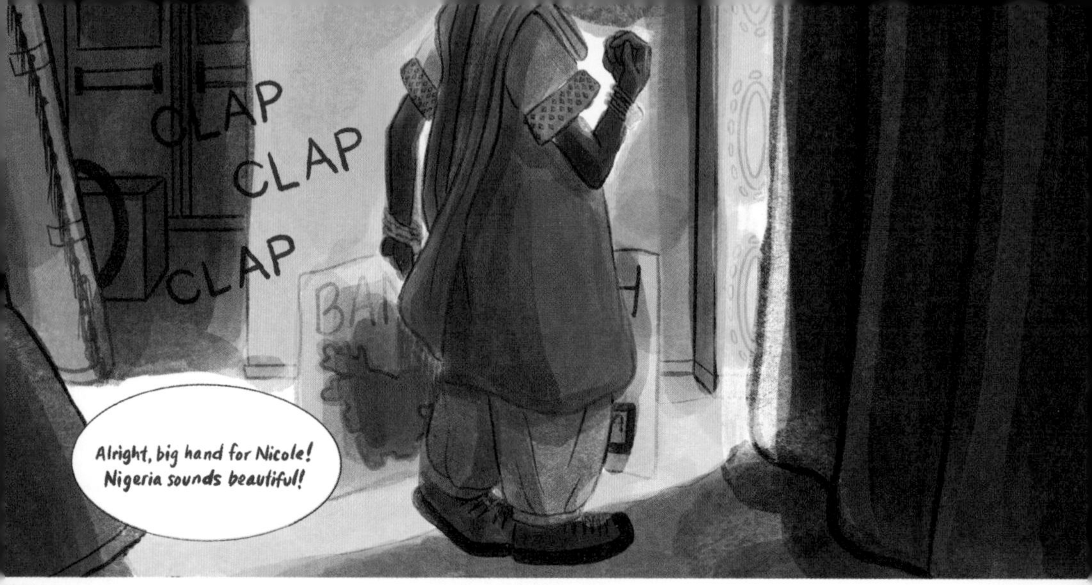
CLAP
CLAP
CLAP
Alright, big hand for Nicole! Nigeria sounds beautiful!

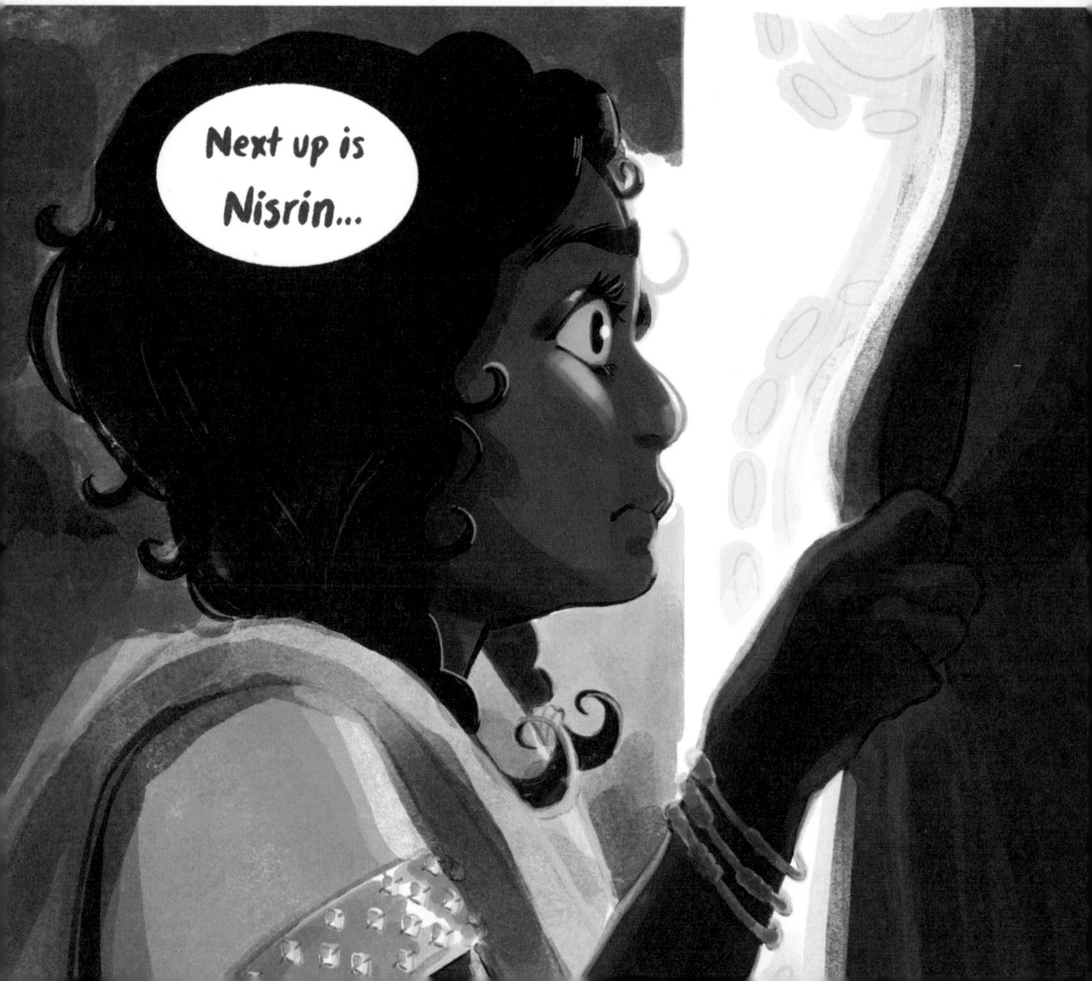
Next up is Nisrin...

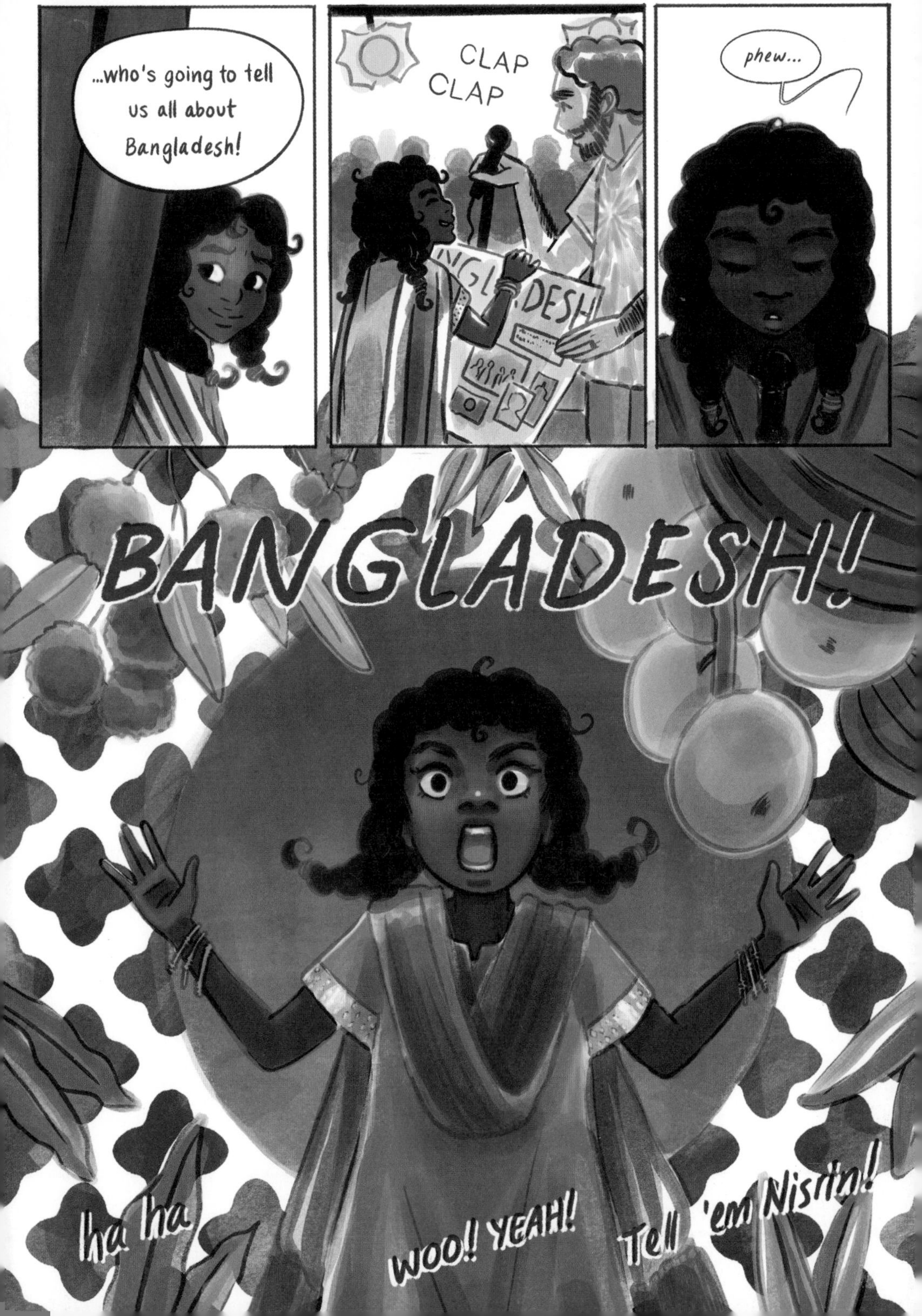
...who's going to tell us all about Bangladesh!
CLAP
CLAP
phew...
BANGLADESH!
ha ha
WOO!! YEAH!
Tell 'em Nisrin!

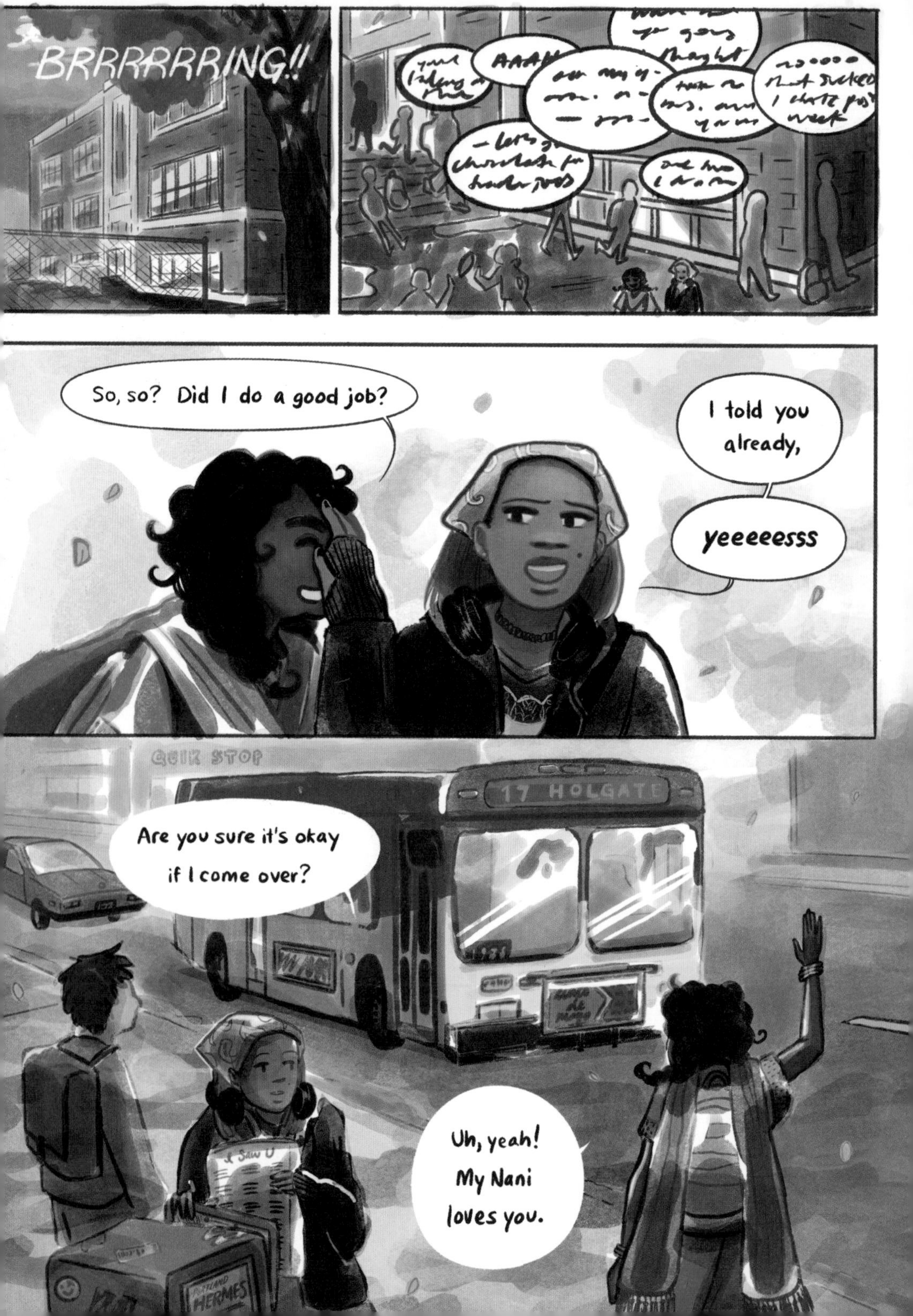
BRRRRRRING!!
So, so? Did I do a good job?
I told you already,
yeeeeesss
QUIK STOP
17 HOLGATE
Are you sure it's okay if I come over?
Uh, yeah! My Nani loves you.

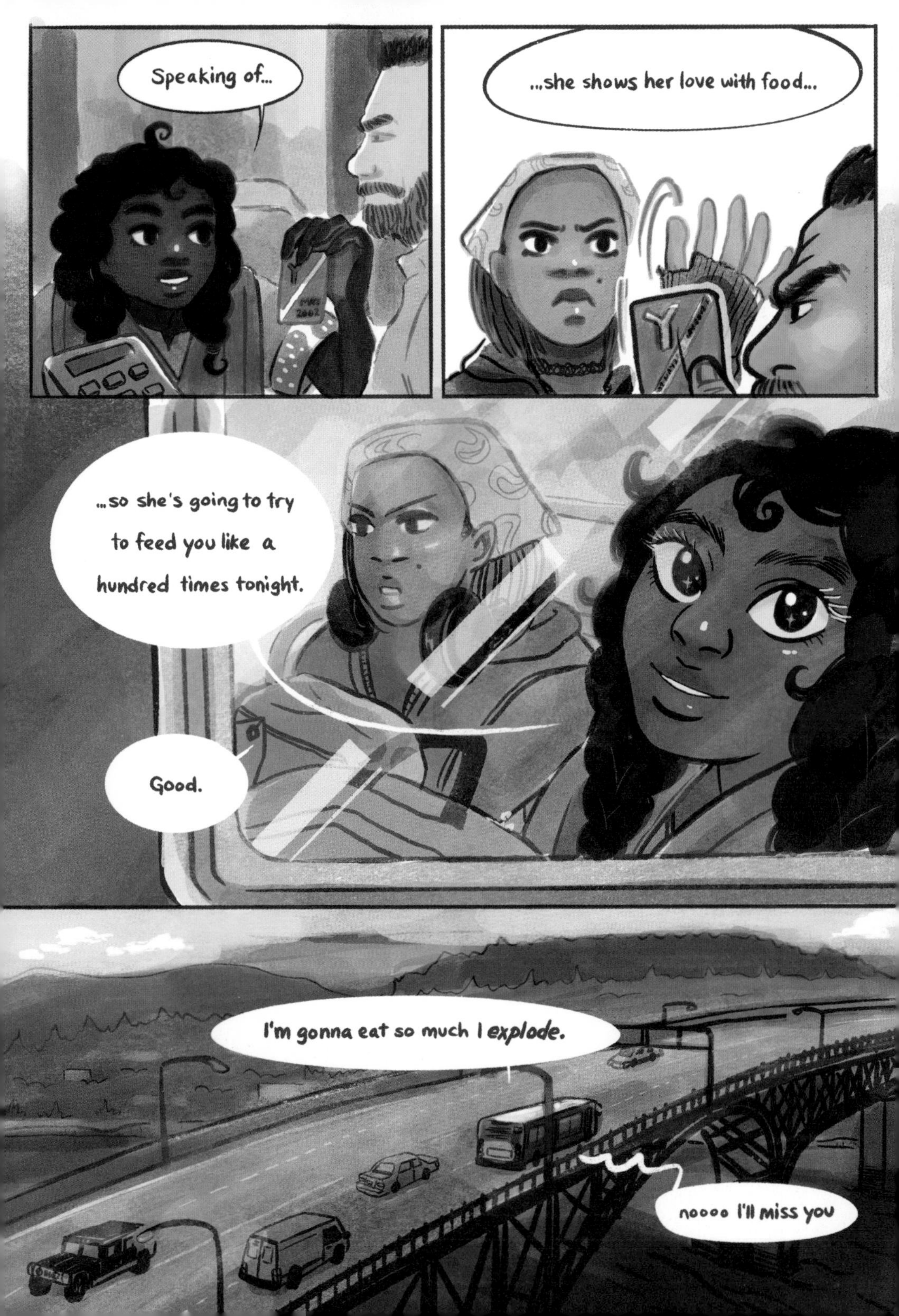
Speaking of...
...she shows her love with food...
...so she's going to try to feed you like a hundred times tonight.
Good.
I'm gonna eat so much I *explode.*
noooo I'll miss you

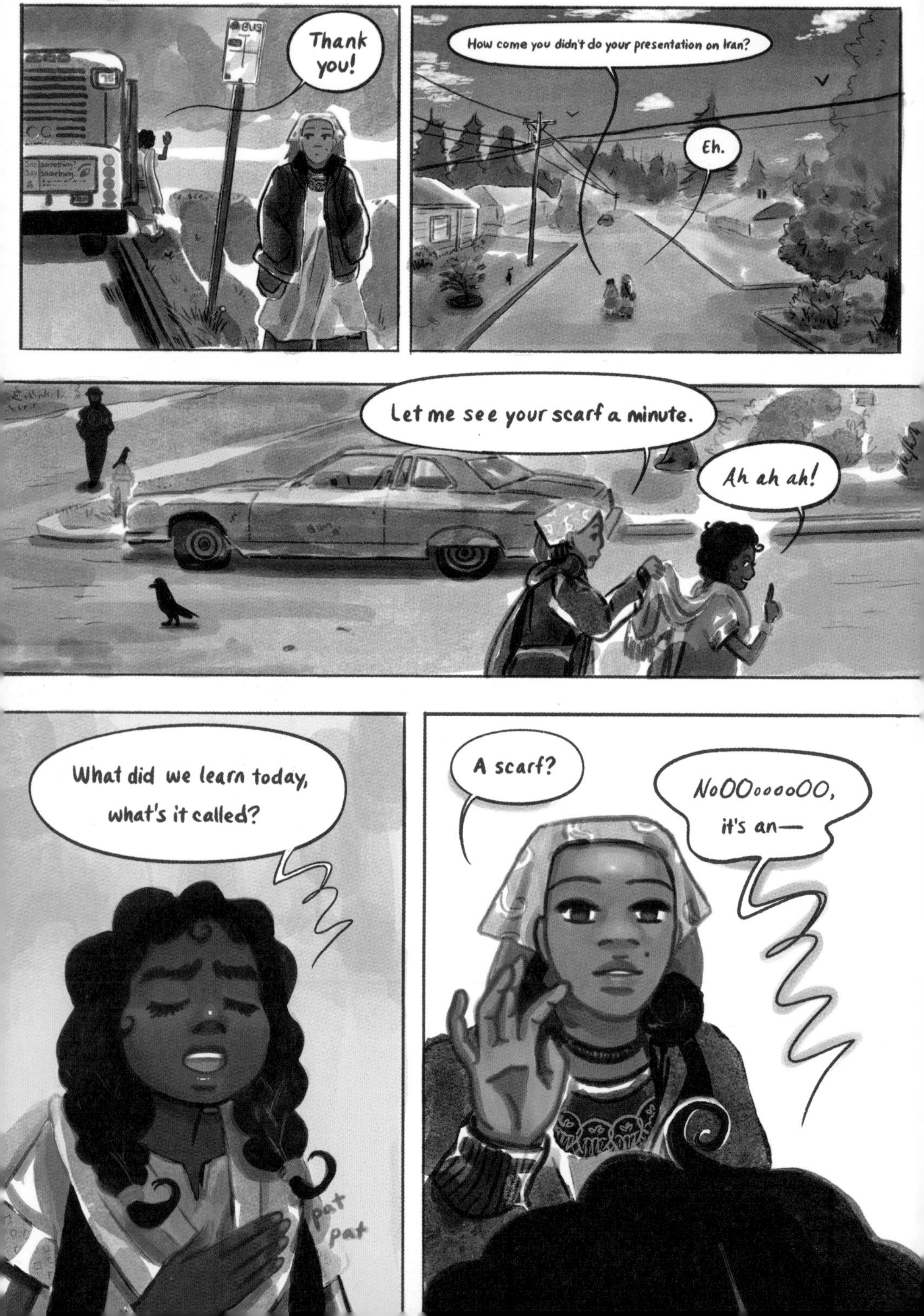
Thank you!
How come you didn't do your presentation on Iran?
Eh.
Let me see your scarf a minute.
Ah ah ah!
What did we learn today, what's it called?
pat pat
A scarf?
NoOOooooOO, it's an—

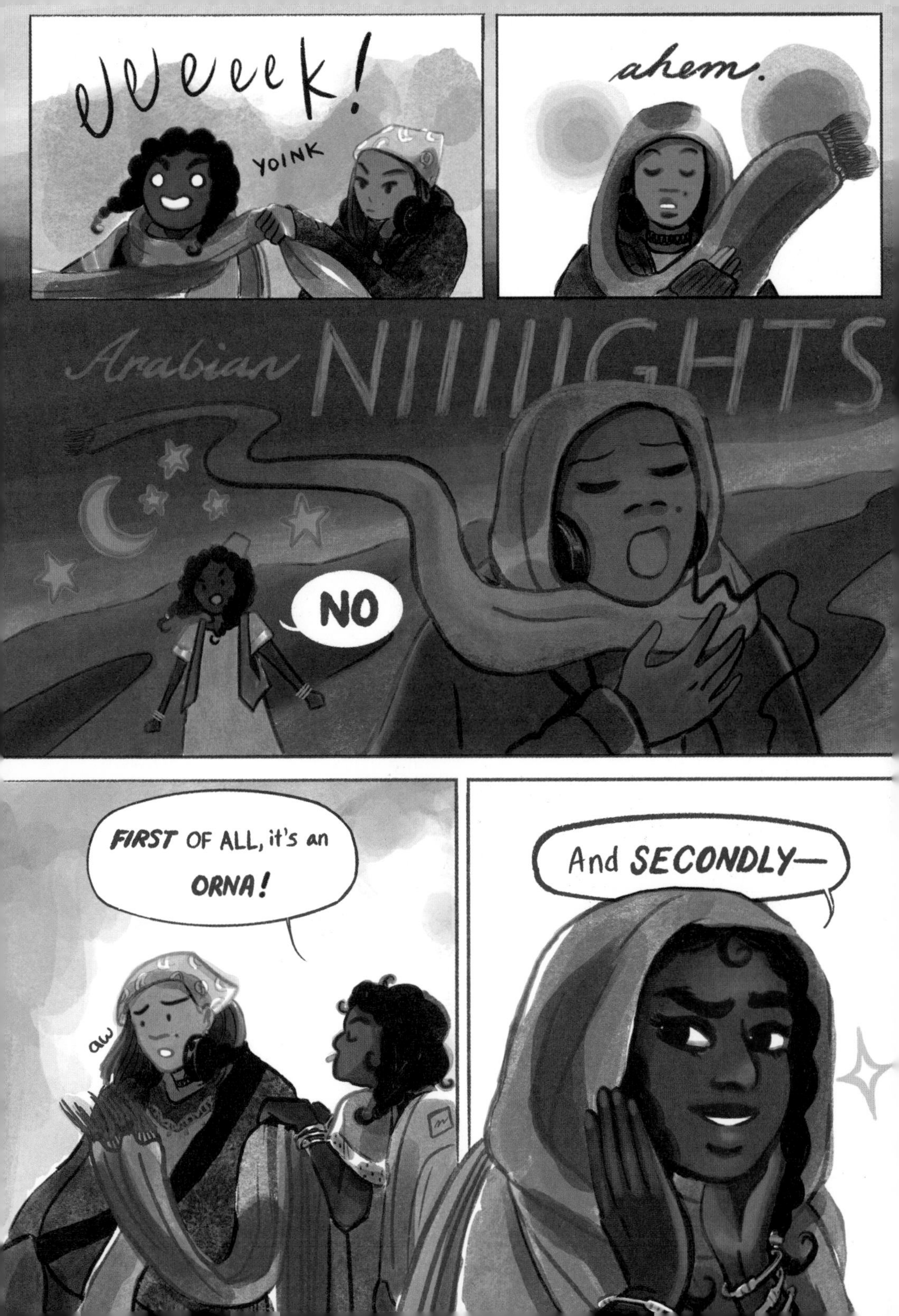

UUeeek!
YOINK
ahem.
Arabian NIIIIGHTS
NO
FIRST OF ALL, it's an ORNA!
aw
And SECONDLY—

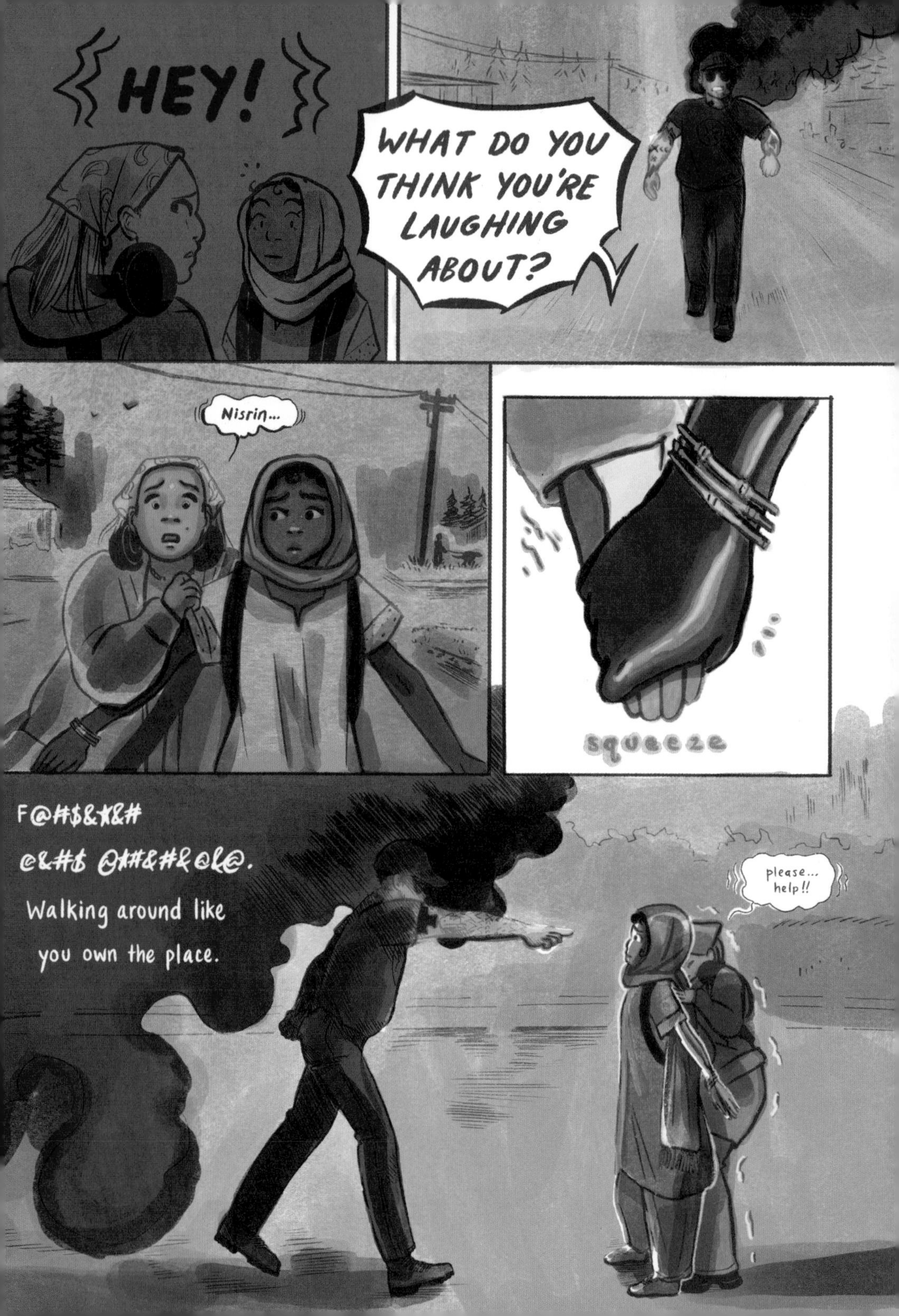
HEY!
WHAT DO YOU THINK YOU'RE LAUGHING ABOUT?
Nisrin...
squeeze
F@#$&★&#
@&#$ @##&#&@&@.
Walking around like you own the place.
please... help!!

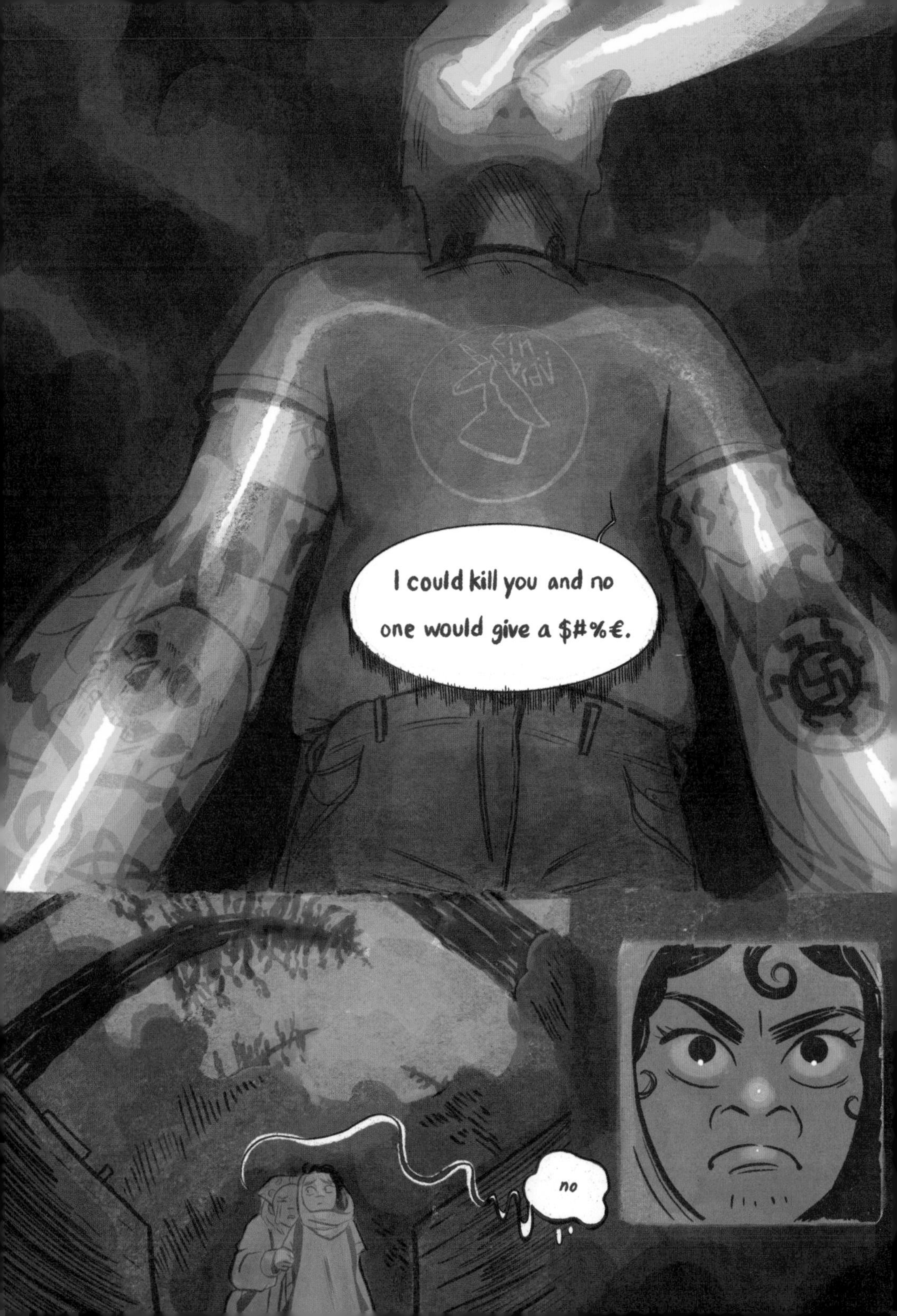
I could kill you and no one would give a $#%€.
no

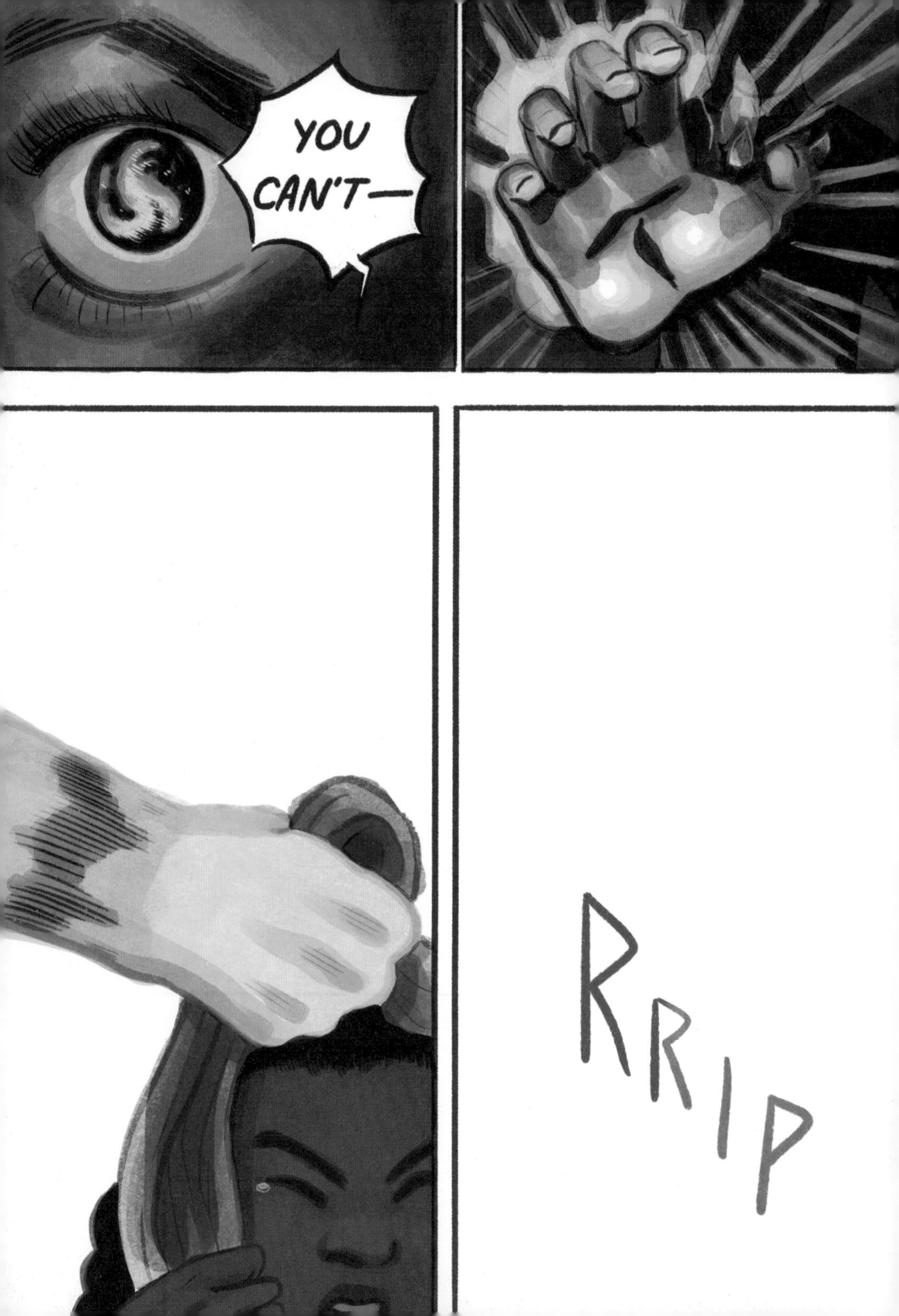
YOU CAN'T—
RRIP

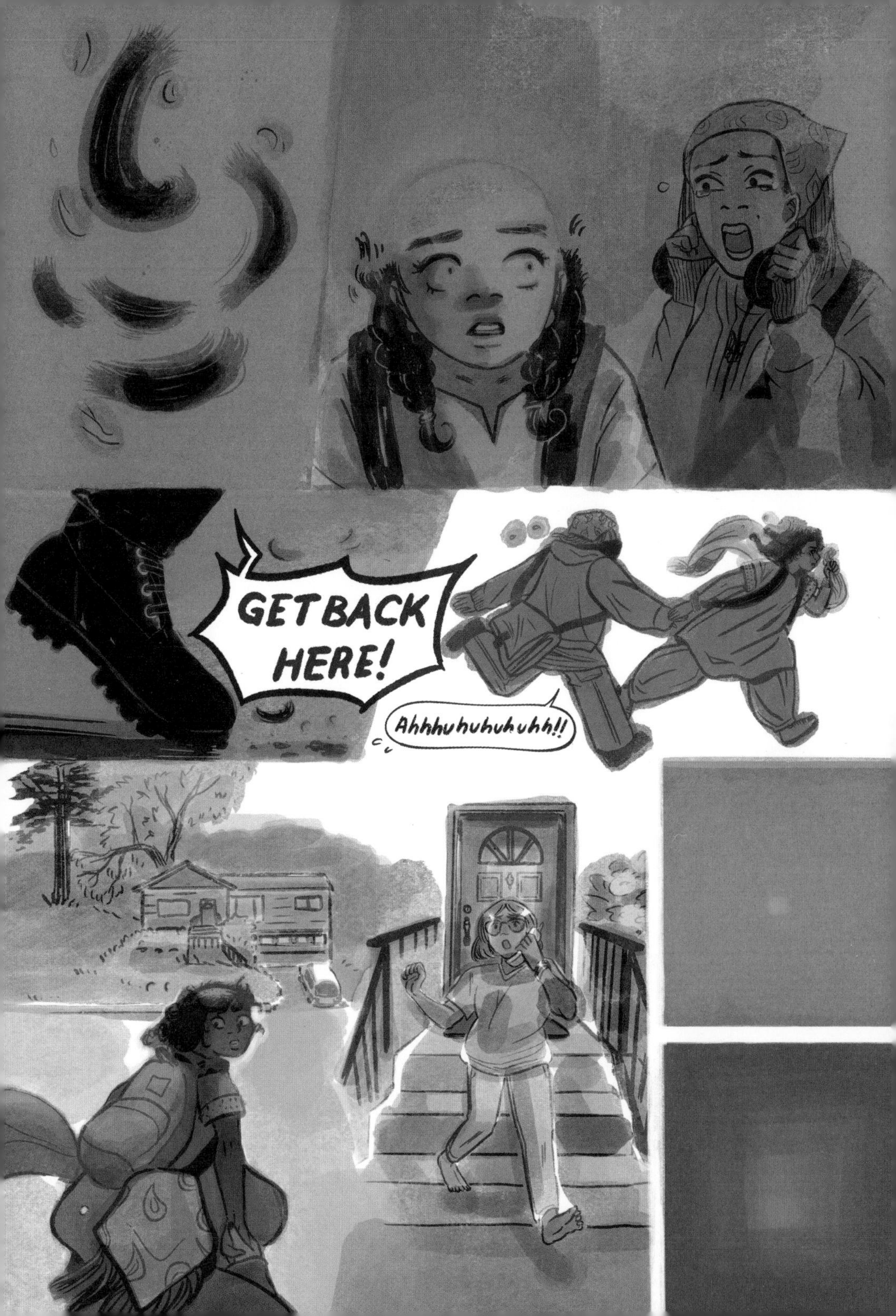
GET BACK HERE!
Ahhhuhuhuhuhh!!

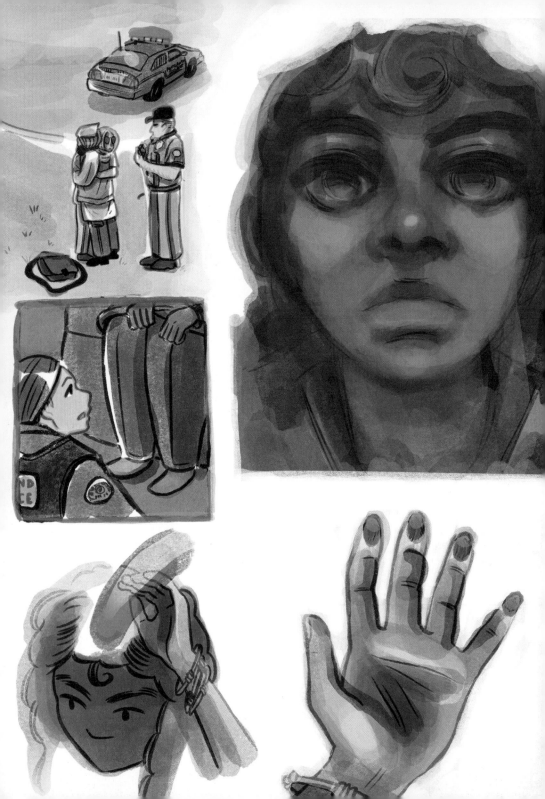

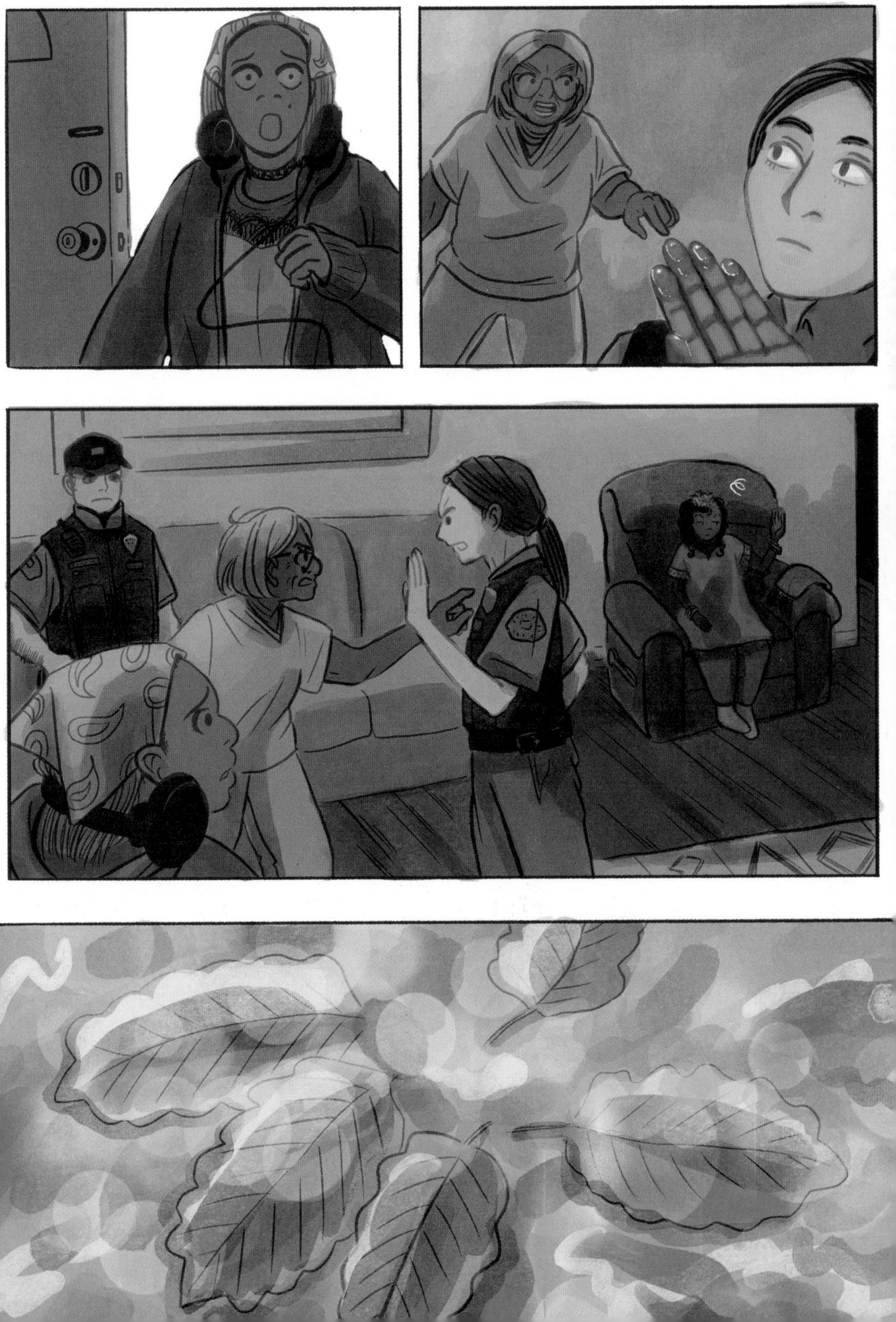

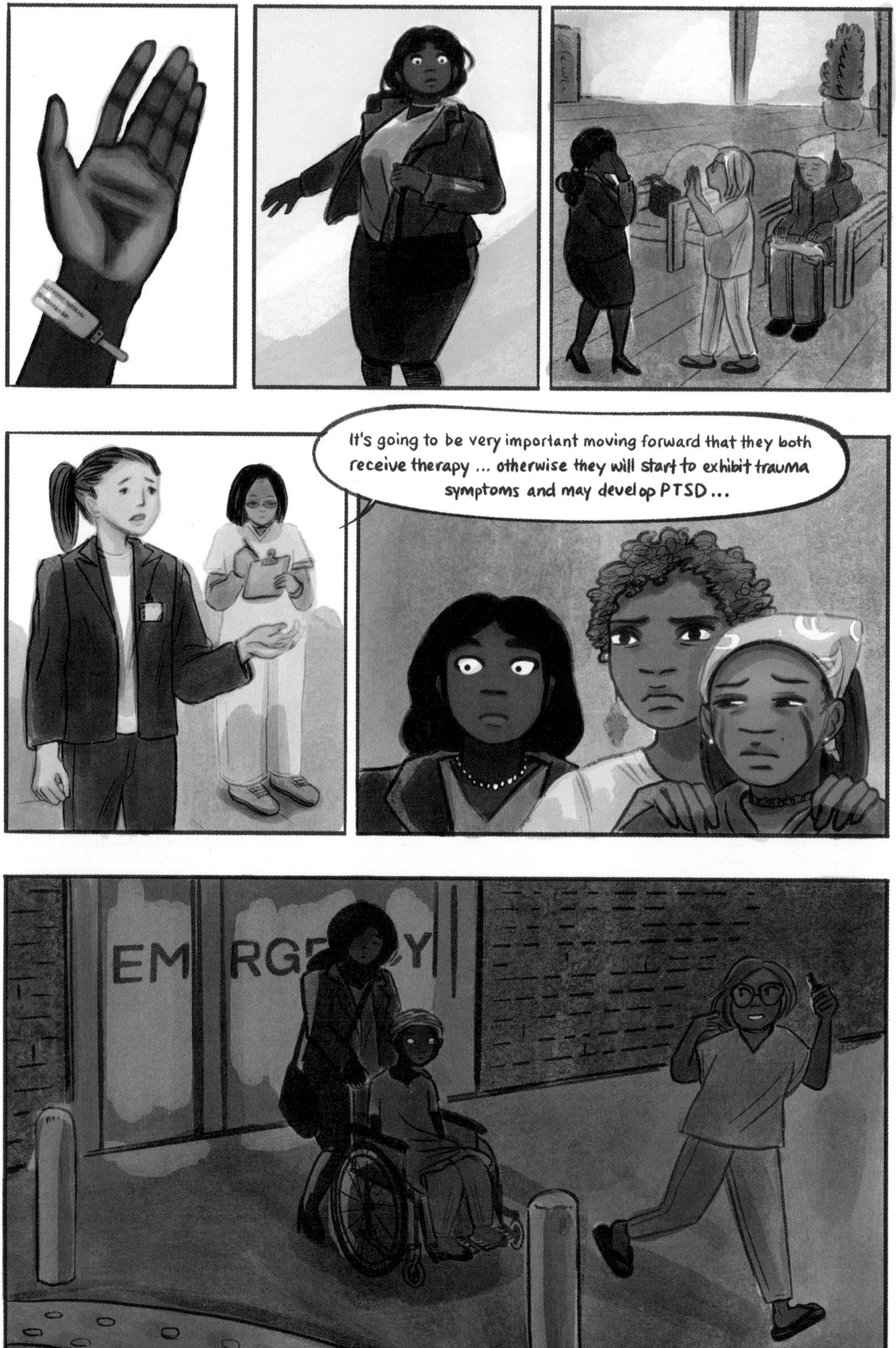
It's going to be very important moving forward that they both receive therapy ... otherwise they will start to exhibit trauma symptoms and may develop PTSD ...
EM RGE Y

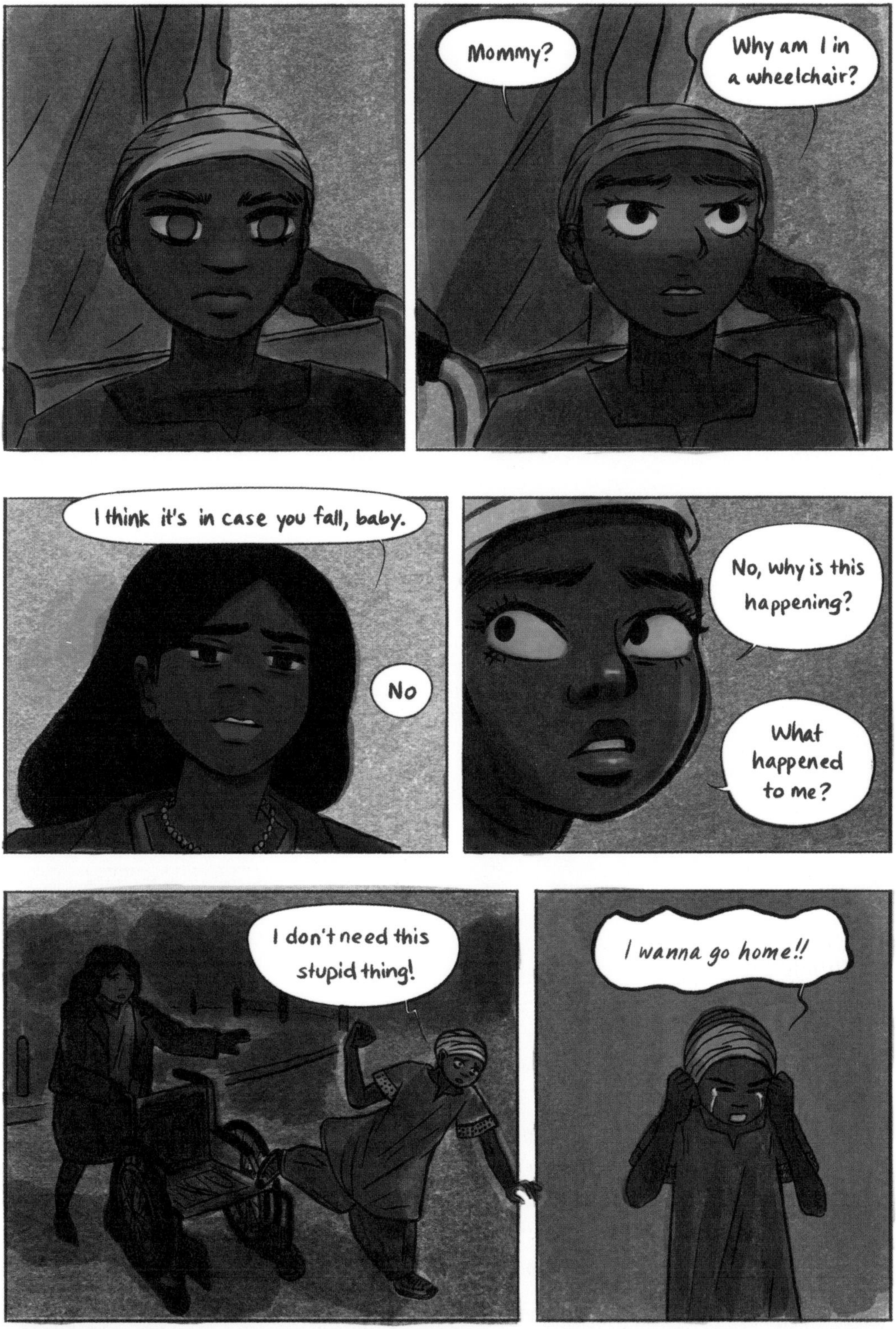
Mommy?
Why am I in a wheelchair?
I think it's in case you fall, baby.
No
No, why is this happening?
What happened to me?
I don't need this stupid thing!
I wanna go home!!

I don't wanna go to therapy!

Too bad, you gotta.

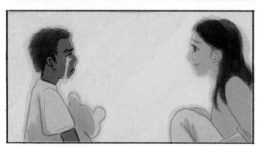

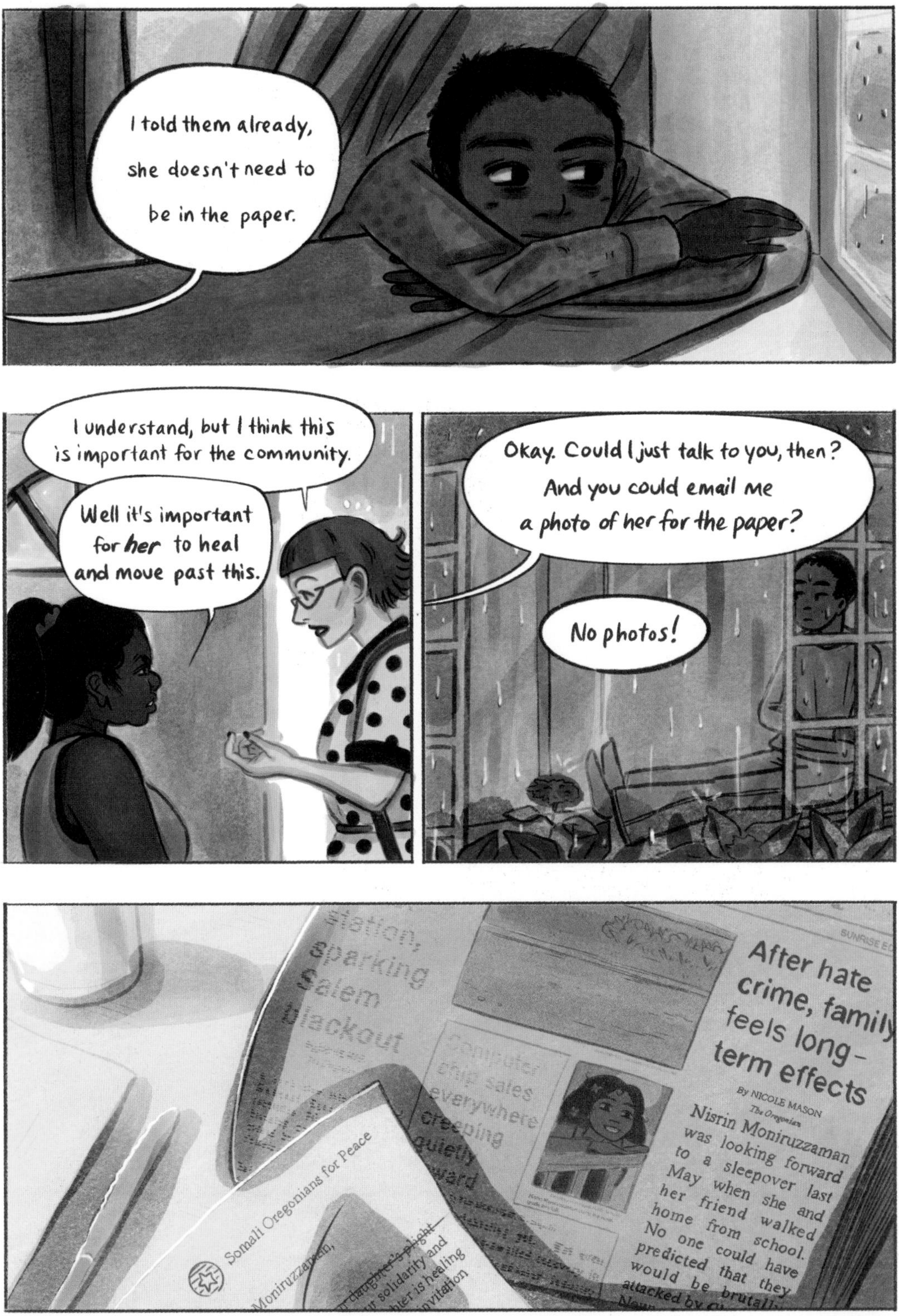
I told them already, she doesn't need to be in the paper.
I understand, but I think this is important for the community.
Well it's important for *her* to heal and move past this.
Okay. Could I just talk to you, then? And you could email me a photo of her for the paper?
No photos!
station, sparking Salem blackout
Computer chip sales everywhere creeping quietly
SUNRISE
After hate crime, family feels long-term effects
By NICOLE MASON
The Oregonian
Nisrin Moniruzzaman was looking forward to a sleepover last May when she and her friend walked home from school. No one could have predicted that they would be brutally attacked by
Somali Oregonians for Peace
Moniruzzaman,
daughter's plight
solidarity and
is healing
invitation

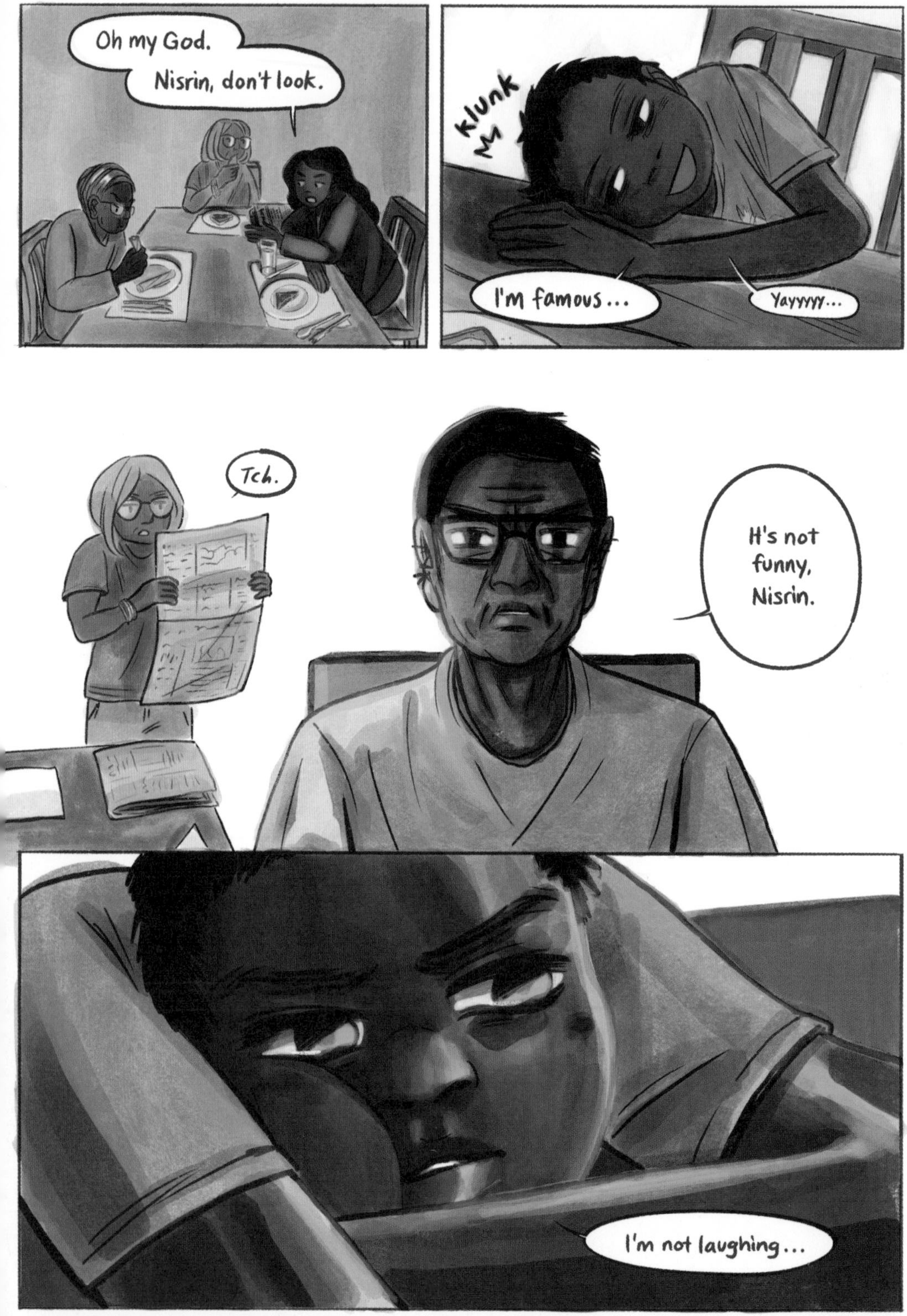
Oh my God.
Nisrin, don't look.
klunk
I'm famous...
Yayyyyy...
Tch.
It's not funny, Nisrin.
I'm not laughing...

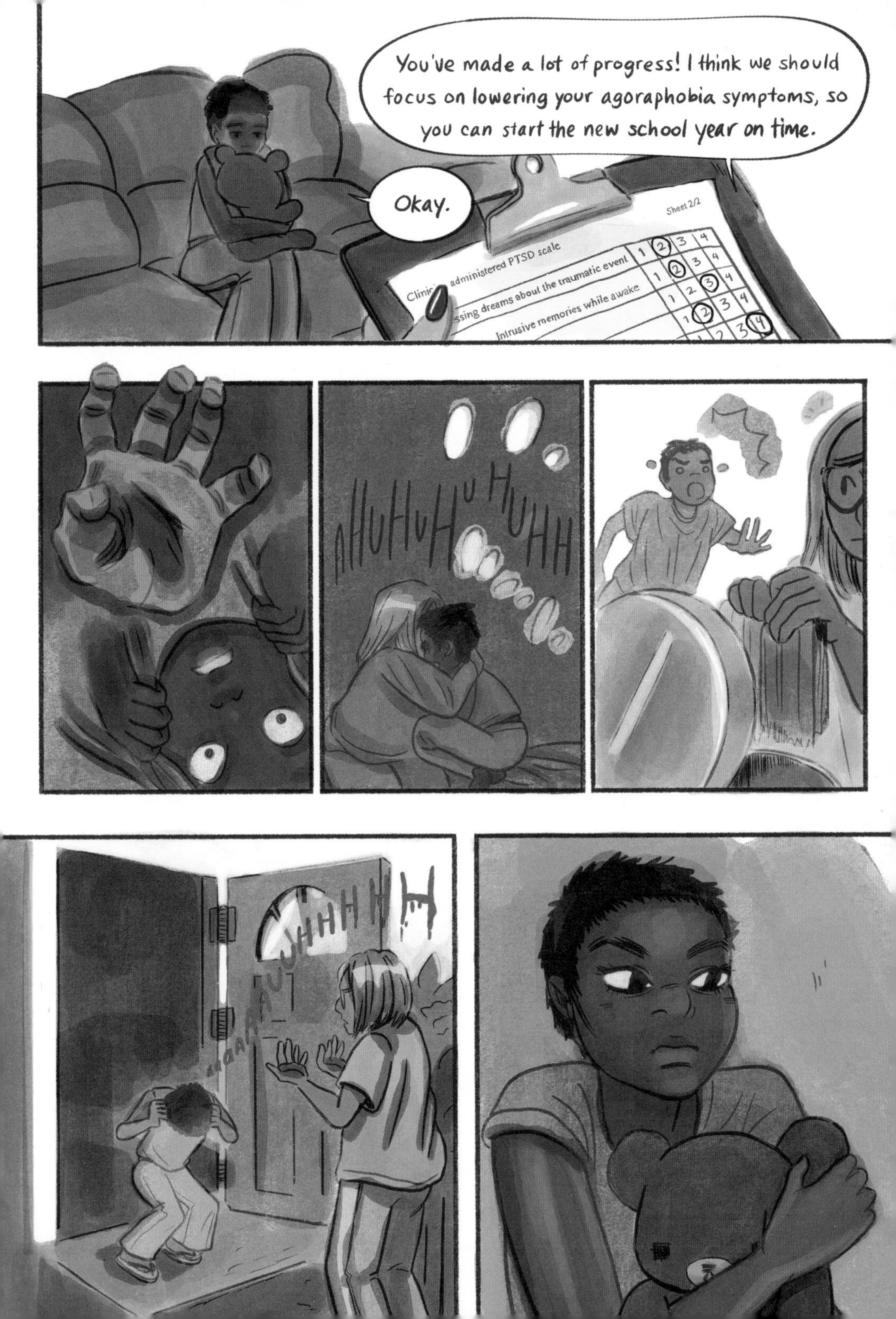

You've made a lot of progress! I think we should focus on lowering your agoraphobia symptoms, so you can start the new school year on time.
Okay.
Sheet 2/2
administered PTSD scale
dreams about the traumatic event
Intrusive memories while awake

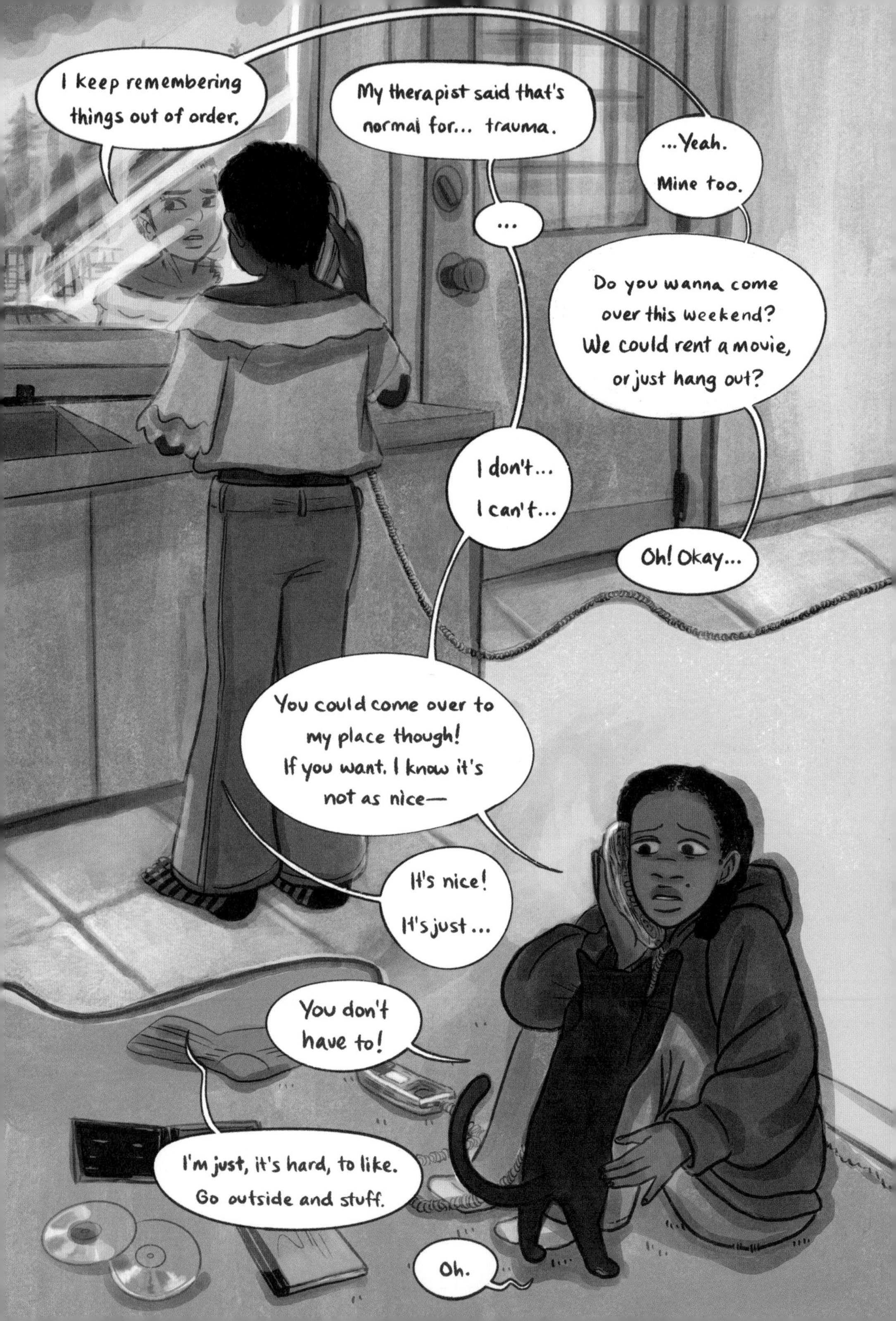
I keep remembering things out of order.
My therapist said that's normal for... trauma.
...Yeah. Mine too.
...
Do you wanna come over this weekend? We could rent a movie, or just hang out?
I don't... I can't...
Oh! Okay...
You could come over to my place though! If you want. I know it's not as nice—
It's nice! It's just...
You don't have to!
I'm just, it's hard, to like. Go outside and stuff.
Oh.

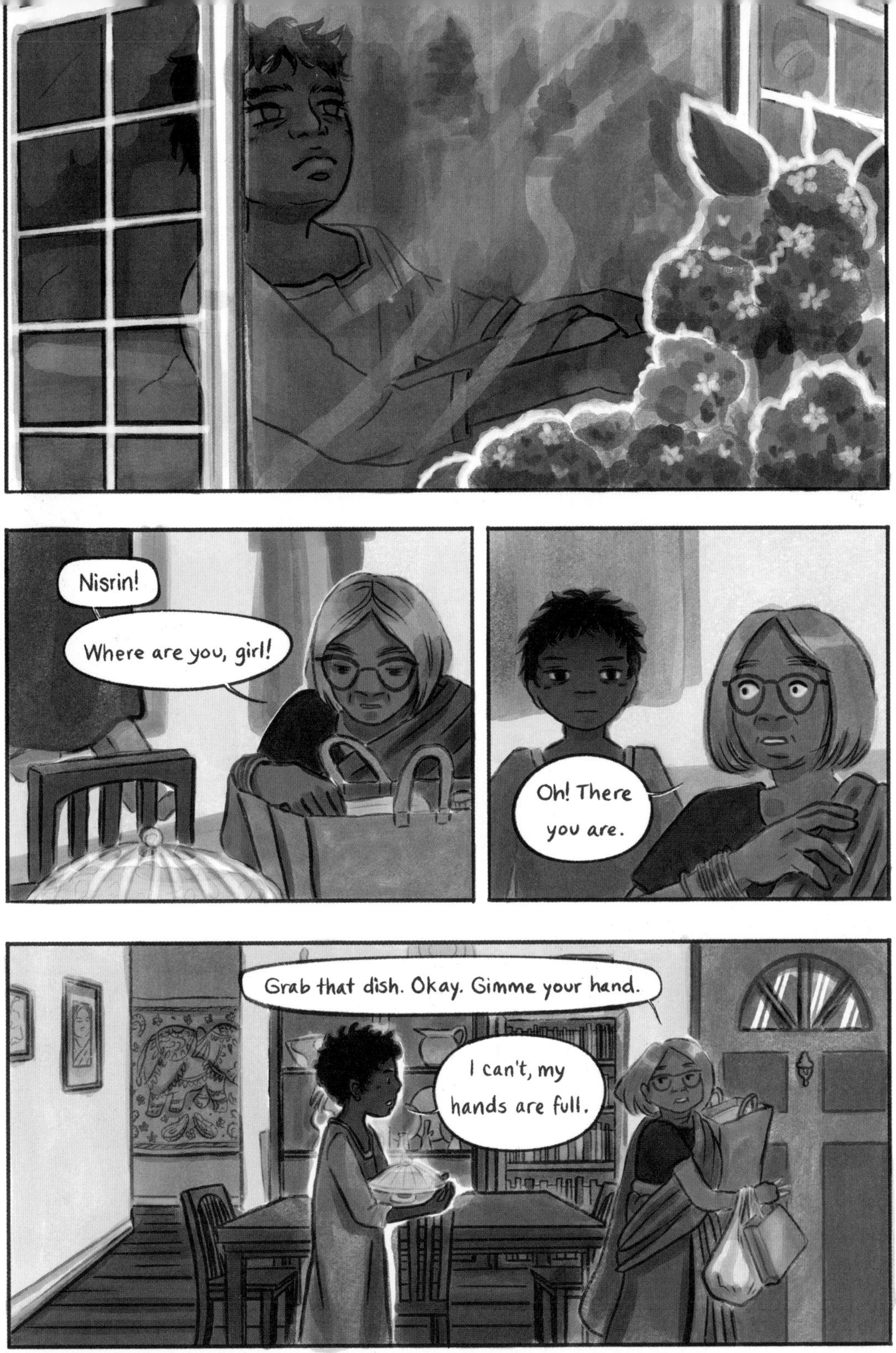
Nisrin!
Where are you, girl!
Oh! There you are.
Grab that dish. Okay. Gimme your hand.
I can't, my hands are full.

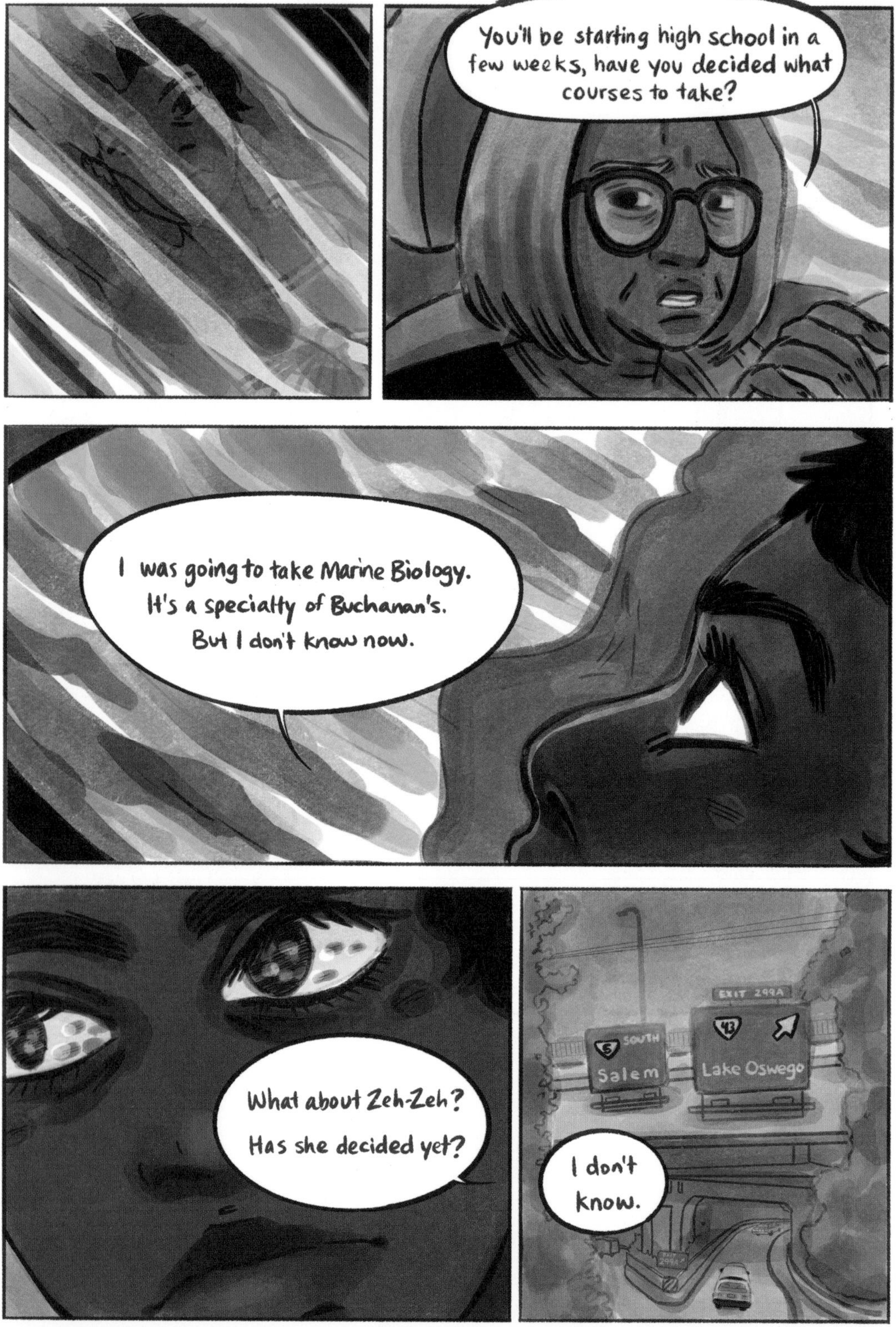
You'll be starting high school in a few weeks, have you decided what courses to take?
I was going to take Marine Biology. It's a specialty of Buchanan's. But I don't know now.
What about Zeh-Zeh? Has she decided yet?
EXIT 299A
5 SOUTH
Salem
43
Lake Oswego
I don't know.

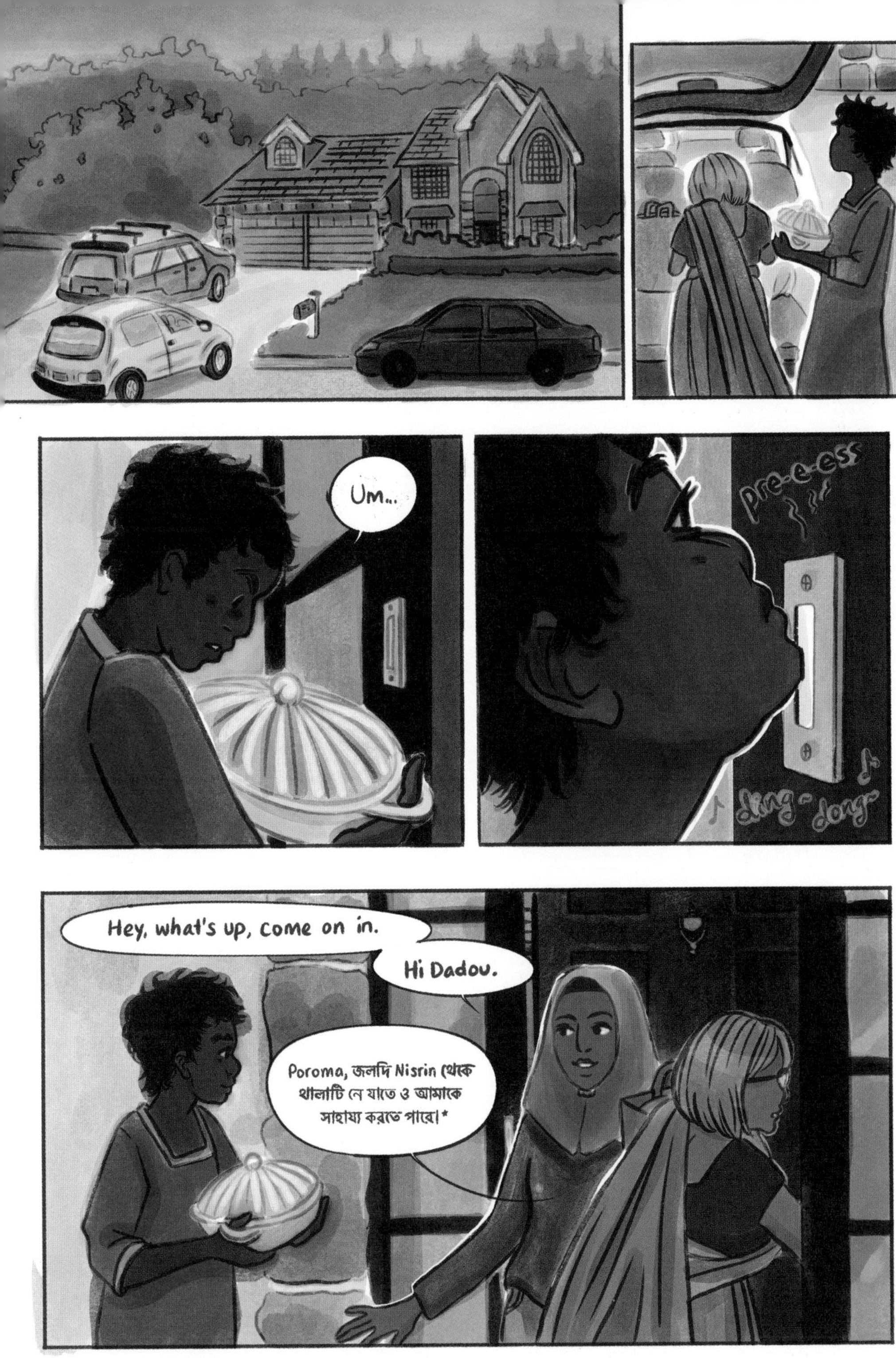
Um...
pre-e-ess
ding-dong-
Hey, what's up, come on in.
Hi Dadou.
Poroma, জলদি Nisrin থেকে থালাটি নে যাতে ও আমাকে সাহায্য করতে পারে।*

*Poroma, grab that dish from Nisrin quickly please, so she can help me.

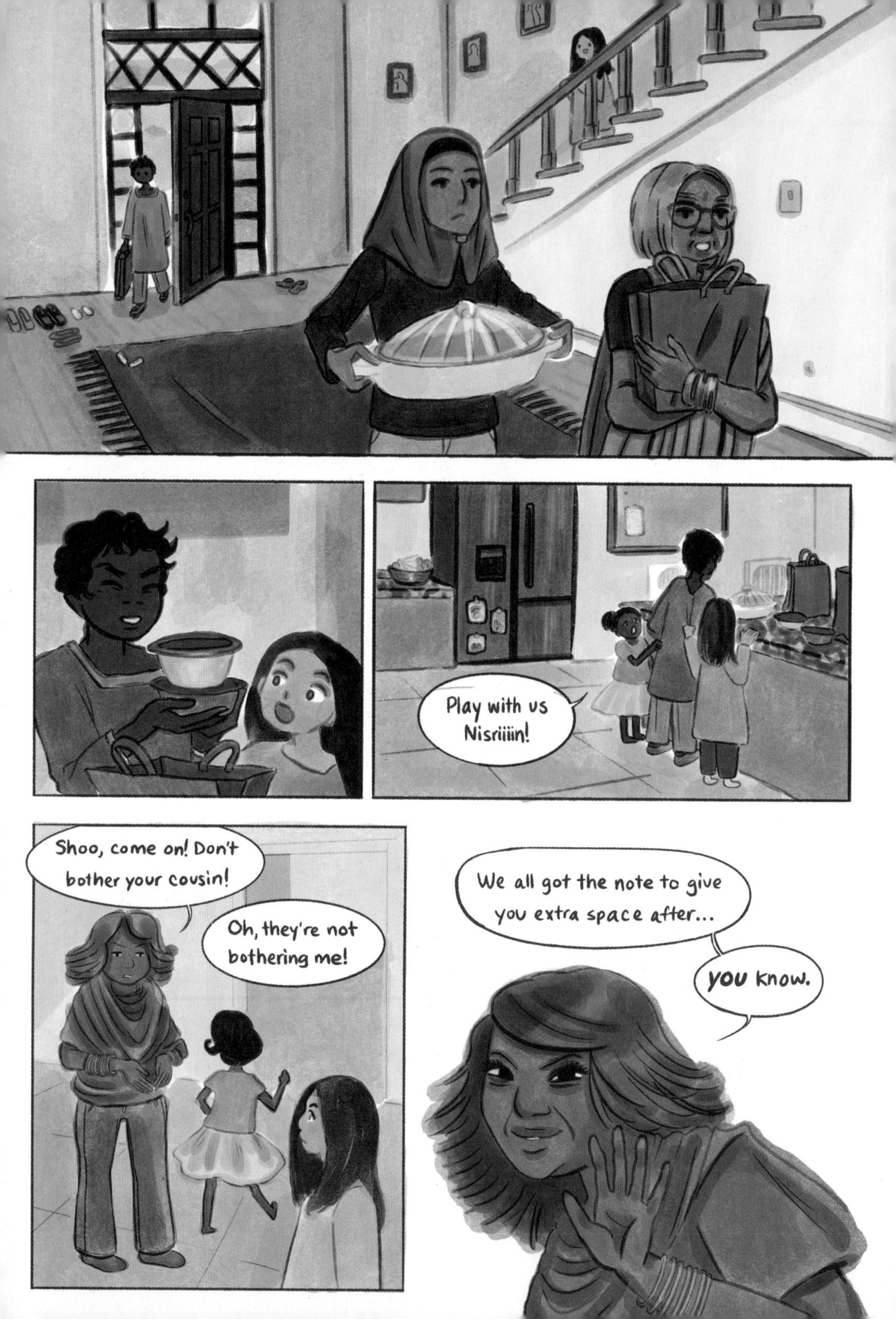
Play with us Nisriiiin!
Shoo, come on! Don't bother your cousin!
Oh, they're not bothering me!
We all got the note to give you extra space after...
YOU know.

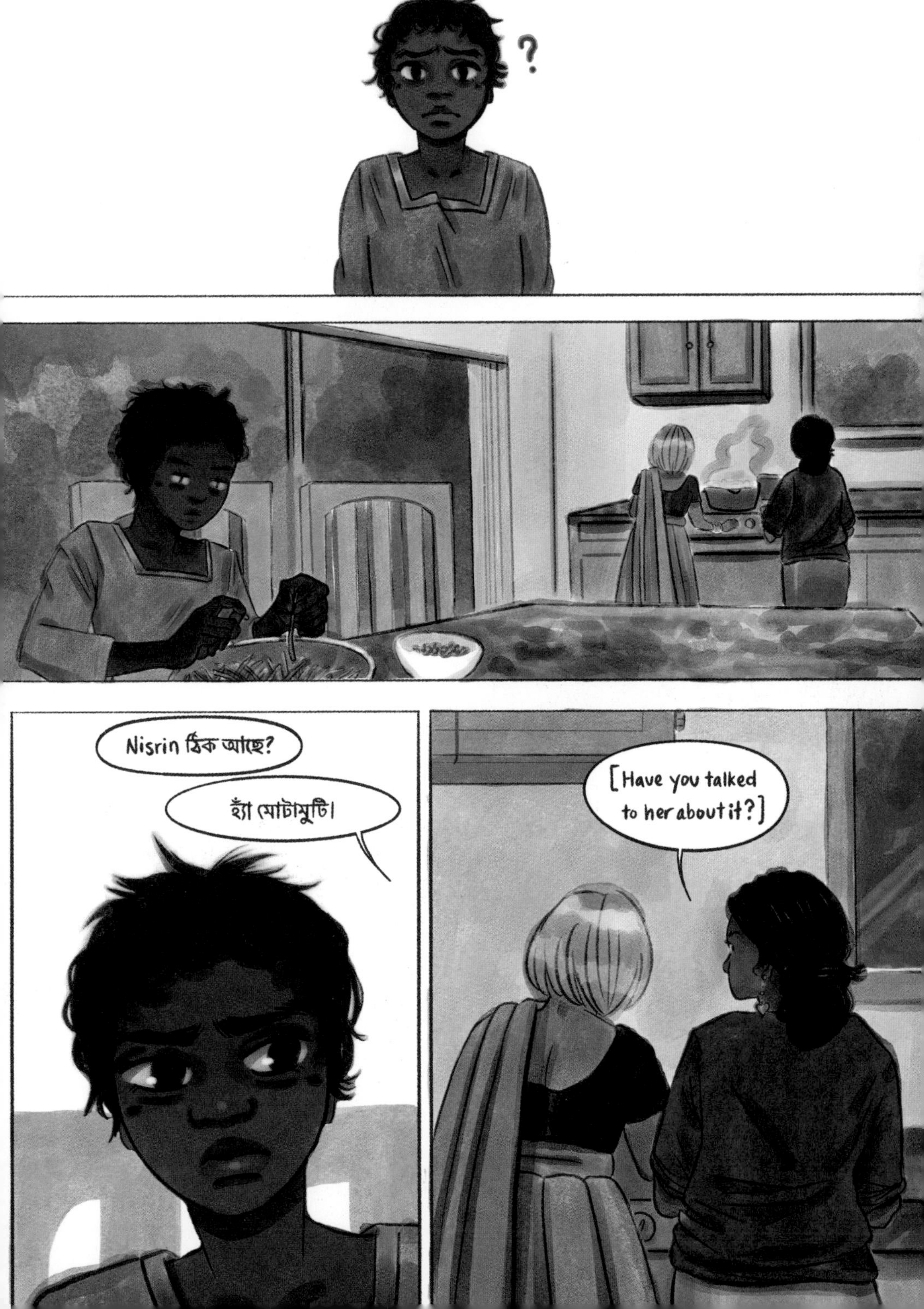
?
Nisrin ঠিক আছে?
হ্যাঁ মোটামুটি।
[Have you talked to her about it?]

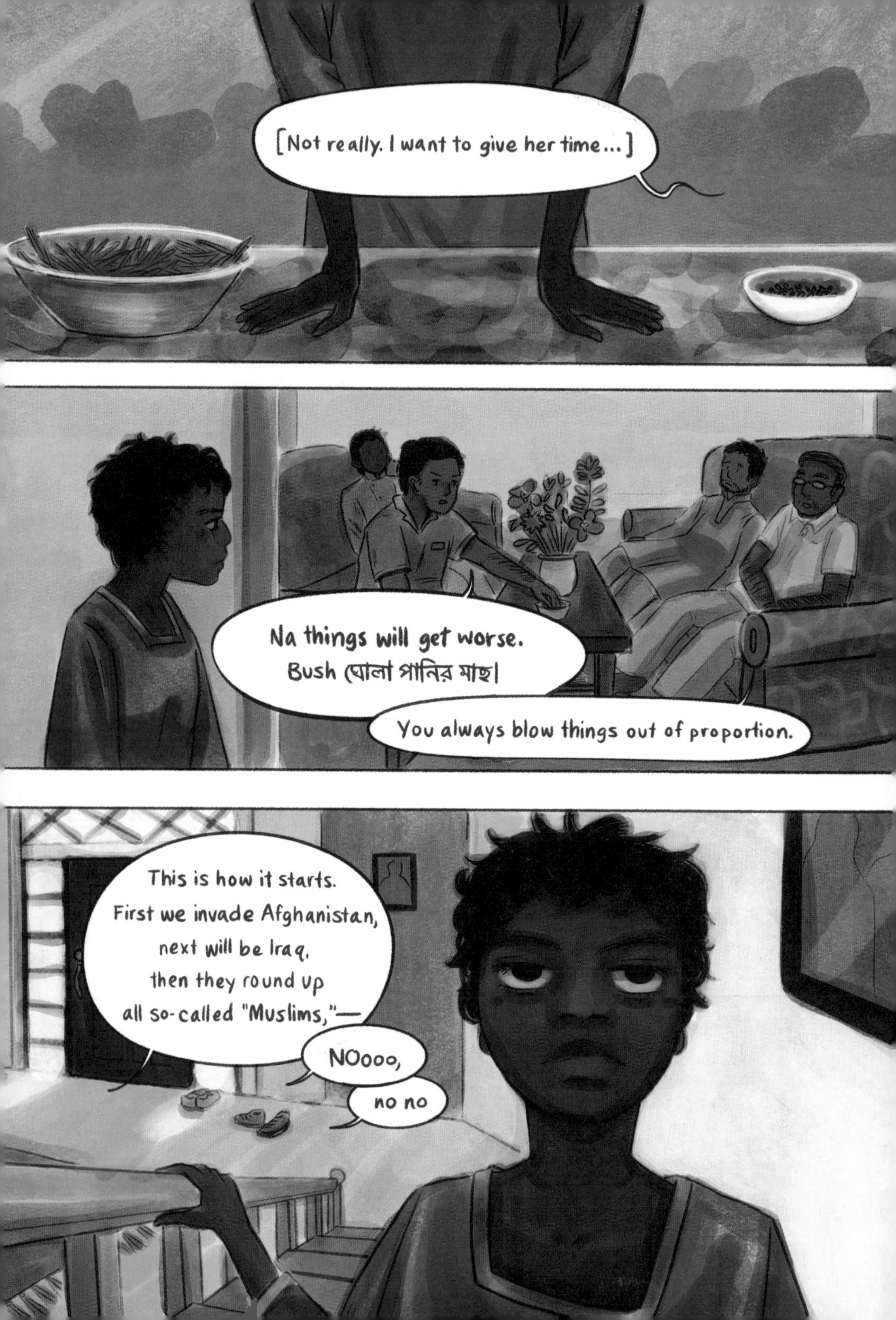
[Not really. I want to give her time...]
Na things will get worse.
Bush ঘোলা পানির মাছ।
You always blow things out of proportion.
This is how it starts. First we invade Afghanistan, next will be Iraq, then they round up all so-called "Muslims,"—
NOooo,
no no

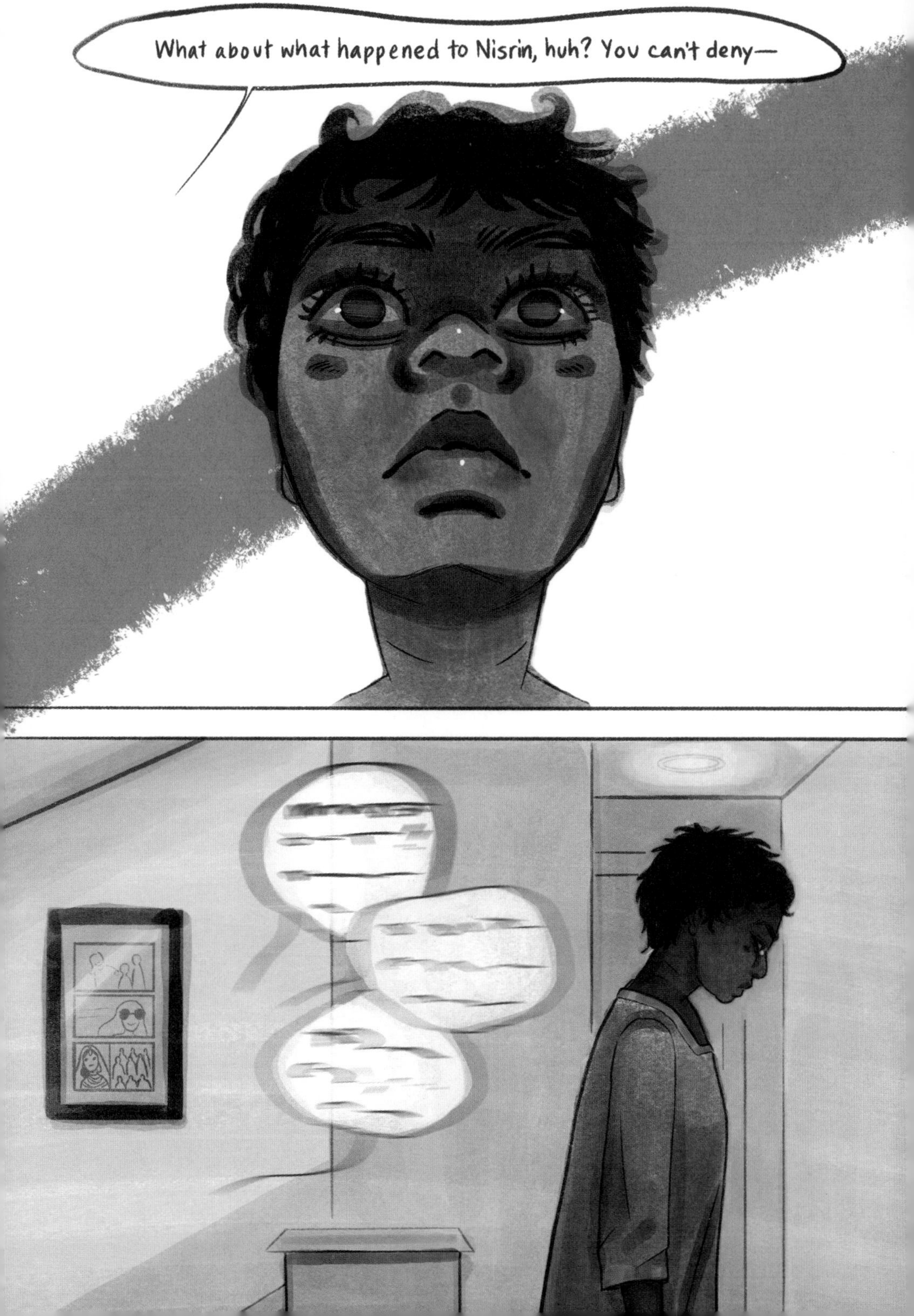
What about what happened to Nisrin, huh? You can't deny—

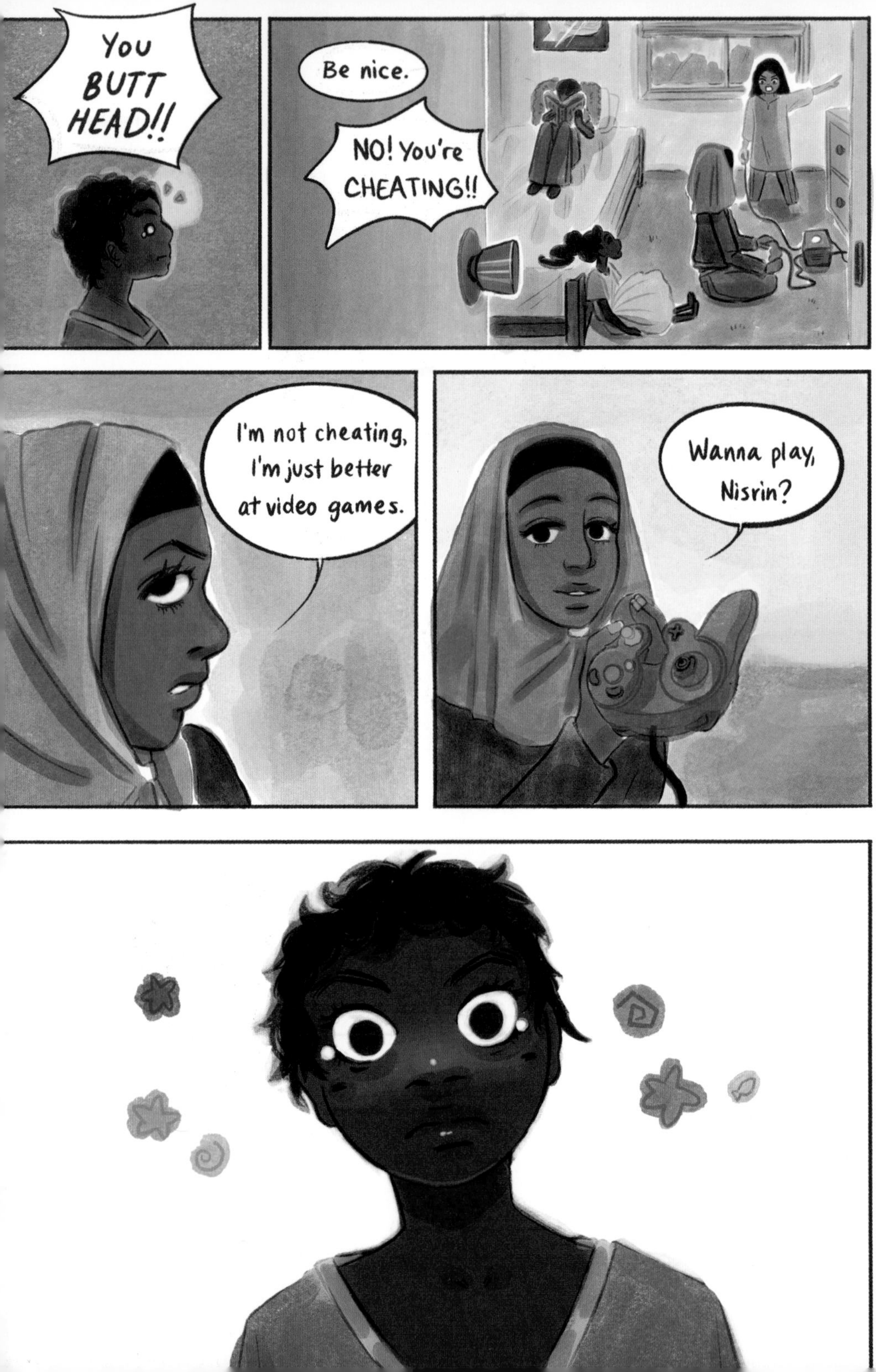
You BUTT HEAD!!
Be nice.
NO! You're CHEATING!!
I'm not cheating, I'm just better at video games.
Wanna play, Nisrin?

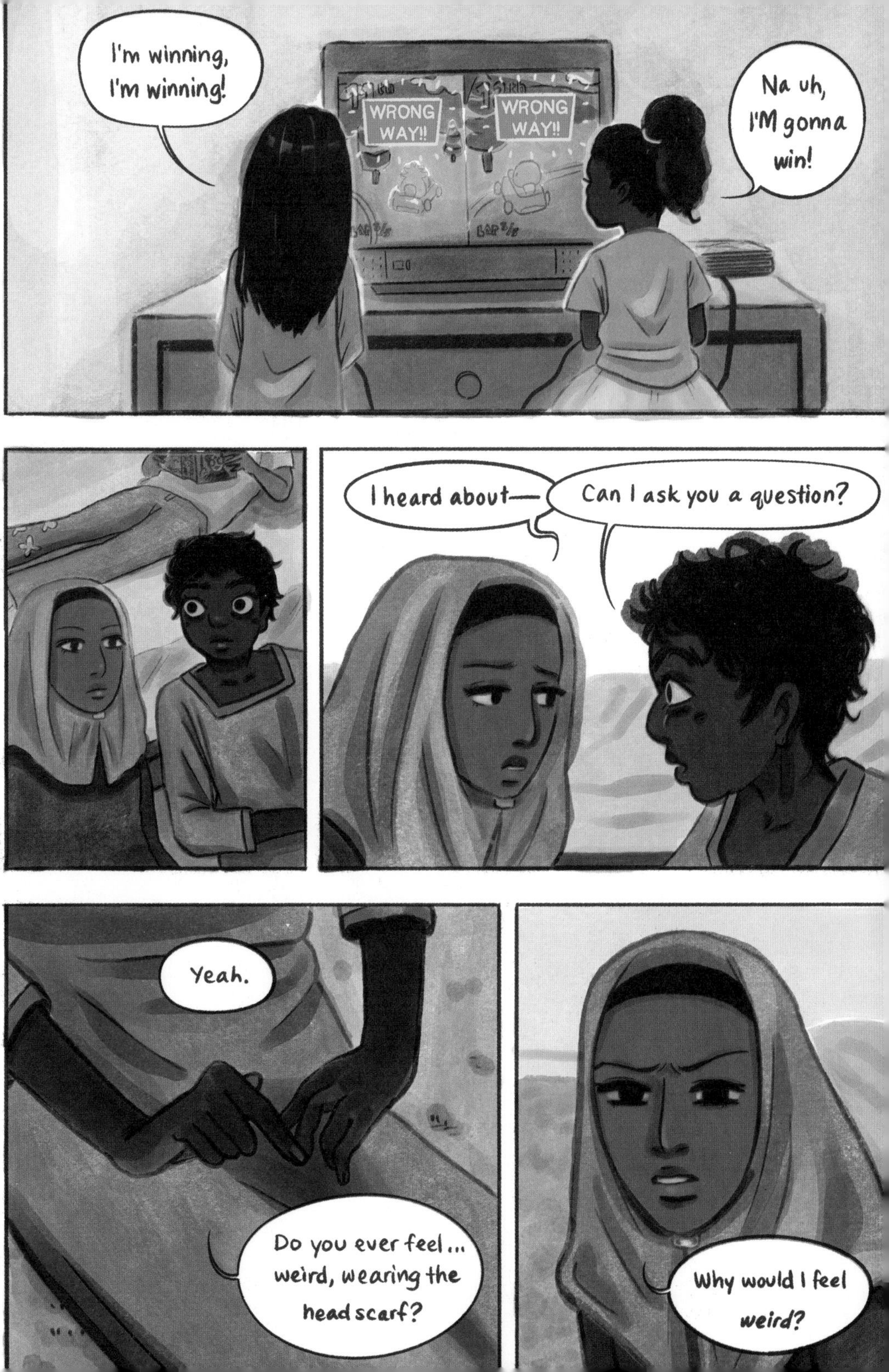
I'm winning, I'm winning!
WRONG WAY!!
WRONG WAY!!
Na uh, I'M gonna win!
I heard about—
Can I ask you a question?
Yeah.
Do you ever feel... weird, wearing the head scarf?
Why would I feel weird?

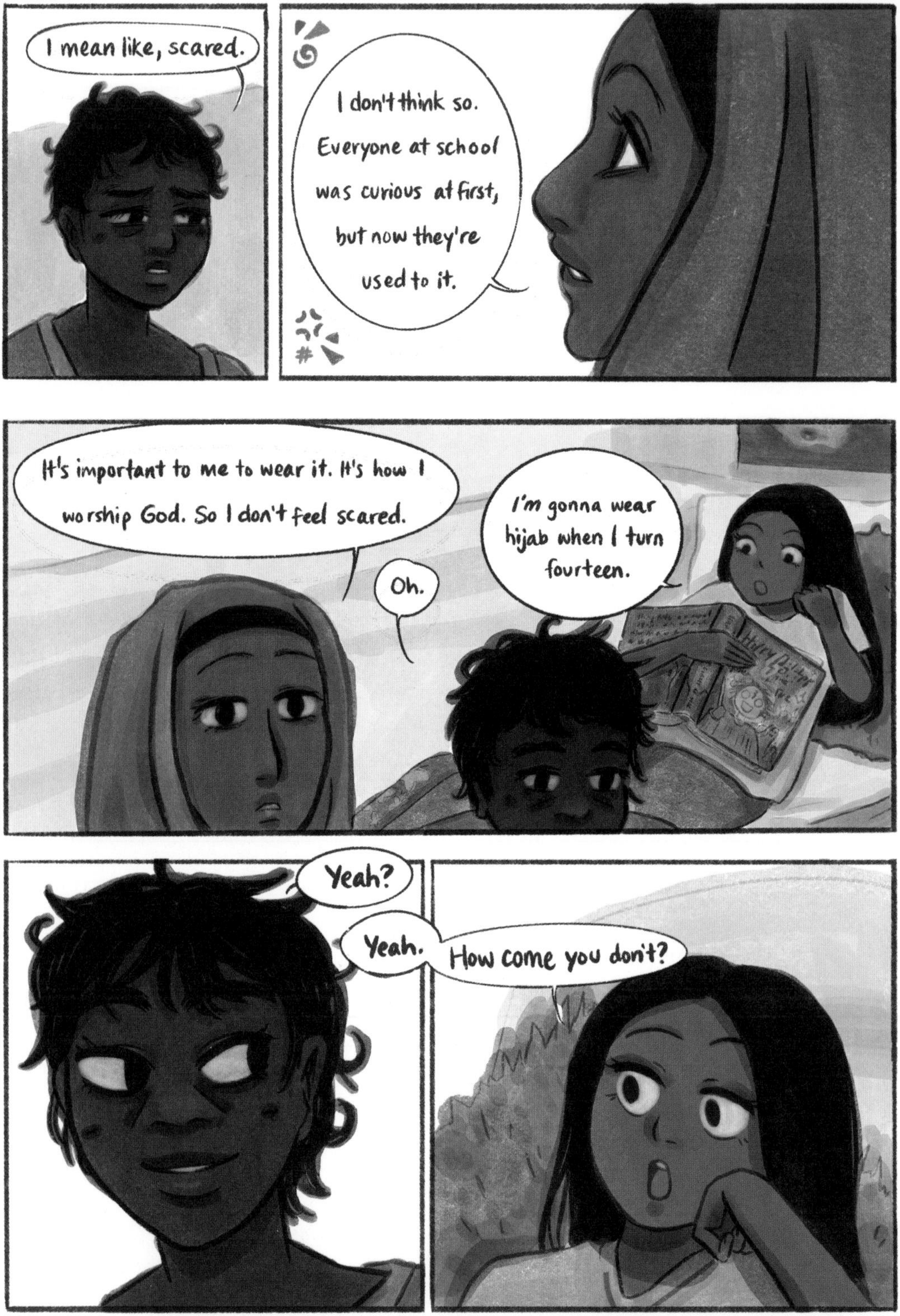
I mean like, scared.
I don't think so. Everyone at school was curious at first, but now they're used to it.
It's important to me to wear it. It's how I worship God. So I don't feel scared.
Oh.
I'm gonna wear hijab when I turn fourteen.
Yeah?
Yeah.
How come you don't?

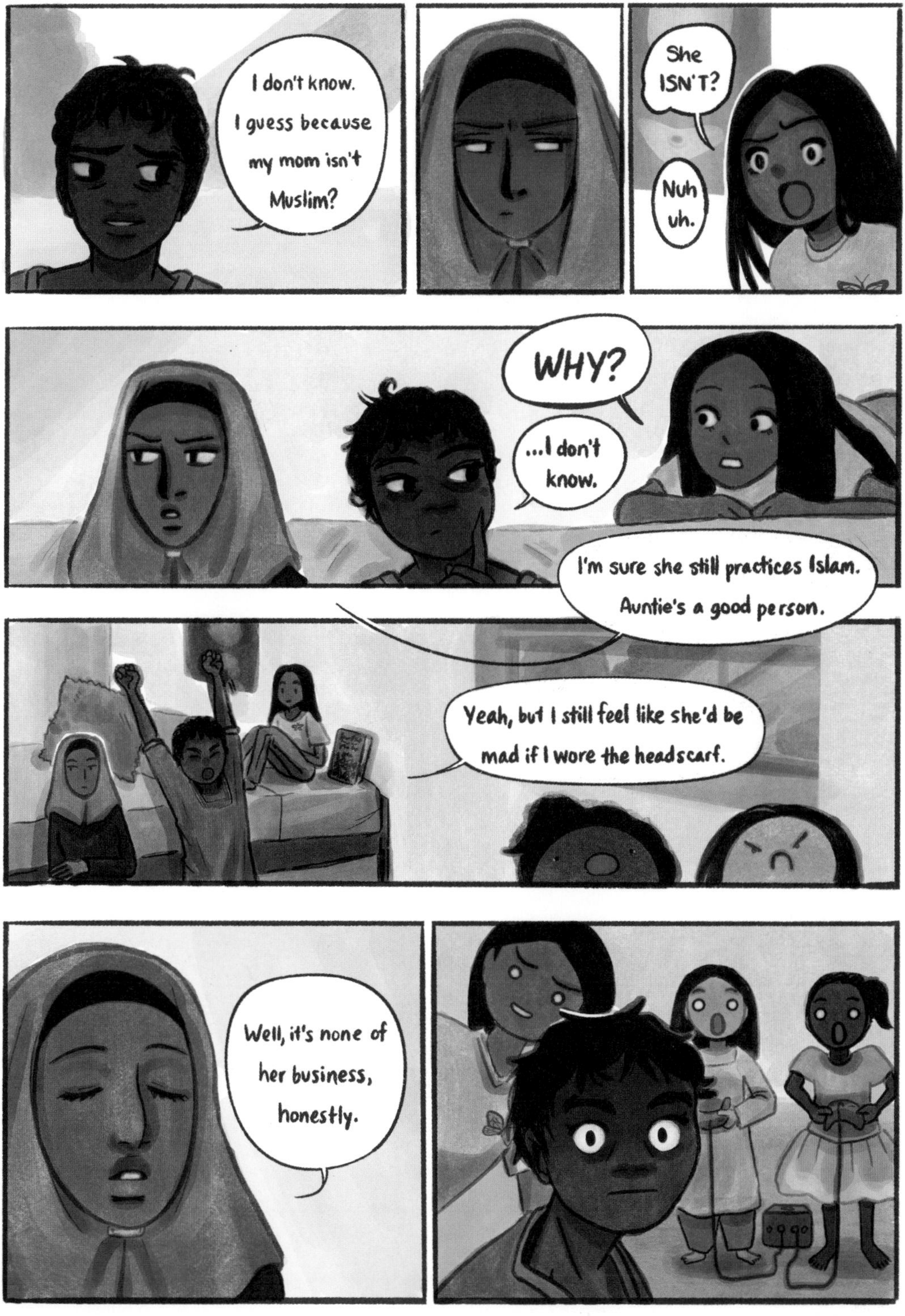
I don't know. I guess because my mom isn't Muslim?
She ISN'T?
Nuh uh.
WHY?
...I don't know.
I'm sure she still practices Islam. Auntie's a good person.
Yeah, but I still feel like she'd be mad if I wore the headscarf.
Well, it's none of her business, honestly.

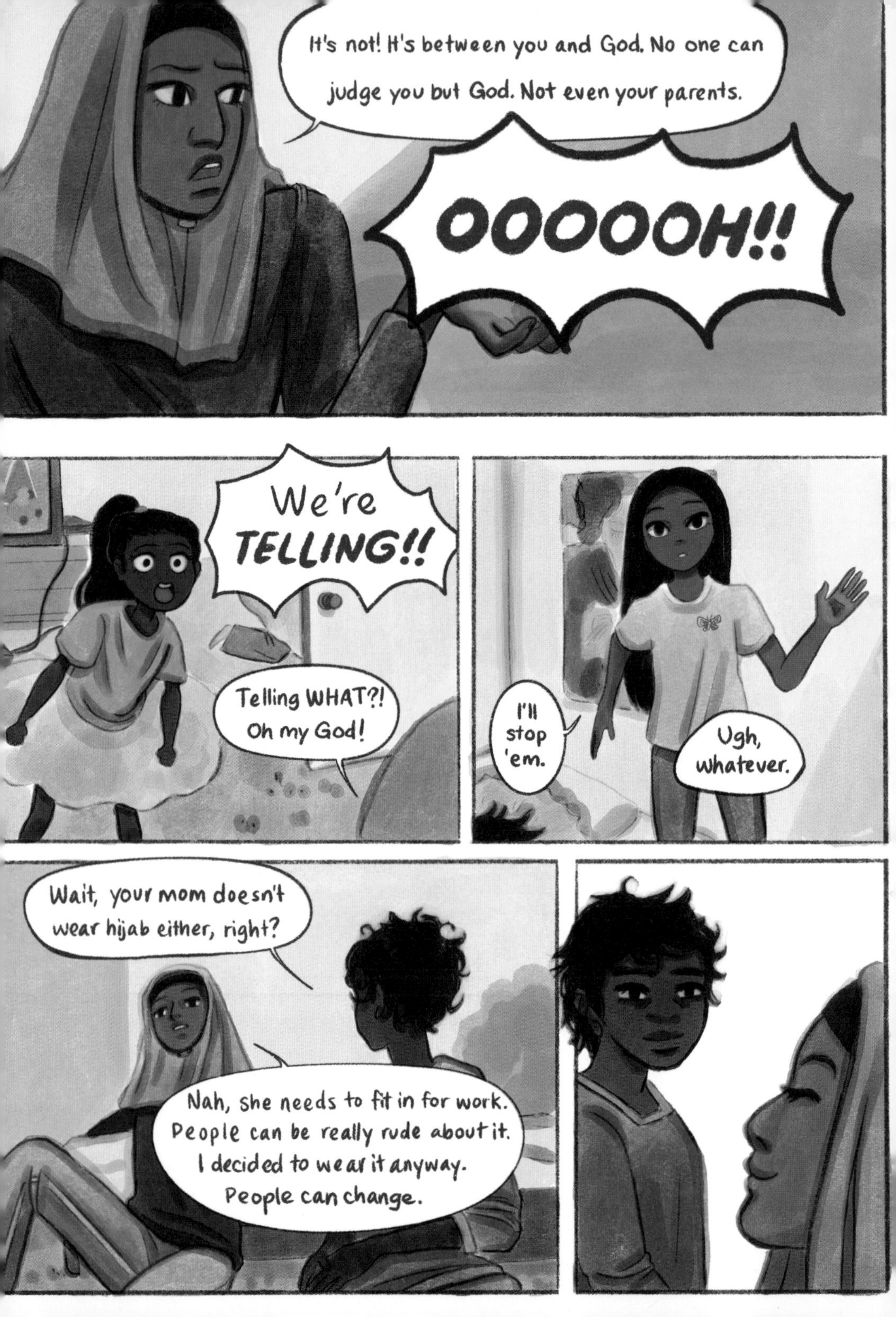
It's not! It's between you and God. No one can judge you but God. Not even your parents.
OOOOOH!!
We're TELLING!!
Telling WHAT?! Oh my God!
I'll stop 'em.
Ugh, whatever.
Wait, your mom doesn't wear hijab either, right?
Nah, she needs to fit in for work. People can be really rude about it. I decided to wear it anyway. People can change.

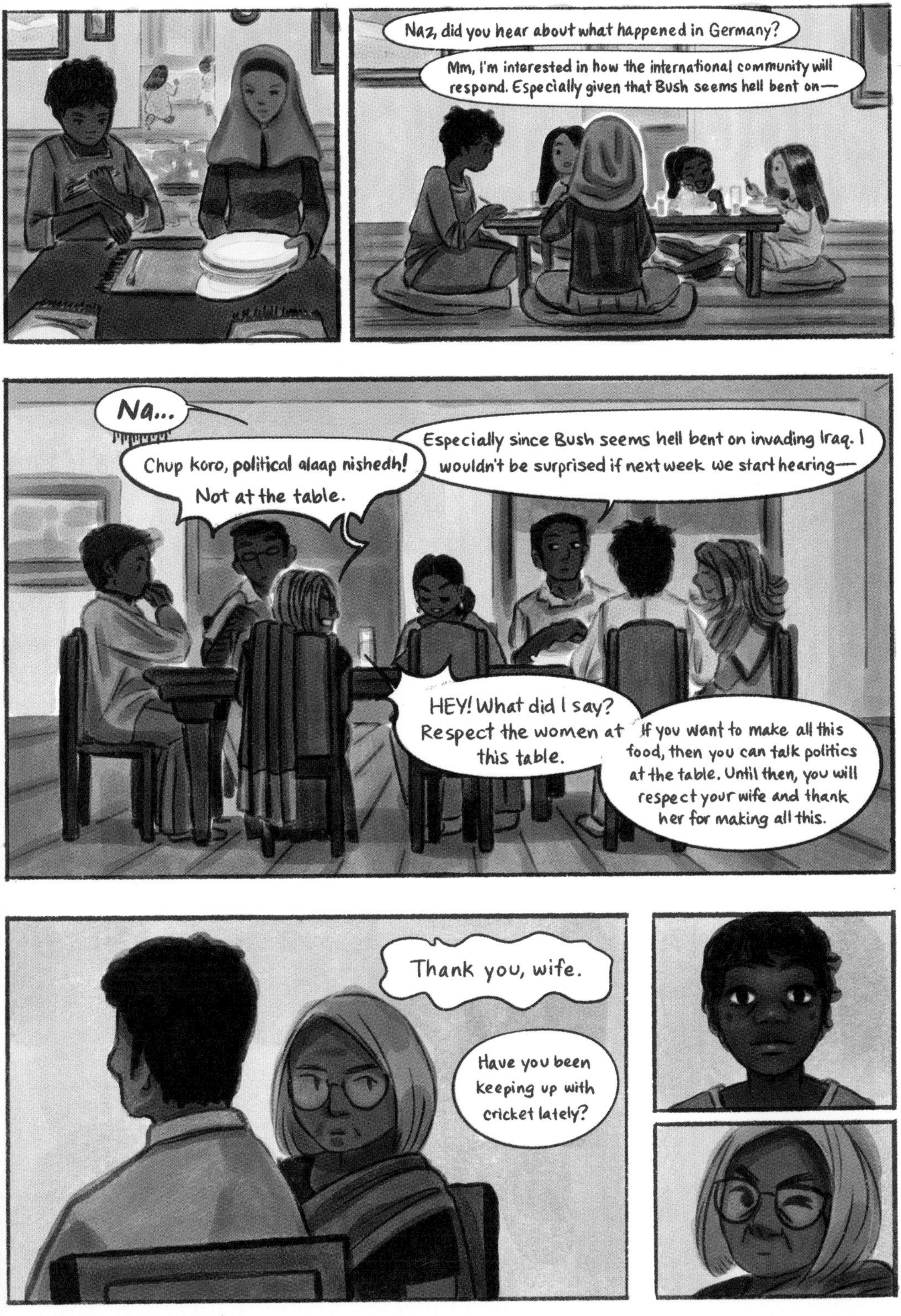
Naz, did you hear about what happened in Germany?
Mm, I'm interested in how the international community will respond. Especially given that Bush seems hell bent on—
Na...
Especially since Bush seems hell bent on invading Iraq. I wouldn't be surprised if next week we start hearing—
Chup koro, political alaap nishedh! Not at the table.
HEY! What did I say? Respect the women at this table.
If you want to make all this food, then you can talk politics at the table. Until then, you will respect your wife and thank her for making all this.
Thank you, wife.
Have you been keeping up with cricket lately?

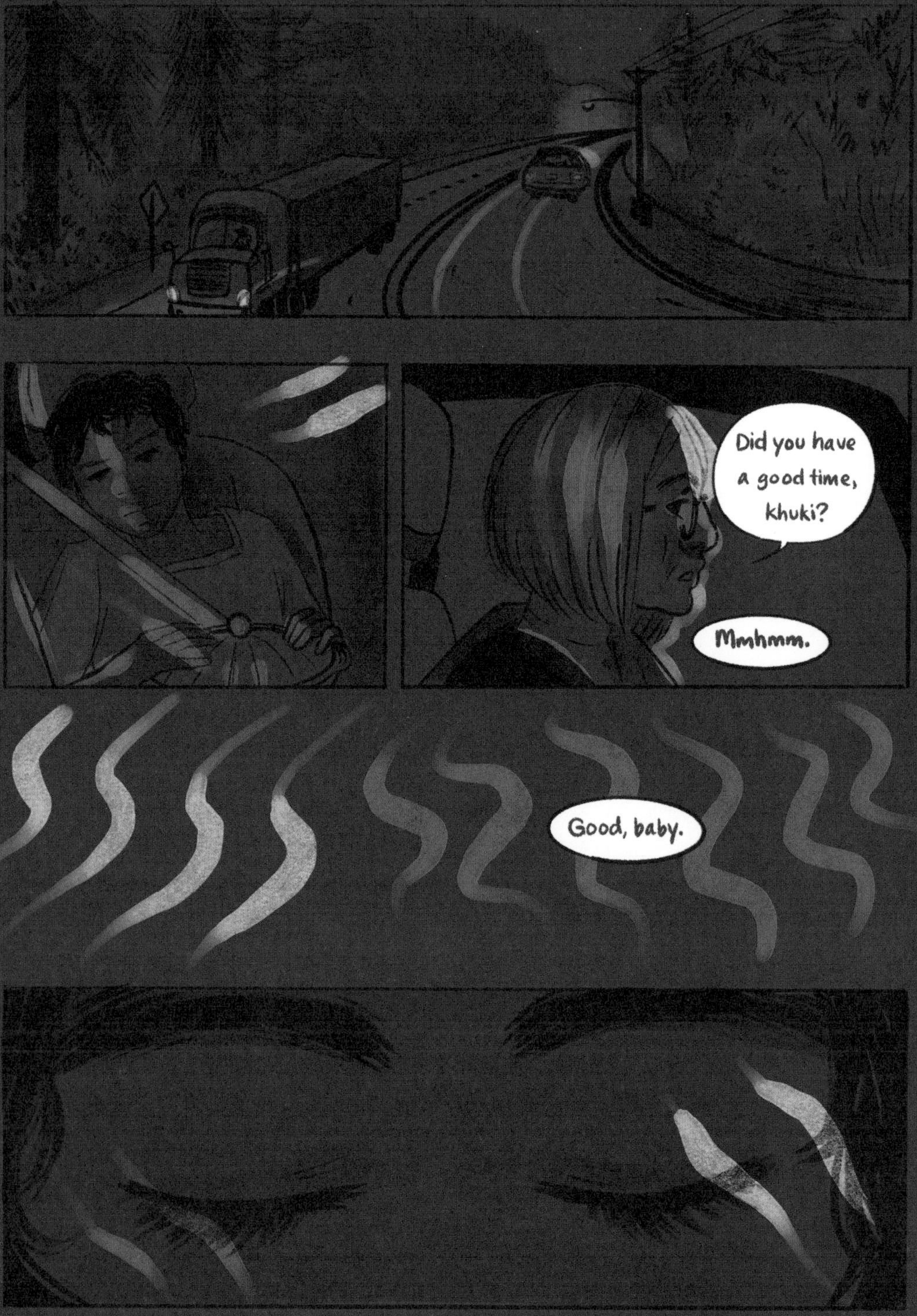
Did you have a good time, khuki?
Mmhmm.
Good, baby.

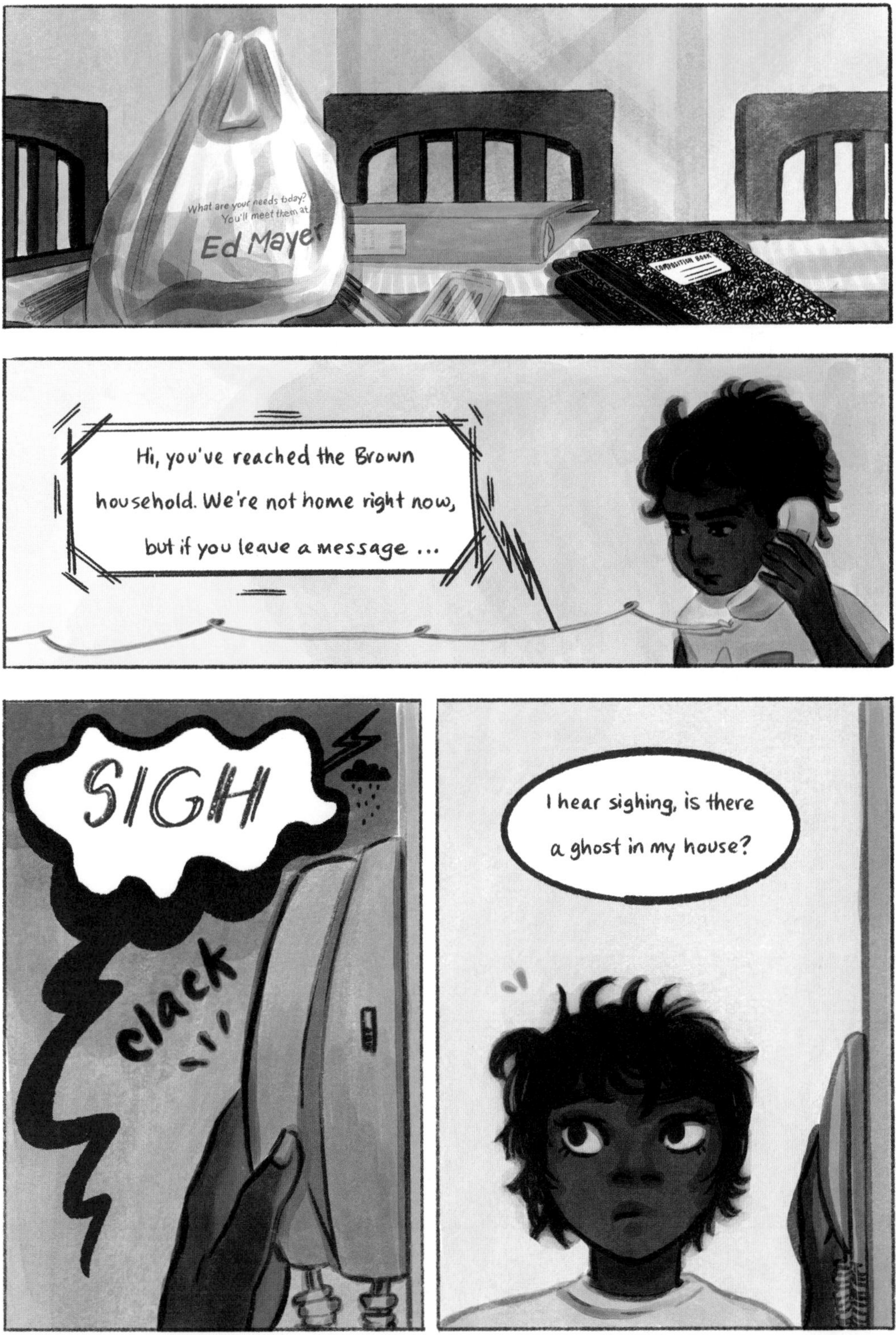
What are your needs today? You'll meet them at
Ed Mayer
Hi, you've reached the Brown household. We're not home right now, but if you leave a message ...
SIGH
clack
I hear sighing, is there a ghost in my house?

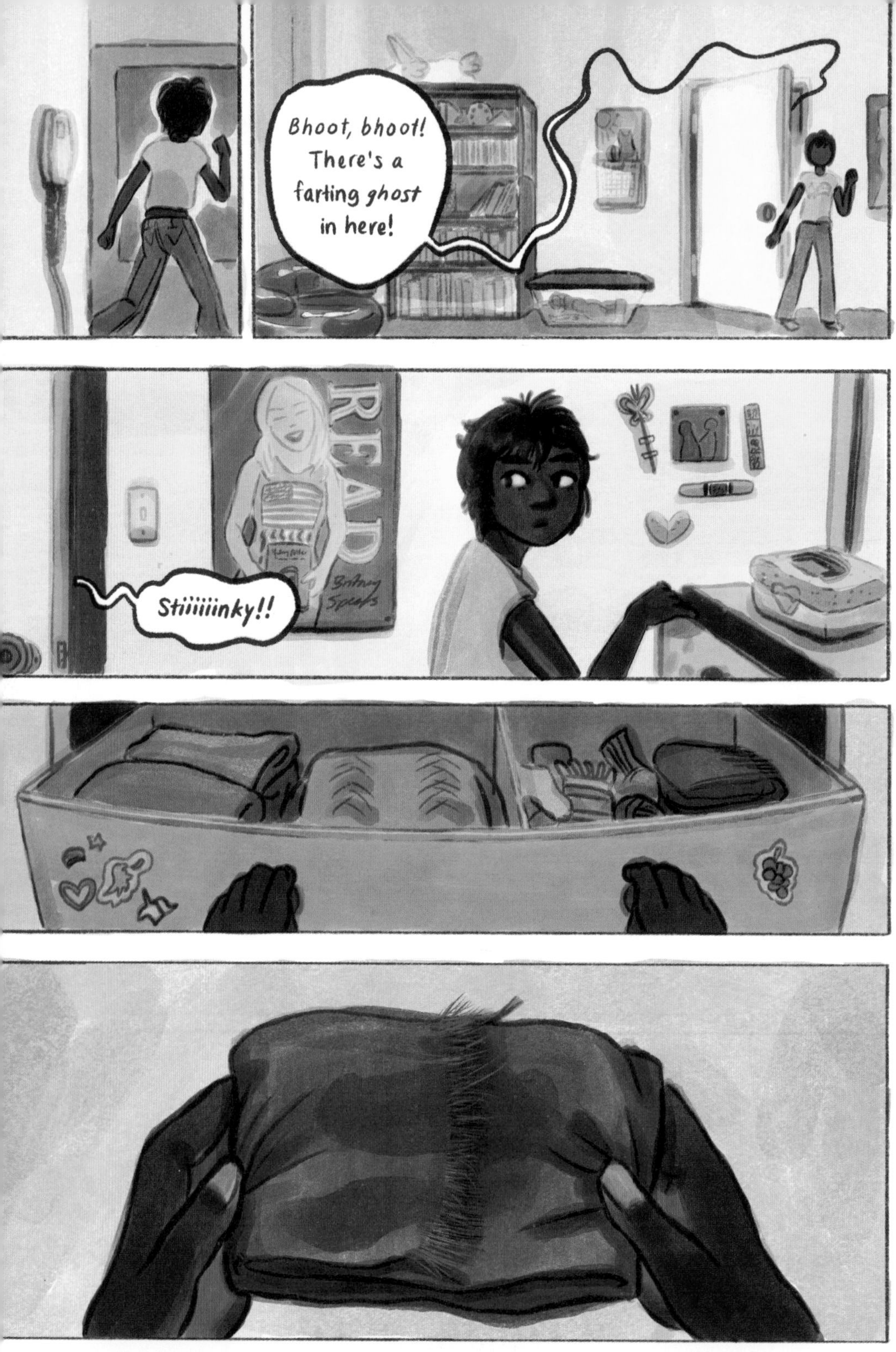
Bhoot, bhoot! There's a farting ghost in here!
READ
Britney Spears
Stiiiiiinky!!

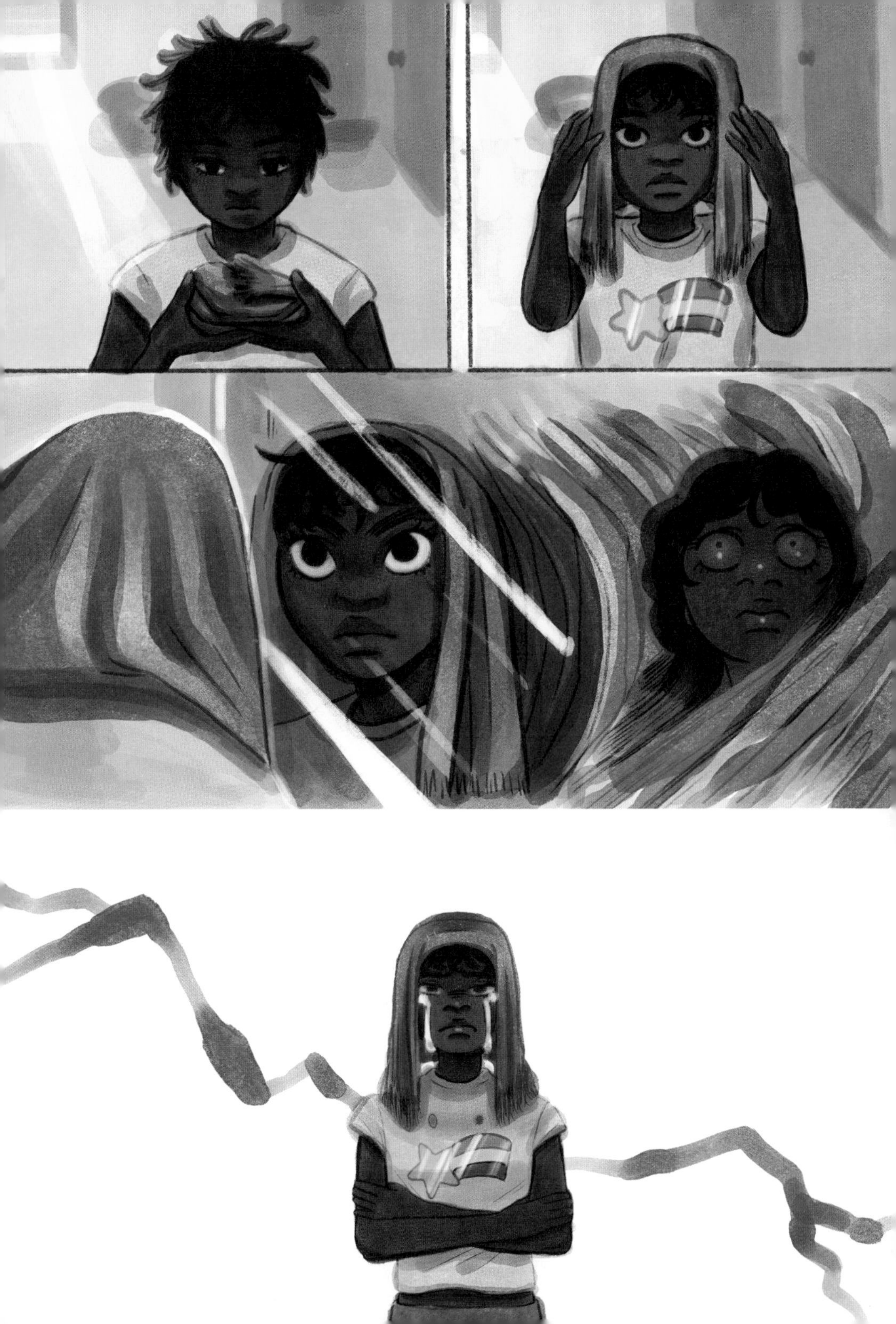

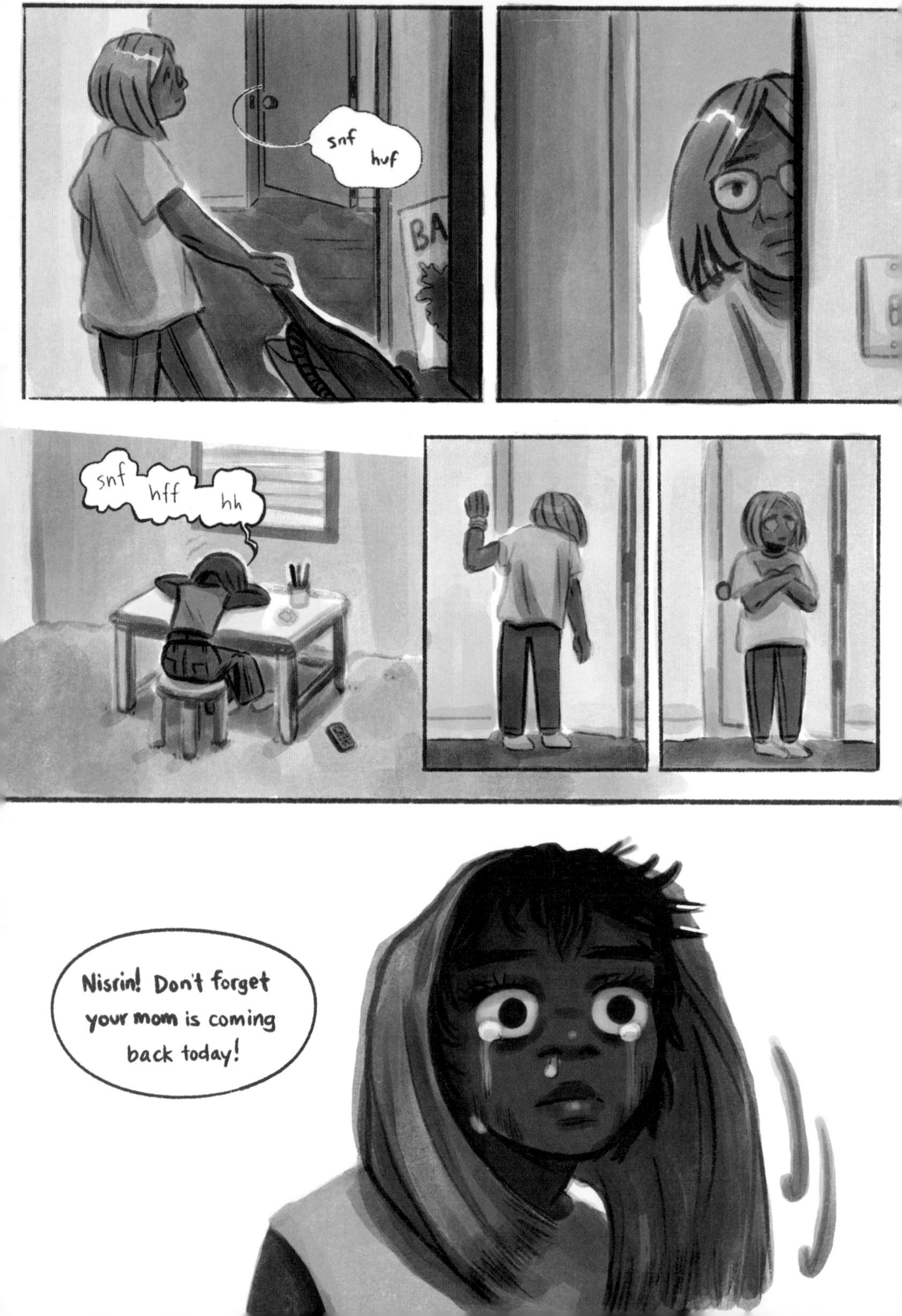
snf huf
snf hff hh
Nisrin! Don't forget your mom is coming back today!

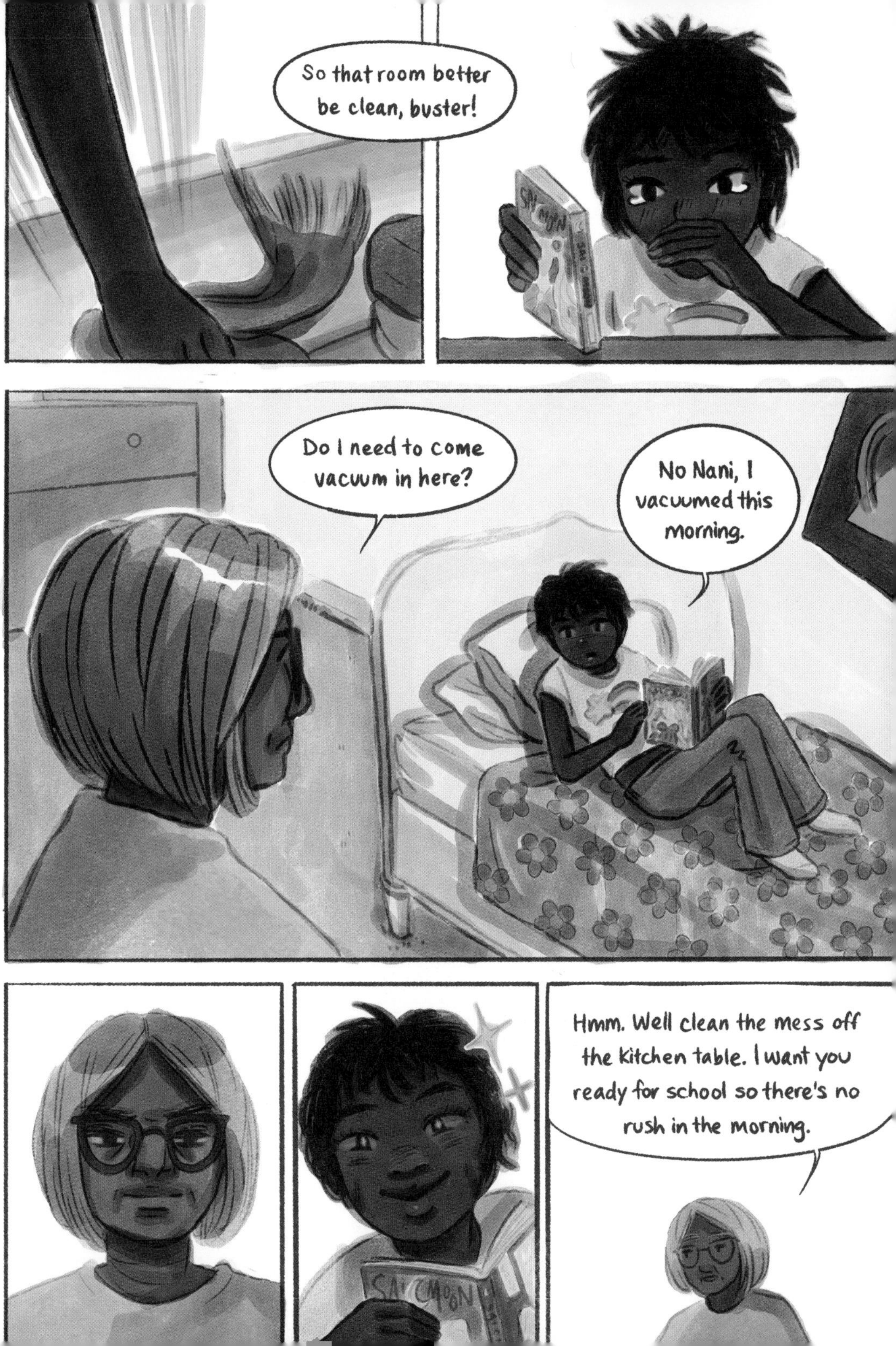
So that room better be clean, buster!
SAI MOON
Do I need to come vacuum in here?
No Nani, I vacuumed this morning.
Hmm. Well clean the mess off the kitchen table. I want you ready for school so there's no rush in the morning.
SAI MOON

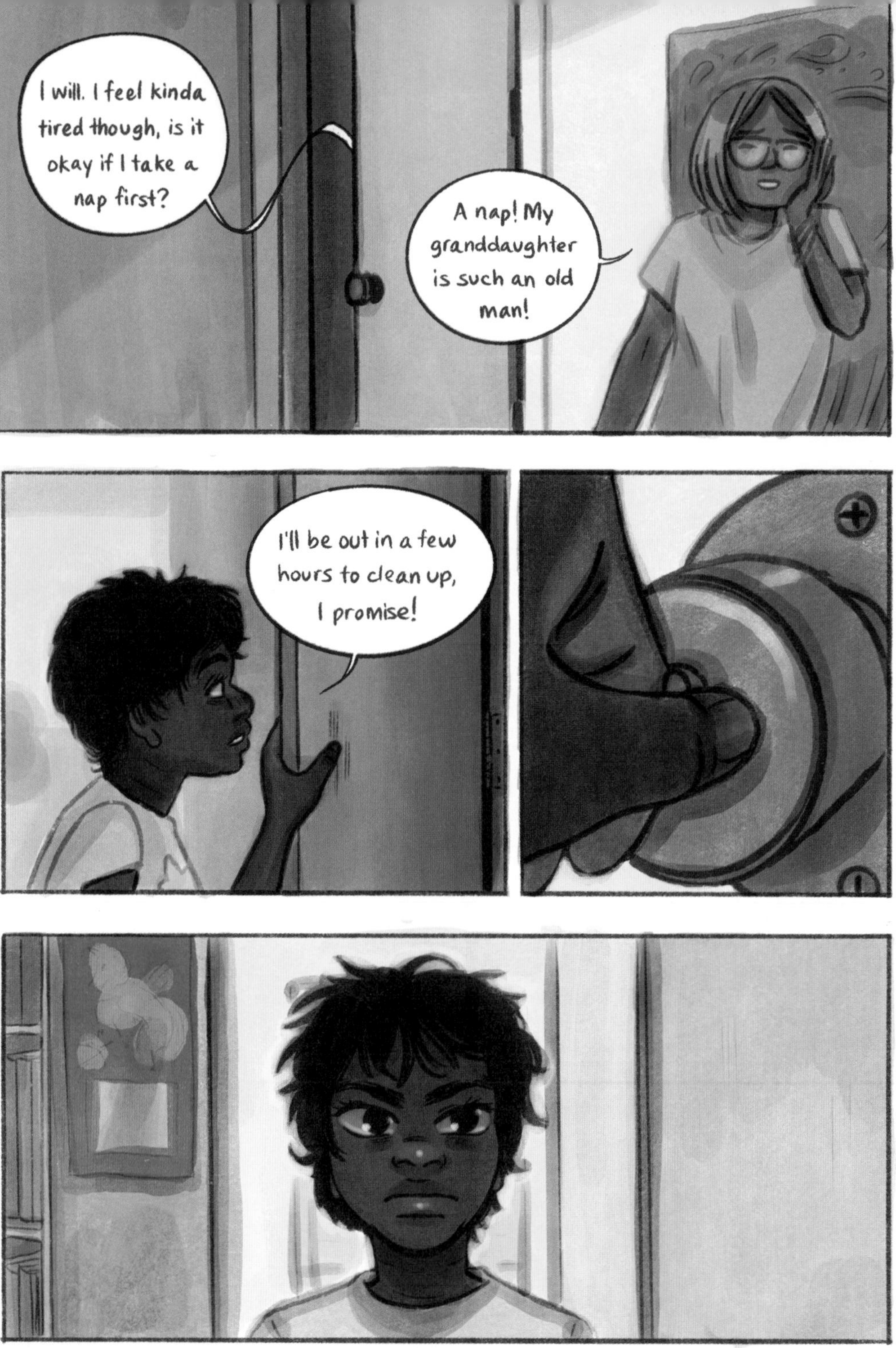
I will. I feel kinda tired though, is it okay if I take a nap first?
A nap! My granddaughter is such an old man!
I'll be out in a few hours to clean up, I promise!

I'm home!!

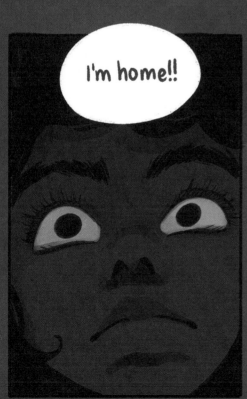

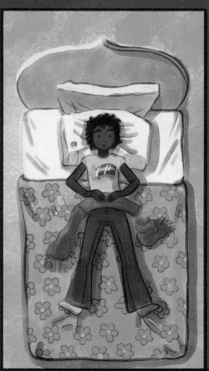

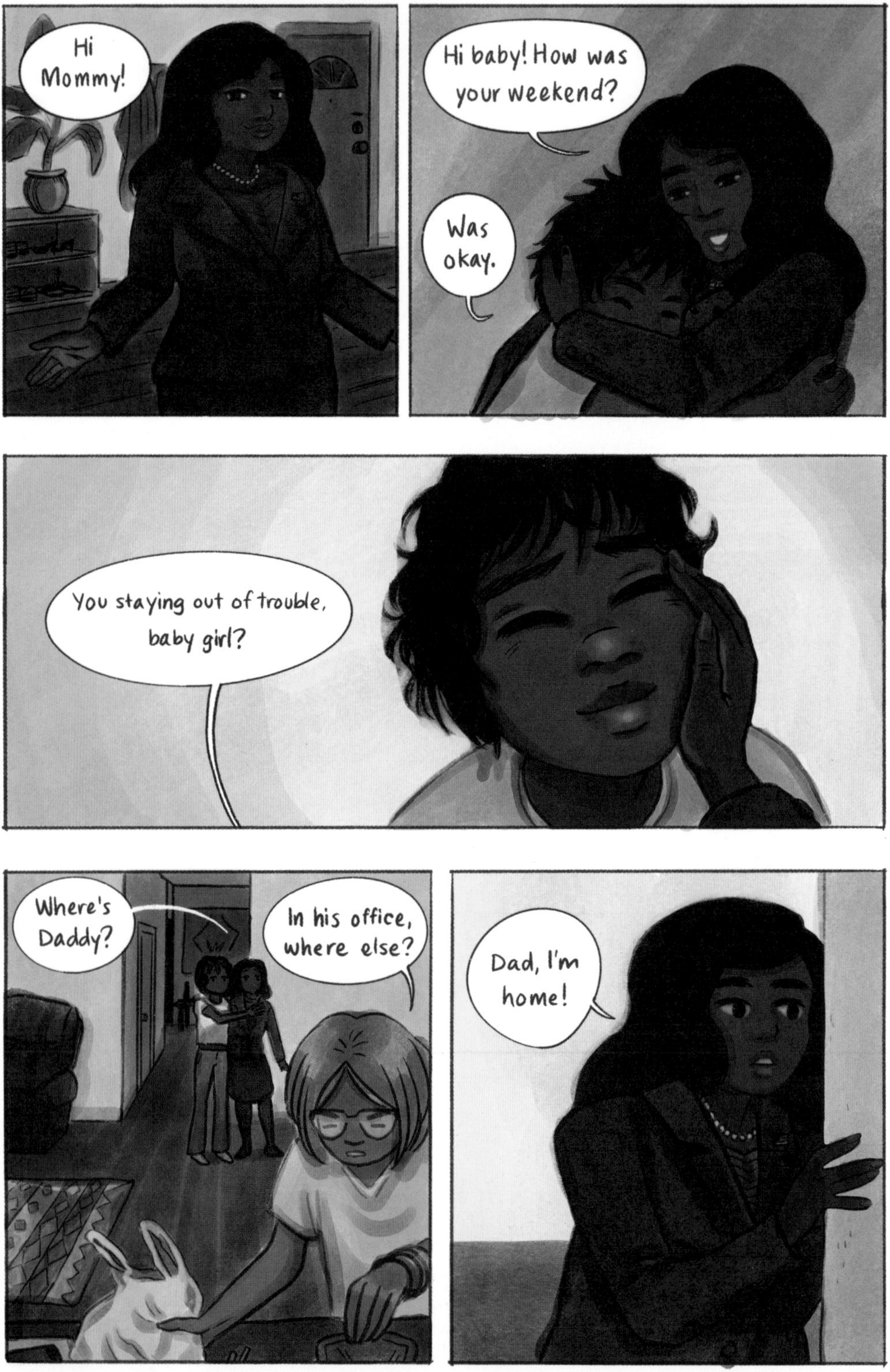
Hi Mommy!
Hi baby! How was your weekend?
Was okay.
You staying out of trouble, baby girl?
Where's Daddy?
In his office, where else?
Dad, I'm home!

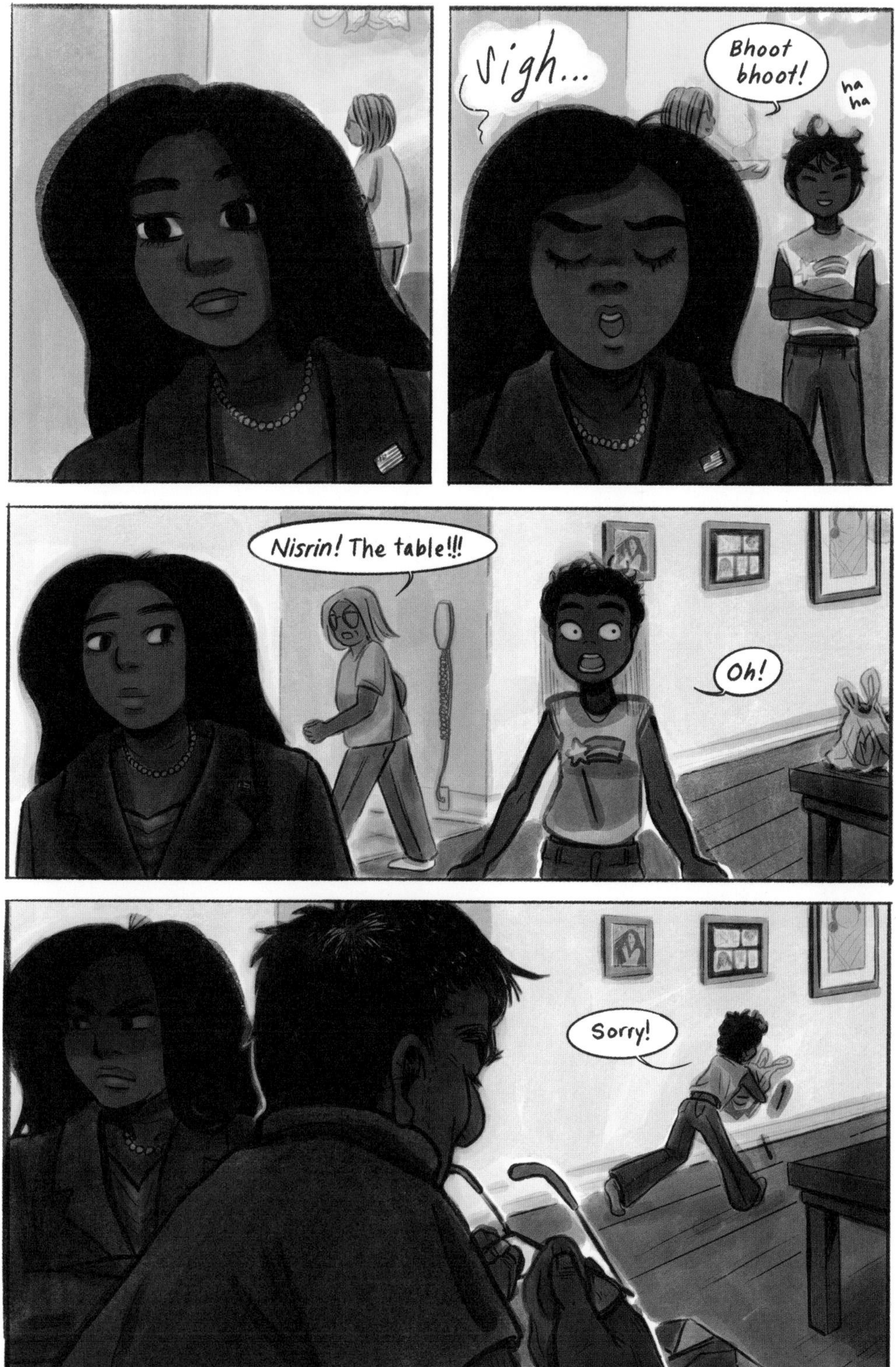
Sigh...
Bhoot bhoot!
ha ha
Nisrin! The table!!!
Oh!
Sorry!

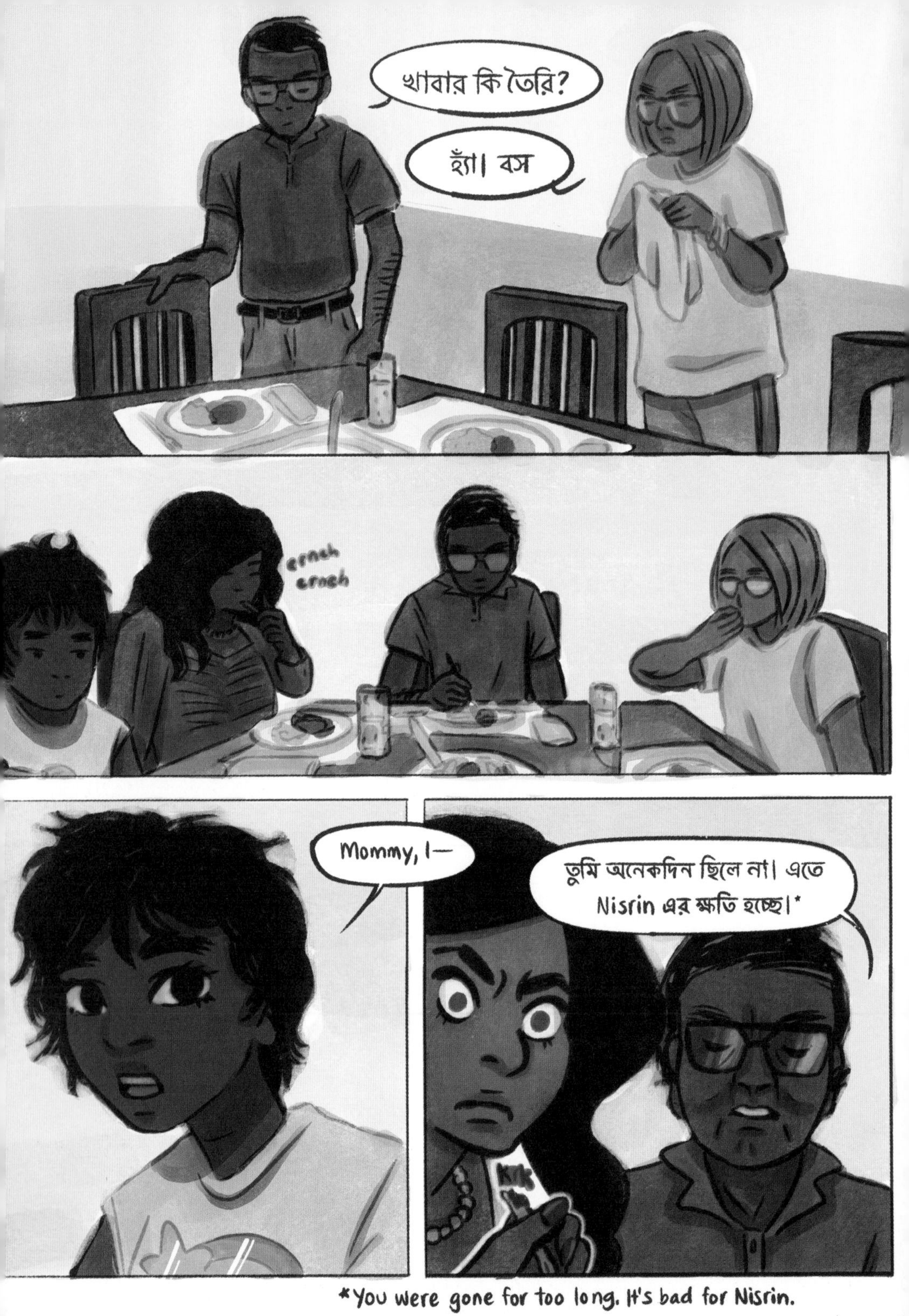
খাবার কি তৈরি?
হ্যাঁ। বস
crnch crnch
Mommy, I—
তুমি অনেকদিন ছিলে না। এতে Nisrin এর ক্ষতি হচ্ছে।*

*You were gone for too long. It's bad for Nisrin.

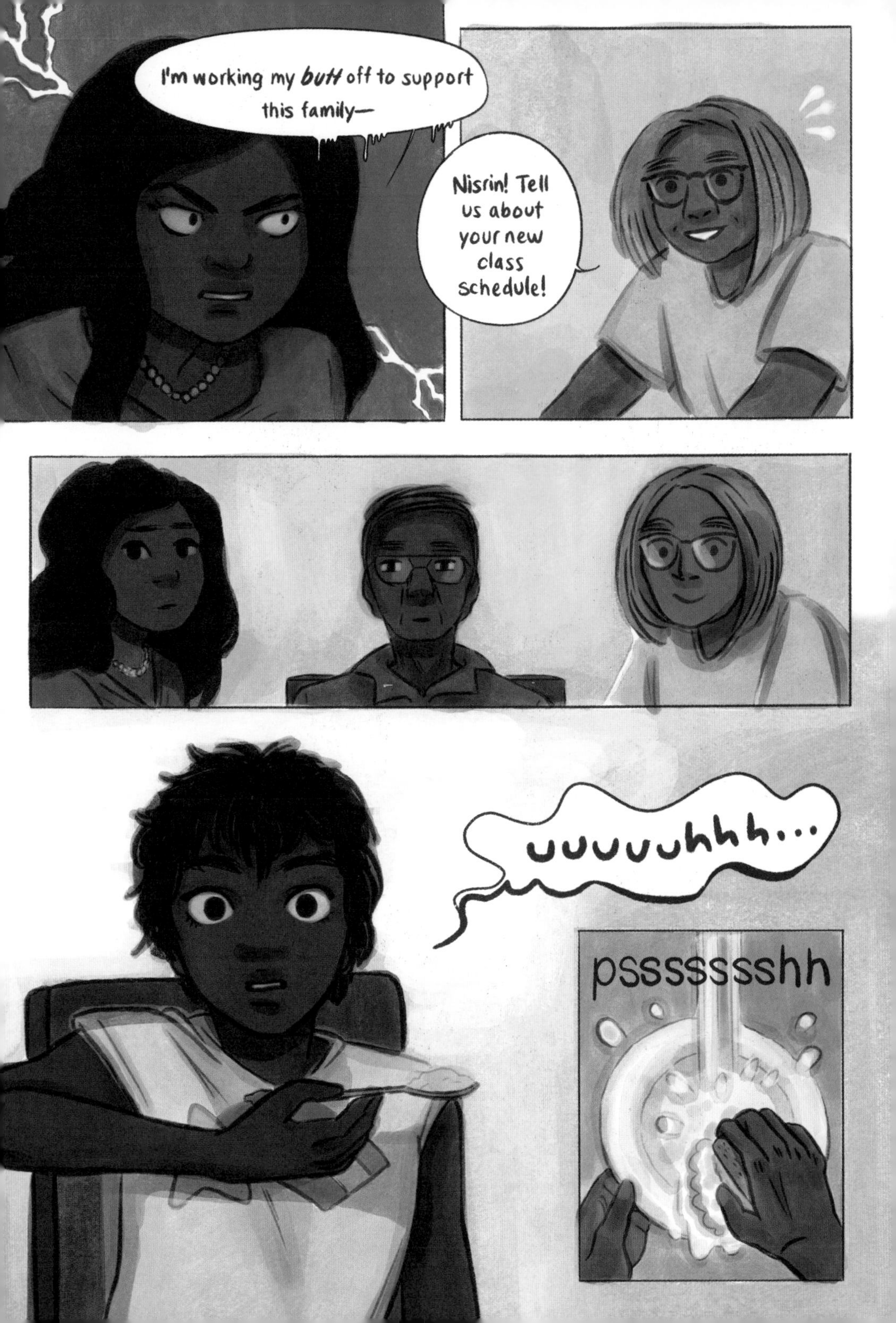
I'm working my *butt* off to support this family—
Nisrin! Tell us about your new class schedule!
uuuuuhhh...
psssssssshh

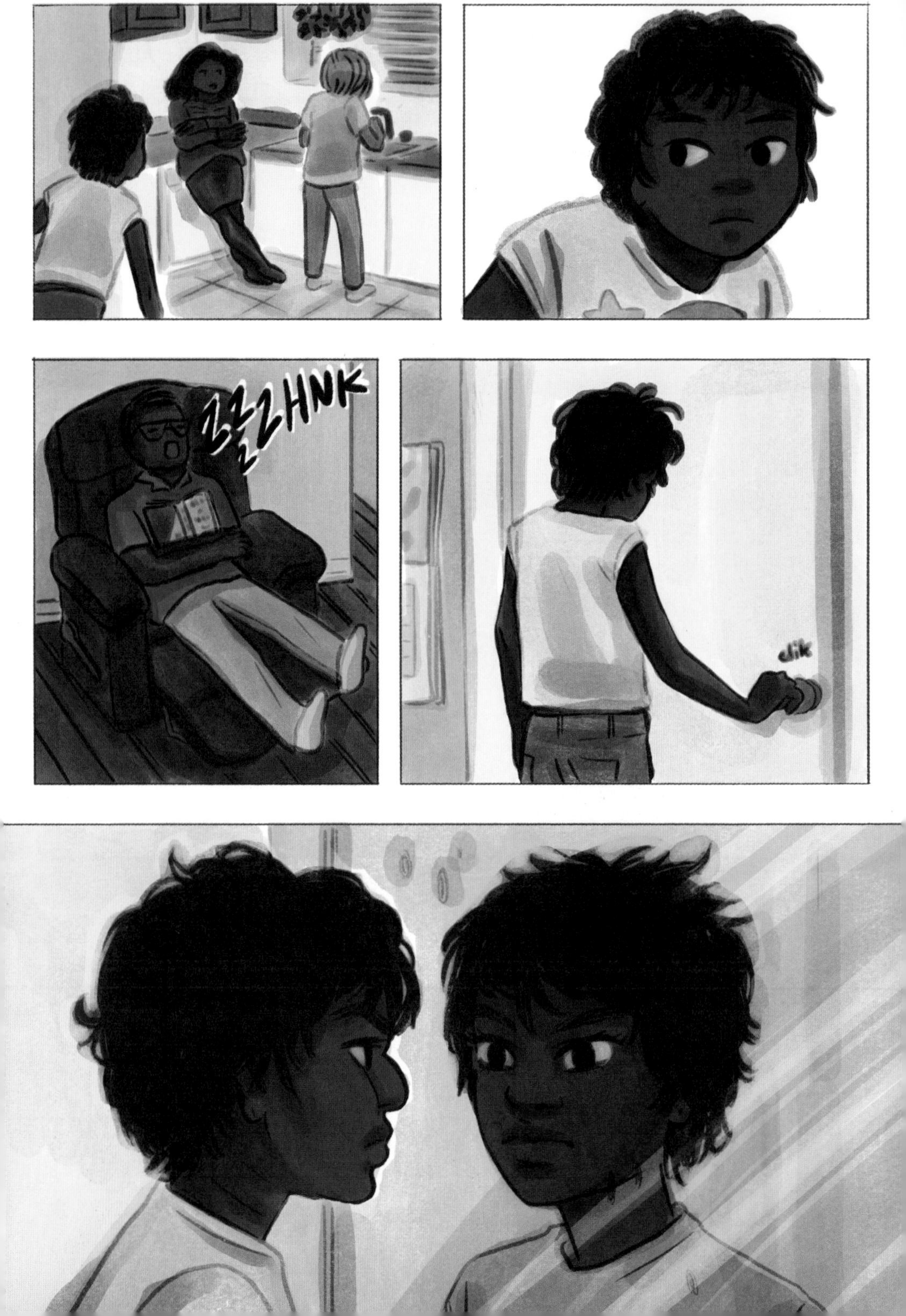

ZZZZHNK
clik

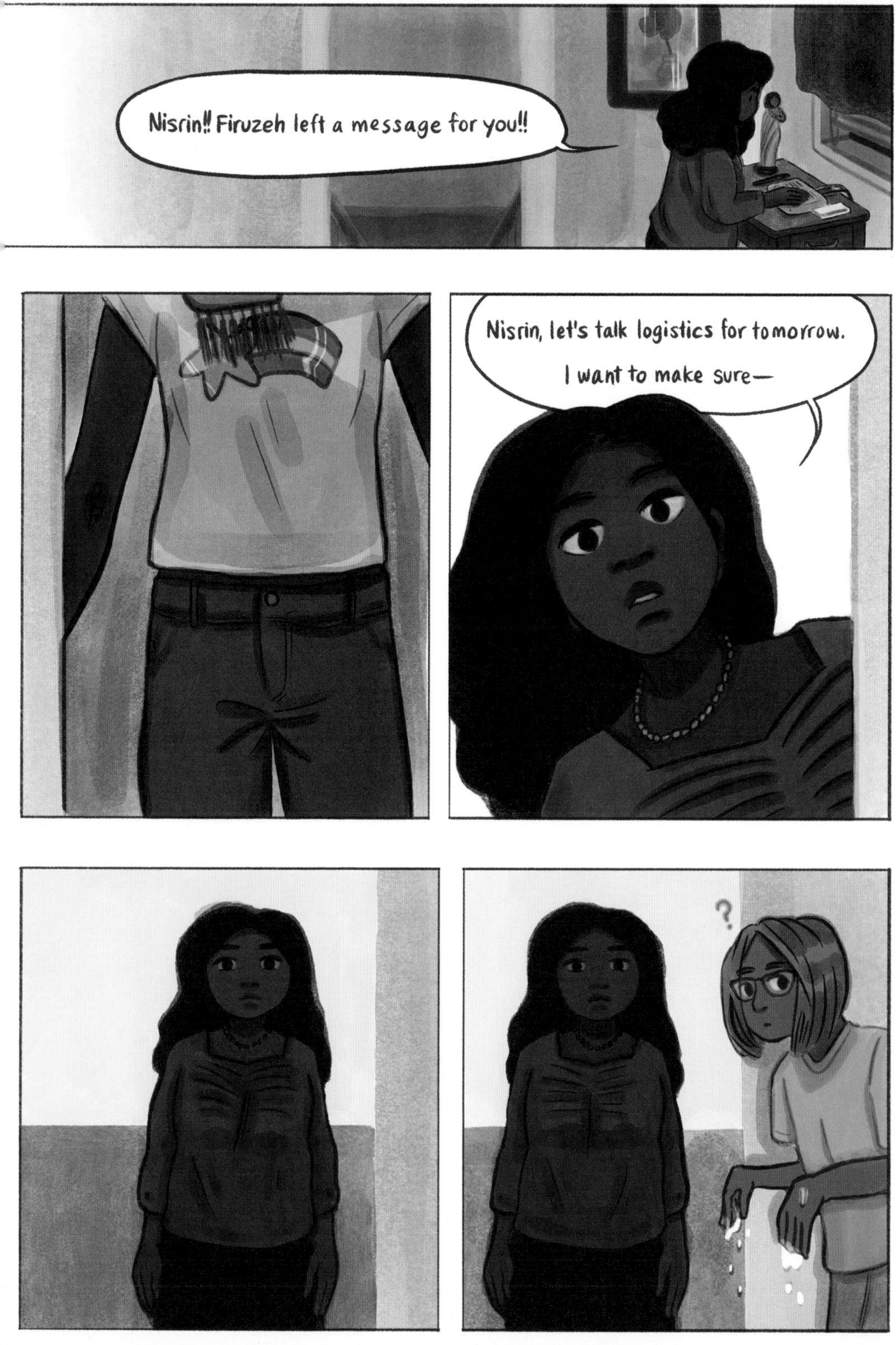
Nisrin!! Firuzeh left a message for you!!
Nisrin, let's talk logistics for tomorrow. I want to make sure—
?

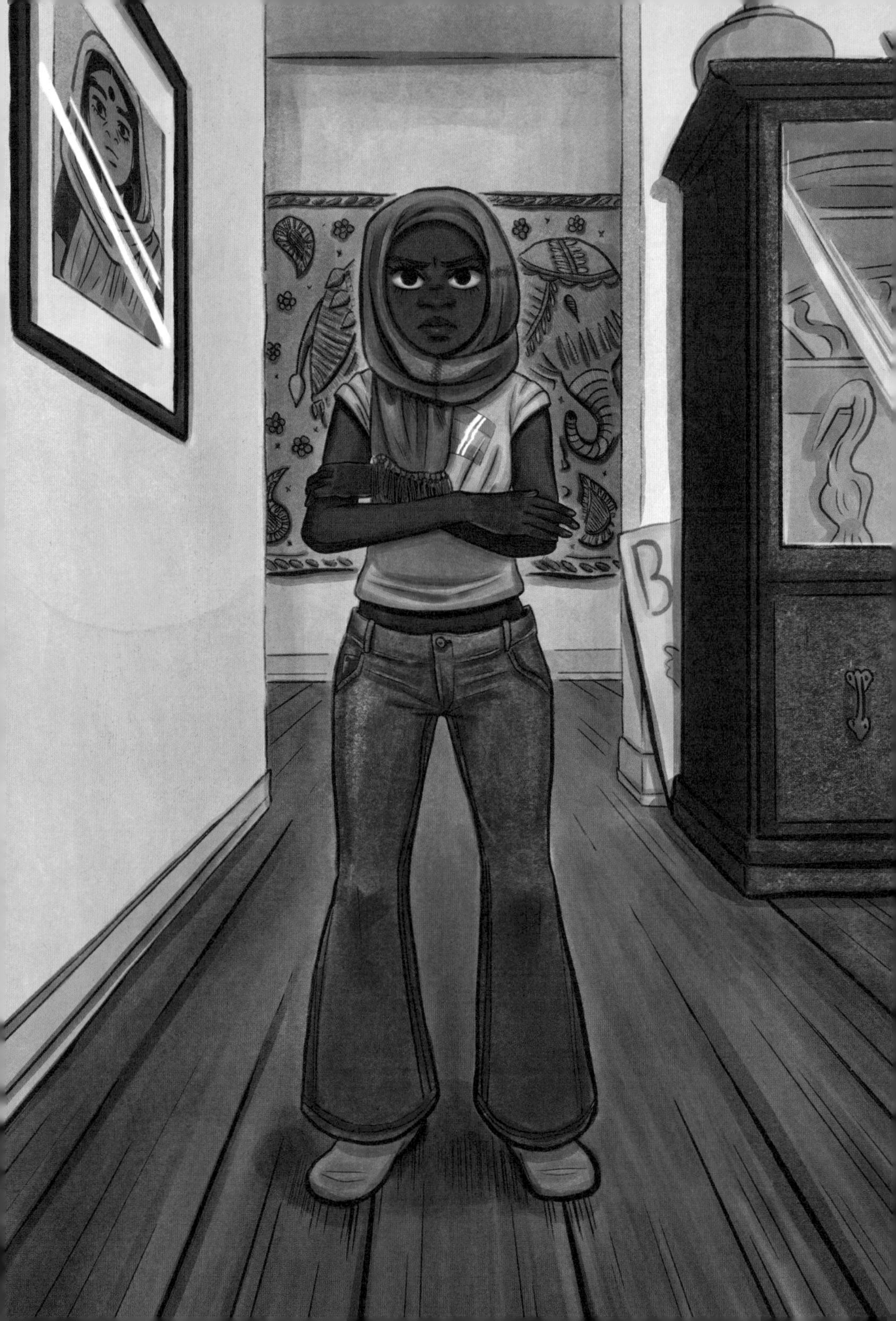

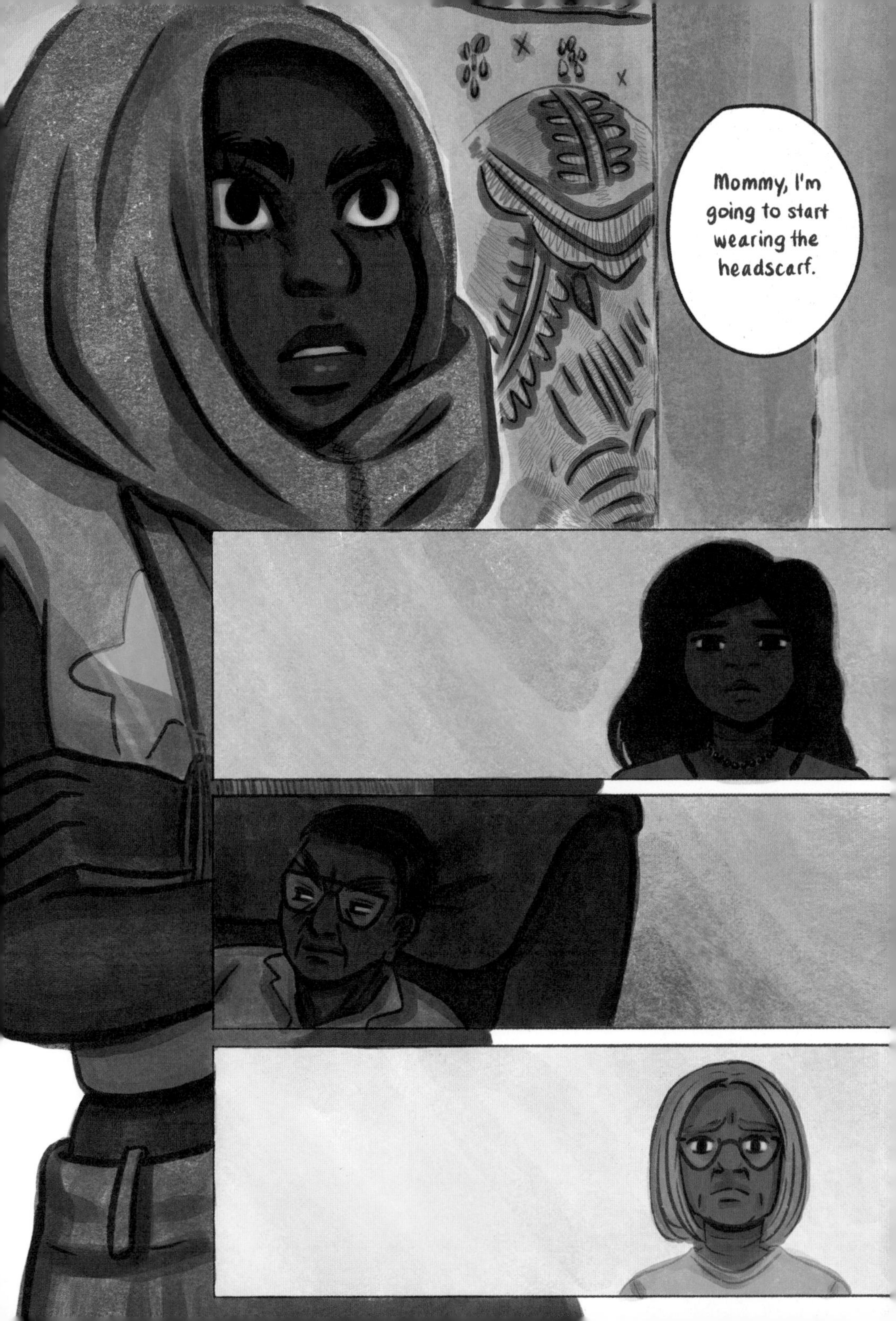
Mommy, I'm going to start wearing the headscarf.

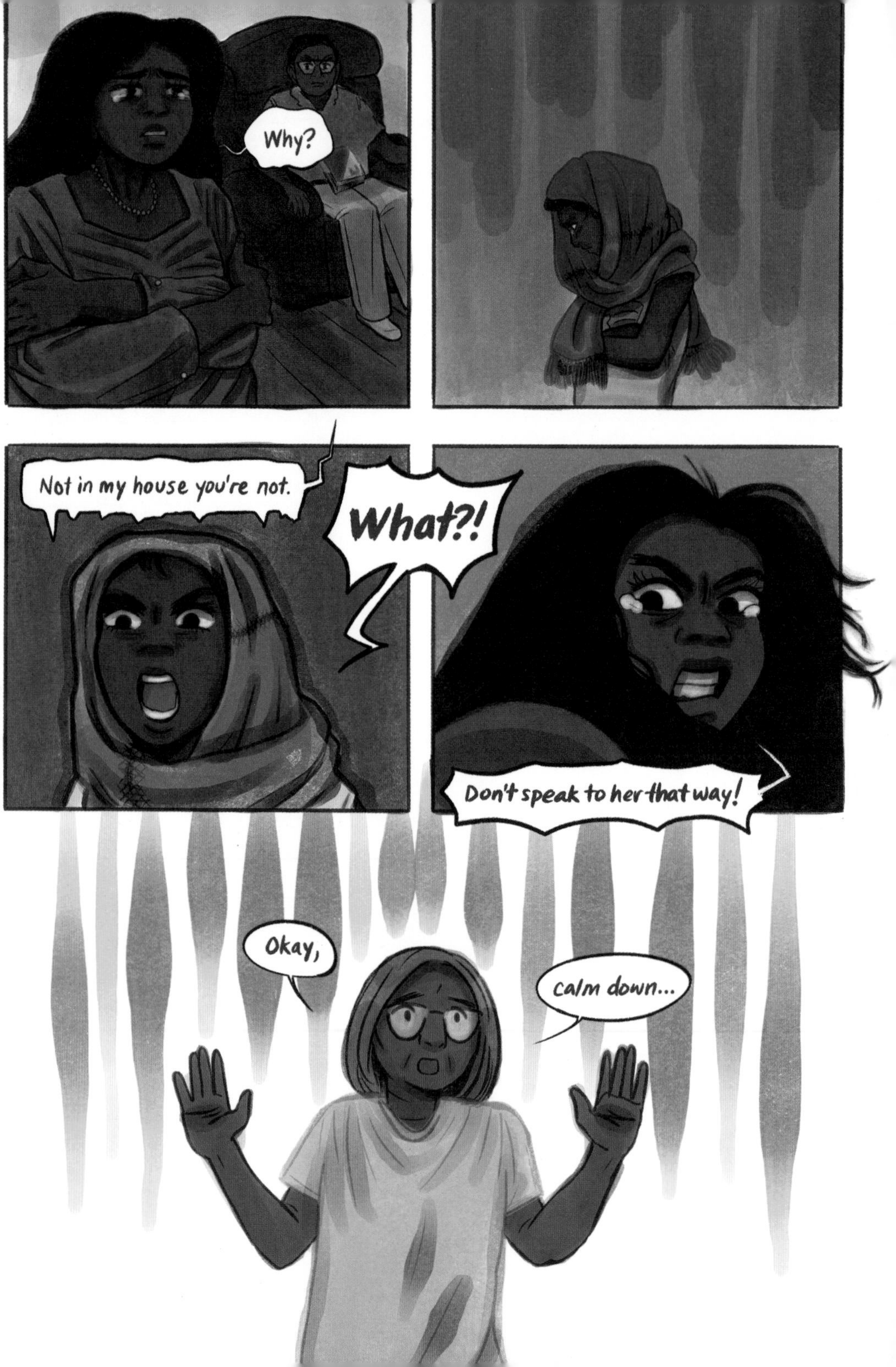
Why?
Not in my house you're not.
What?!
Don't speak to her that way!
Okay,
calm down...

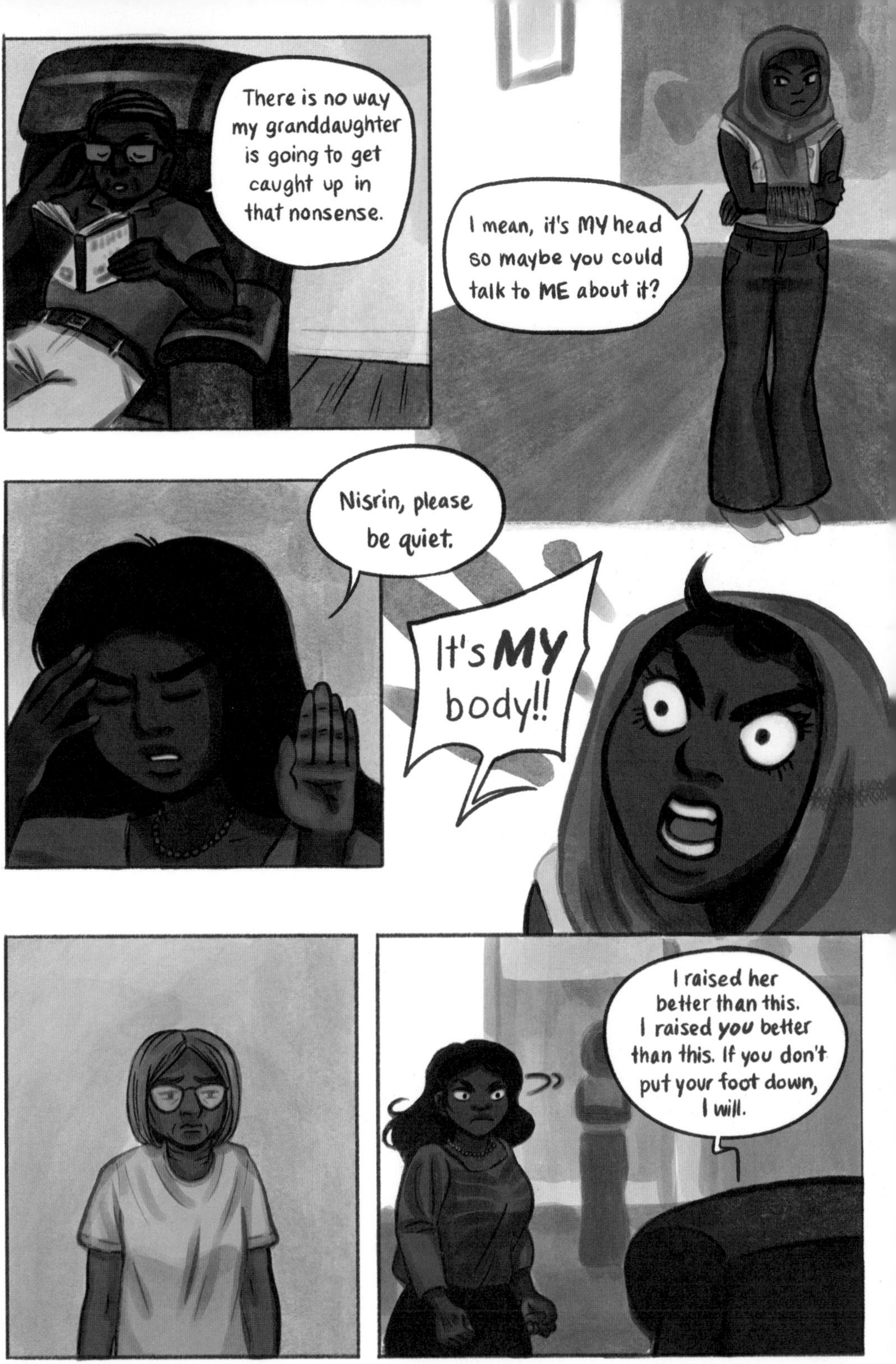
There is no way my granddaughter is going to get caught up in that nonsense.
I mean, it's MY head so maybe you could talk to ME about it?
Nisrin, please be quiet.
It's **MY** body!!
I raised her better than this. I raised *you* better than this. If you don't put your foot down, I will.

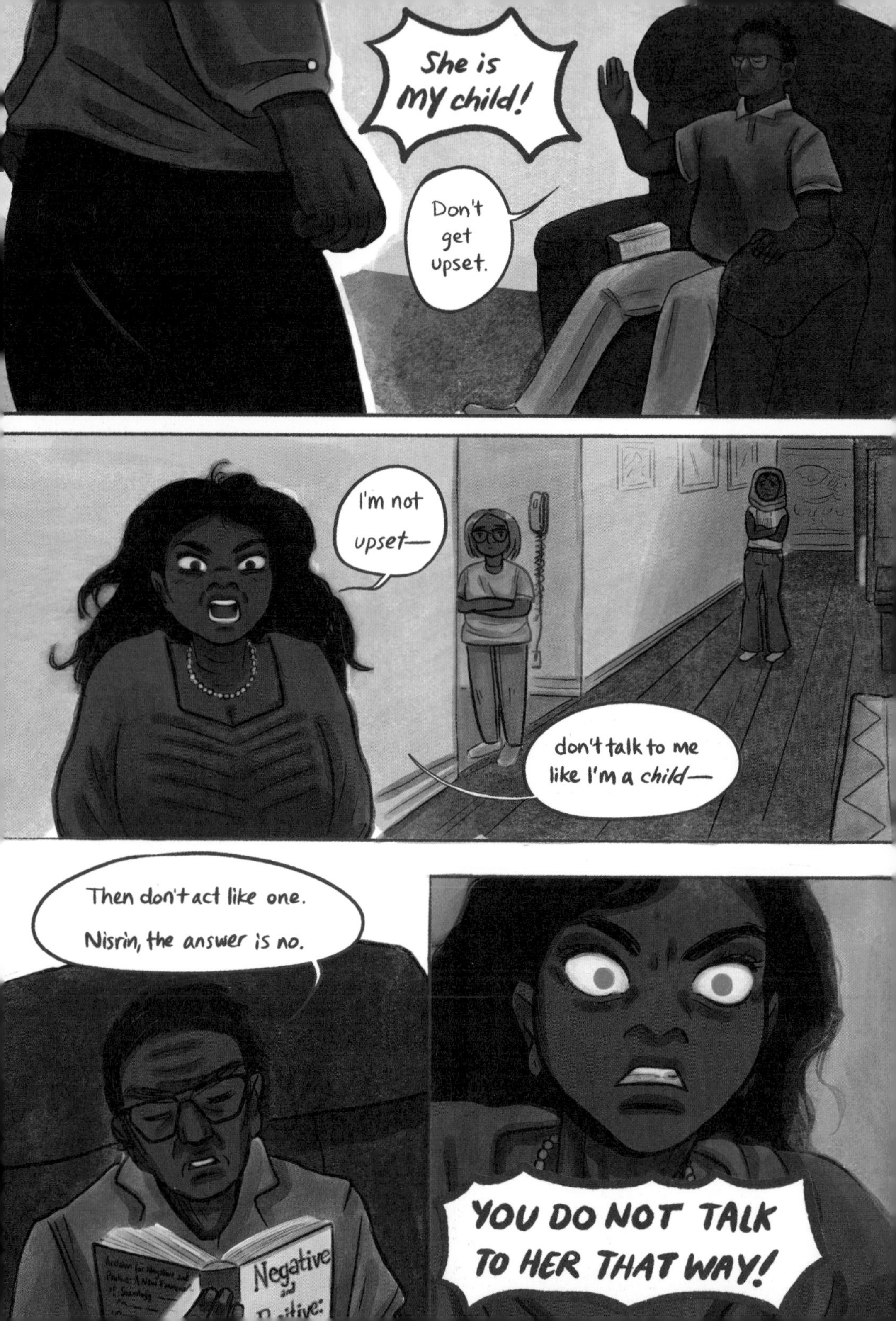
She is MY child!
Don't get upset.
I'm not upset—
don't talk to me like I'm a child—
Then don't act like one.
Nisrin, the answer is no.
Negative and Positive:
YOU DO NOT TALK TO HER THAT WAY!

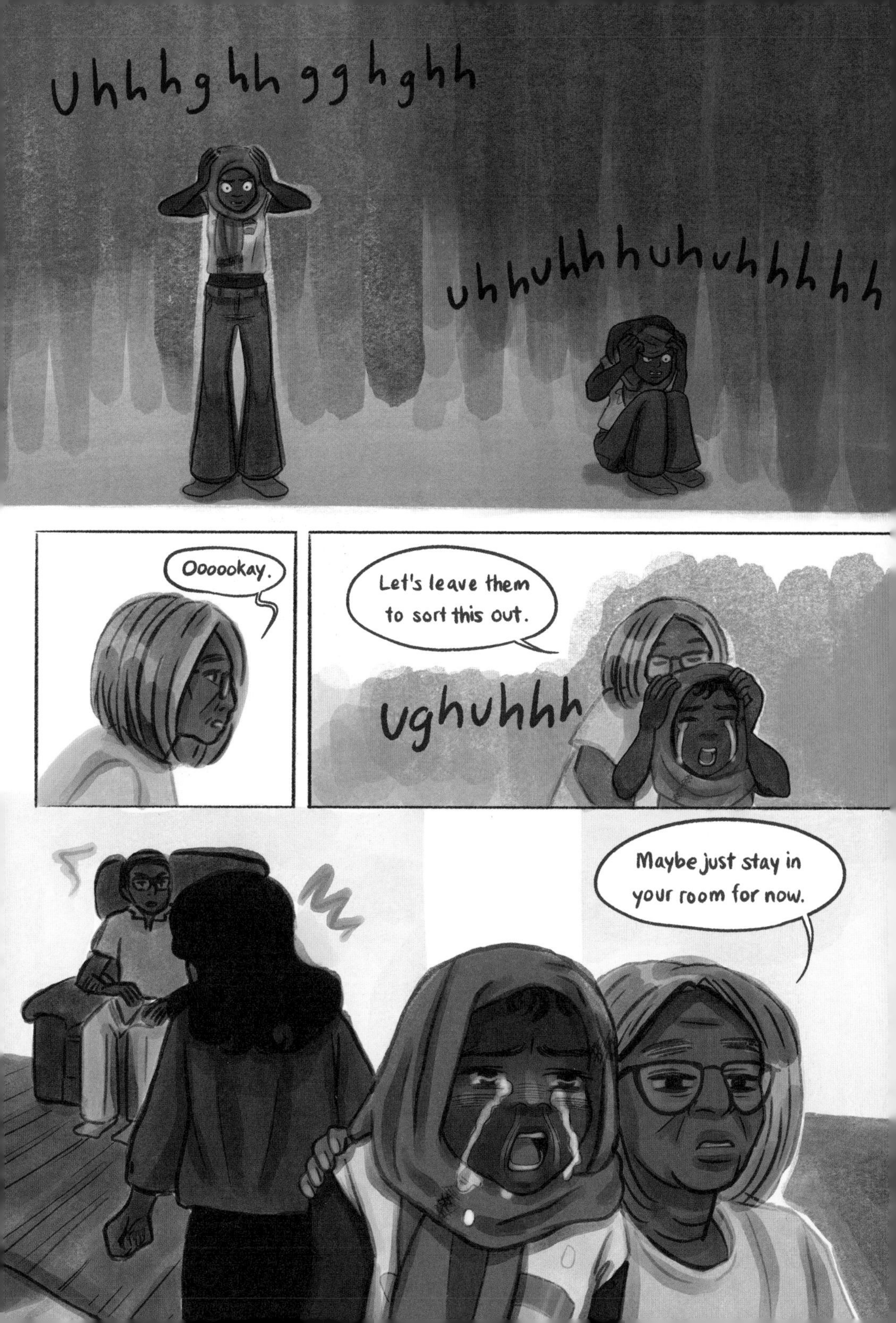
Uhhhghh gghghh
uhhuhhhuhuhhhhh
Oooookay.
Let's leave them to sort this out.
ughuhhh
Maybe just stay in your room for now.

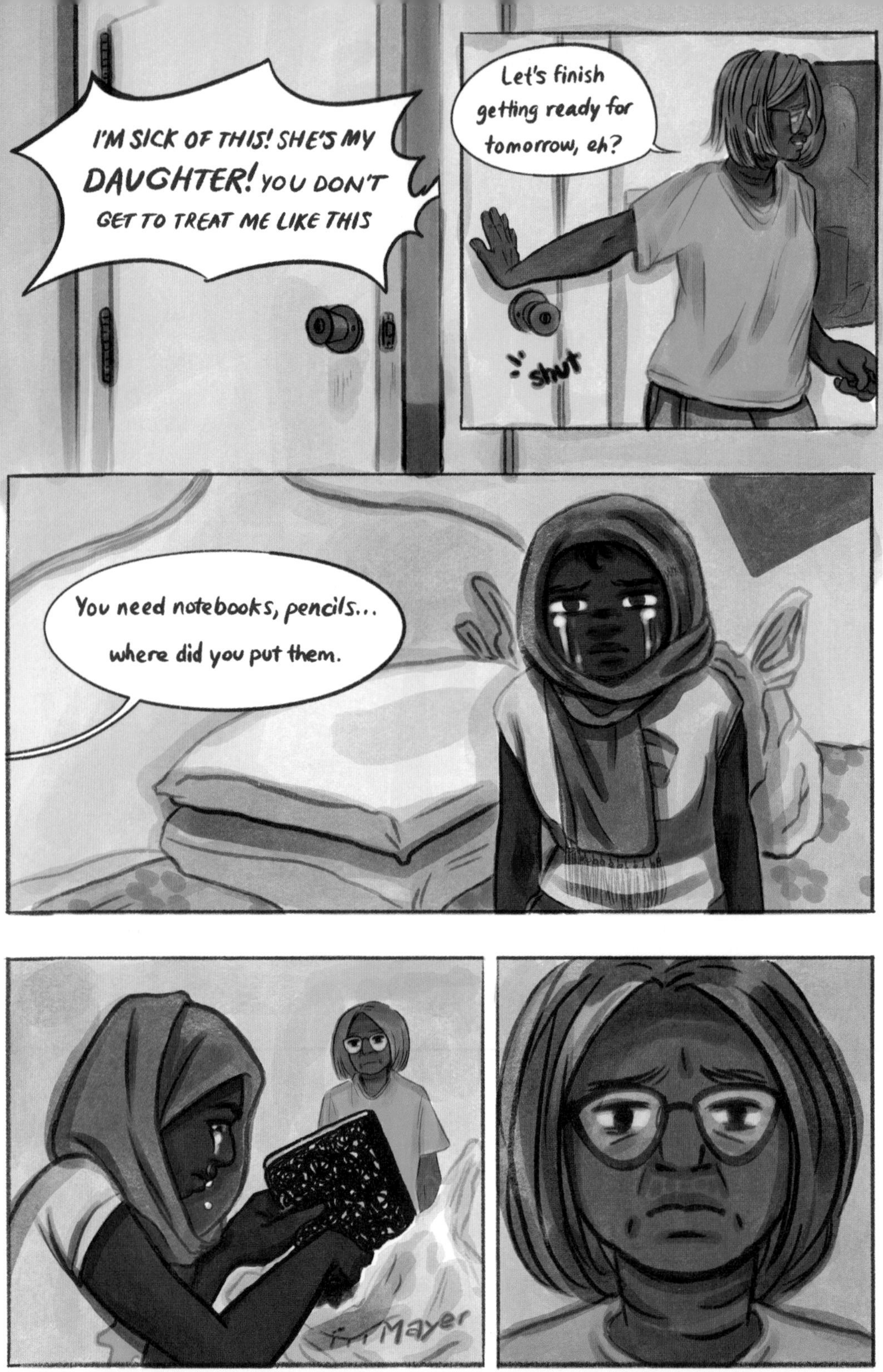
I'M SICK OF THIS! SHE'S MY DAUGHTER! YOU DON'T GET TO TREAT ME LIKE THIS
Let's finish getting ready for tomorrow, eh?
shut
You need notebooks, pencils... where did you put them.

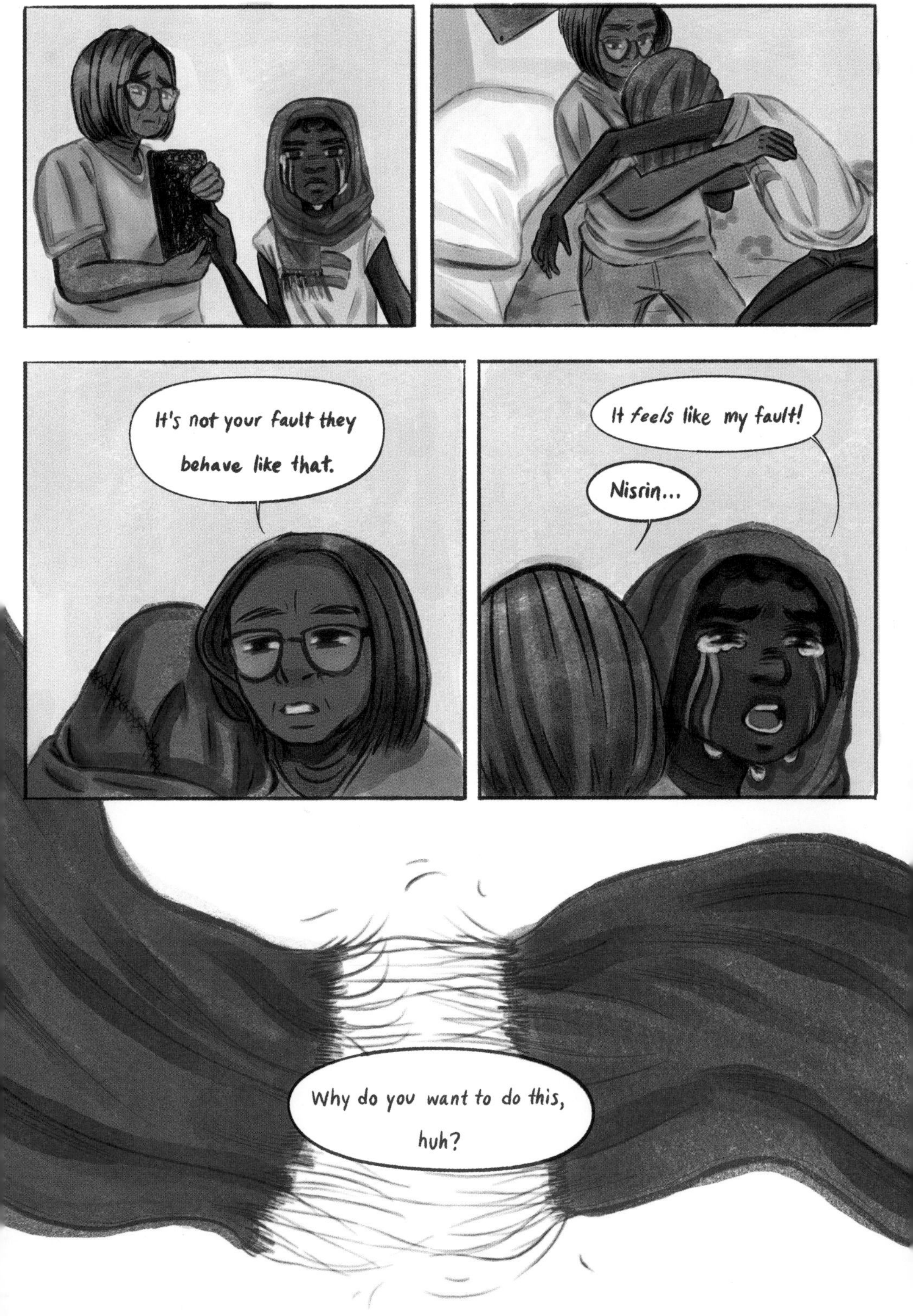
It's not your fault they behave like that.
It feels like my fault!
Nisrin...
Why do you want to do this, huh?

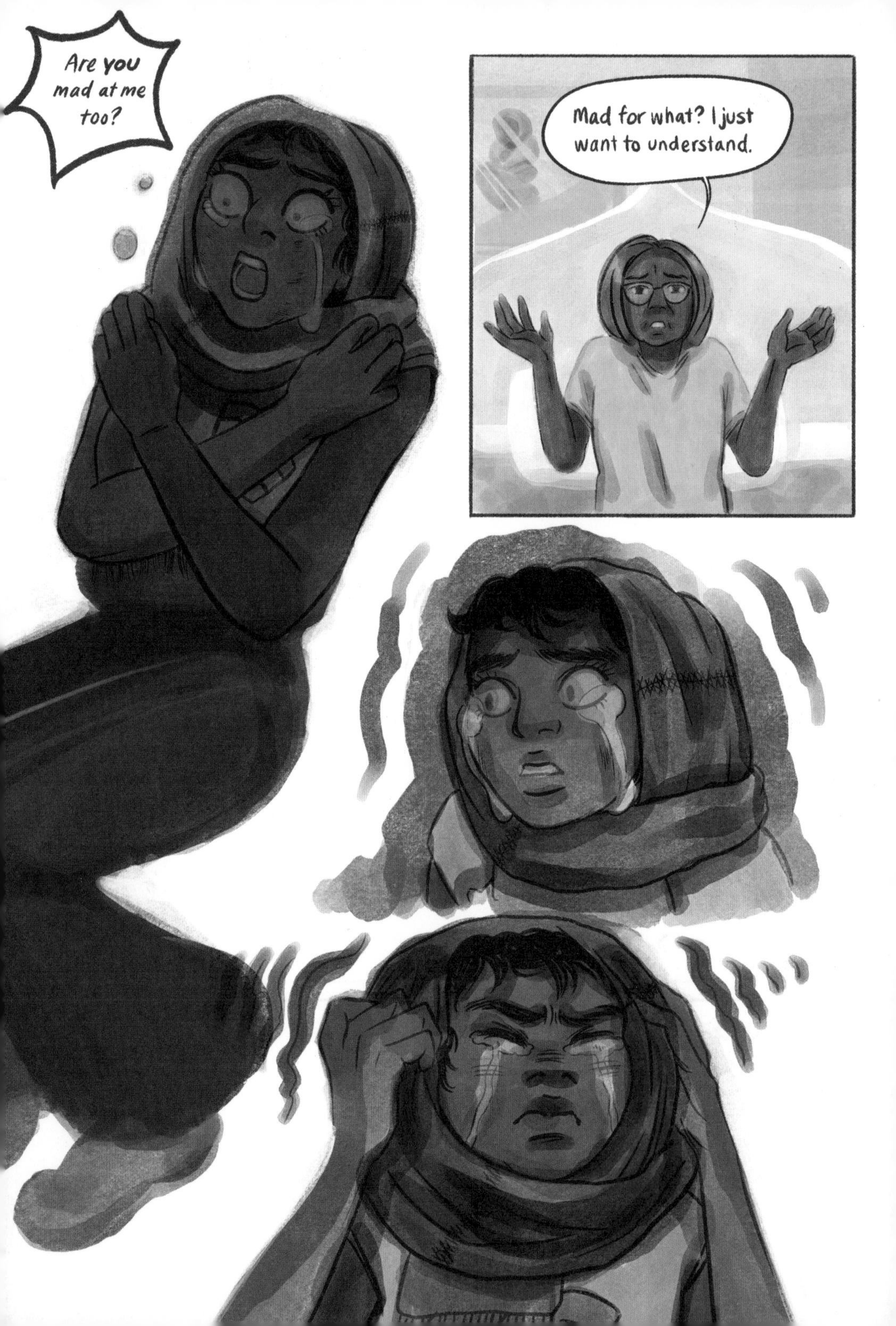
Are you mad at me too?
Mad for what? I just want to understand.

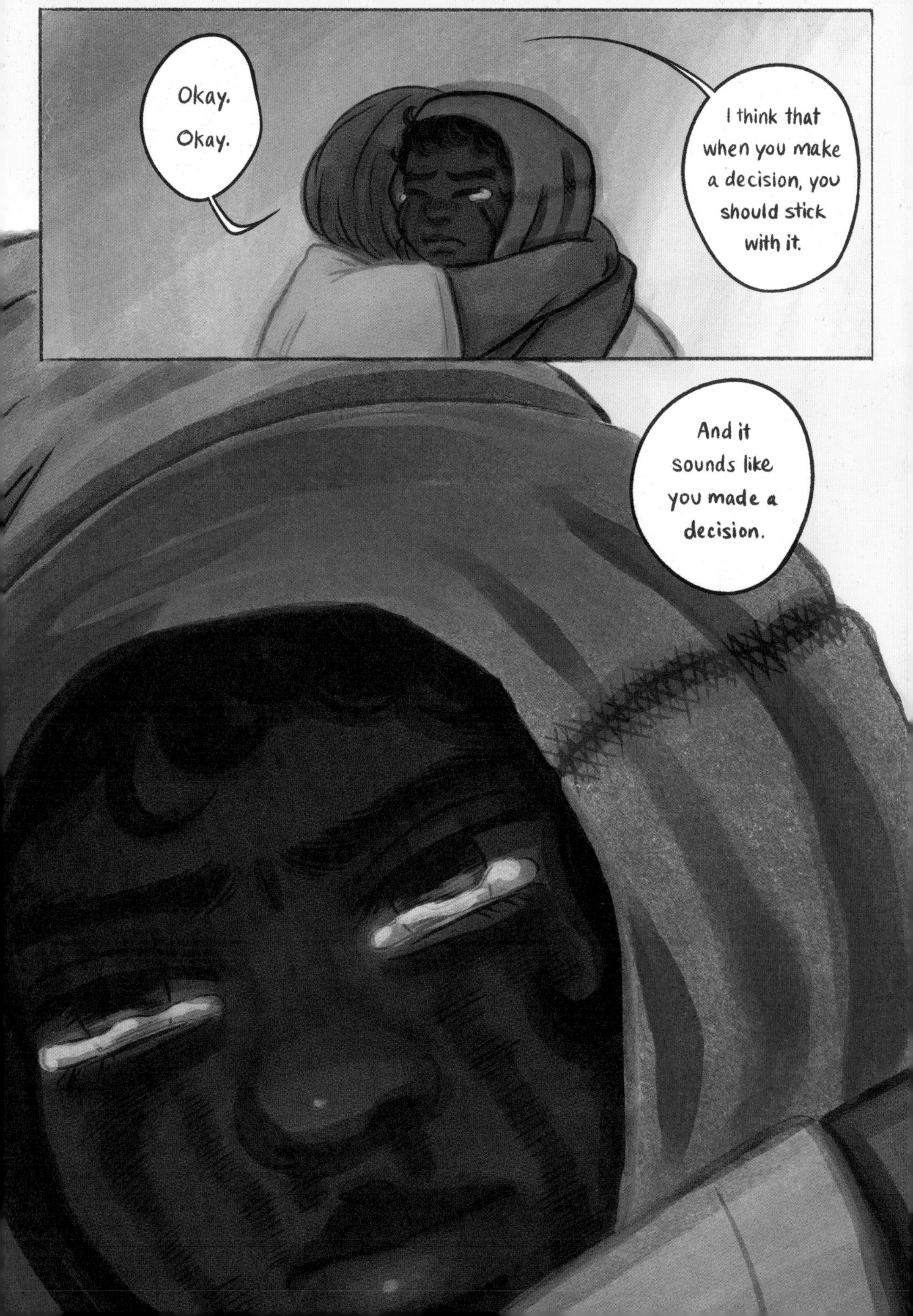
Okay.
Okay.
I think that when you make a decision, you should stick with it.
And it sounds like you made a decision.

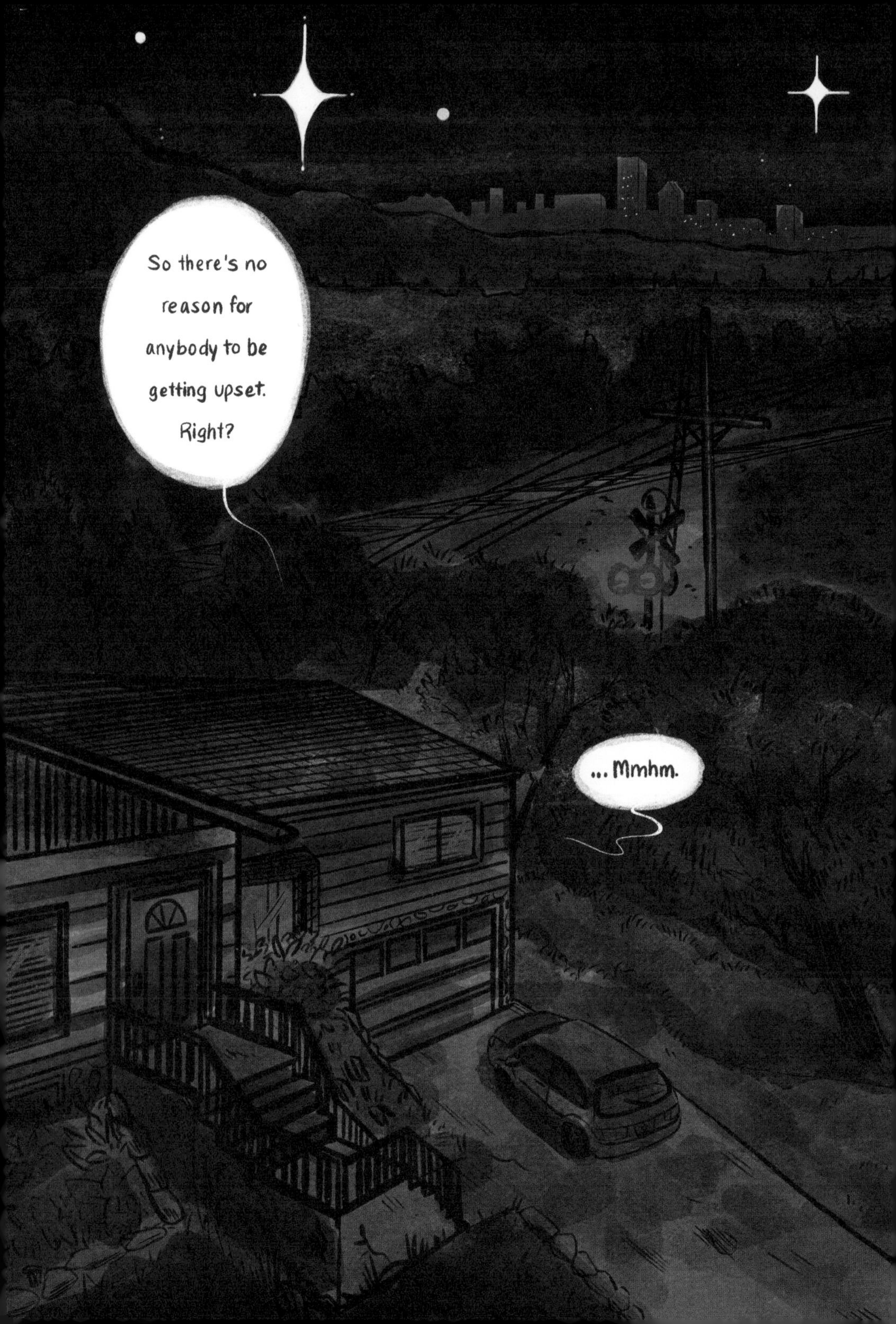
So there's no reason for anybody to be getting upset. Right?
...Mmhm.

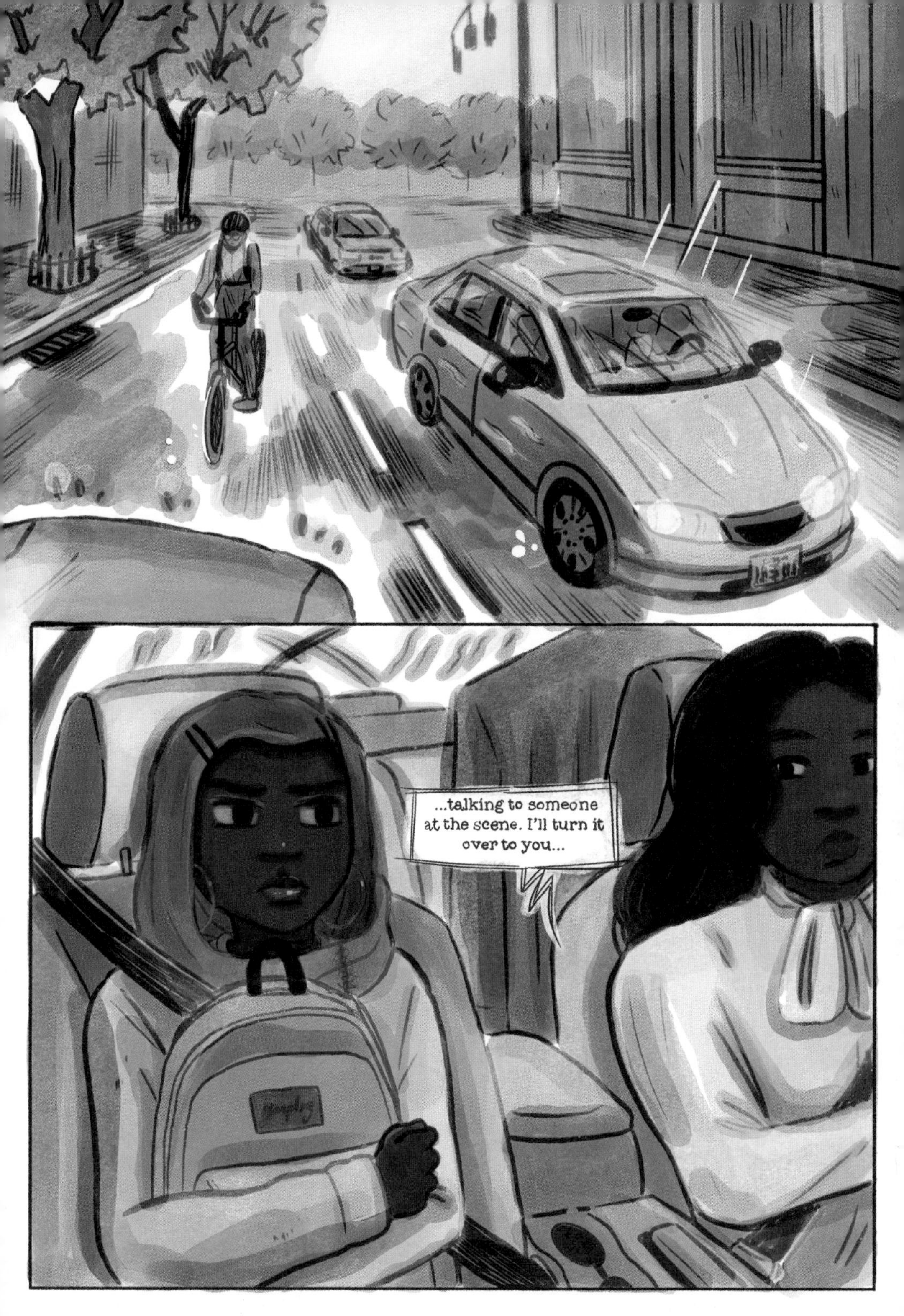
...talking to someone at the scene. I'll turn it over to you...

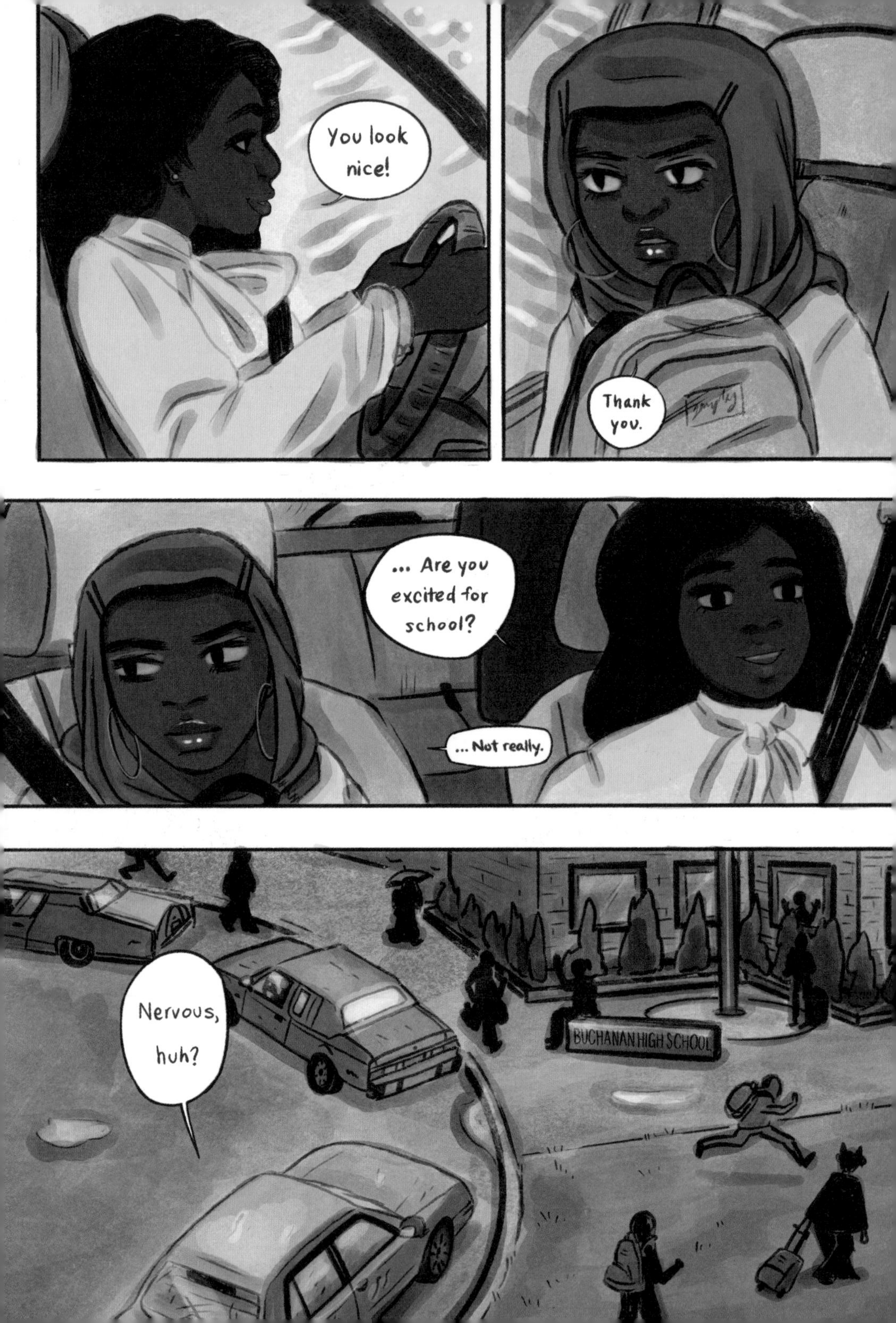
You look nice!
Thank you.
... Are you excited for school?
... Not really.
BUCHANAN HIGH SCHOOL
Nervous, huh?

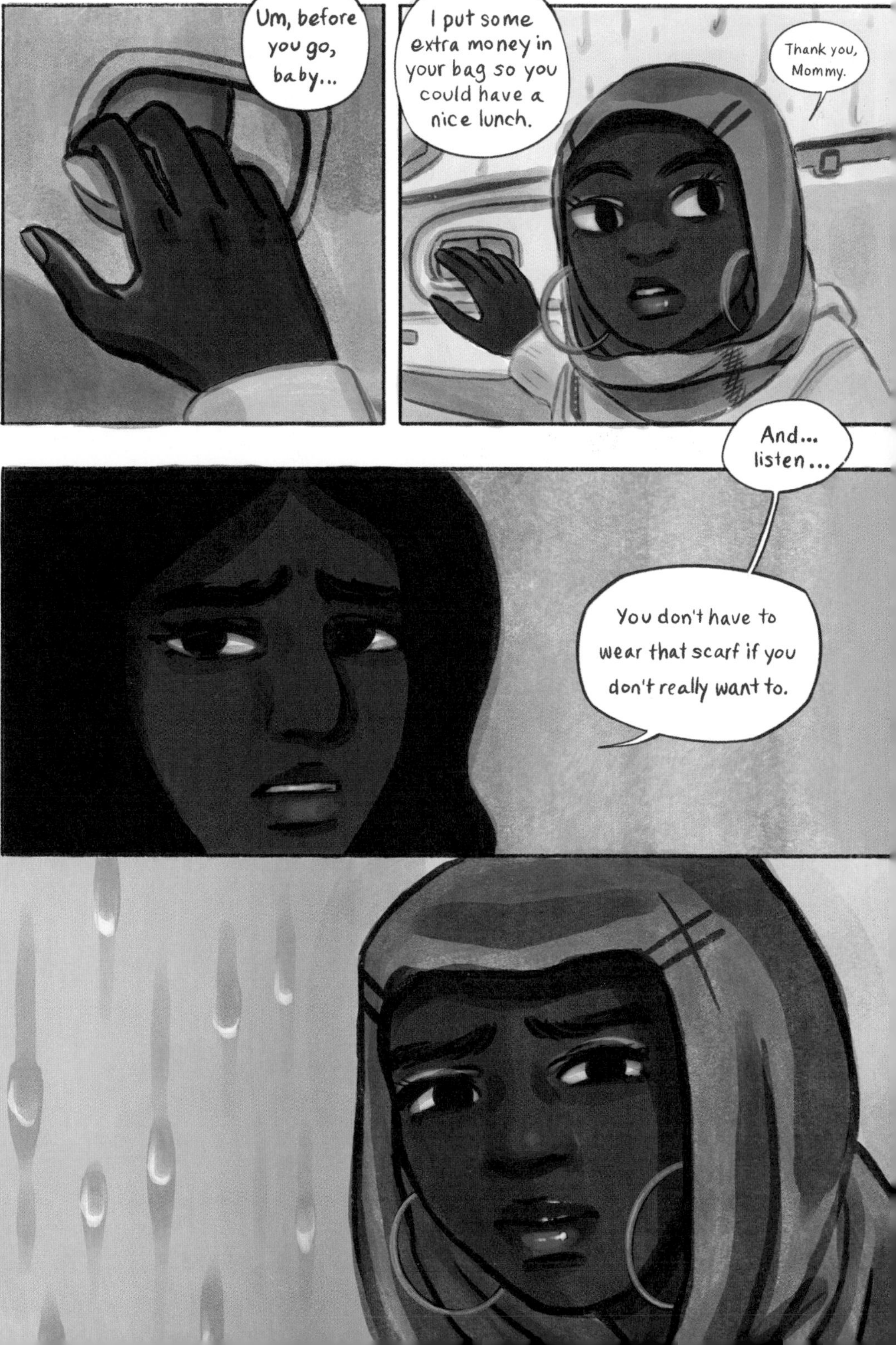
Um, before you go, baby...
I put some extra money in your bag so you could have a nice lunch.
Thank you, Mommy.
And... listen...
You don't have to wear that scarf if you don't really want to.

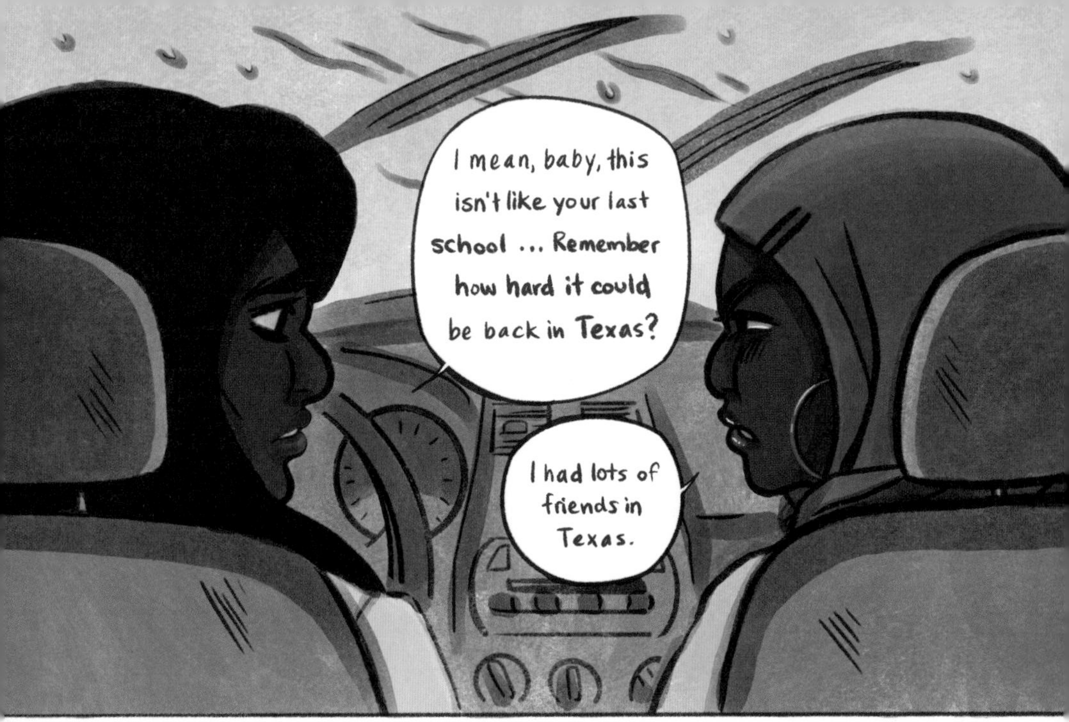
I mean, baby, this isn't like your last school ... Remember how hard it could be back in Texas?
I had lots of friends in Texas.

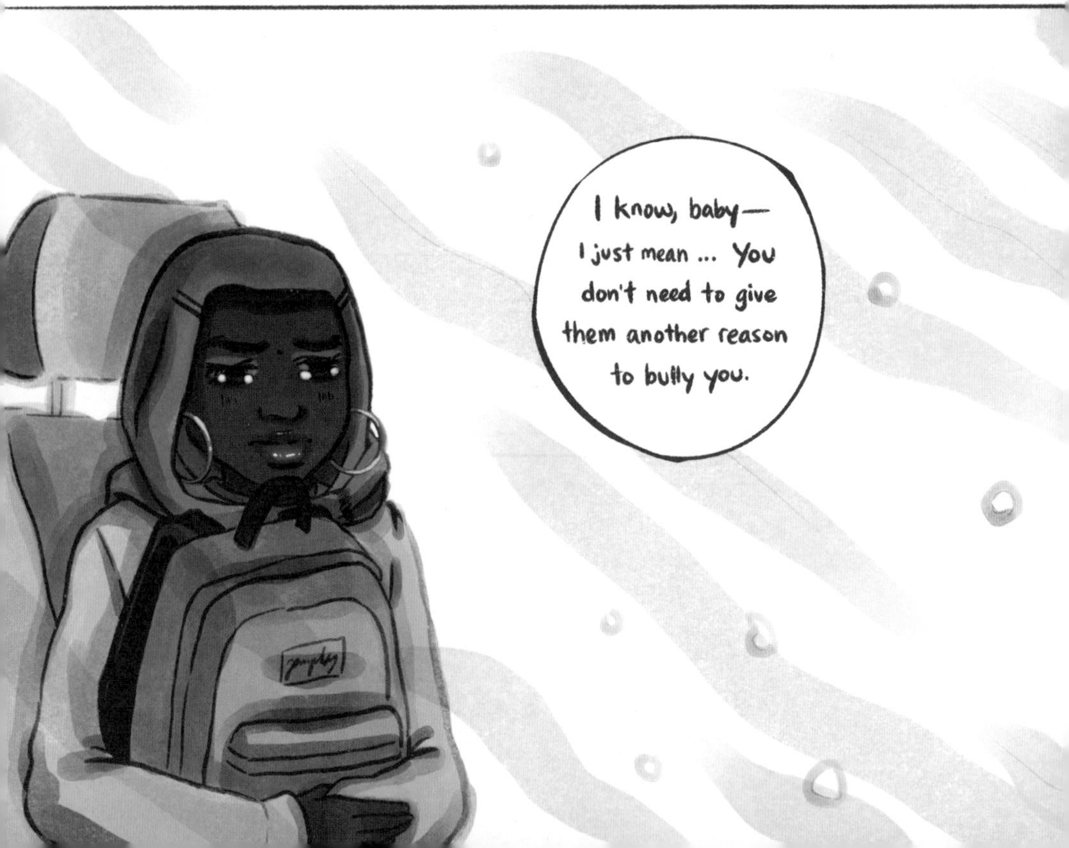
I know, baby— I just mean ... You don't need to give them another reason to bully you.

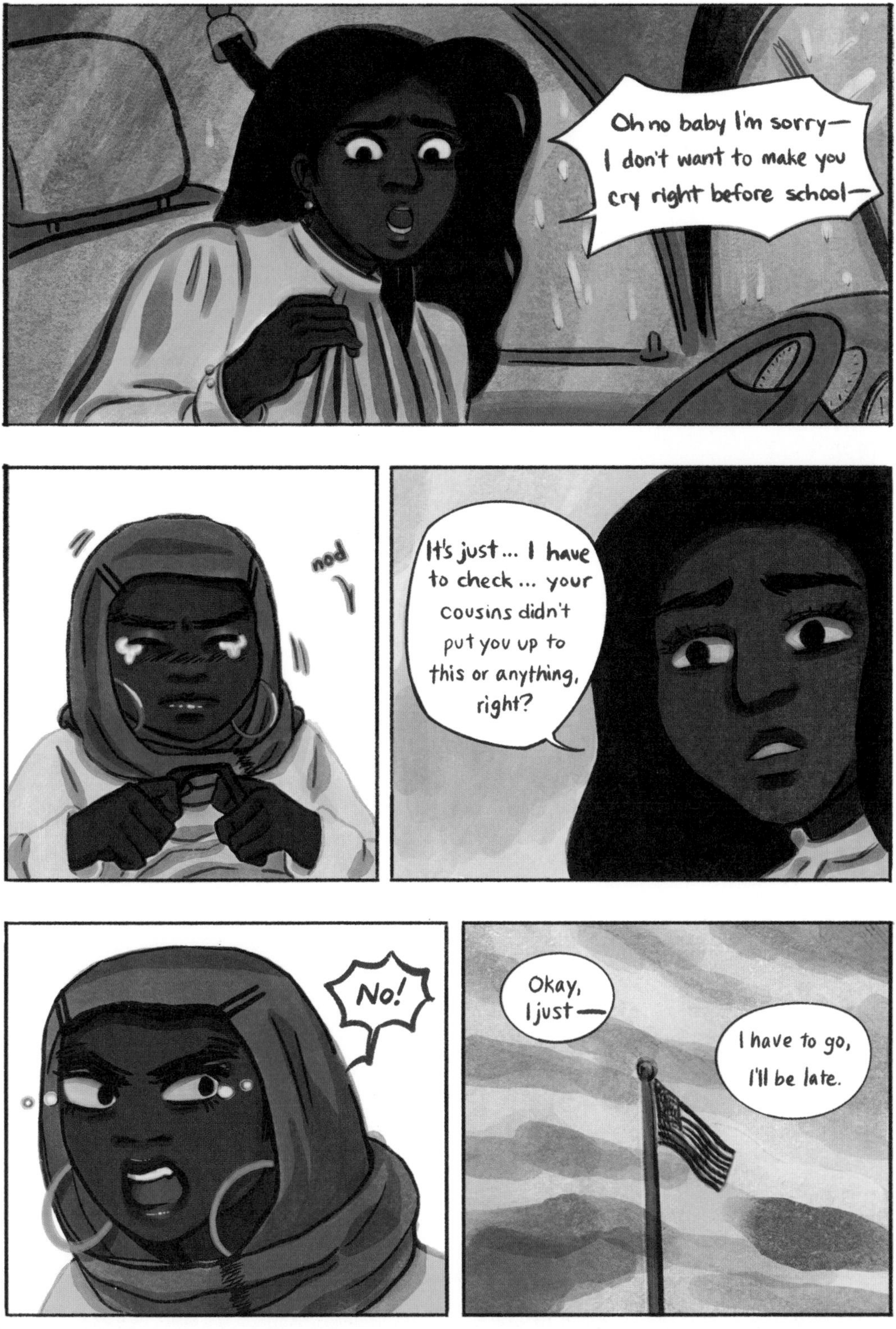
Oh no baby I'm sorry—
I don't want to make you cry right before school—
nod
It's just... I have to check... your cousins didn't put you up to this or anything, right?
No!
Okay, I just—
I have to go, I'll be late.

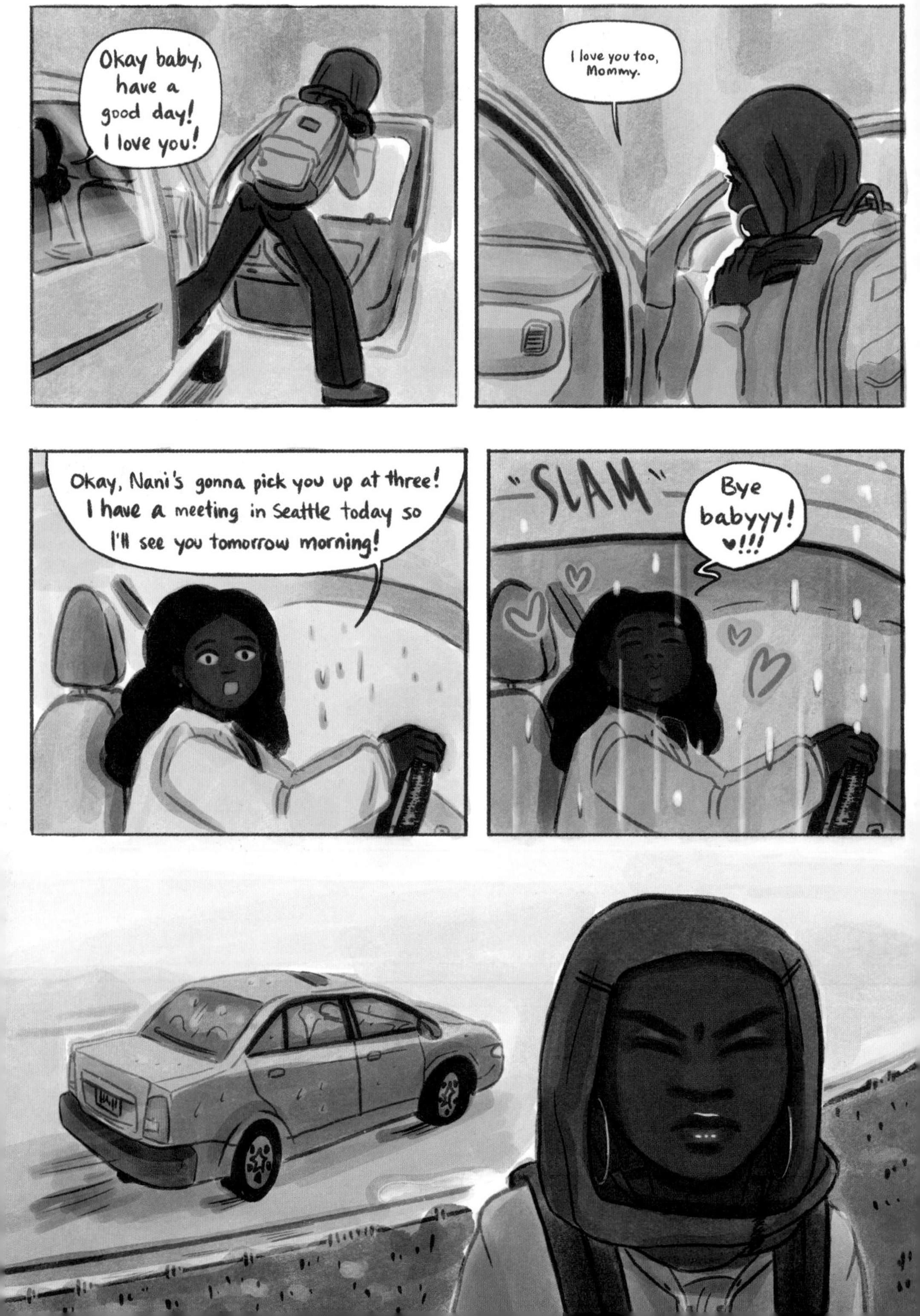

Okay baby, have a good day! I love you!
I love you too, Mommy.
Okay, Nani's gonna pick you up at three! I have a meeting in Seattle today so I'll see you tomorrow morning!
"SLAM"
Bye babyyy! ♥!!!

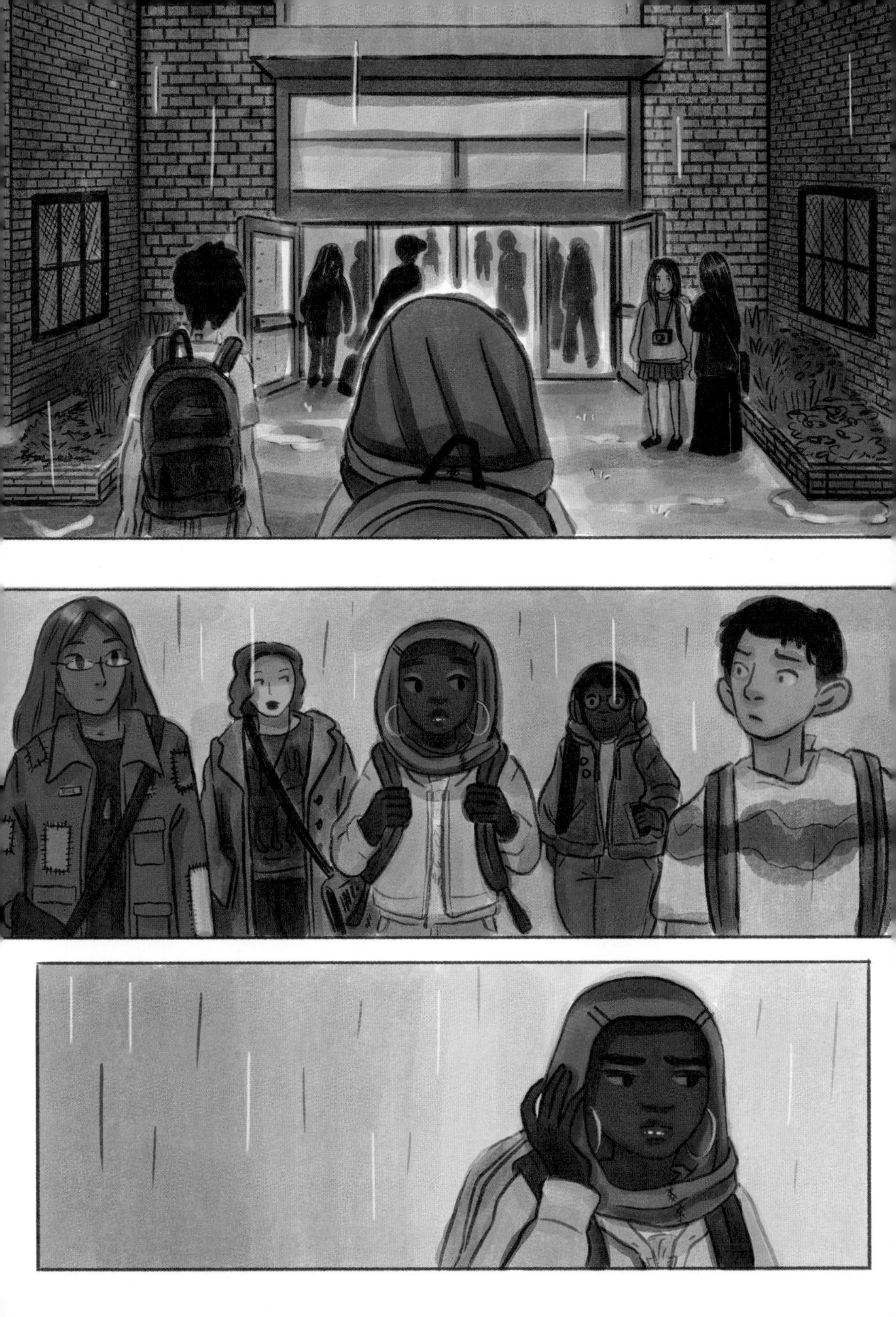

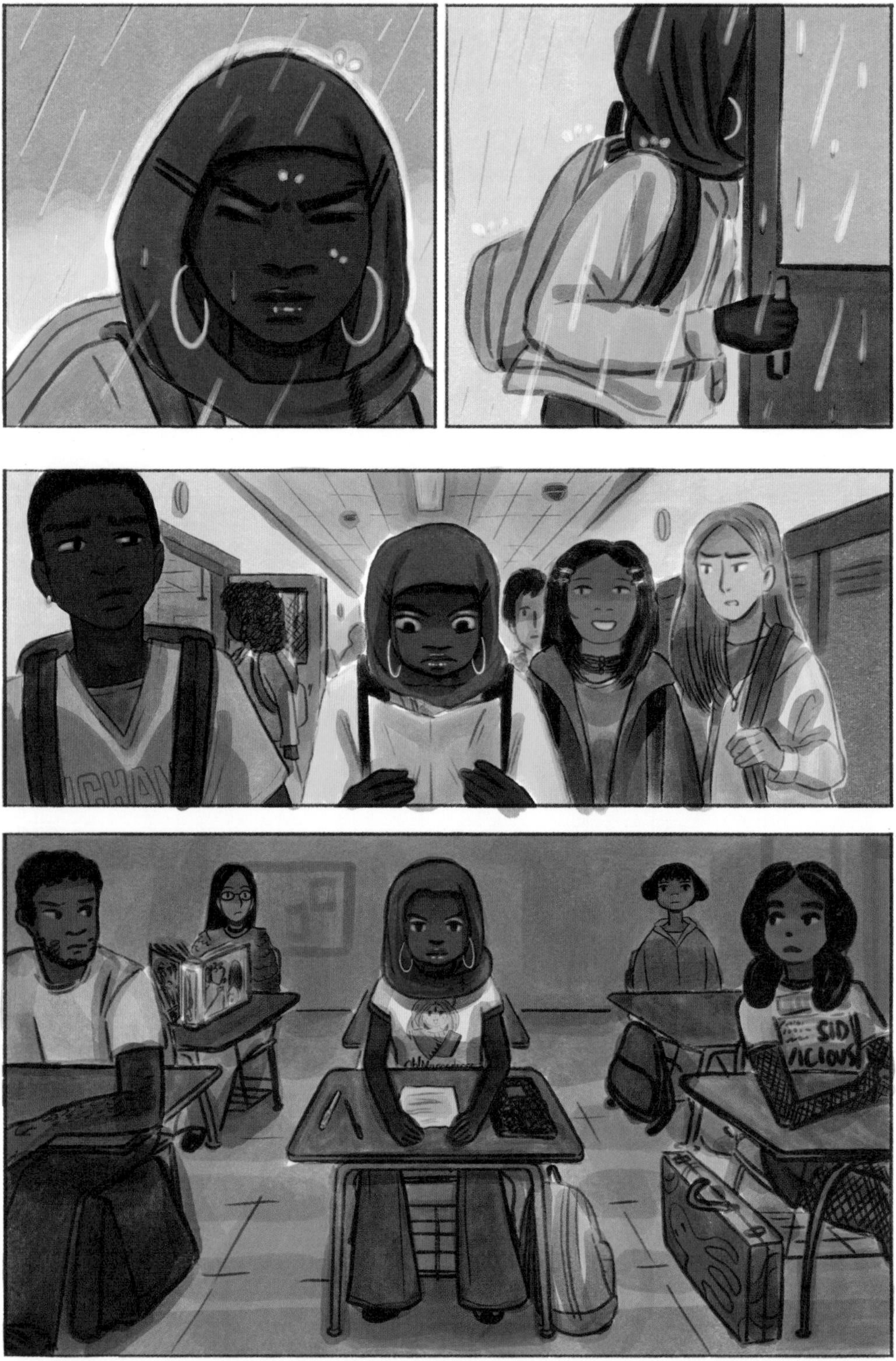
SID

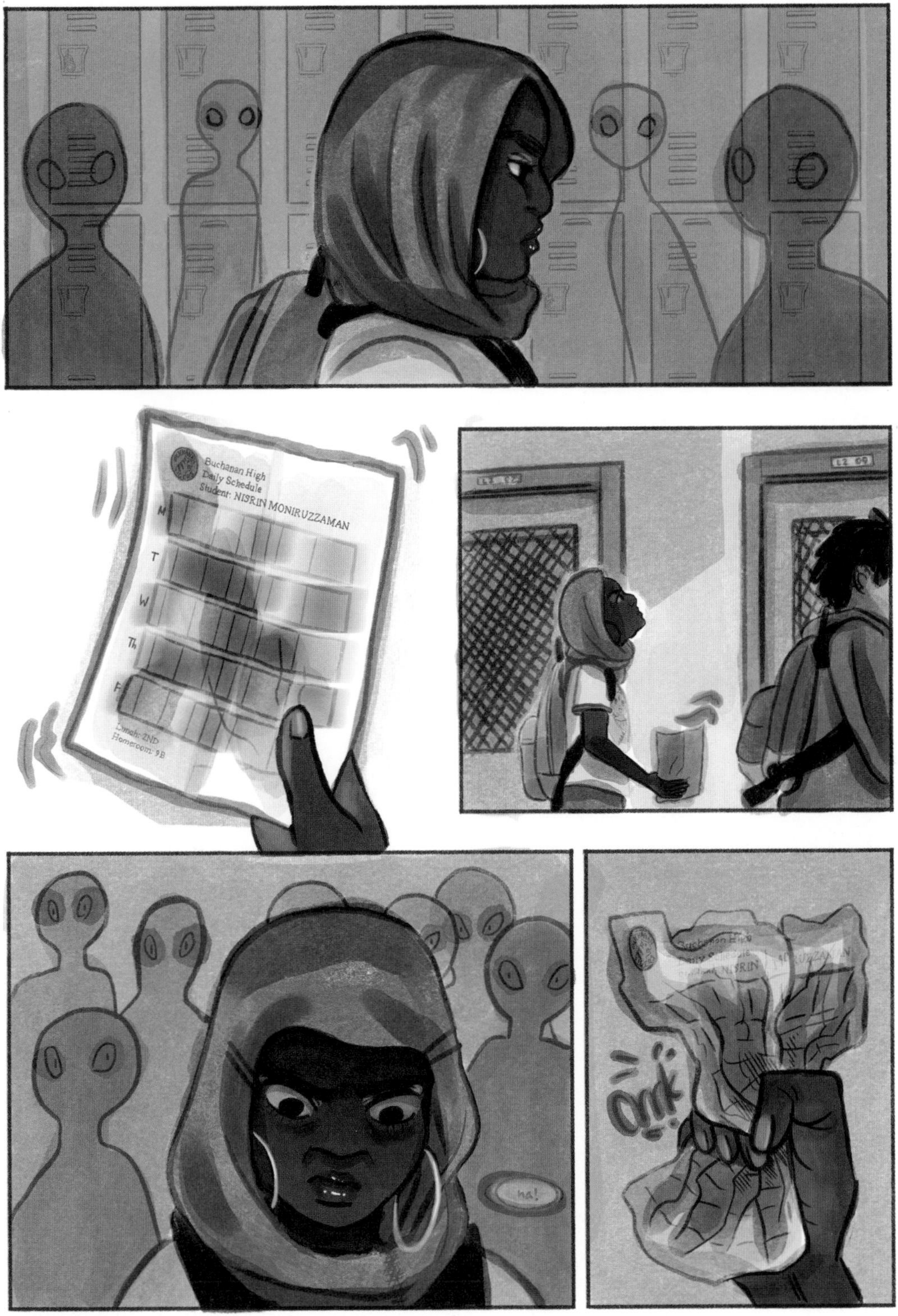

Buchanan High
Daily Schedule
Student: NISRIN MONIRUZZAMAN
M
T
W
Th
F
Lunch: 2ND
Homeroom: 9B
L2 09
ha!
Crk

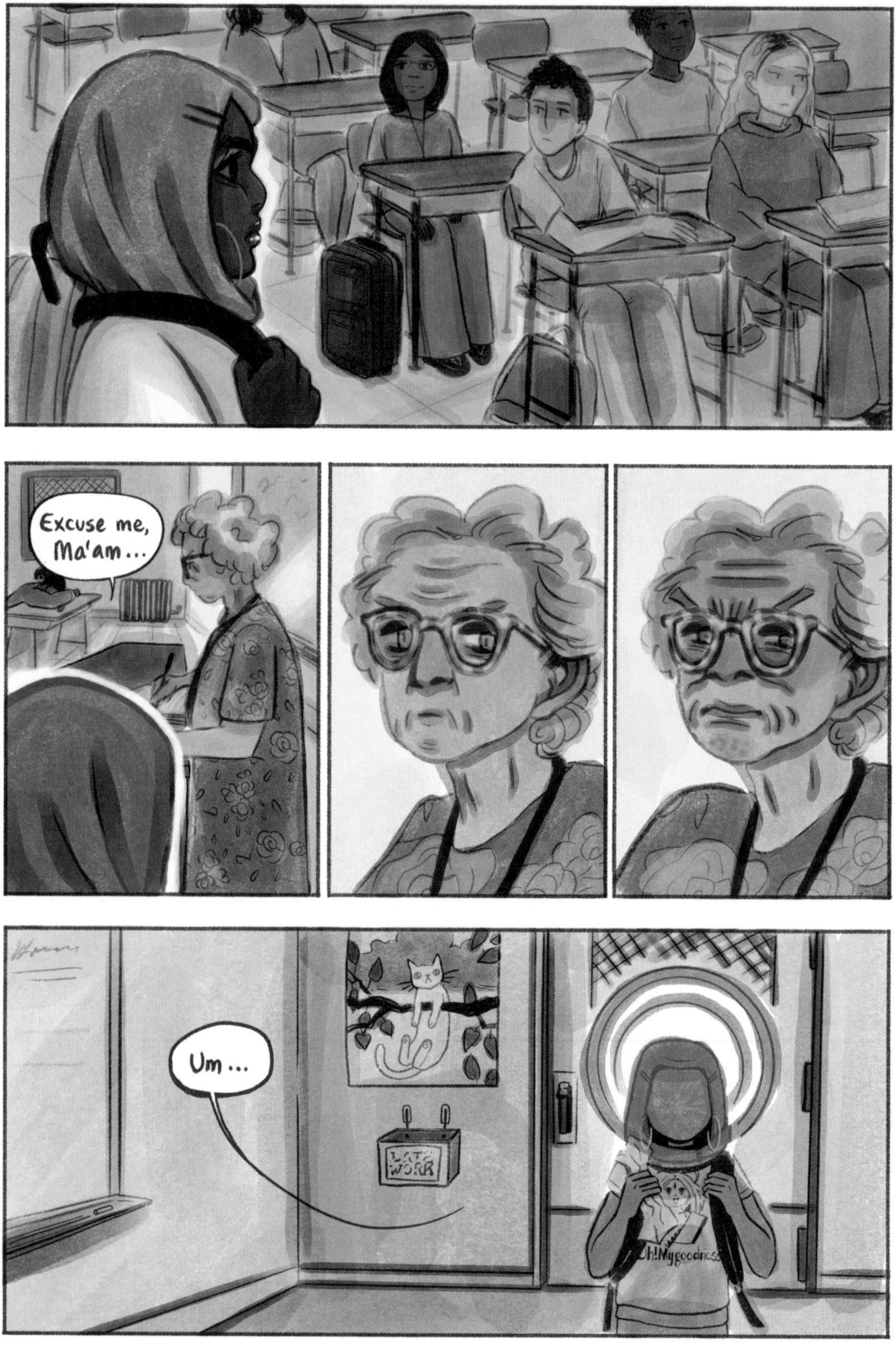
Excuse me, Ma'am...
Um...
LATE WORK
Oh! My goodness

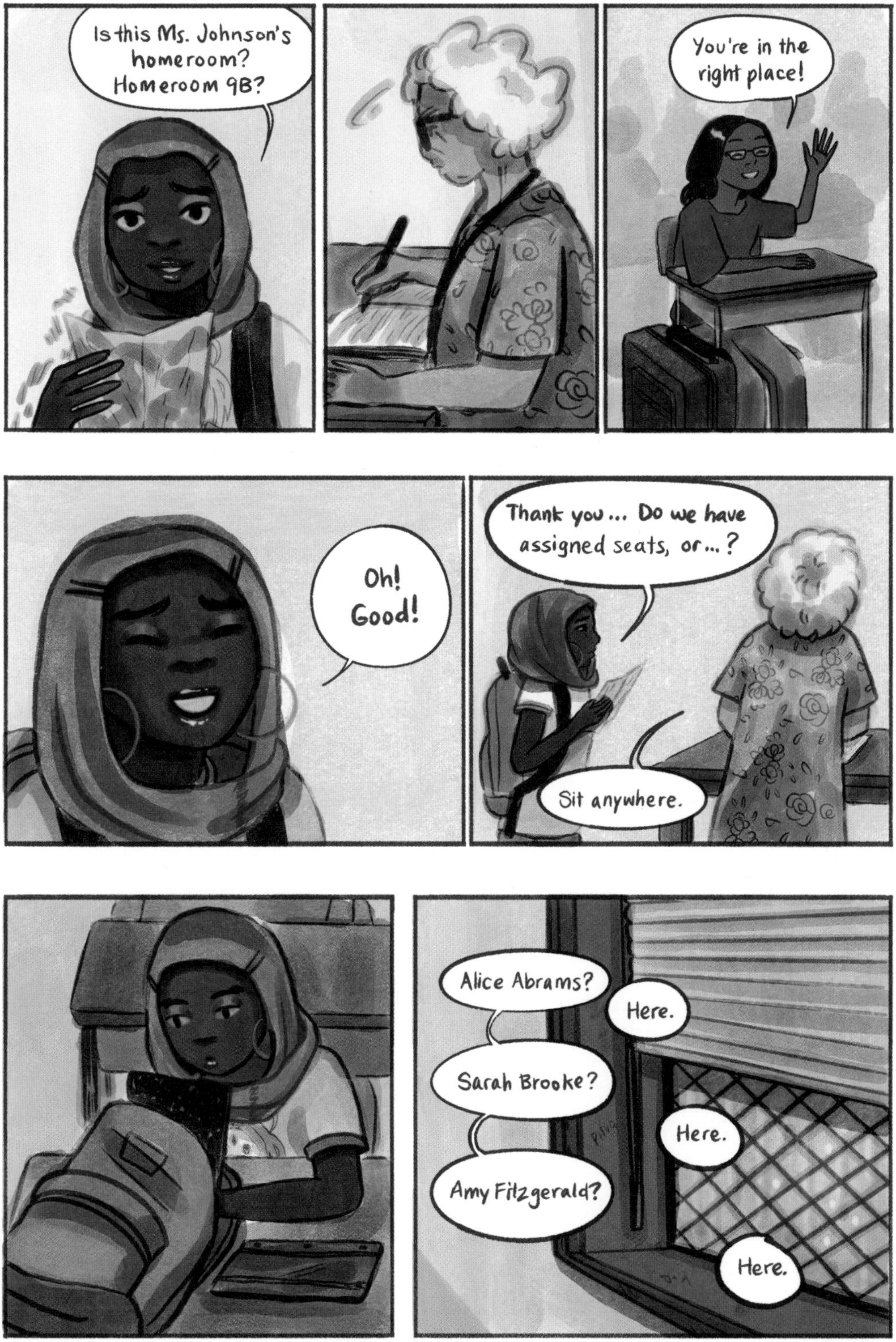
Is this Ms. Johnson's homeroom? Homeroom 9B?
You're in the right place!
Oh! Good!
Thank you... Do we have assigned seats, or...?
Sit anywhere.
Alice Abrams?
Here.
Sarah Brooke?
Here.
Amy Fitzgerald?
Here.

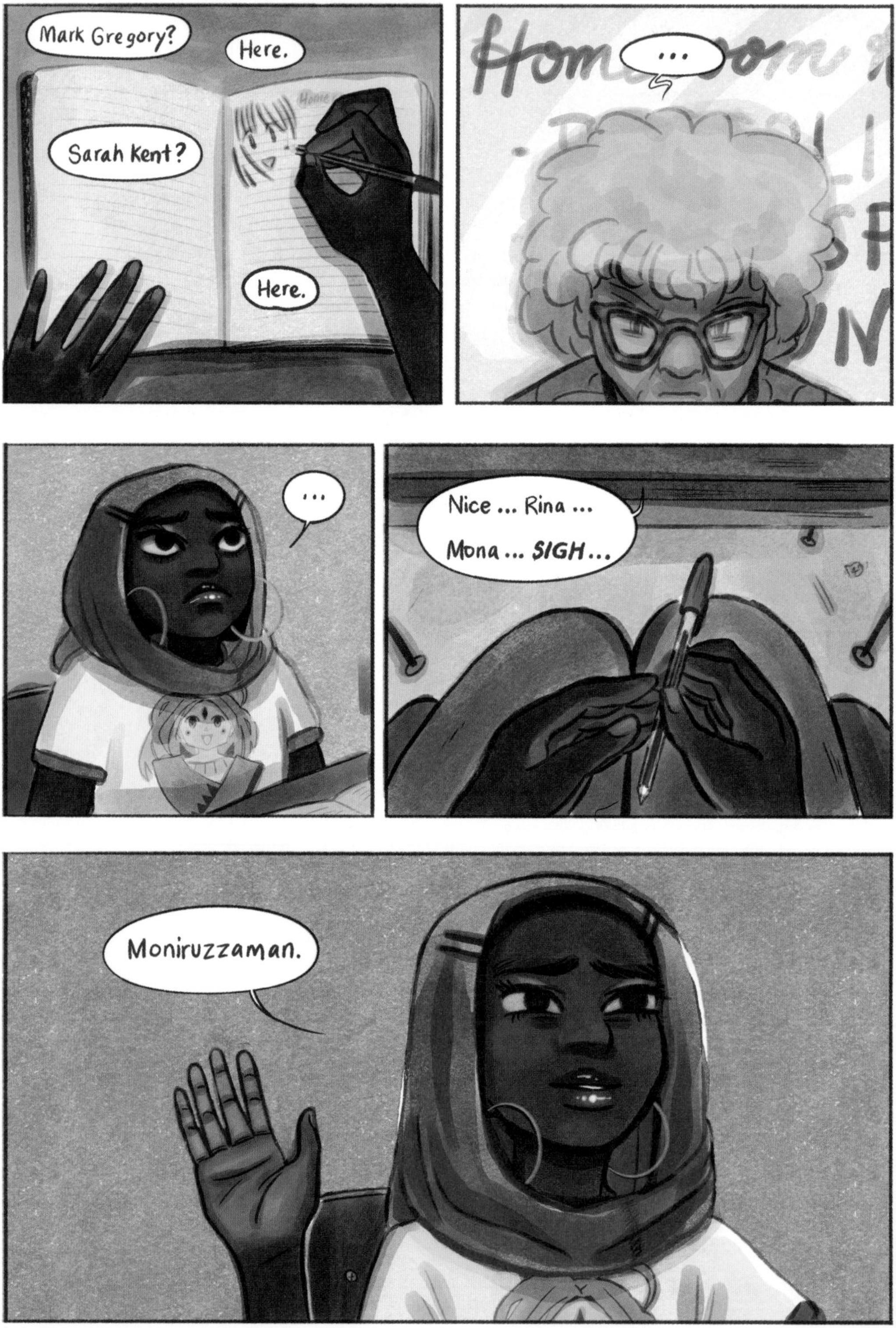

Mark Gregory?
Here.
Sarah Kent?
Here.
...
...
Nice ... Rina ... Mona ... SIGH ...
Moniruzzaman.

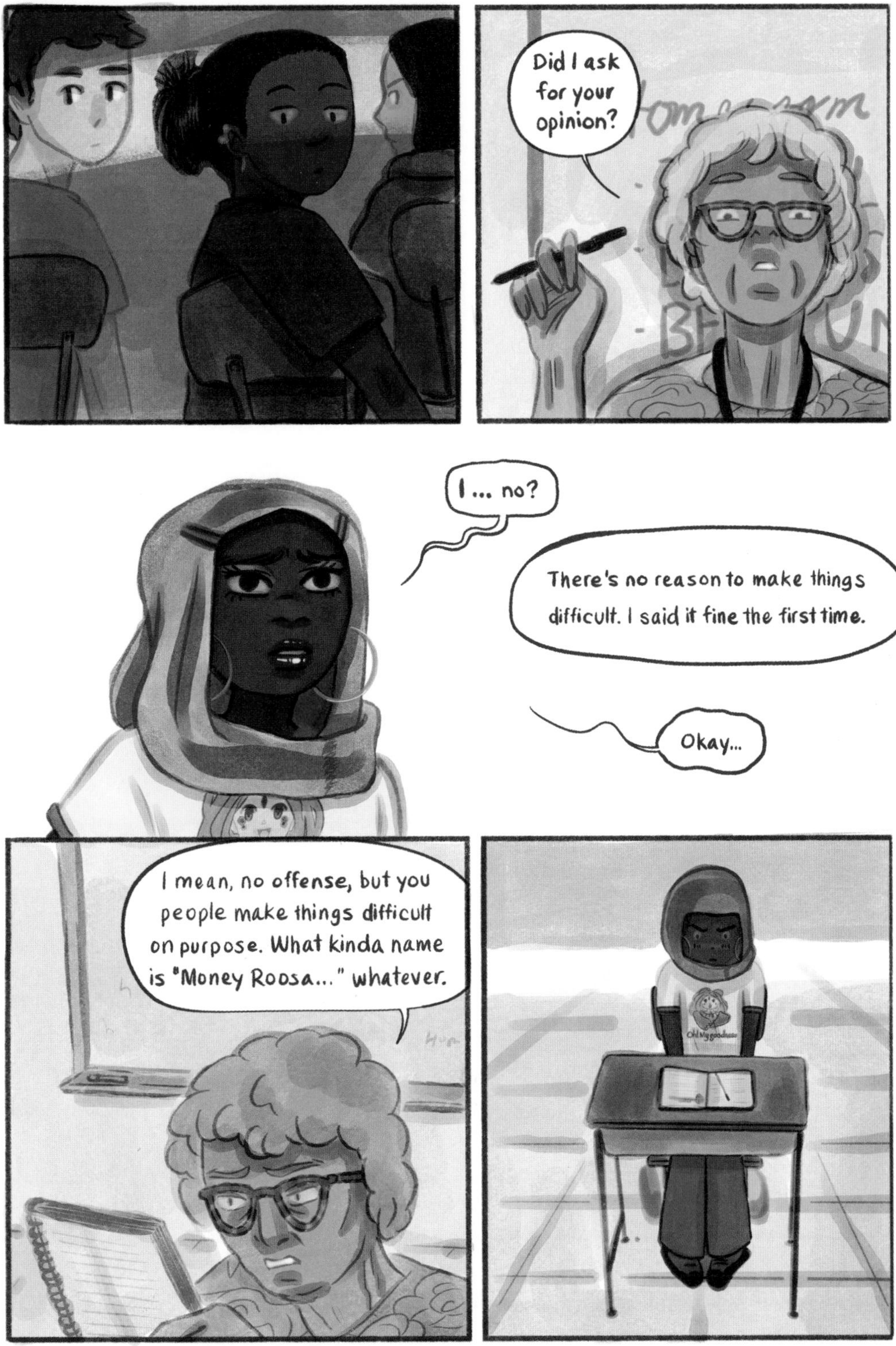
Did I ask for your opinion?
I... no?
There's no reason to make things difficult. I said it fine the first time.
Okay...
I mean, no offense, but you people make things difficult on purpose. What kinda name is "Money Roosa..." whatever.

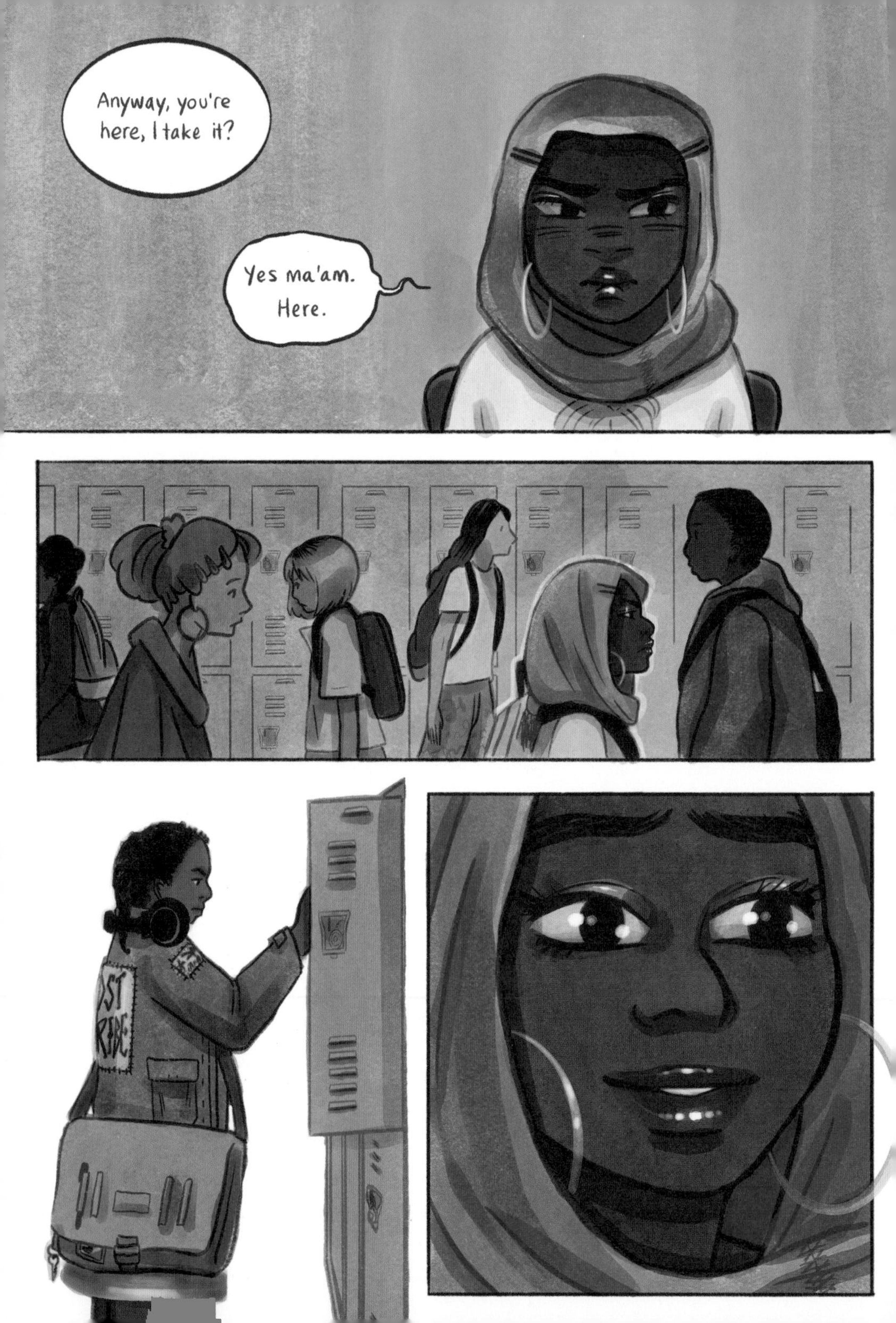
Anyway, you're here, I take it?
Yes ma'am. Here.

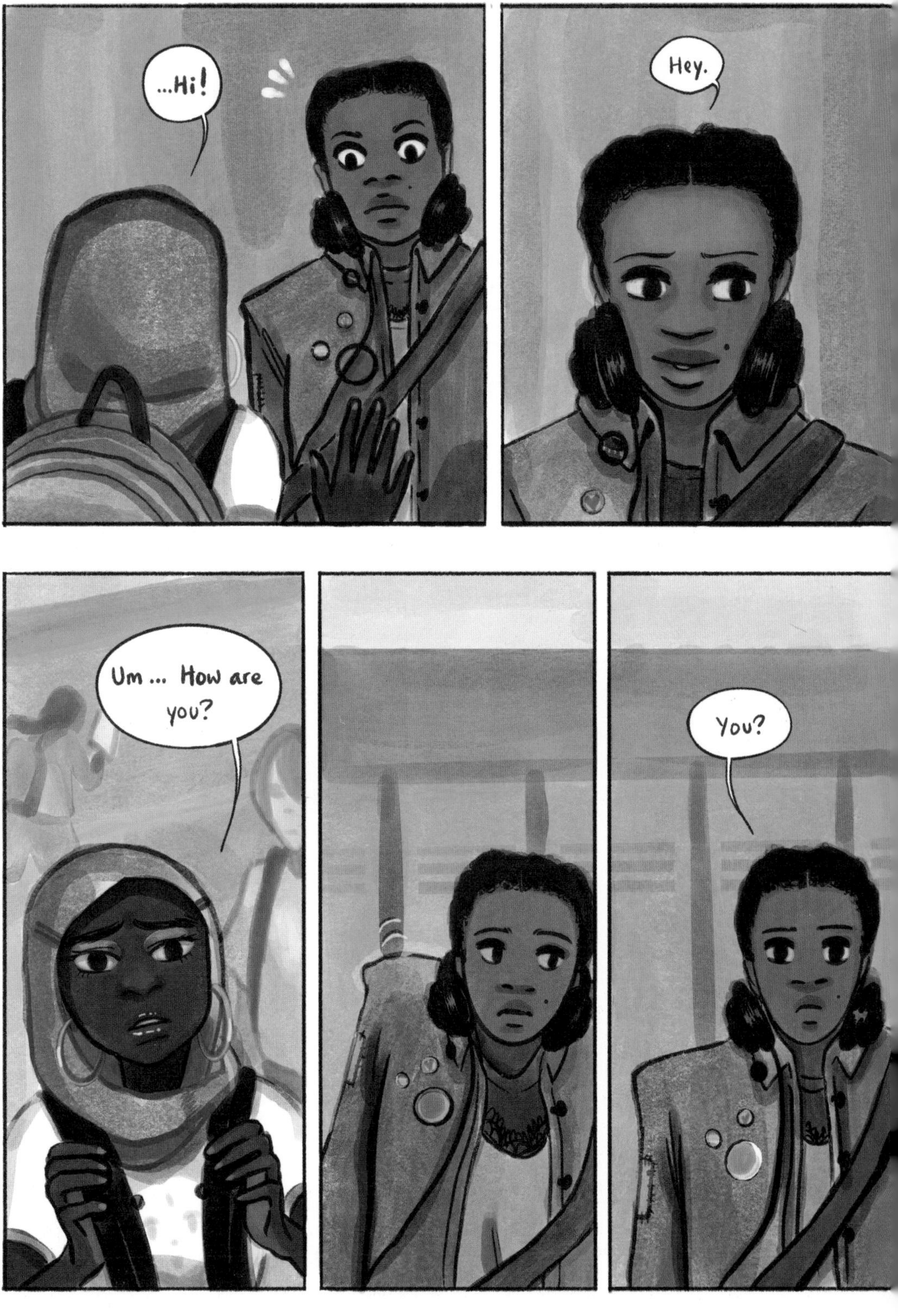
...Hi!
Hey.
Um ... How are you?
You?

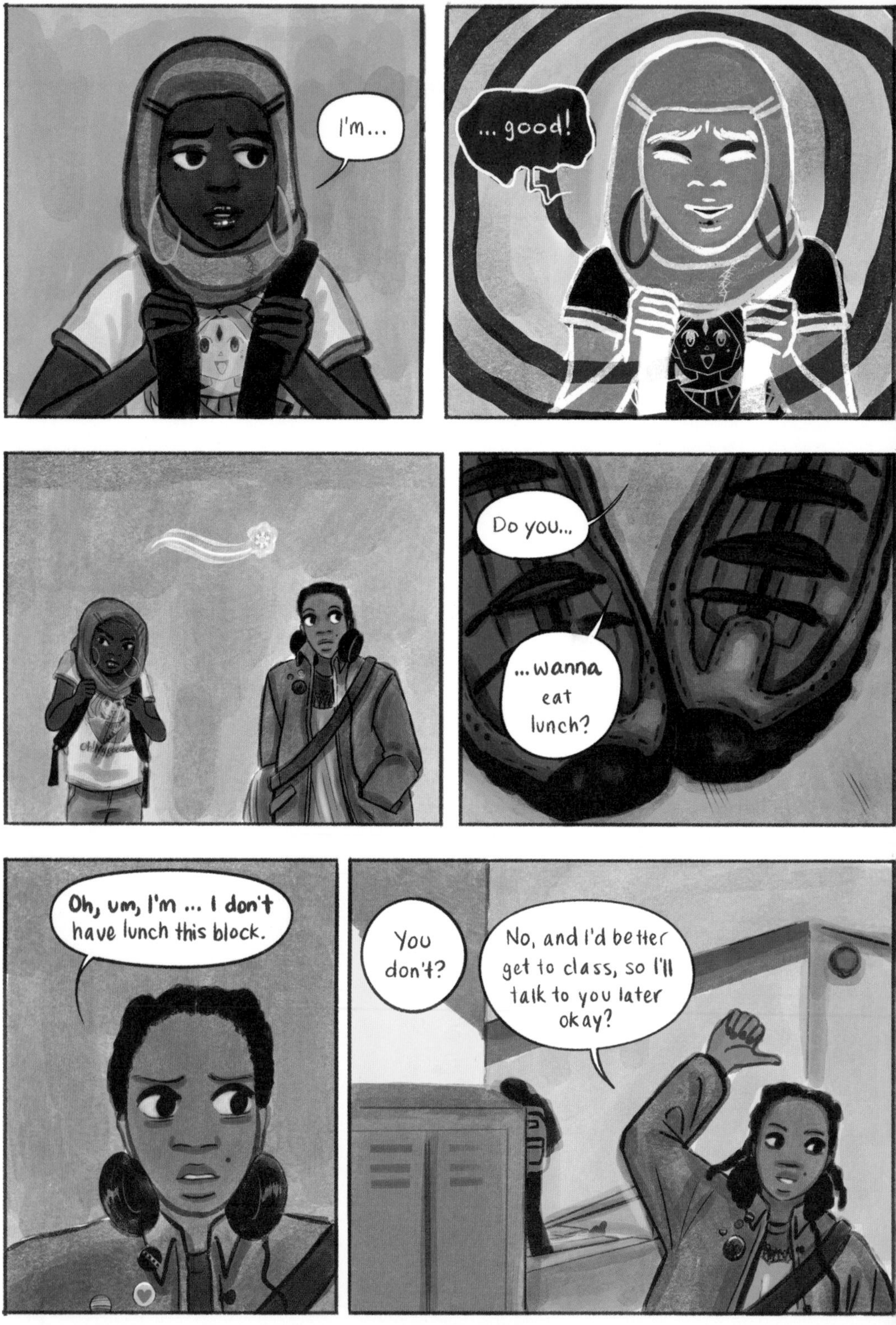
I'm...
...good!
Do you...
...wanna eat lunch?
Oh, um, I'm ... I don't have lunch this block.
You don't?
No, and I'd better get to class, so I'll talk to you later okay?

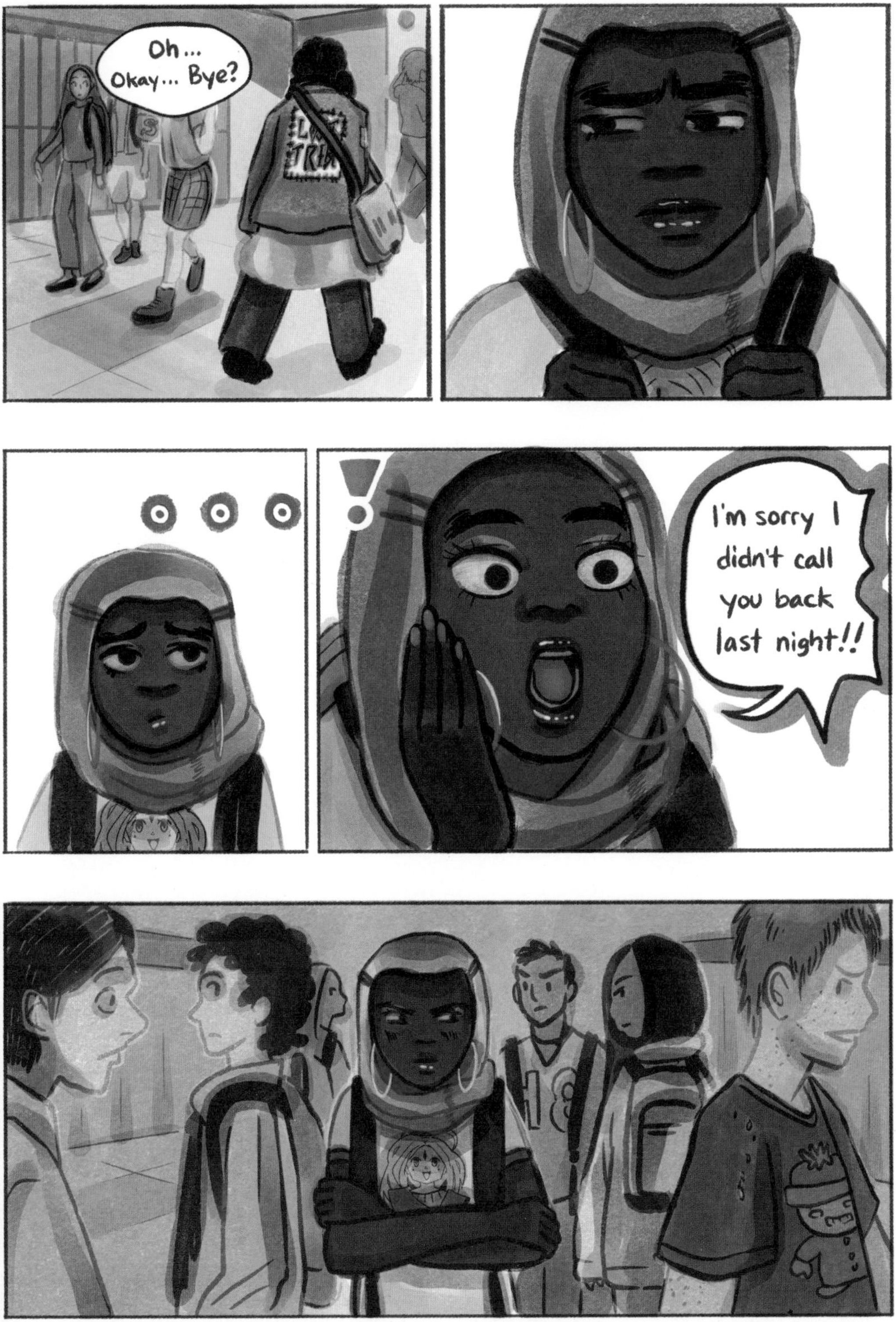
Oh...
Okay... Bye?
I'm sorry I didn't call you back last night!!

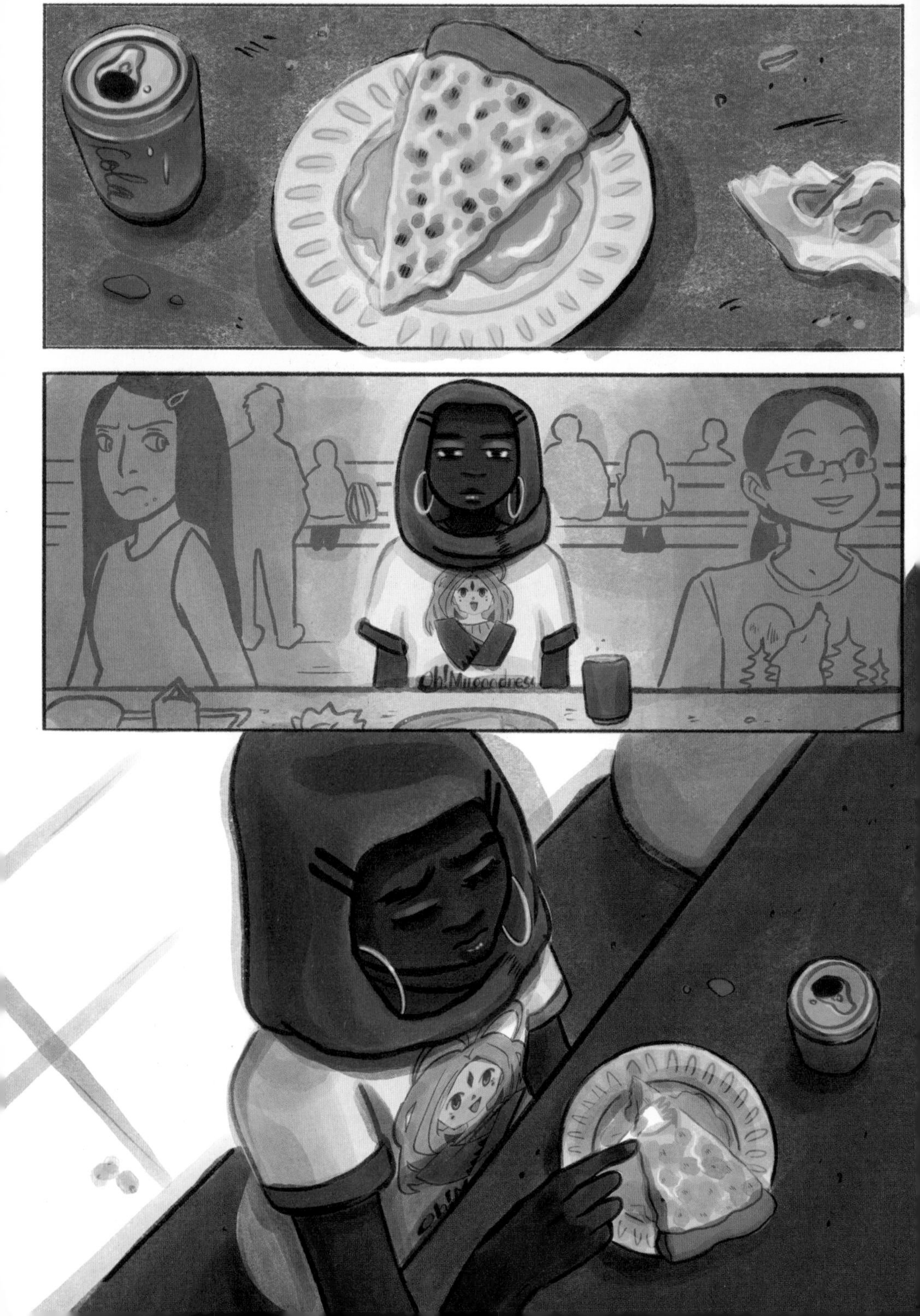
Cola

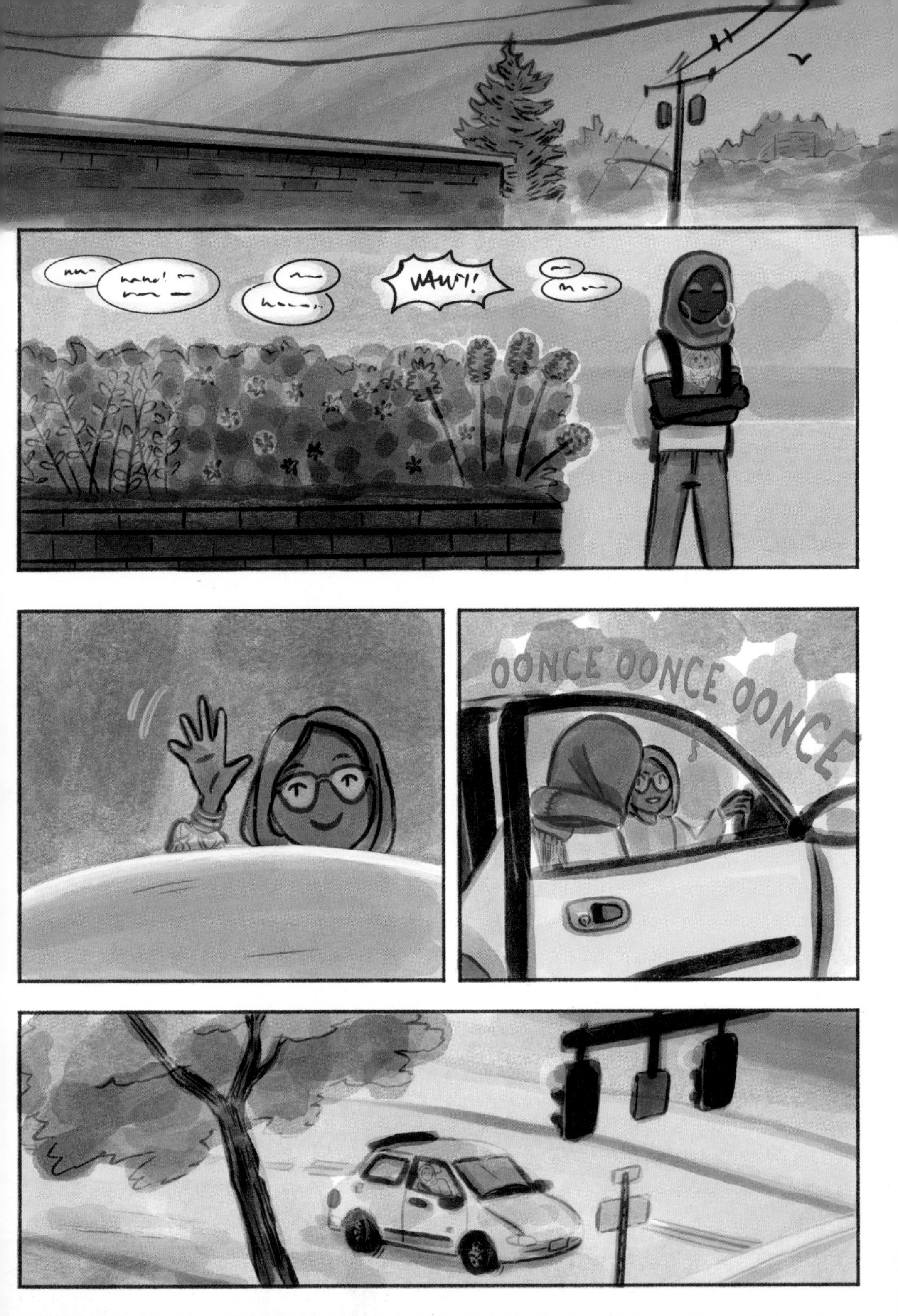
OONCE OONCE OONCE OONCE

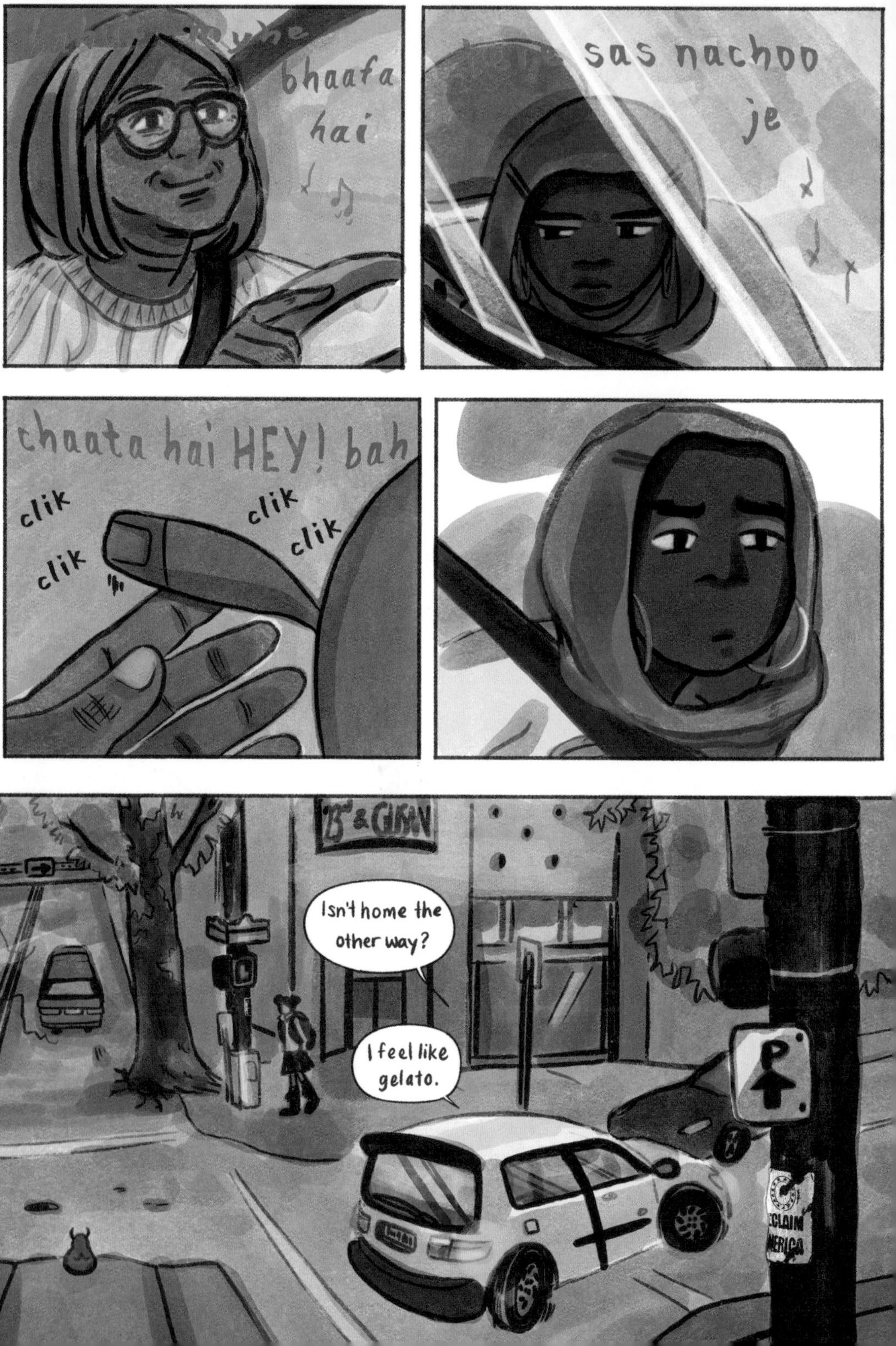

bhaata
hai
sas nachoo
je
chaata hai HEY! bah
clik
clik
clik
clik
Isn't home the other way?
I feel like gelato.

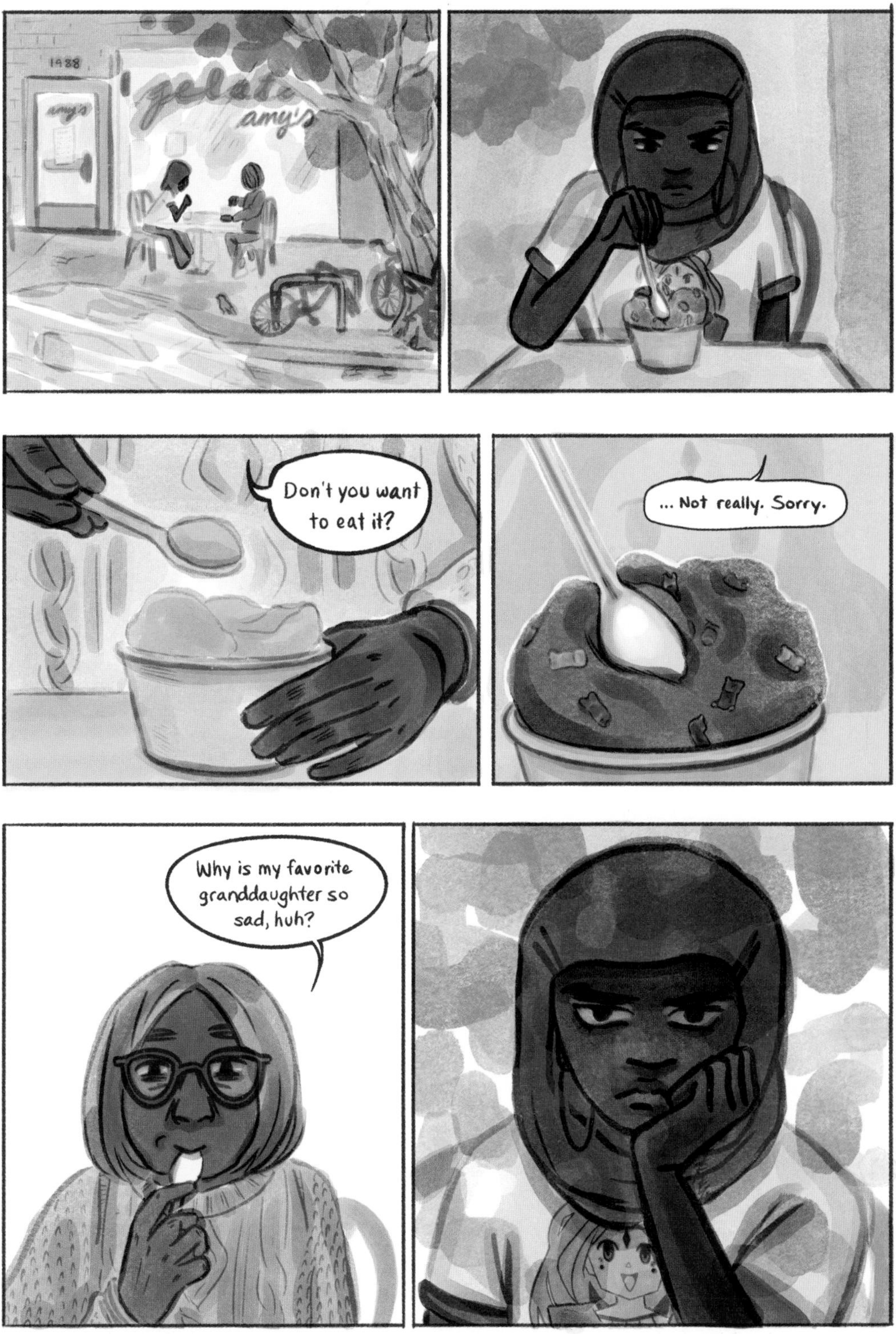
1988
gelato
amy's
amy's
Don't you want to eat it?
... Not really. Sorry.
Why is my favorite granddaughter so sad, huh?

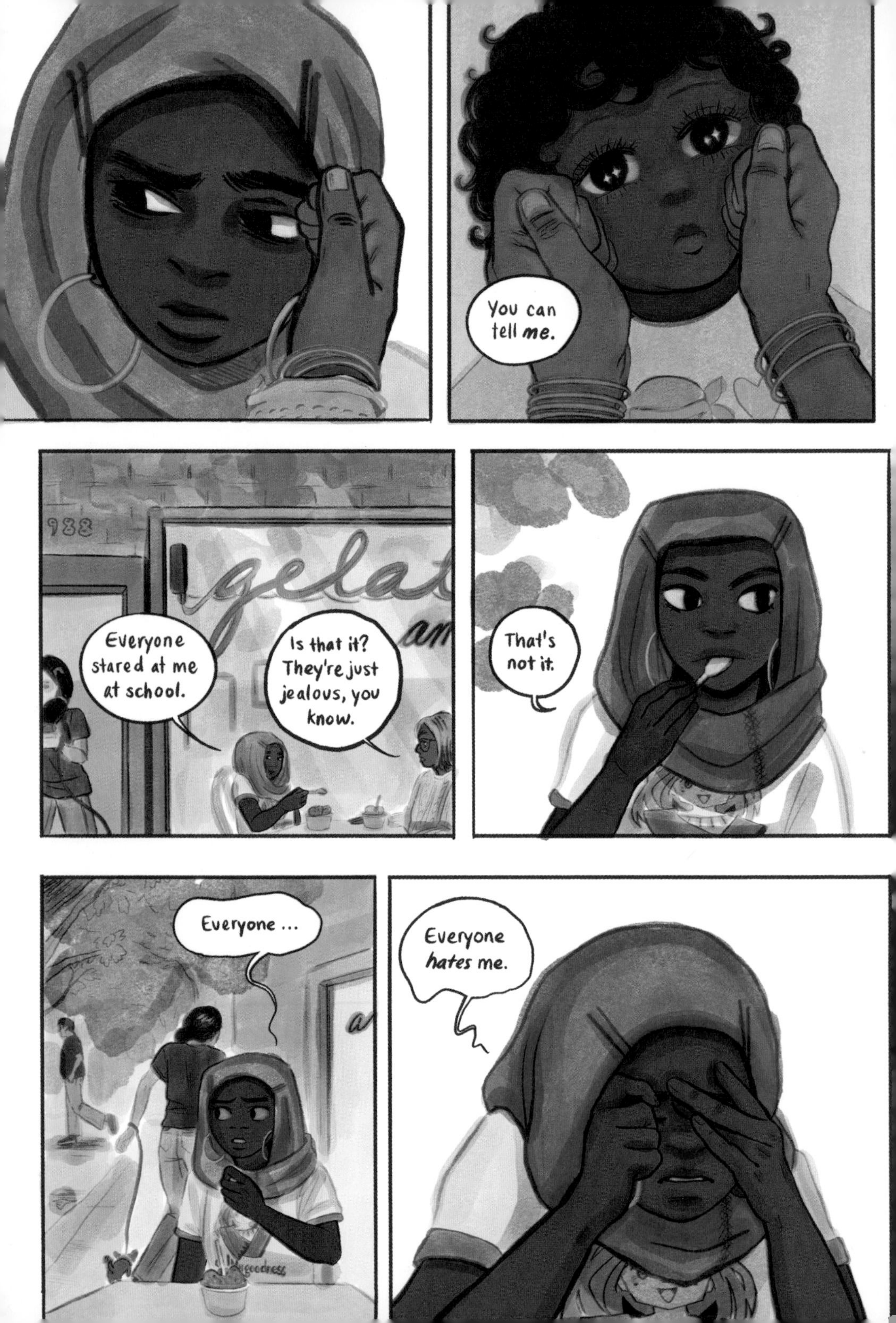
You can tell me.
Everyone stared at me at school.
Is that it? They're just jealous, you know.
That's not it.
Everyone ...
Everyone hates me.

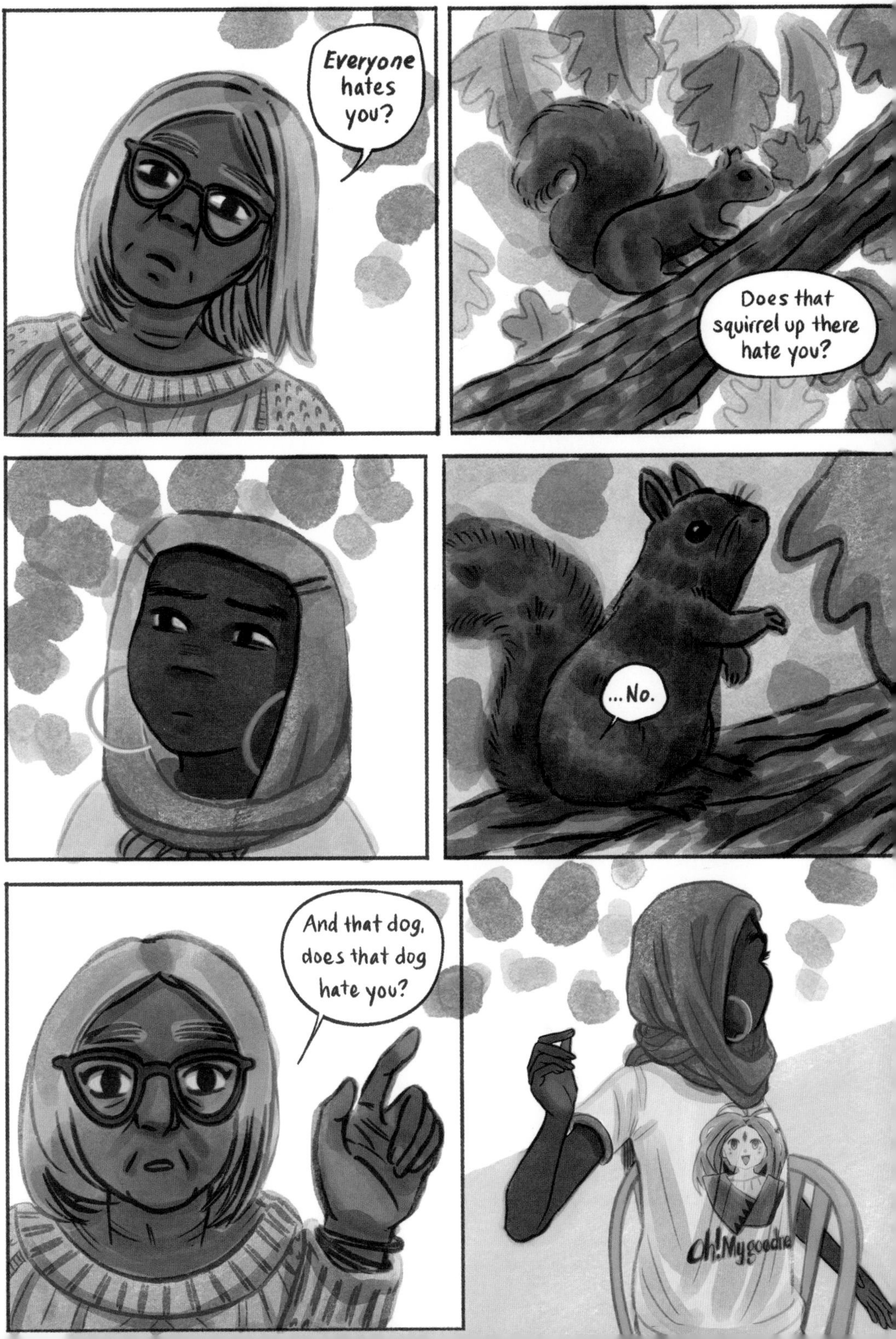
Everyone hates you?
Does that squirrel up there hate you?
...No.
And that dog, does that dog hate you?
Oh! My goddess

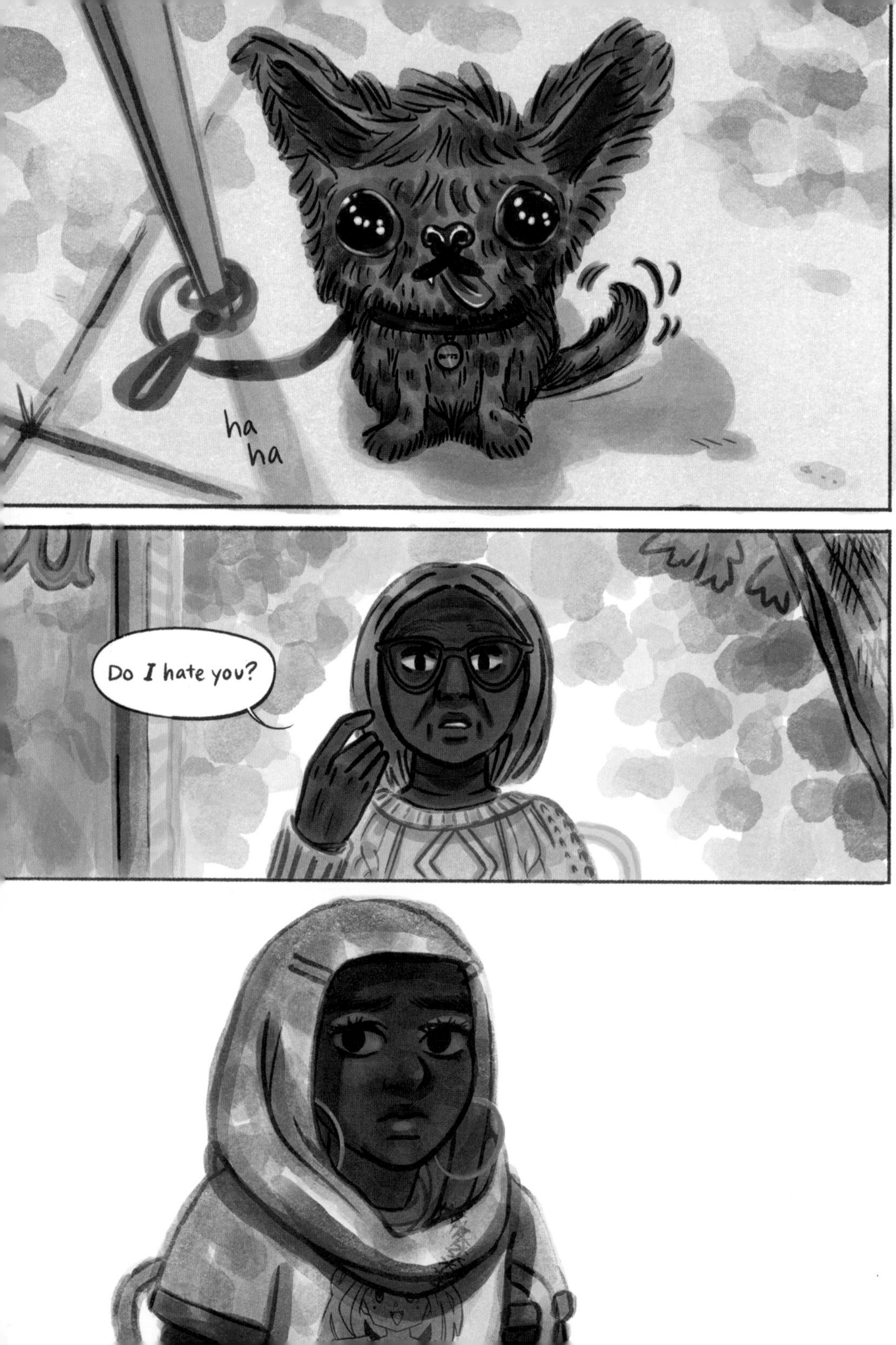
ha
ha
Do I hate you?

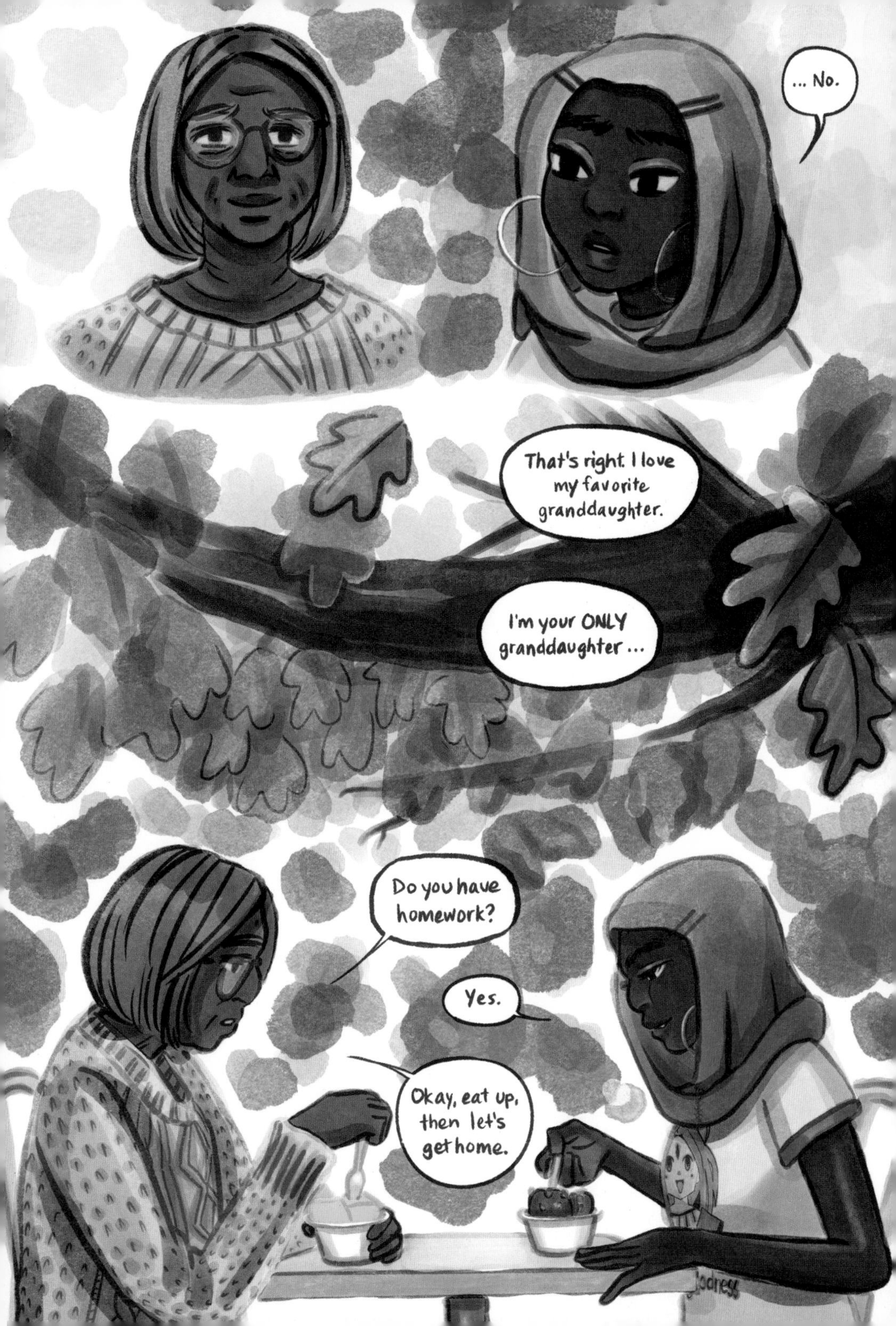
... No.
That's right. I love my favorite granddaughter.
I'm your ONLY granddaughter ...
Do you have homework?
Yes.
Okay, eat up, then let's get home.

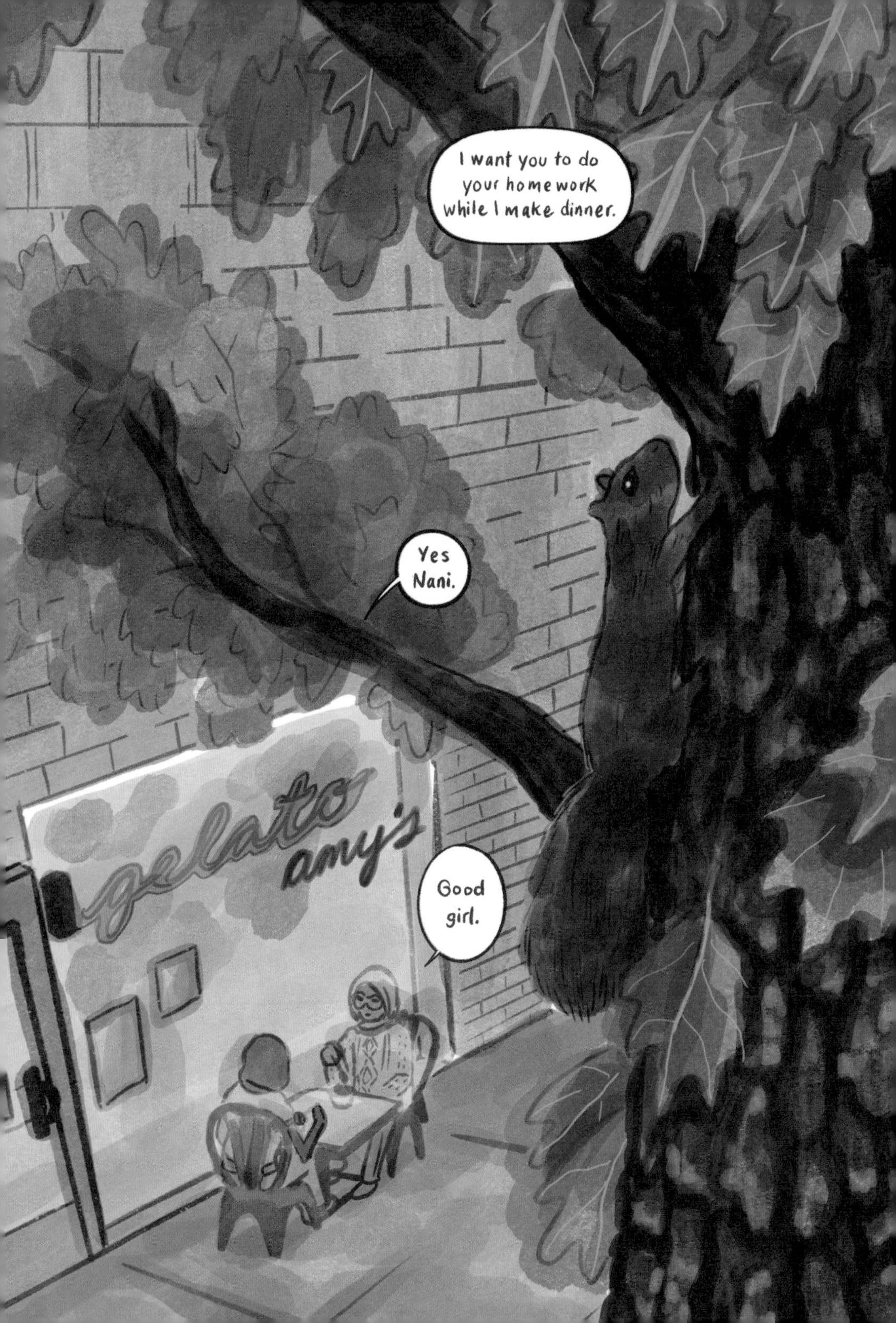
I want you to do your homework while I make dinner.
Yes Nani.
gelato
amy's
Good girl.

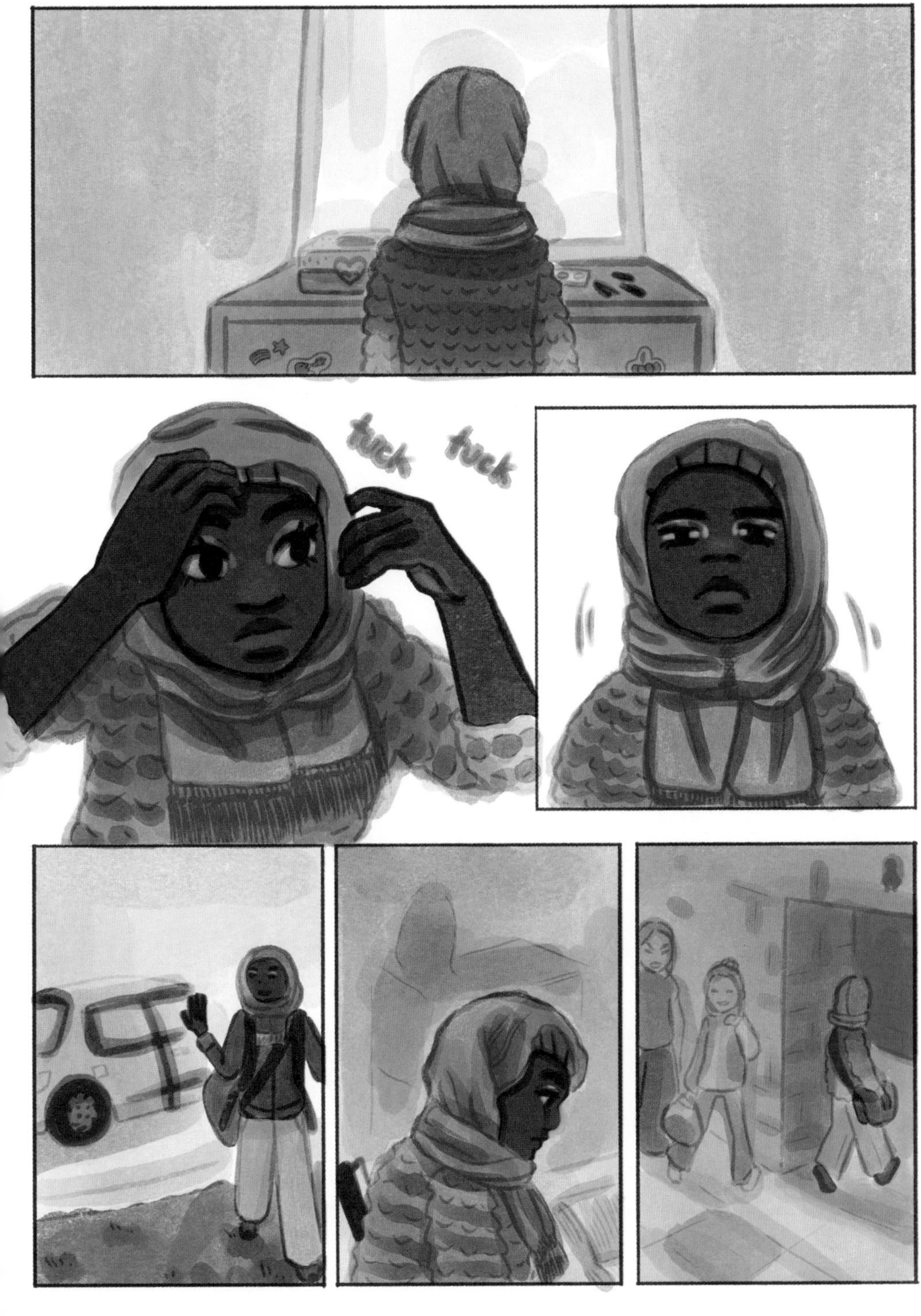
tuck tuck

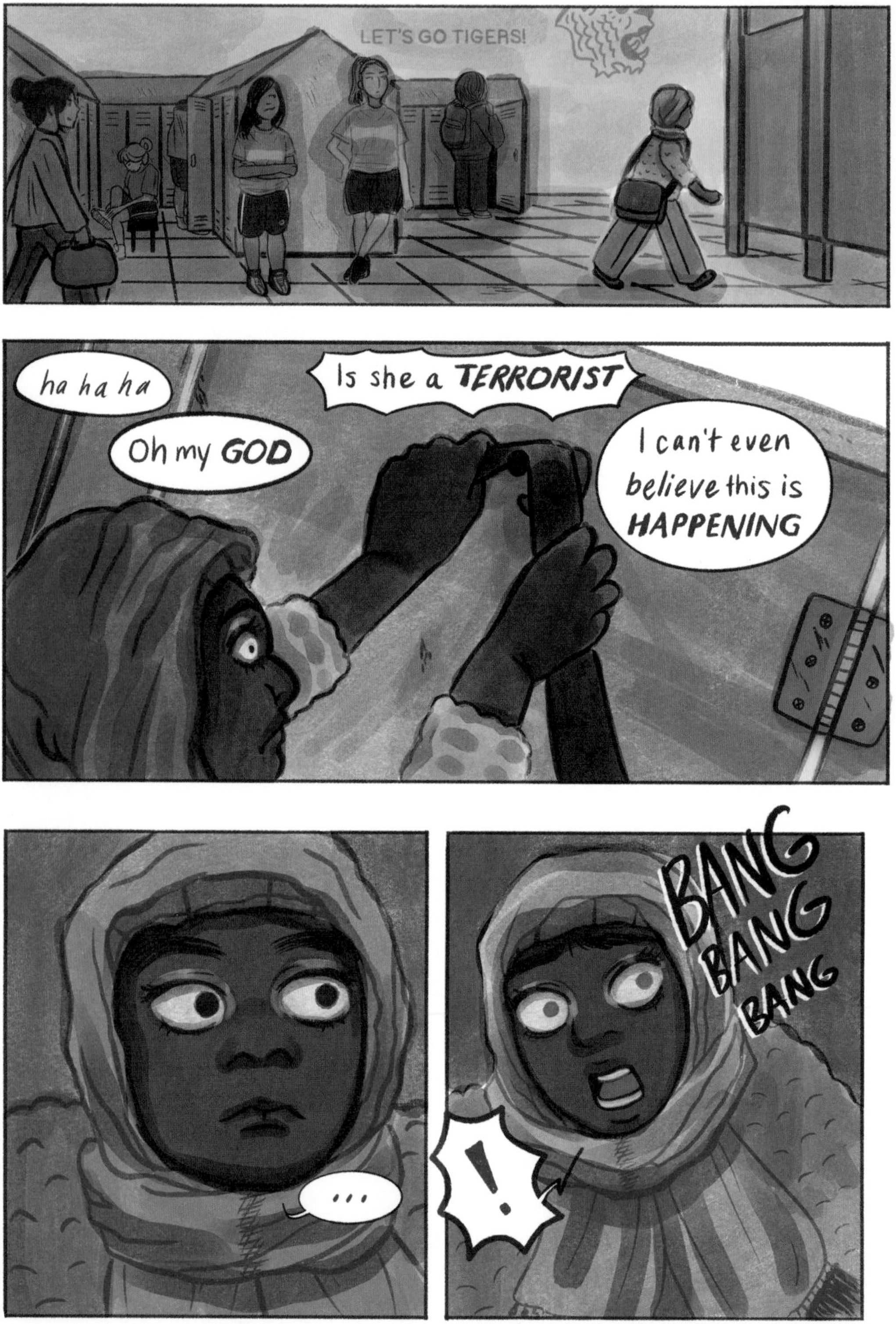
LET'S GO TIGERS!
ha ha ha
Is she a TERRORIST
Oh my GOD
I can't even believe this is HAPPENING
...
!
BANG
BANG
BANG

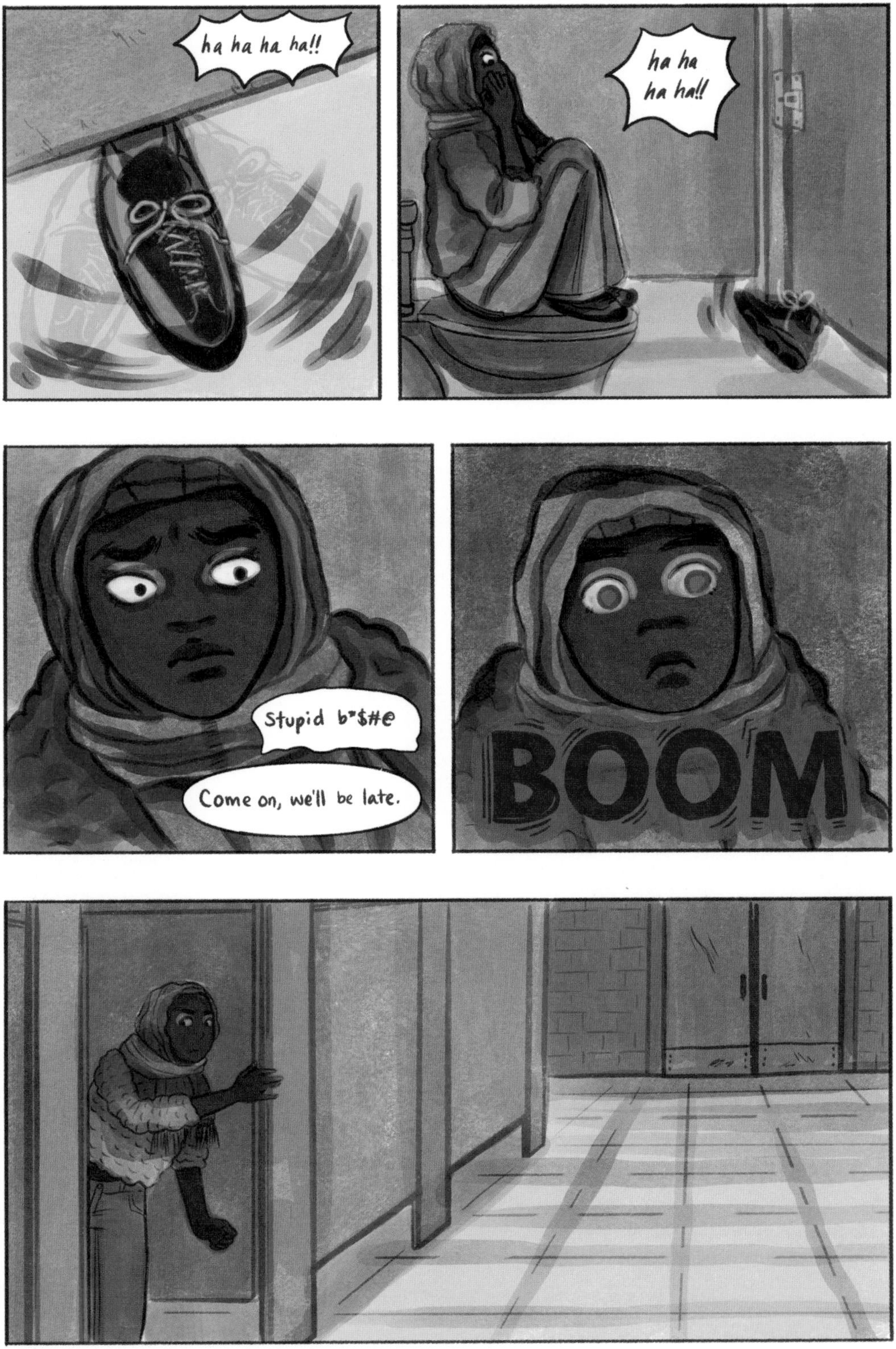
ha ha ha ha!!
ha ha
ha ha!!
Stupid b*$#@
Come on, we'll be late.
BOOM

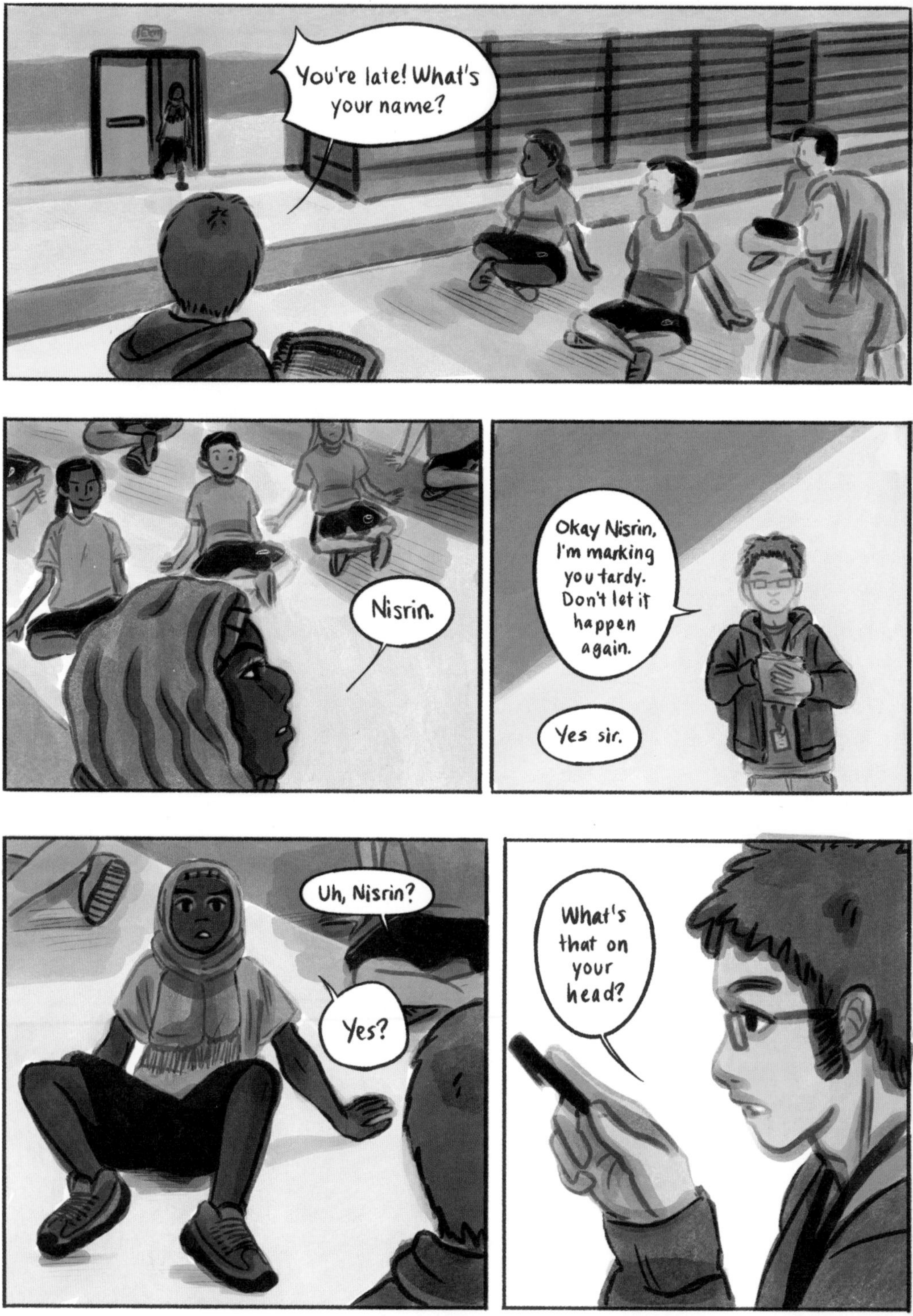
You're late! What's your name?
Nisrin.
Okay Nisrin, I'm marking you tardy. Don't let it happen again.
Yes sir.
Uh, Nisrin?
Yes?
What's that on your head?

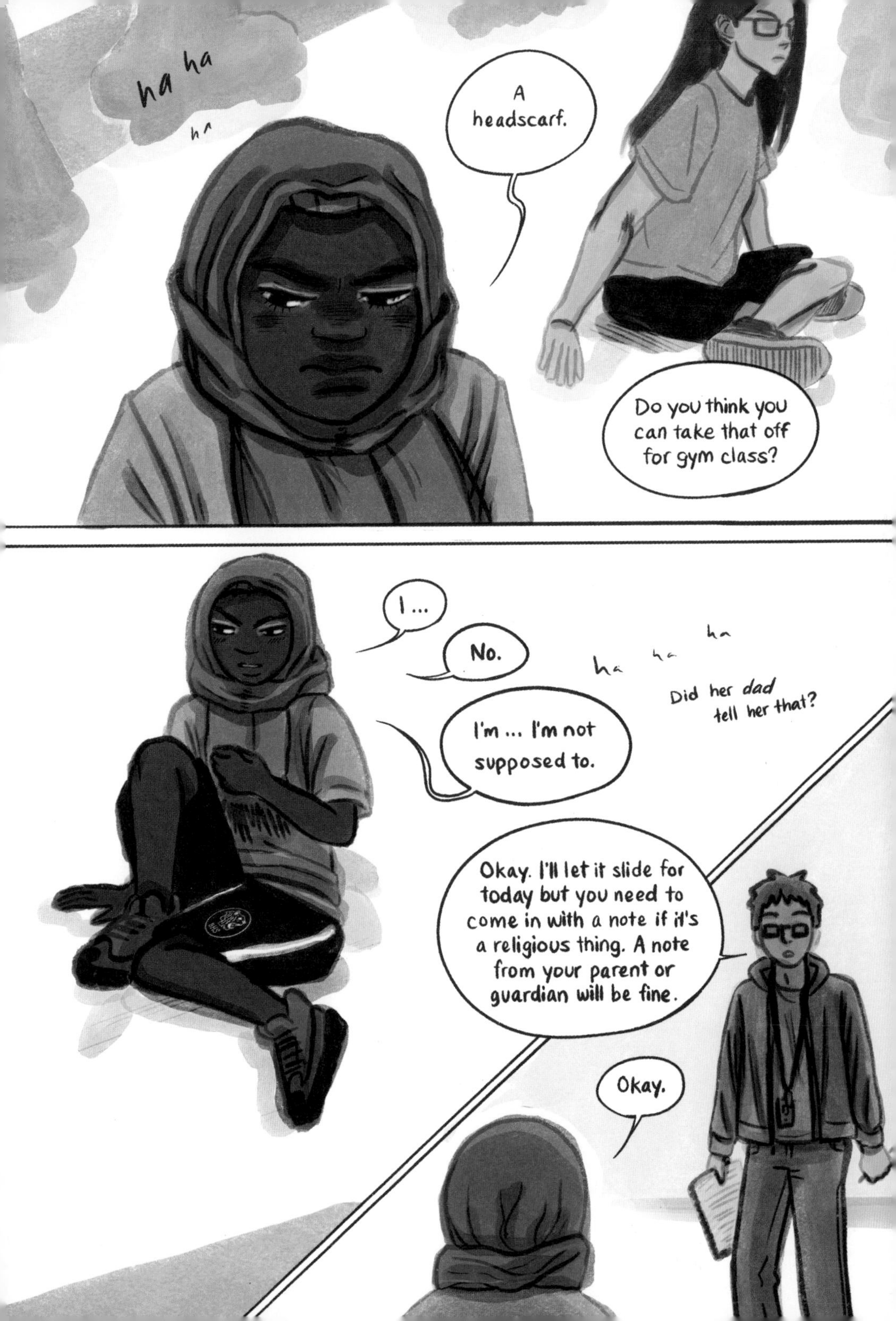
ha ha
ha
A headscarf.
Do you think you can take that off for gym class?
I...
No.
ha ha ha
Did her *dad* tell her that?
I'm ... I'm not supposed to.
Okay. I'll let it slide for today but you need to come in with a note if it's a religious thing. A note from your parent or guardian will be fine.
Okay.

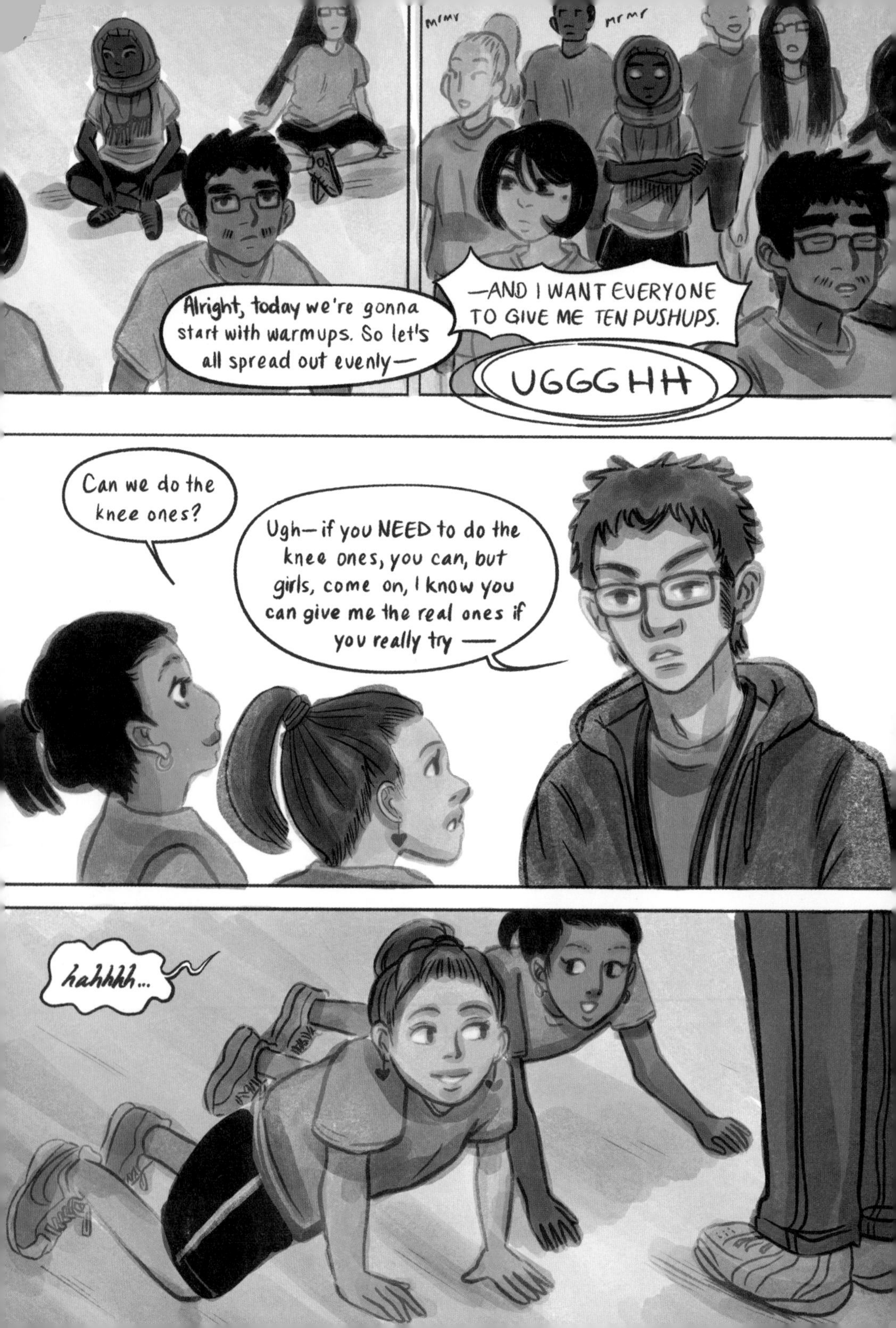
mrmr
mrmr
Alright, today we're gonna start with warmups. So let's all spread out evenly—
—AND I WANT EVERYONE TO GIVE ME TEN PUSHUPS.
UGGGHH
Can we do the knee ones?
Ugh— if you NEED to do the knee ones, you can, but girls, come on, I know you can give me the real ones if you really try —
hahhhh...

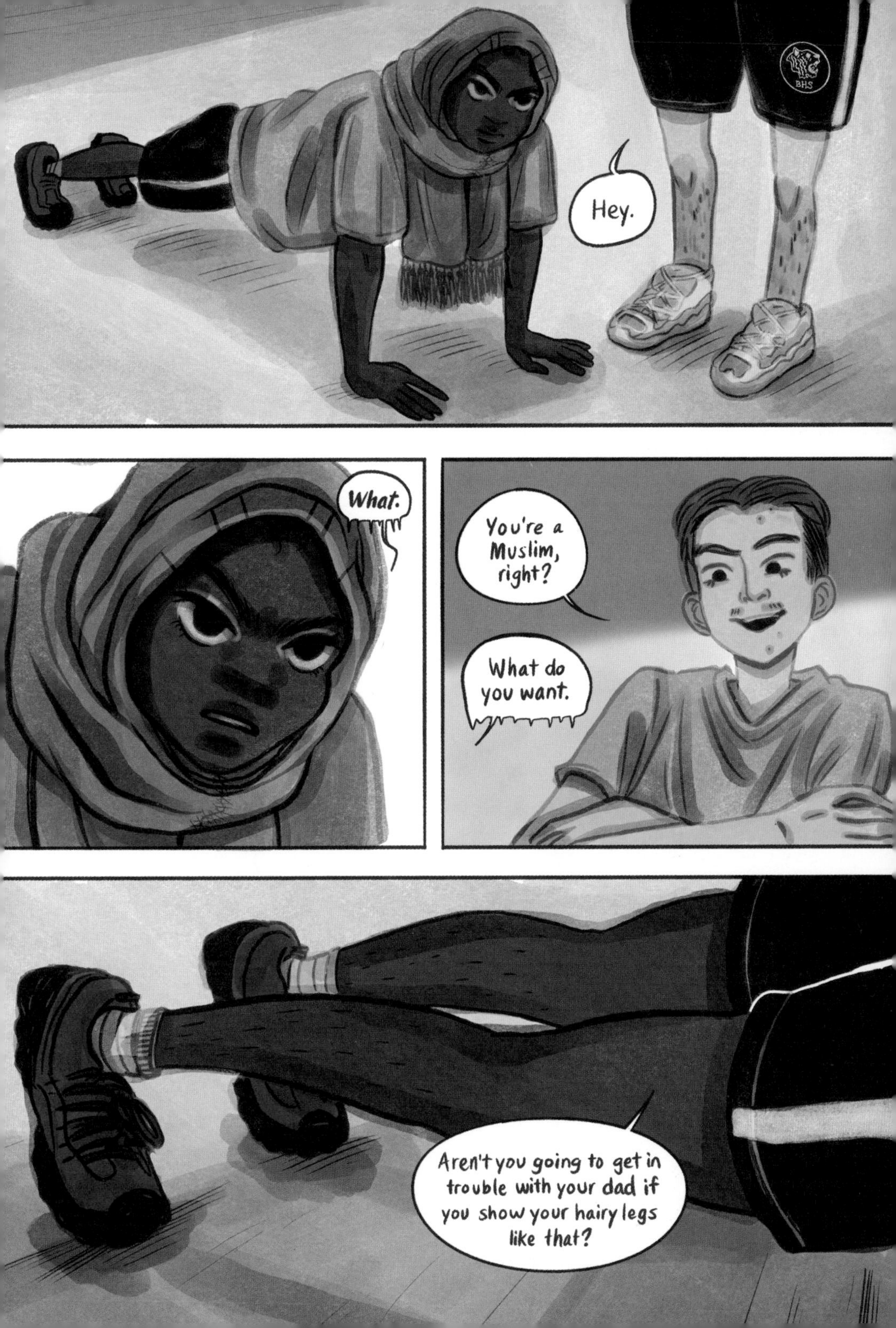
Hey.
What.
You're a Muslim, right?
What do you want.
Aren't you going to get in trouble with your dad if you show your hairy legs like that?

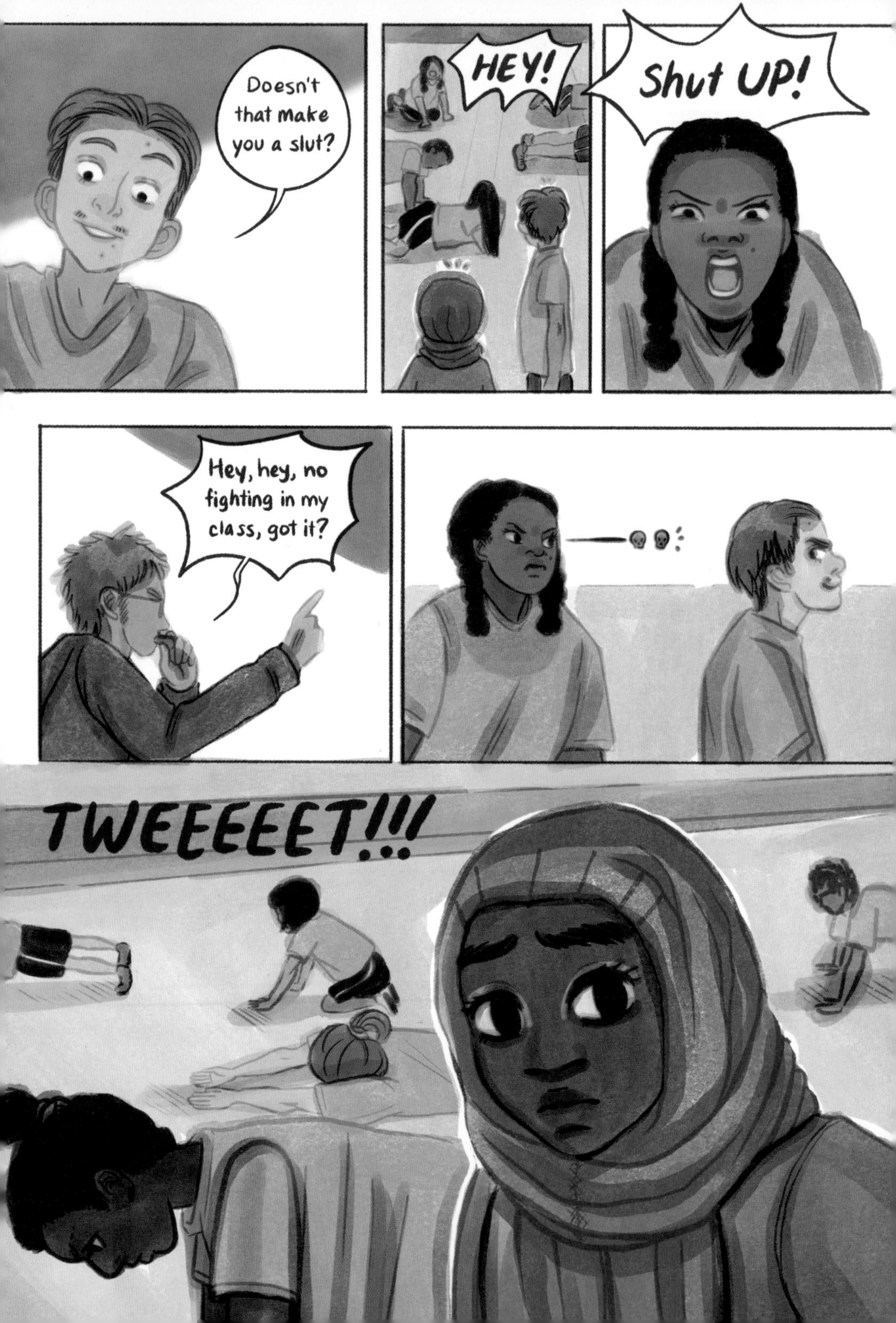

Doesn't that make you a slut?
HEY!
Shut UP!
Hey, hey, no fighting in my class, got it?
TWEEEEET!!!

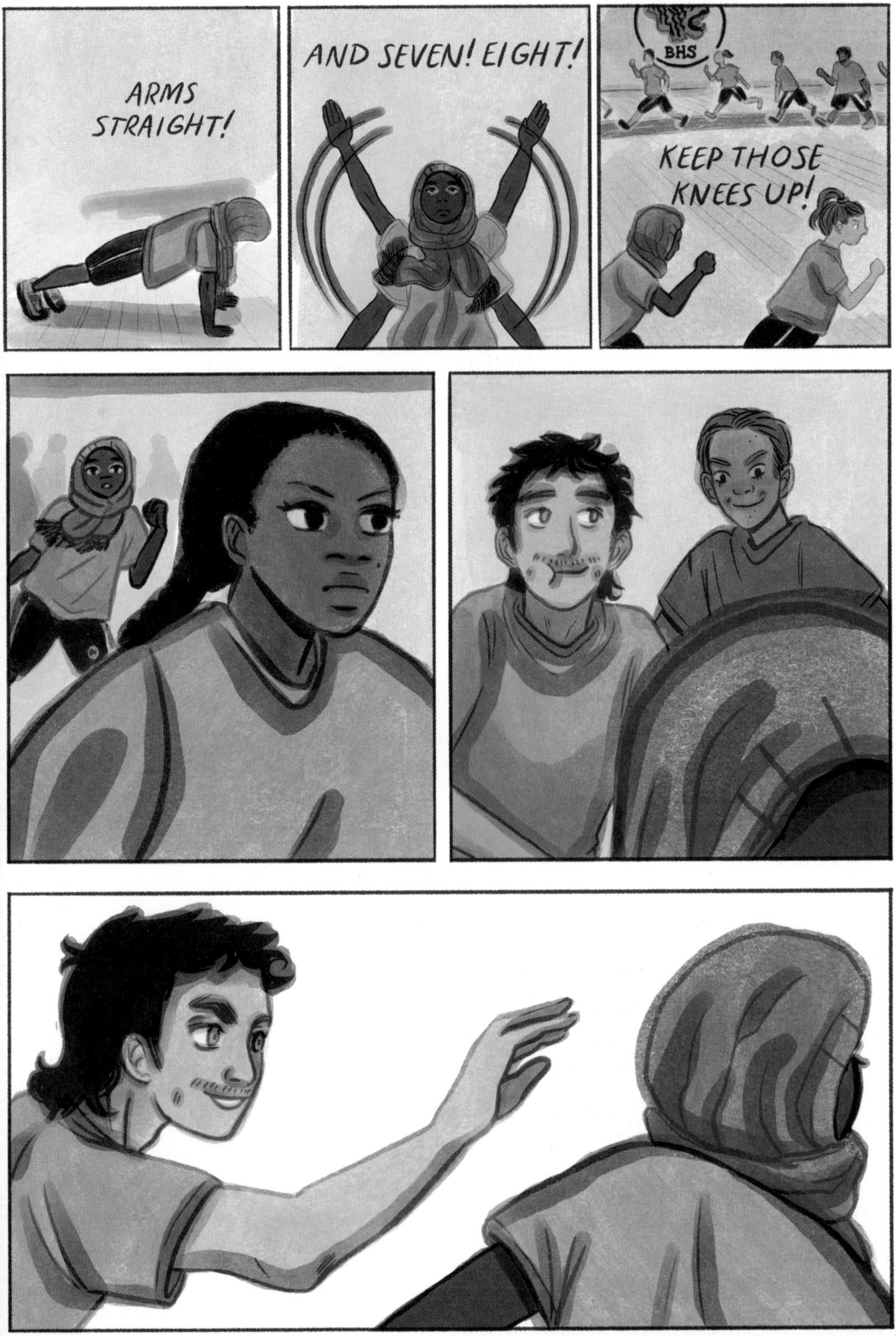
ARMS STRAIGHT!
AND SEVEN! EIGHT!
BHS
KEEP THOSE KNEES UP!

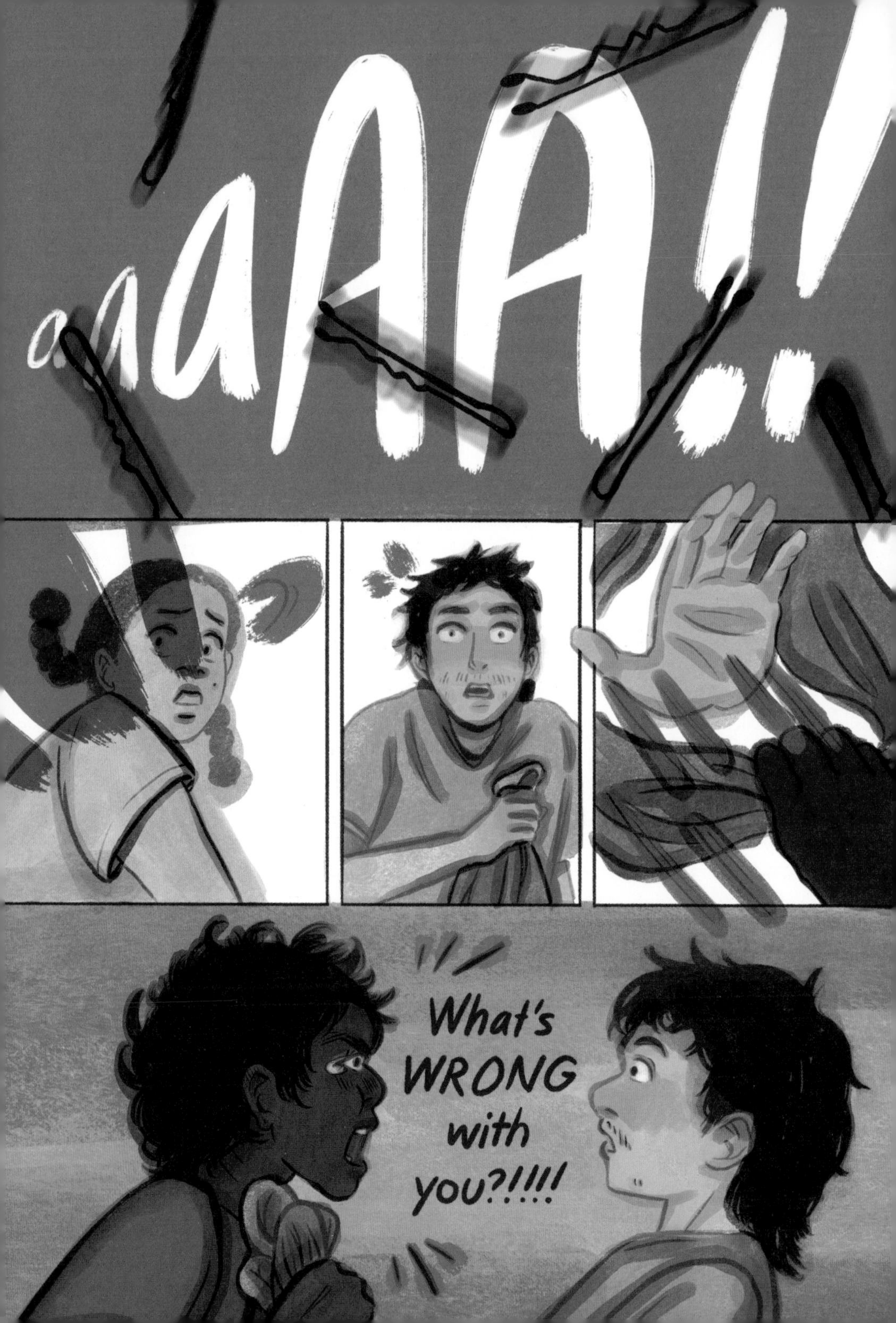
aaaAA!!
What's WRONG with you?!!!!

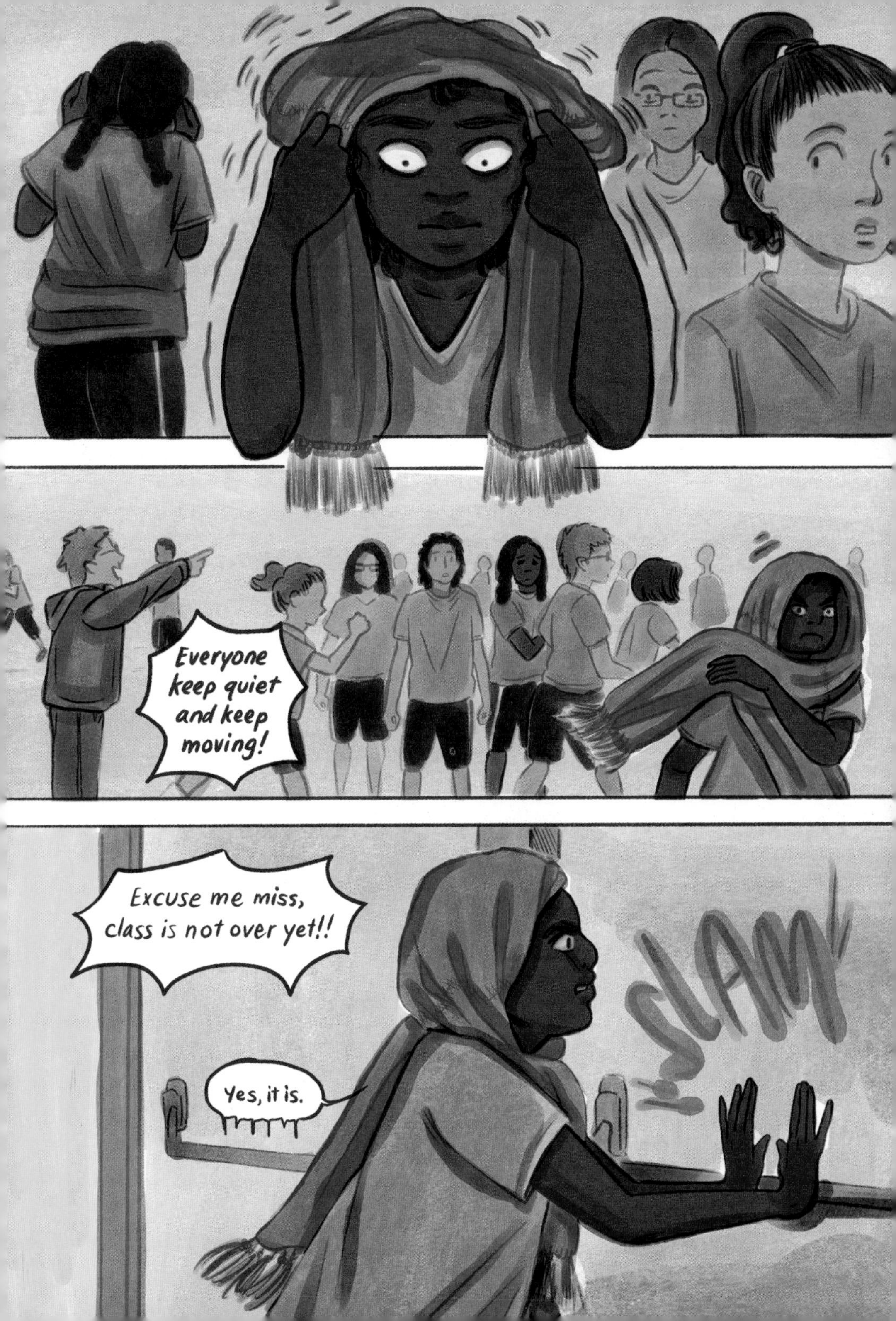
Everyone keep quiet and keep moving!
Excuse me miss, class is not over yet!!
SLAM
Yes, it is.

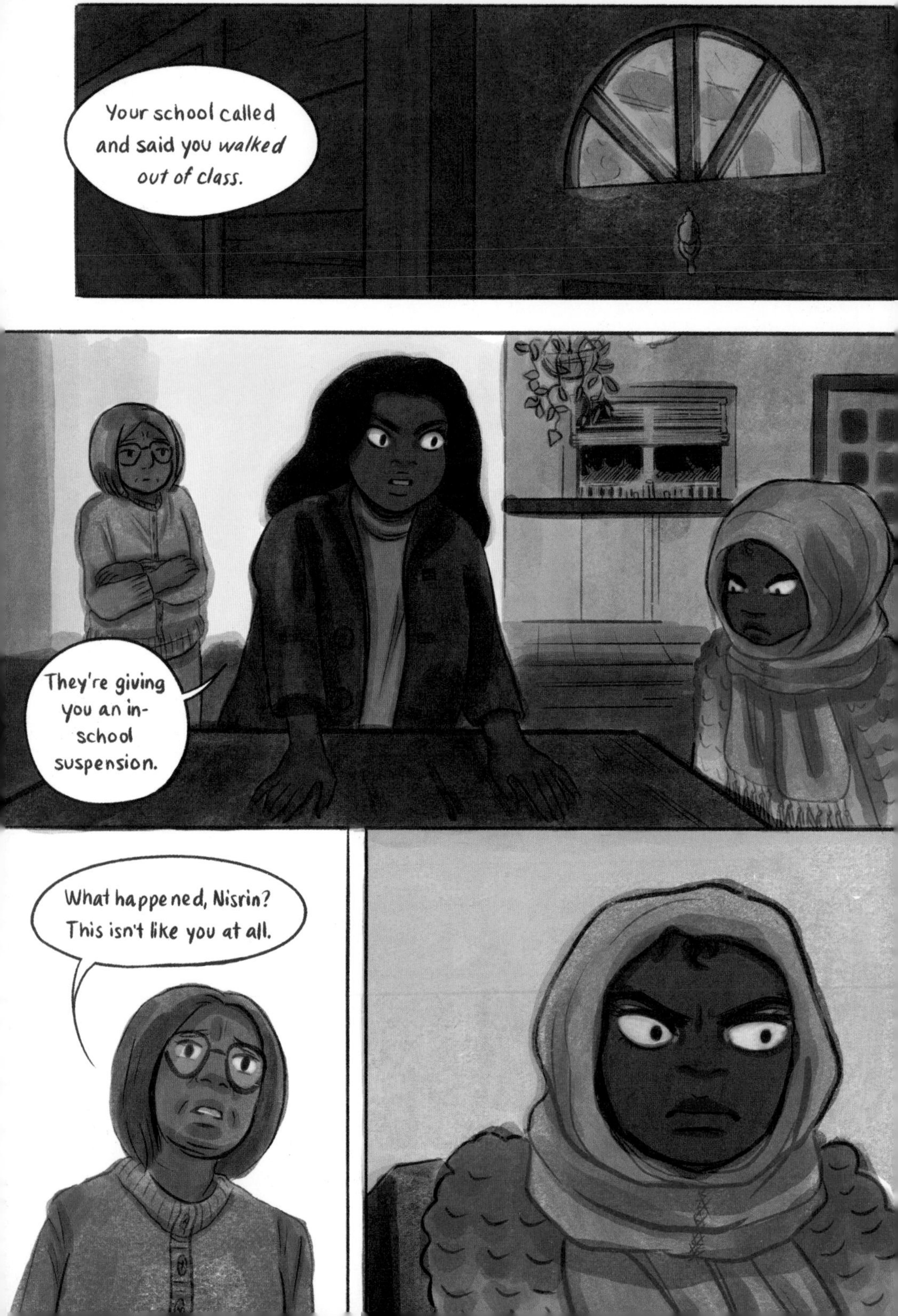
Your school called and said you *walked* out of class.
They're giving you an in-school suspension.
What happened, Nisrin? This isn't like you at all.

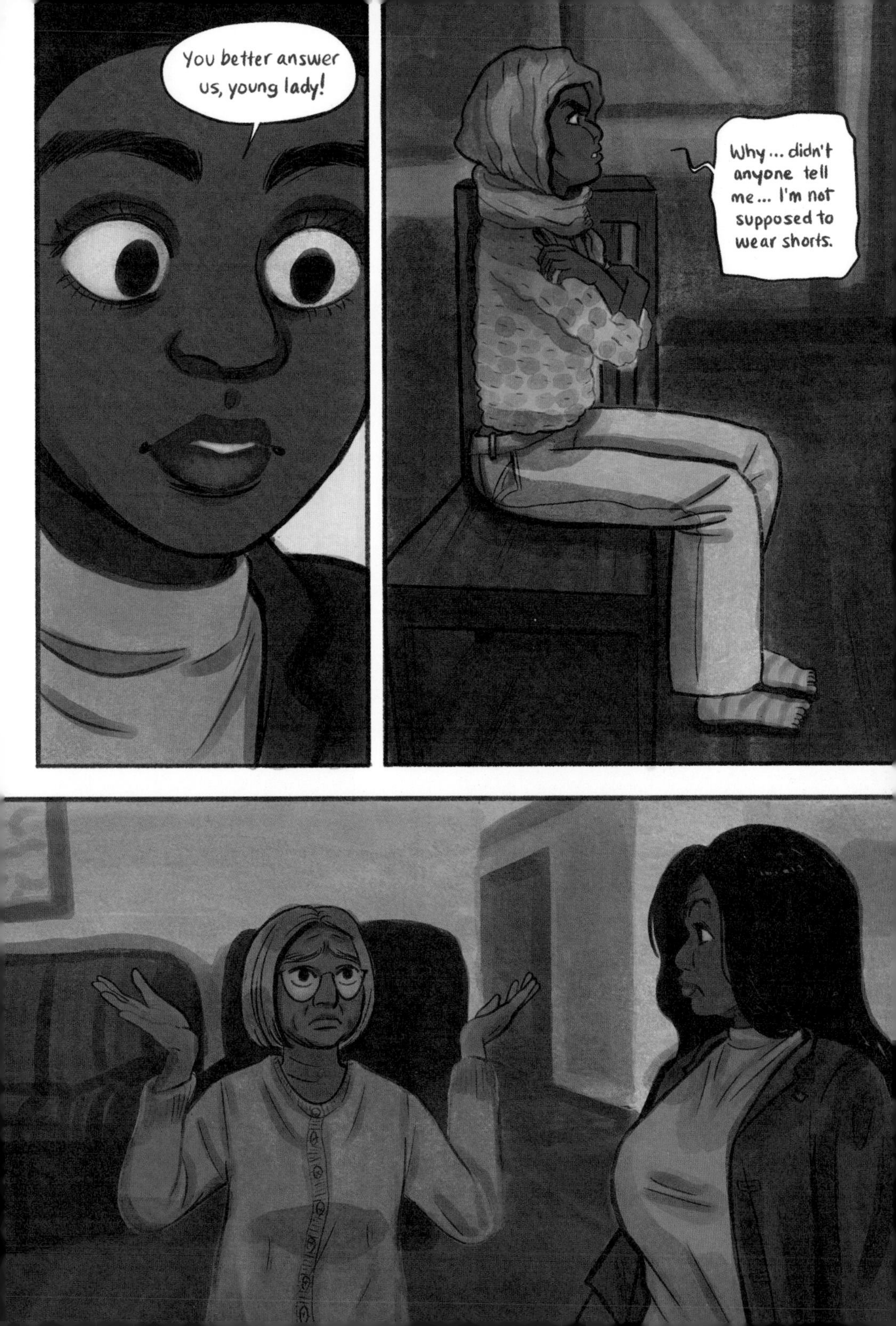
You better answer us, young lady!
Why... didn't anyone tell me... I'm not supposed to wear shorts.

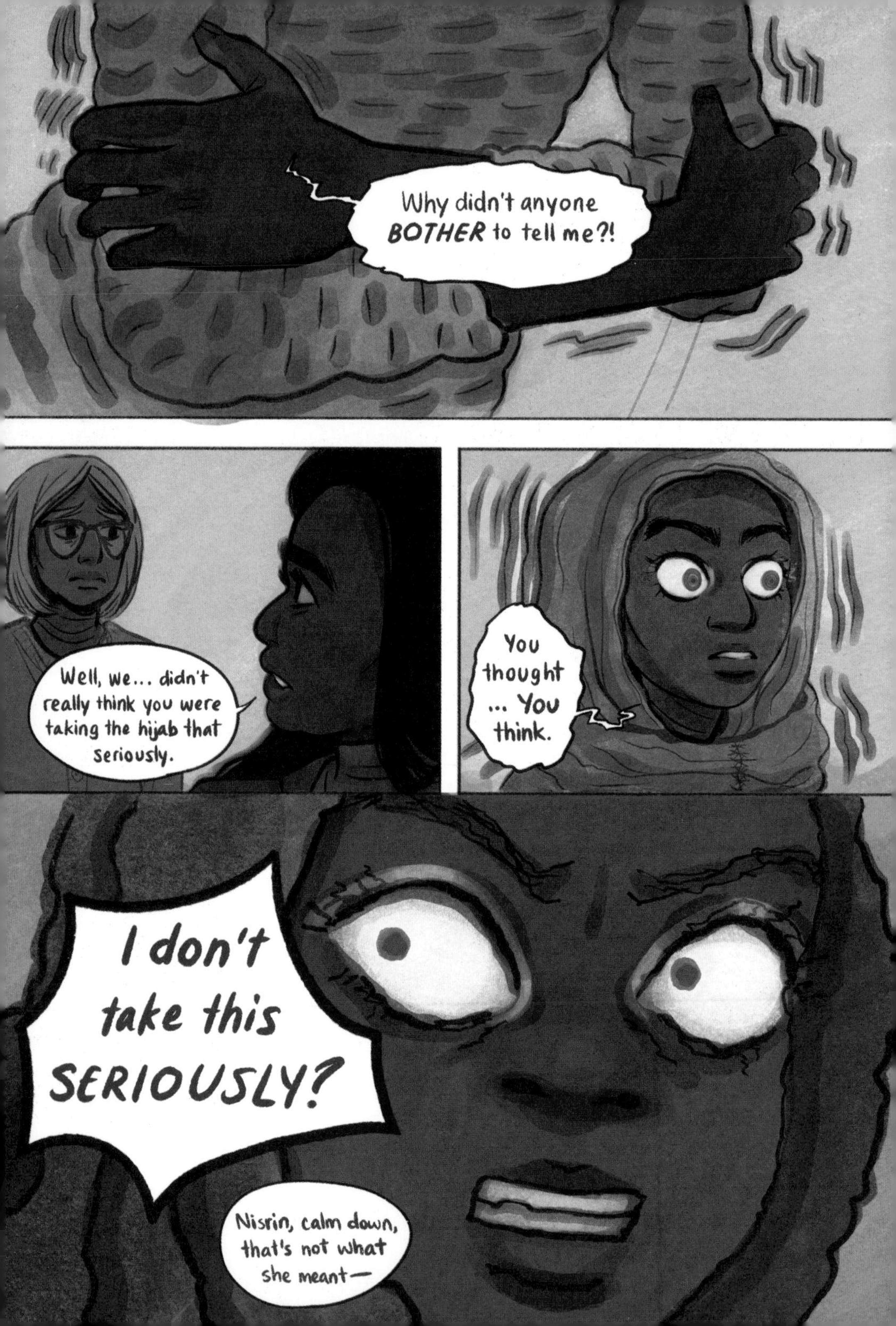
Why didn't anyone BOTHER to tell me?!
Well, we... didn't really think you were taking the hijab that seriously.
You thought ... You think.
I don't take this SERIOUSLY?
Nisrin, calm down, that's not what she meant—

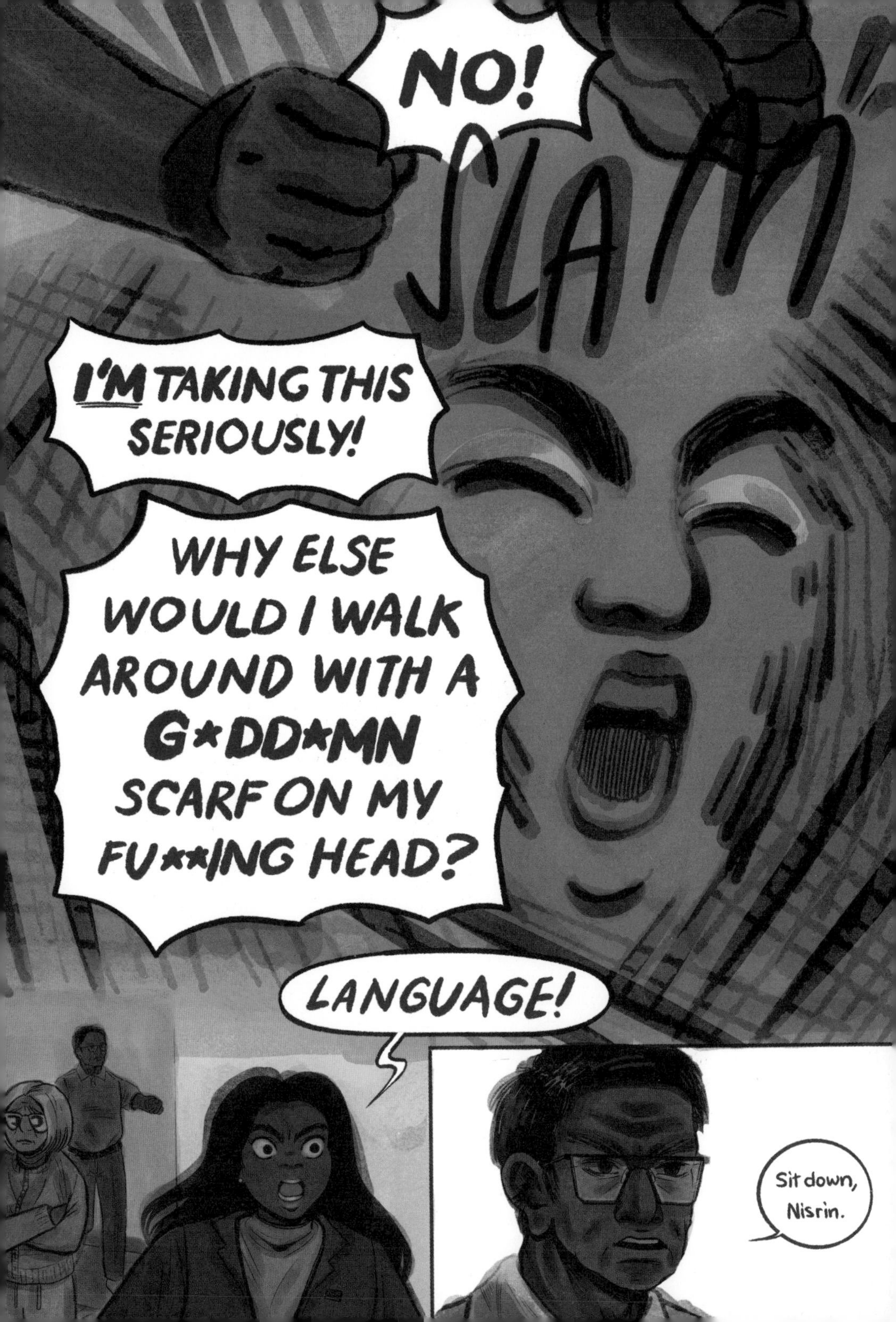
NO!
SLAM
I'M TAKING THIS SERIOUSLY!
WHY ELSE WOULD I WALK AROUND WITH A G*DD*MN SCARF ON MY FU**ING HEAD?
LANGUAGE!
Sit down, Nisrin.

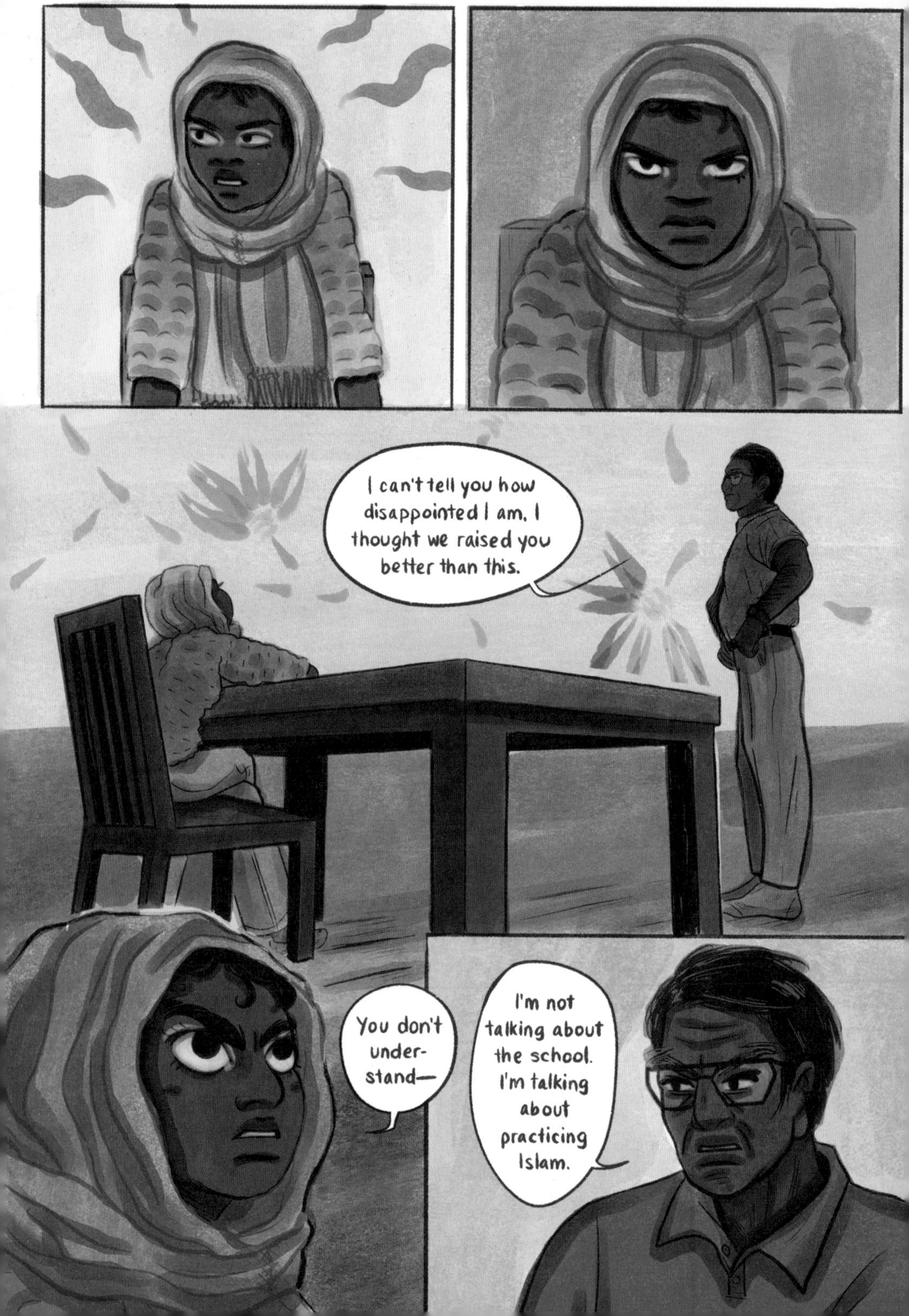
I can't tell you how disappointed I am. I thought we raised you better than this.
You don't under-stand—
I'm not talking about the school. I'm talking about practicing Islam.

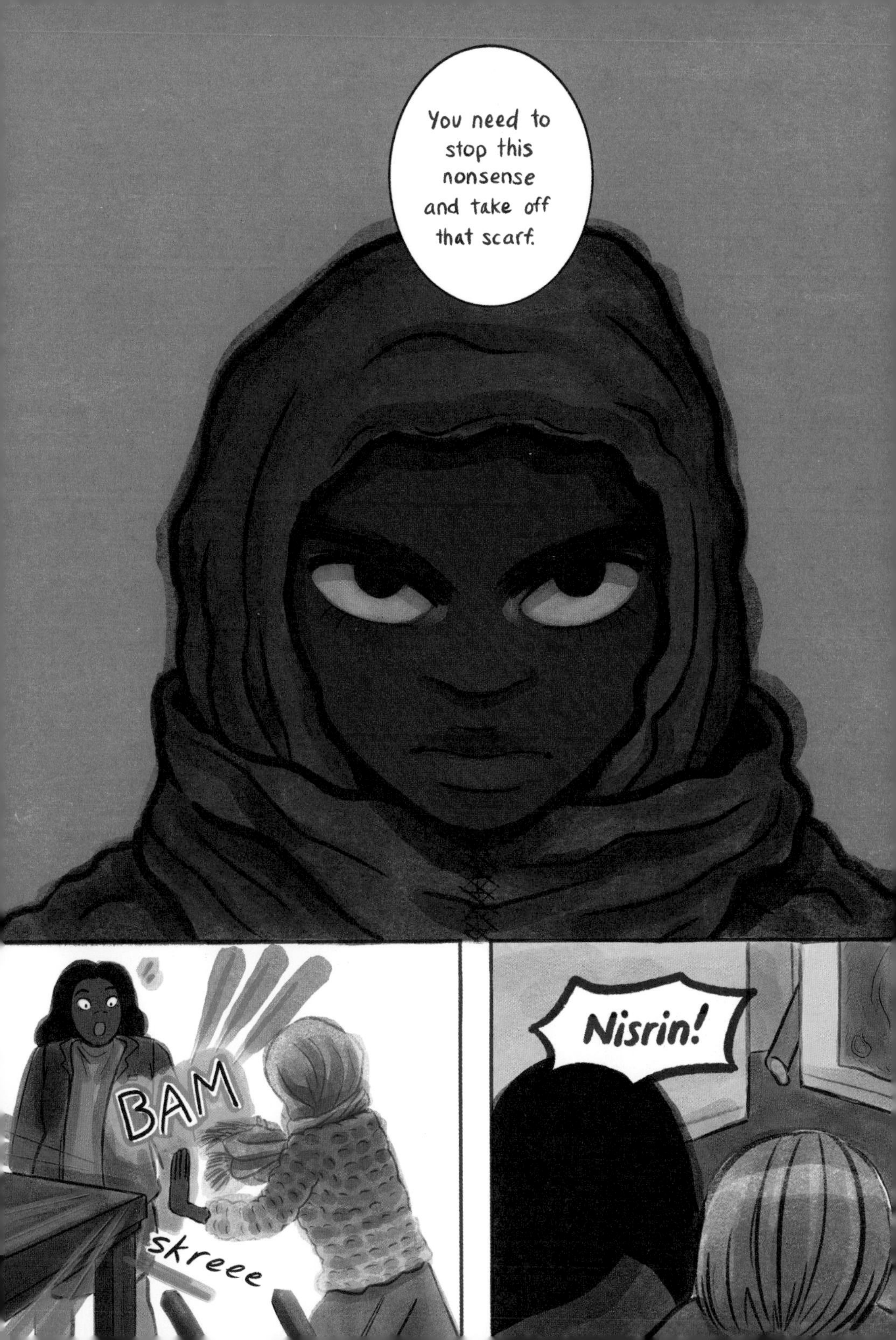
You need to stop this nonsense and take off that scarf.
BAM
skreeee
Nisrin!

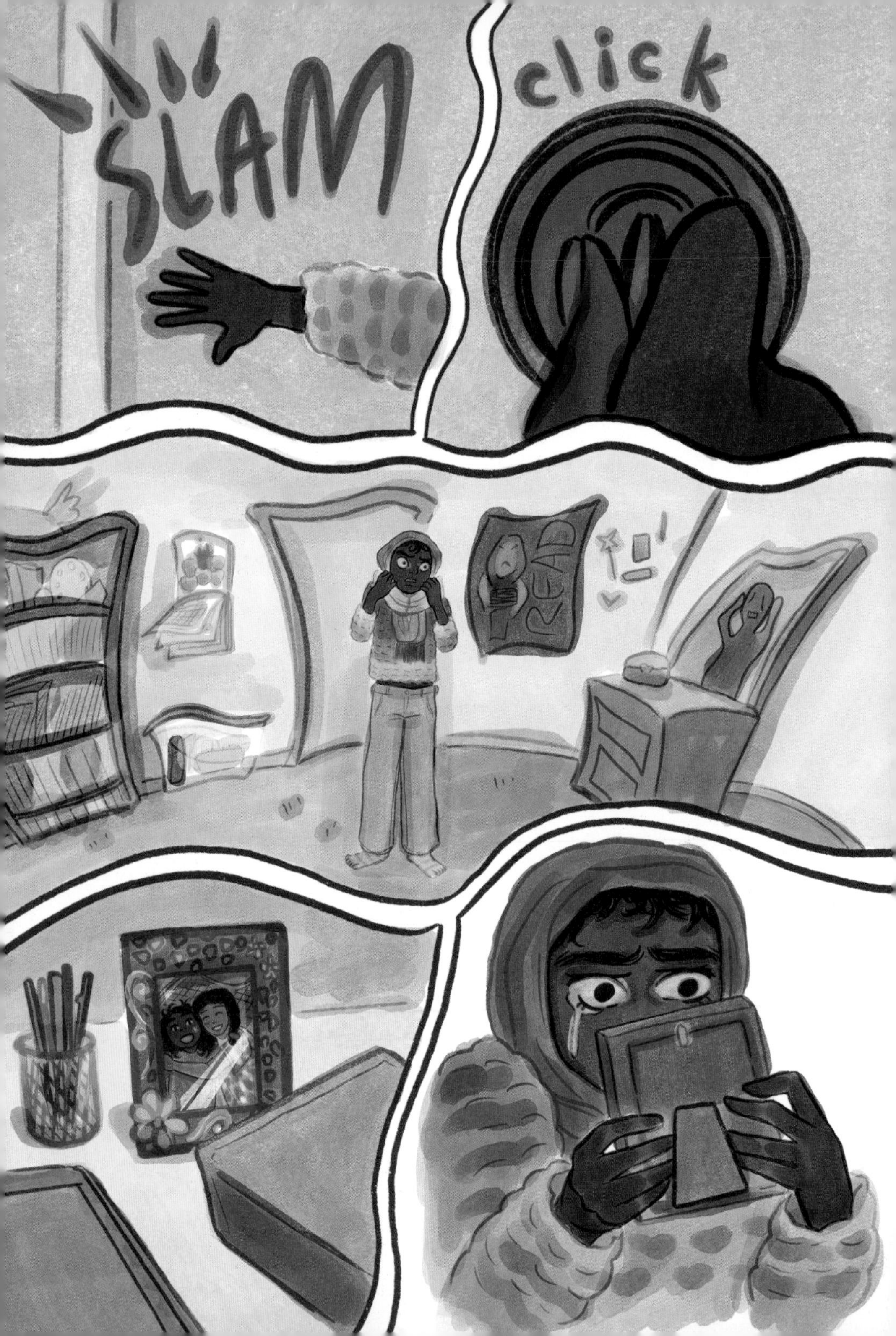
SLAM
click
READ

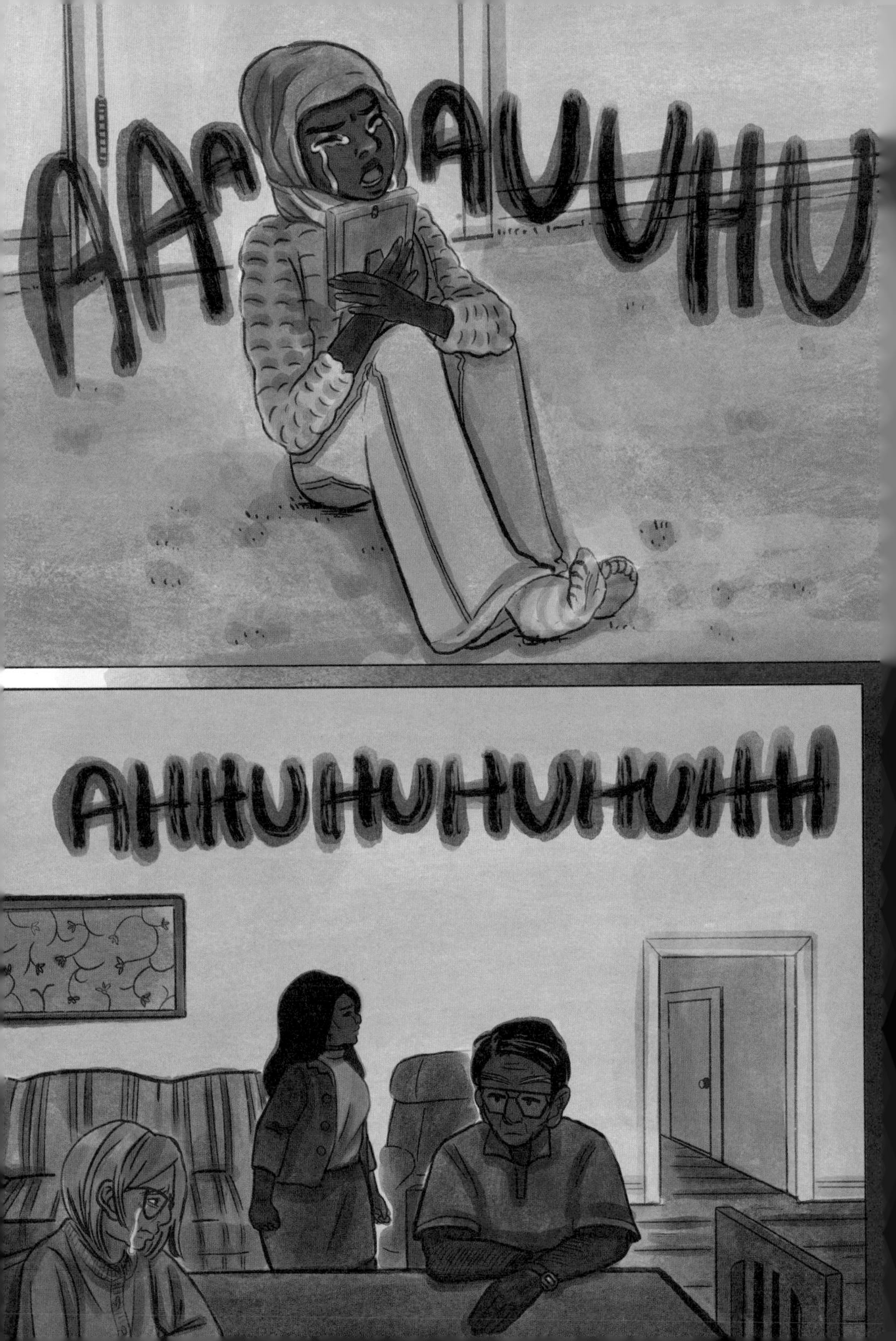
AAAAUUHU
AHHUHUHUHUHH

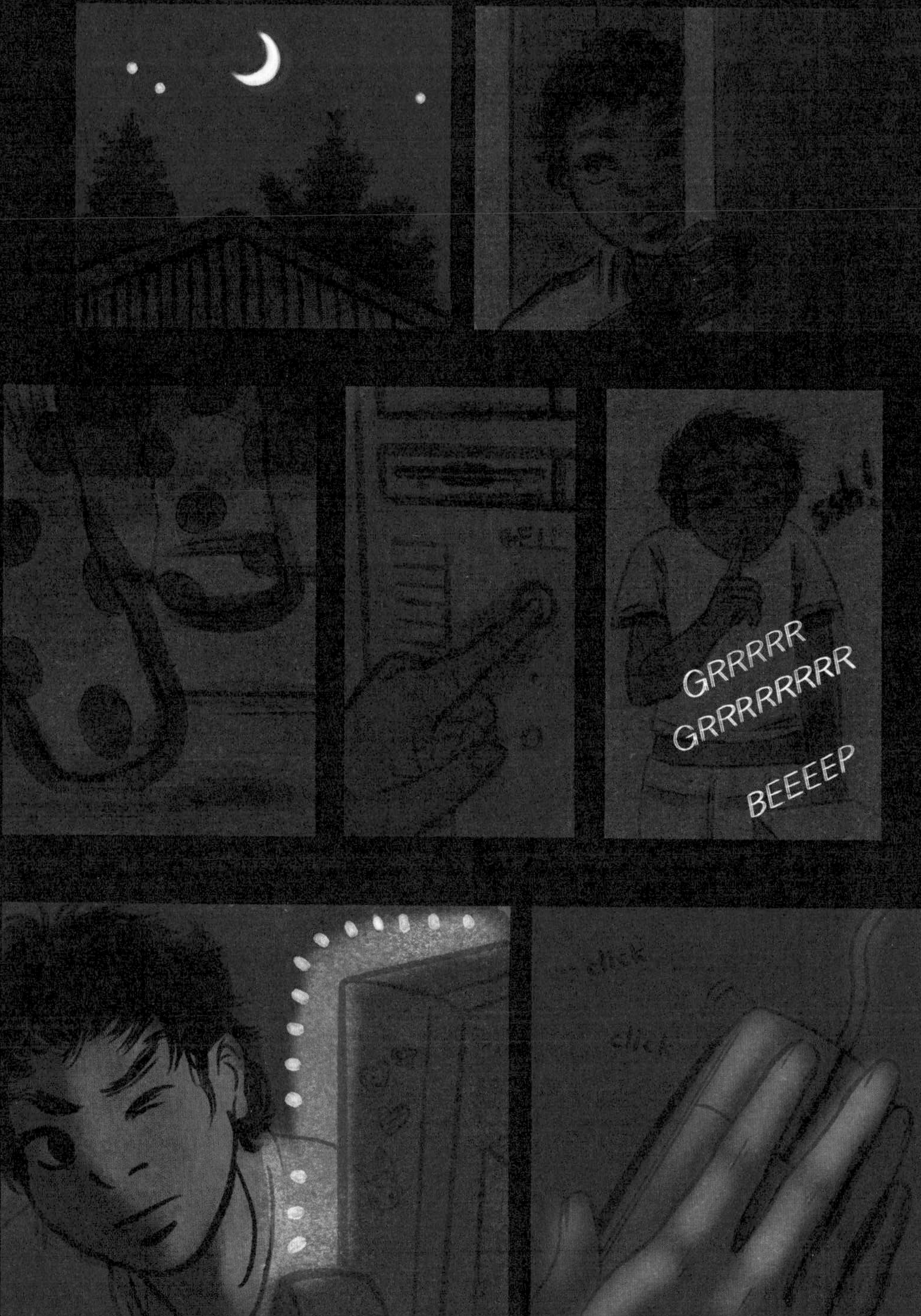
GRRRRR
GRRRRRRRR
BEEEEP
click
click

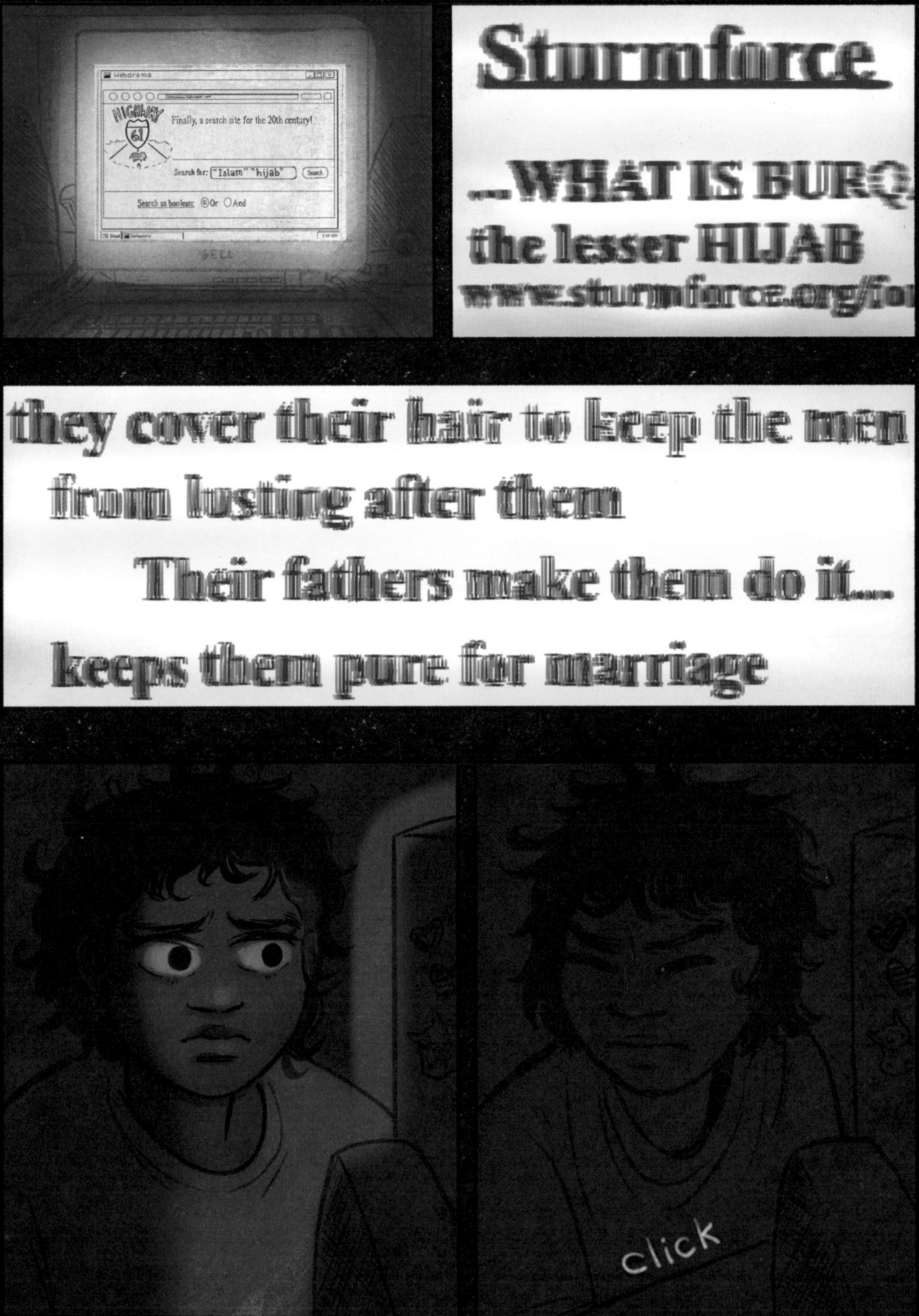
Webdrama
HIGHWAY 61
Finally, a search site for the 20th century!
Search for: "Islam" "hijab"
Search
Search as boolean: Or And
Sturmforce
...WHAT IS BURQ
the lesser HIJAB
www.sturmforce.org/fo
they cover their hair to keep the men
from lusting after them
Their fathers make them do it....
keeps them pure for marriage
click

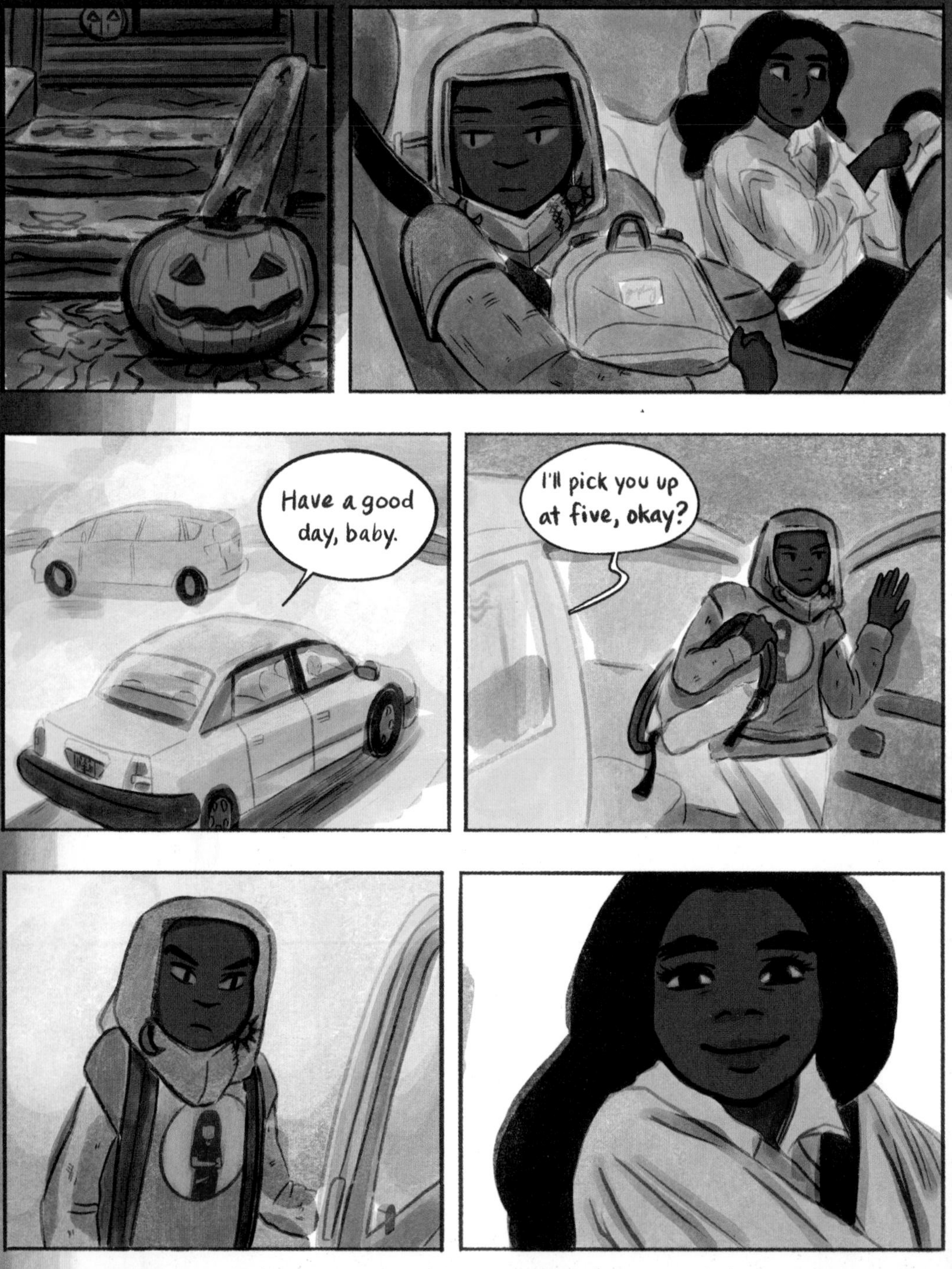
Have a good day, baby.
I'll pick you up at five, okay?

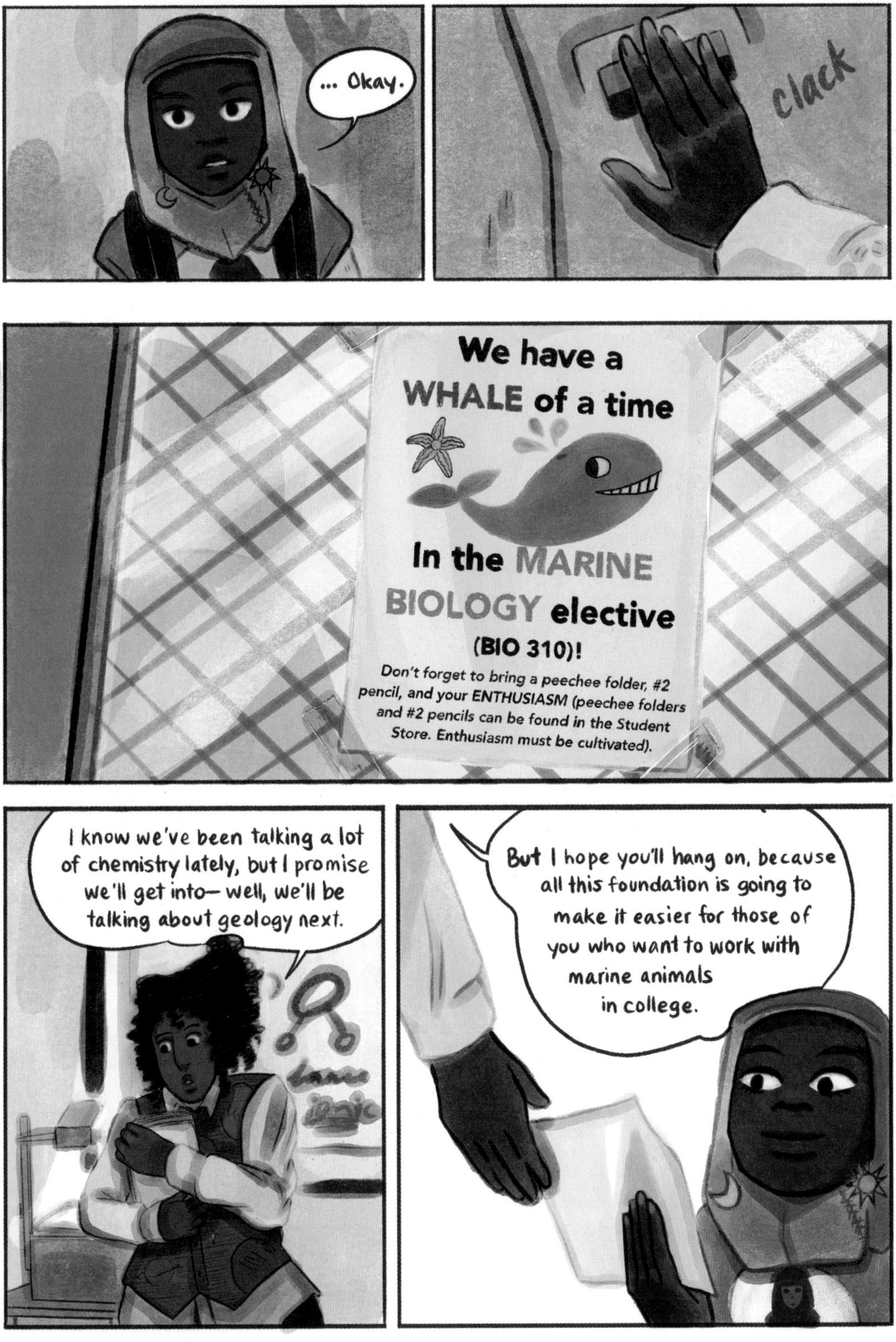

... Okay.
clack
We have a WHALE of a time In the MARINE BIOLOGY elective (BIO 310)!
Don't forget to bring a peechee folder, #2 pencil, and your ENTHUSIASM (peechee folders and #2 pencils can be found in the Student Store. Enthusiasm must be cultivated).
I know we've been talking a lot of chemistry lately, but I promise we'll get into— well, we'll be talking about geology next.
But I hope you'll hang on, because all this foundation is going to make it easier for those of you who want to work with marine animals in college.

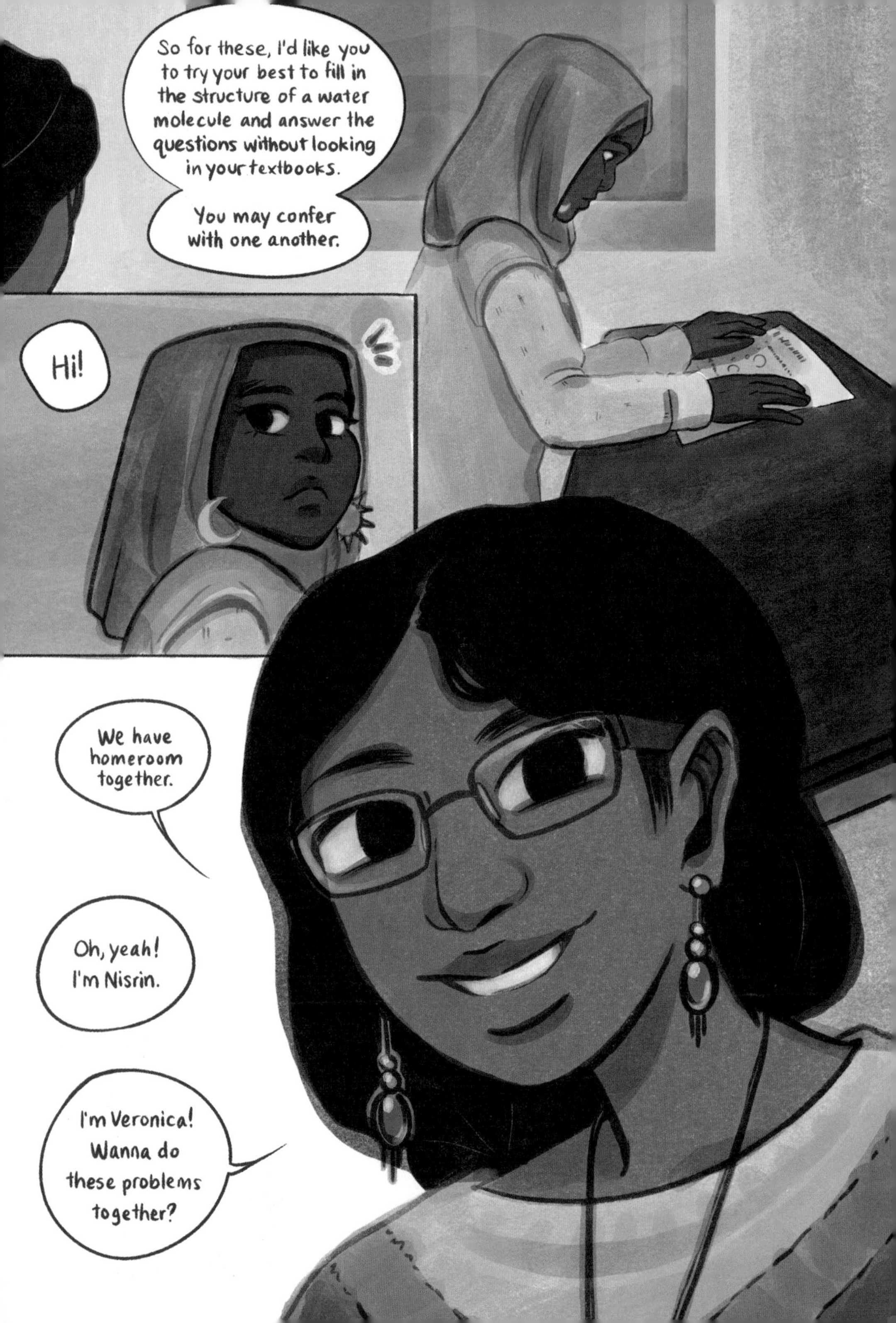
So for these, I'd like you to try your best to fill in the structure of a water molecule and answer the questions without looking in your textbooks.
You may confer with one another.
Hi!
We have homeroom together.
Oh, yeah! I'm Nisrin.
I'm Veronica! Wanna do these problems together?

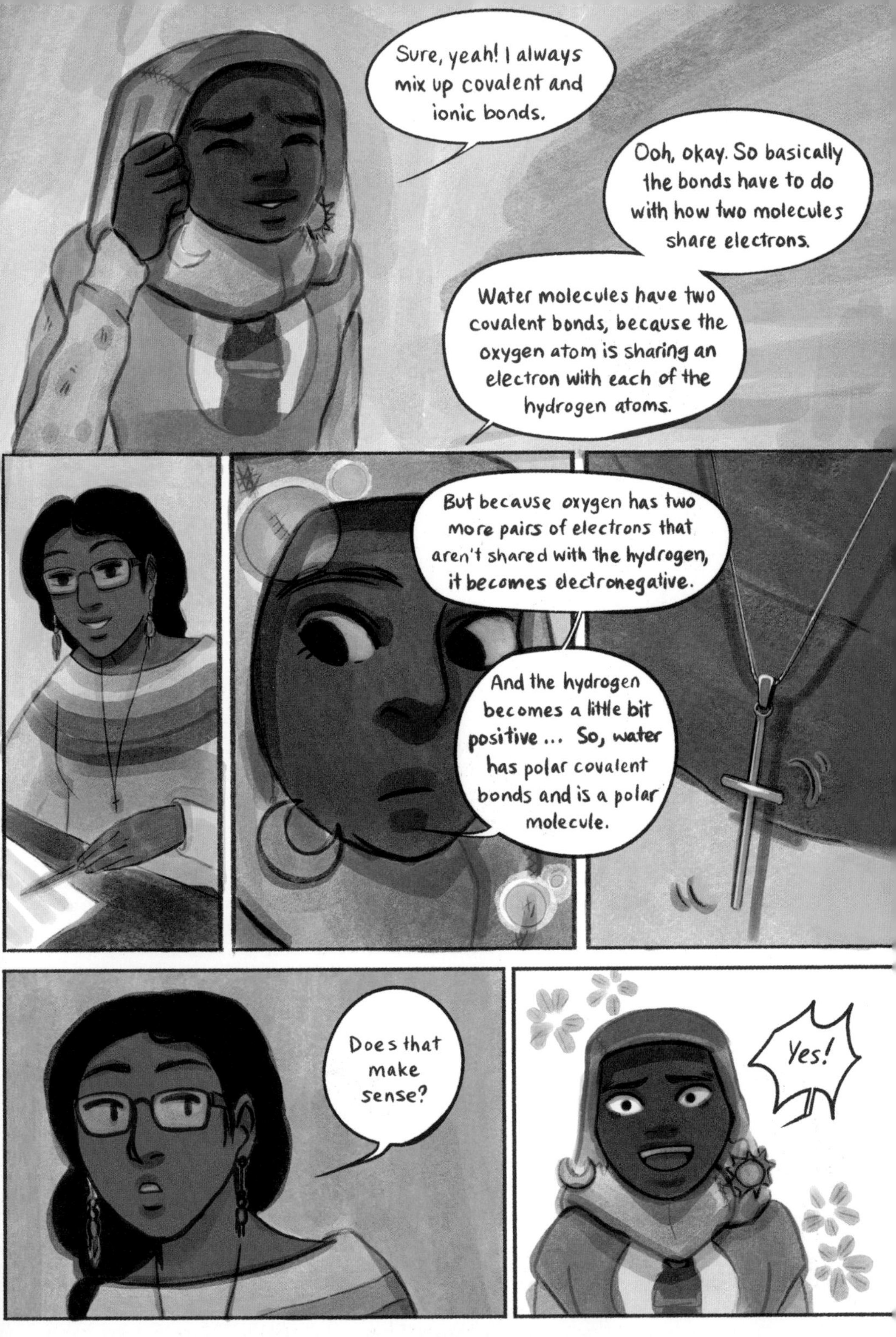
Sure, yeah! I always mix up covalent and ionic bonds.
Ooh, okay. So basically the bonds have to do with how two molecules share electrons.
Water molecules have two covalent bonds, because the oxygen atom is sharing an electron with each of the hydrogen atoms.
But because oxygen has two more pairs of electrons that aren't shared with the hydrogen, it becomes electronegative.
And the hydrogen becomes a little bit positive ... So, water has polar covalent bonds and is a polar molecule.
Does that make sense?
Yes!

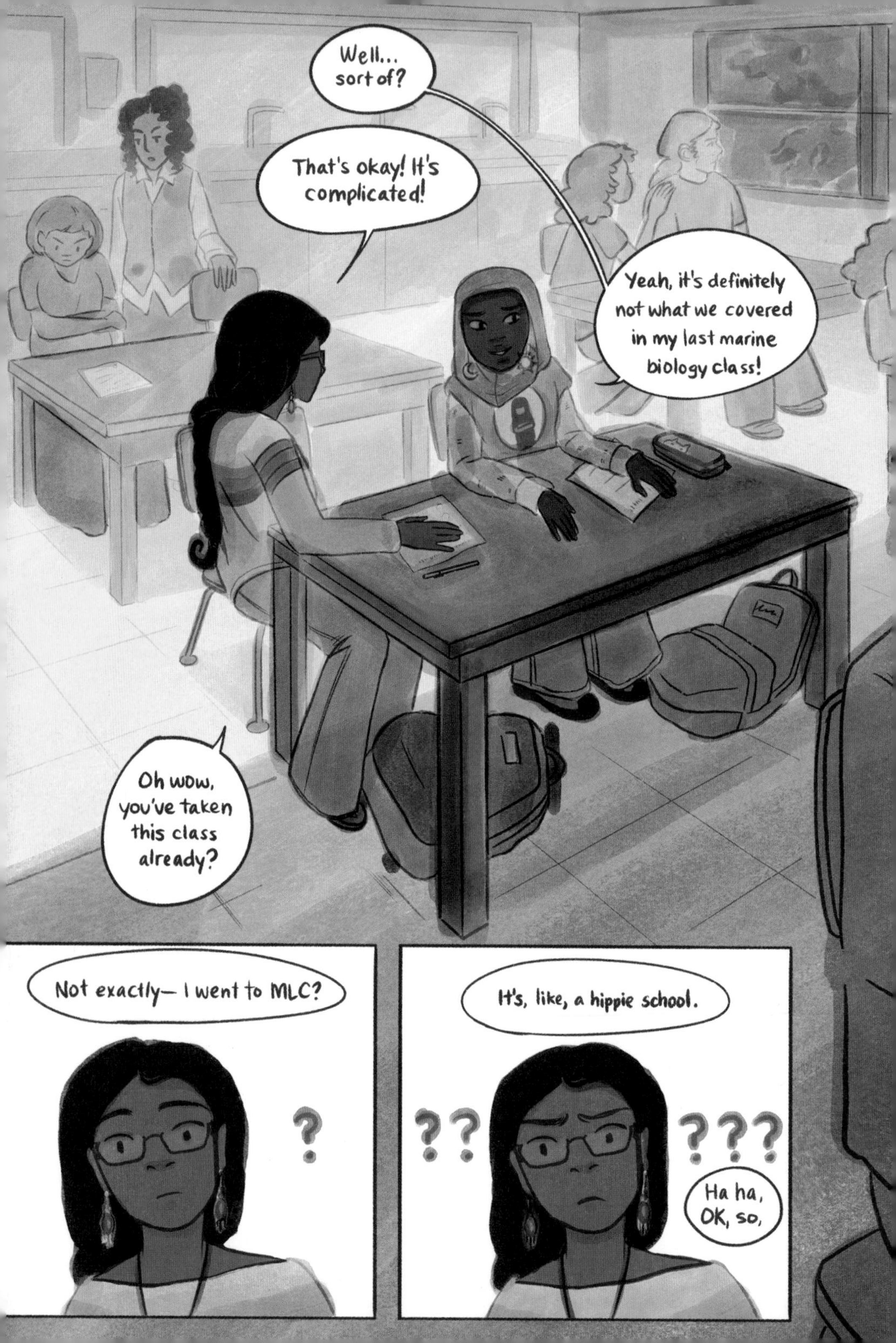
Oh wow, you've taken this class already?
Well... sort of?
That's okay! It's complicated!
Yeah, it's definitely not what we covered in my last marine biology class!
Not exactly— I went to MLC?
?
It's, like, a hippie school.
??
???
Ha ha, OK, so,

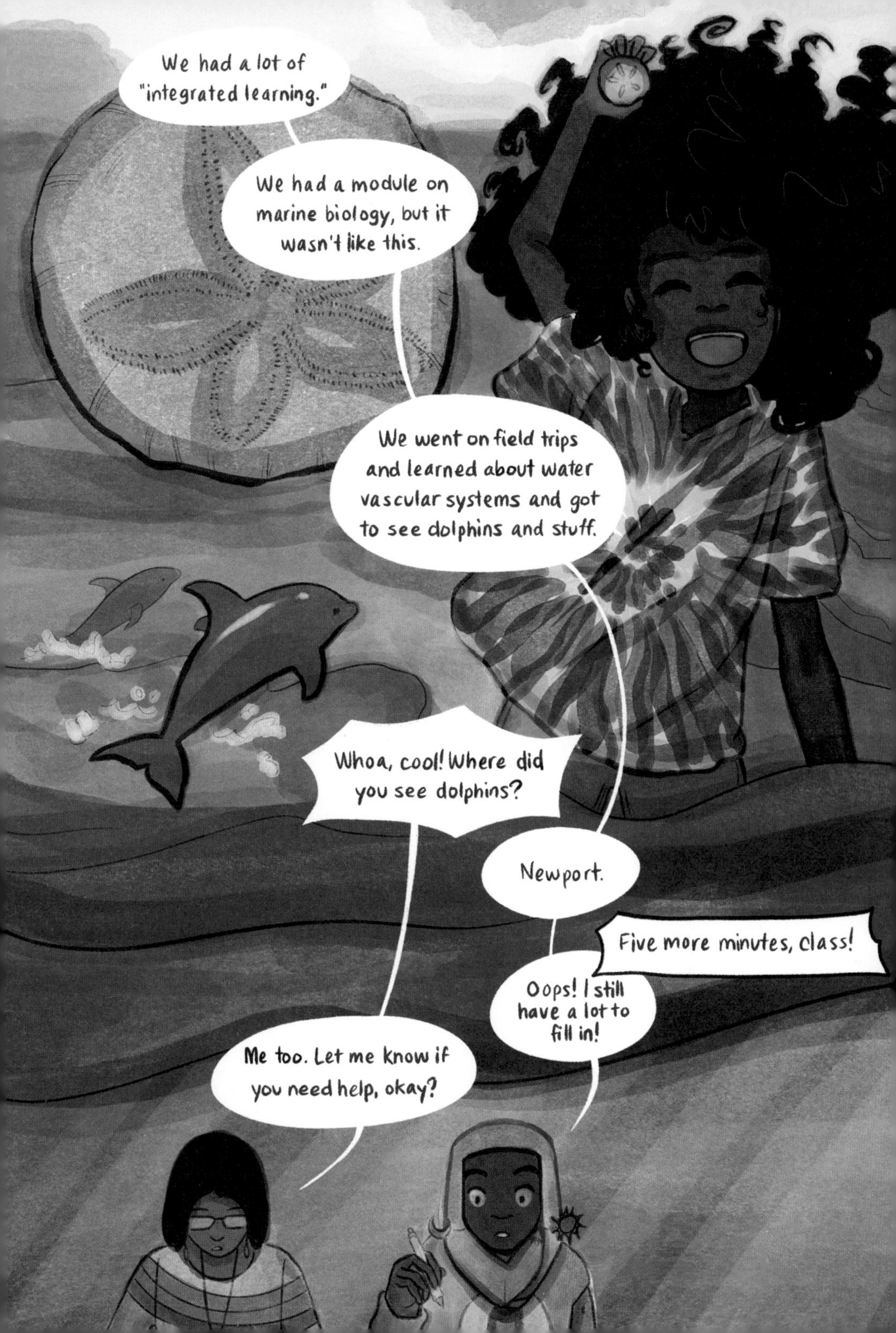
We had a lot of "integrated learning."
We had a module on marine biology, but it wasn't like this.
We went on field trips and learned about water vascular systems and got to see dolphins and stuff.
Whoa, cool! Where did you see dolphins?
Newport.
Five more minutes, class!
Oops! I still have a lot to fill in!
Me too. Let me know if you need help, okay?

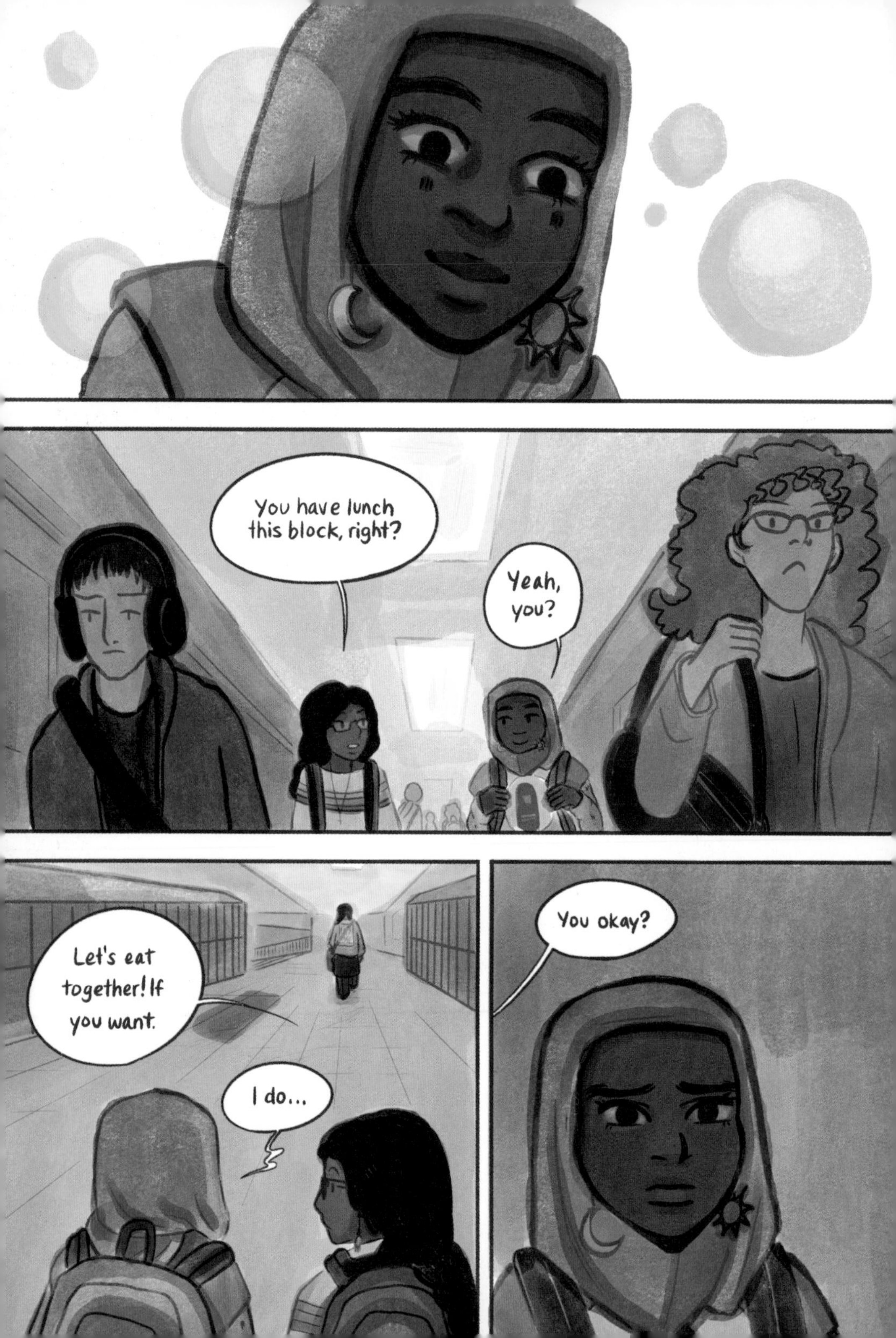
You have lunch this block, right?
Yeah, you?
Let's eat together! If you want.
I do...
You okay?

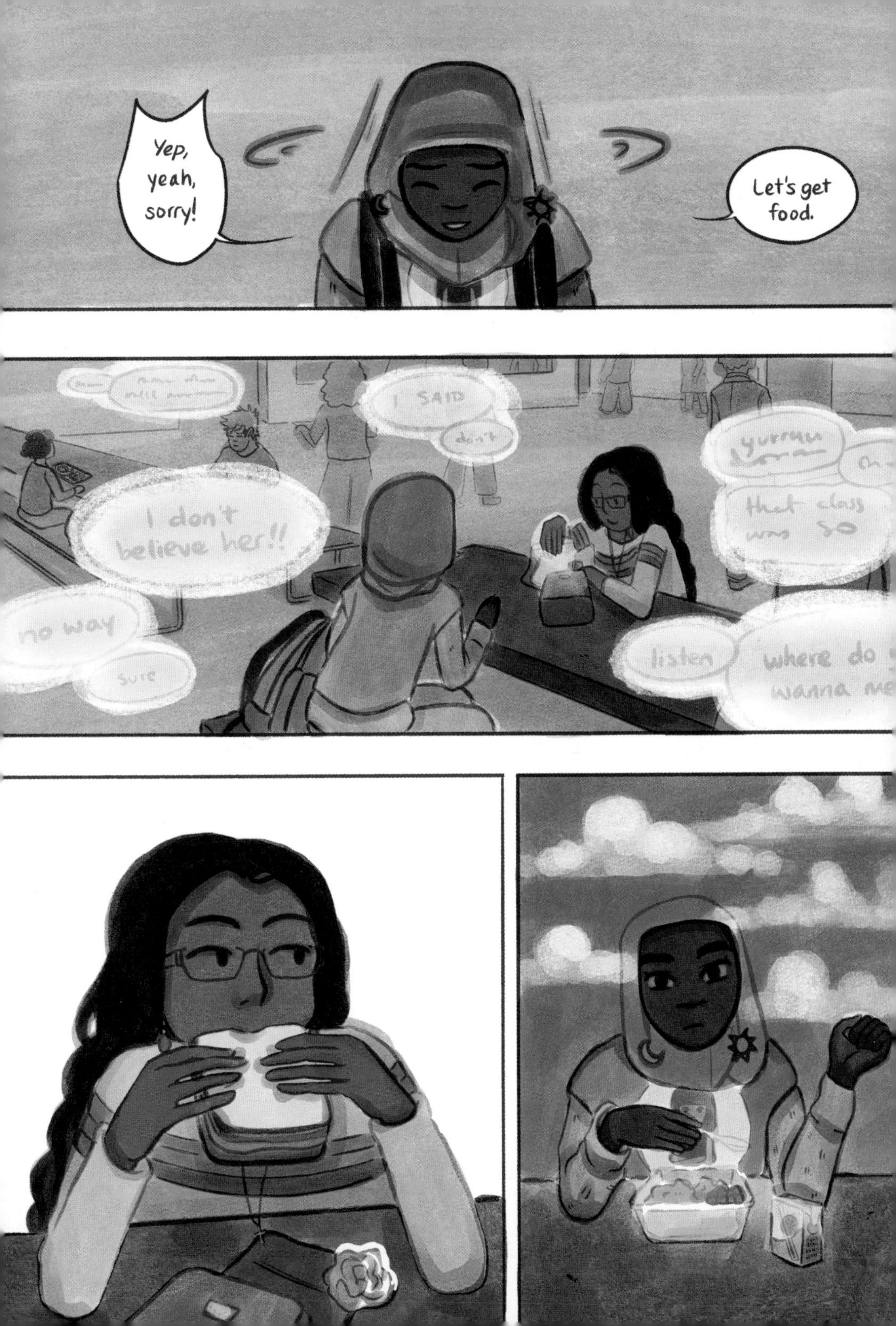
Yep, yeah, sorry!
Let's get food.
I SAID
don't
I don't believe her!!
that class was SO
no way
sure
listen
where do

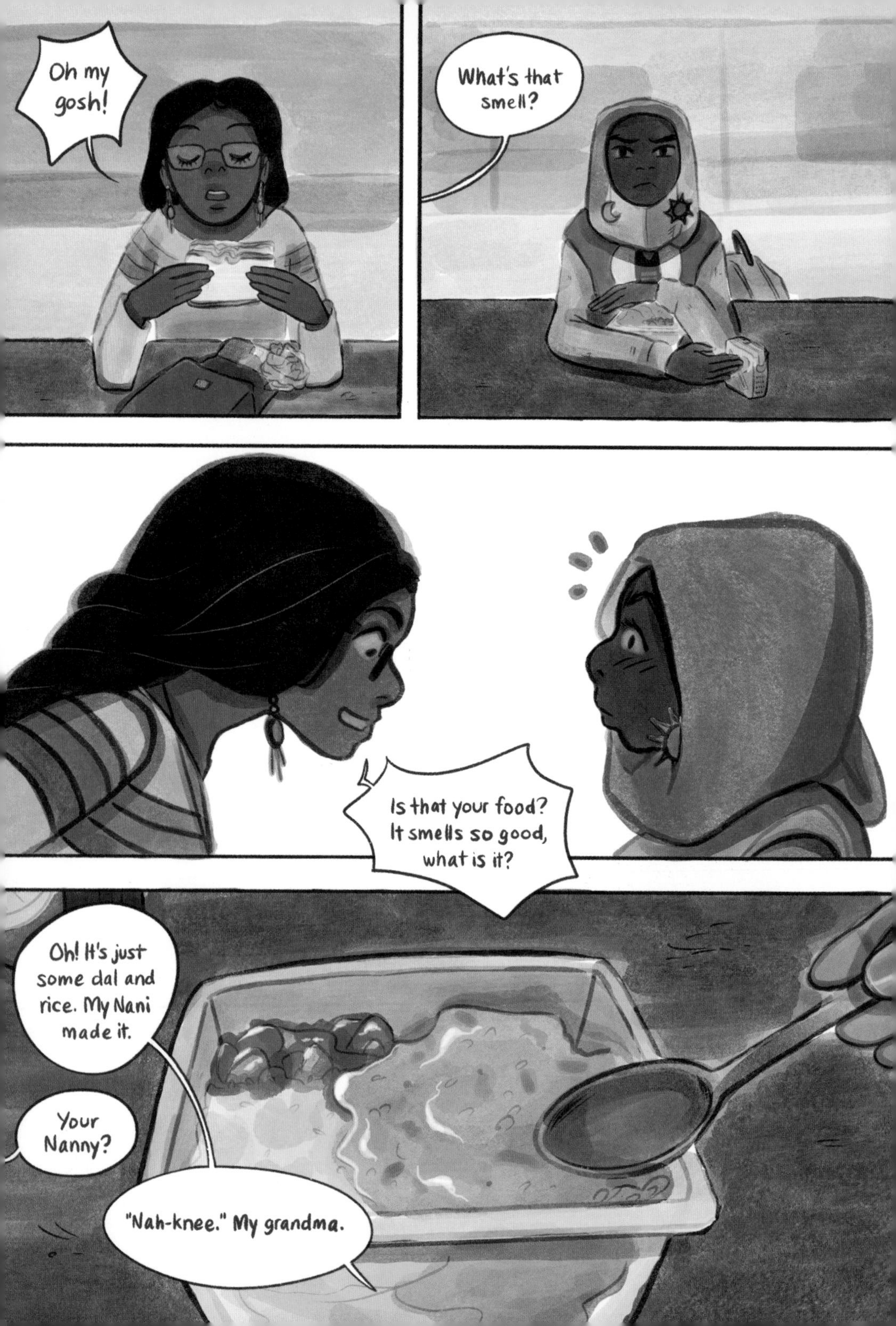
Oh my gosh!
What's that smell?
Is that your food? It smells so good, what is it?
Oh! It's just some dal and rice. My Nani made it.
Your Nanny?
"Nah-knee." My grandma.

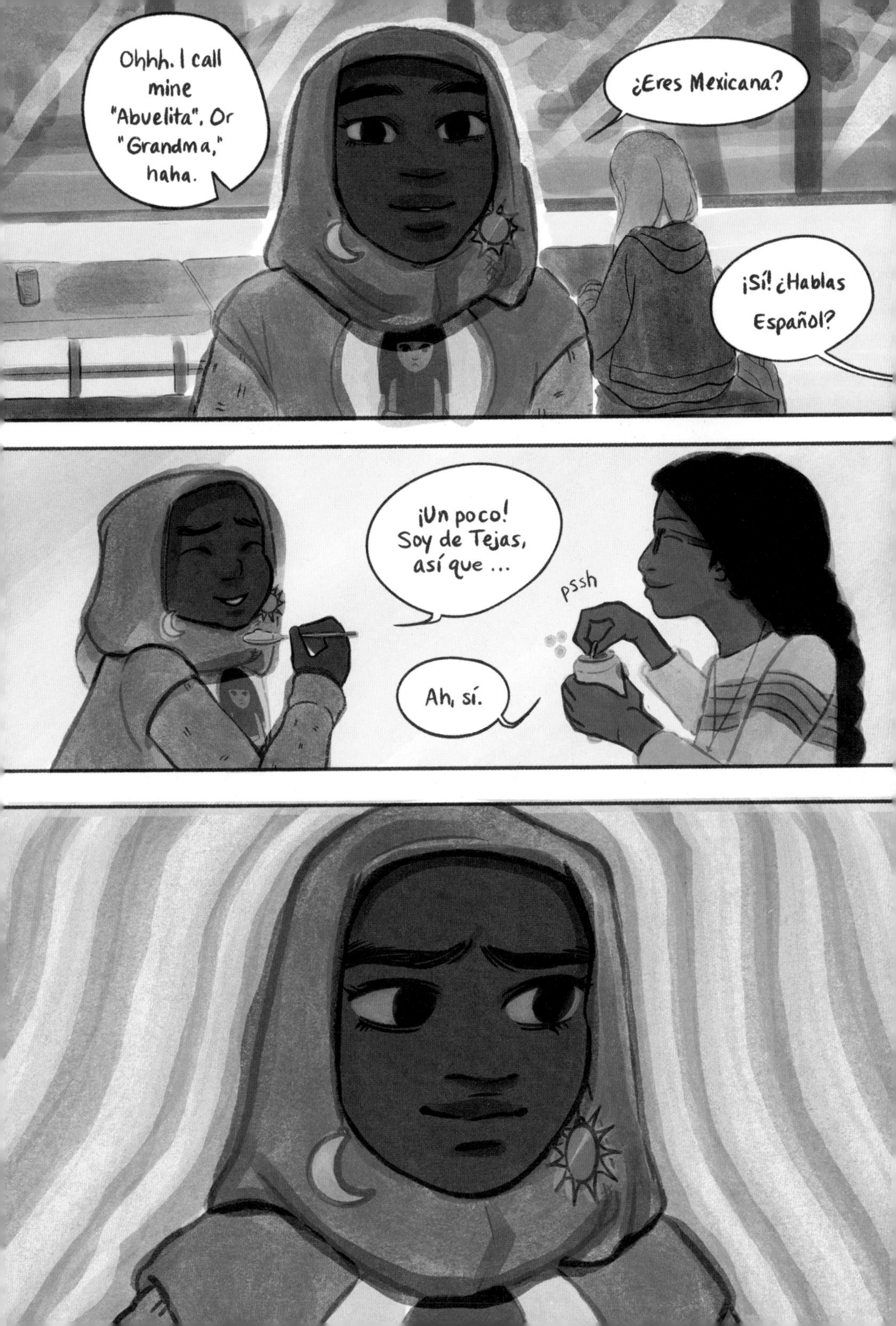

Ohhh. I call mine "Abuelita". Or "Grandma," haha.
¿Eres Mexicana?
¡Sí! ¿Hablas Español?
¡Un poco! Soy de Tejas, así que ...
pssh
Ah, sí.

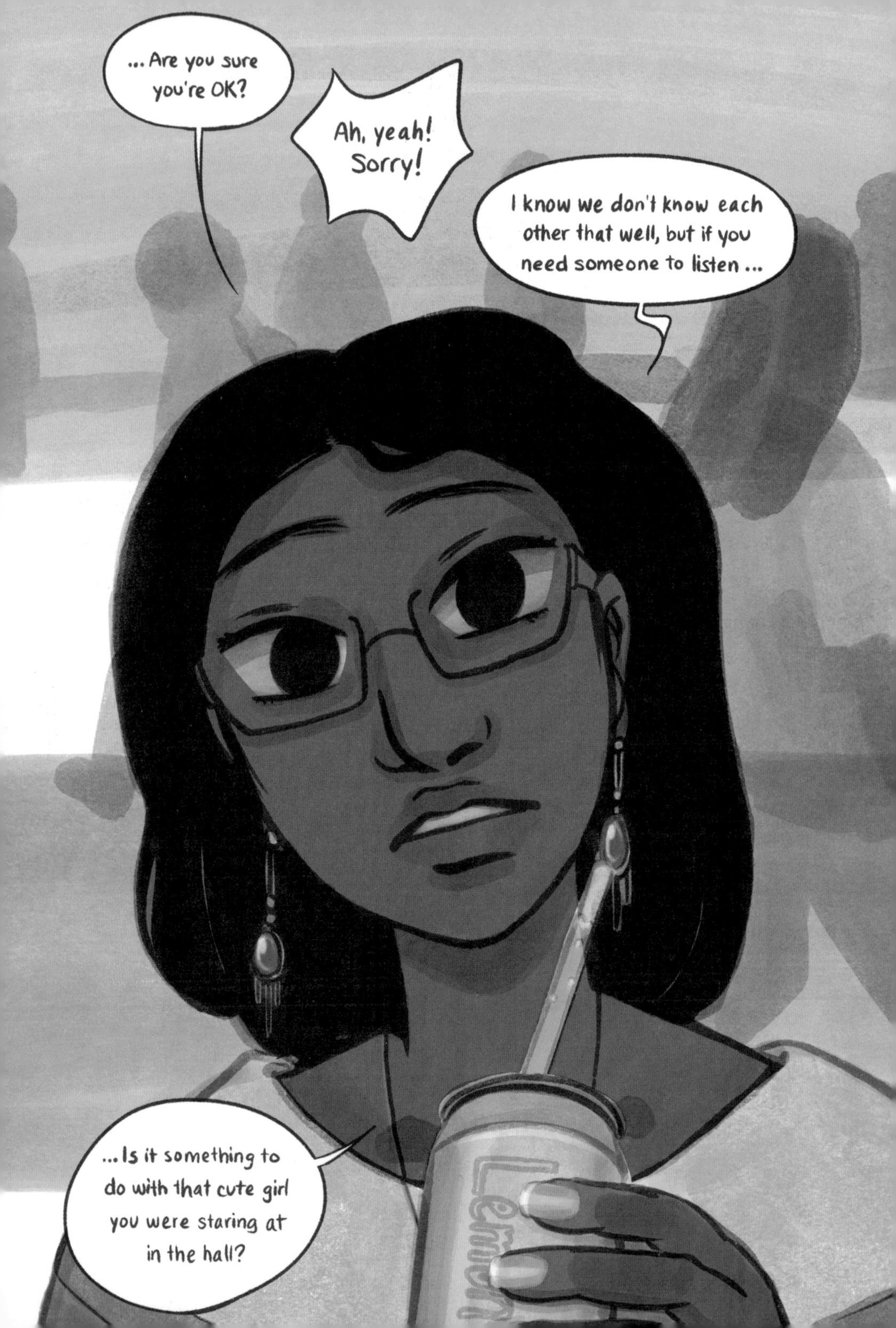
...Are you sure you're OK?
Ah, yeah! Sorry!
I know we don't know each other that well, but if you need someone to listen ...
...Is it something to do with that cute girl you were staring at in the hall?
Lemon

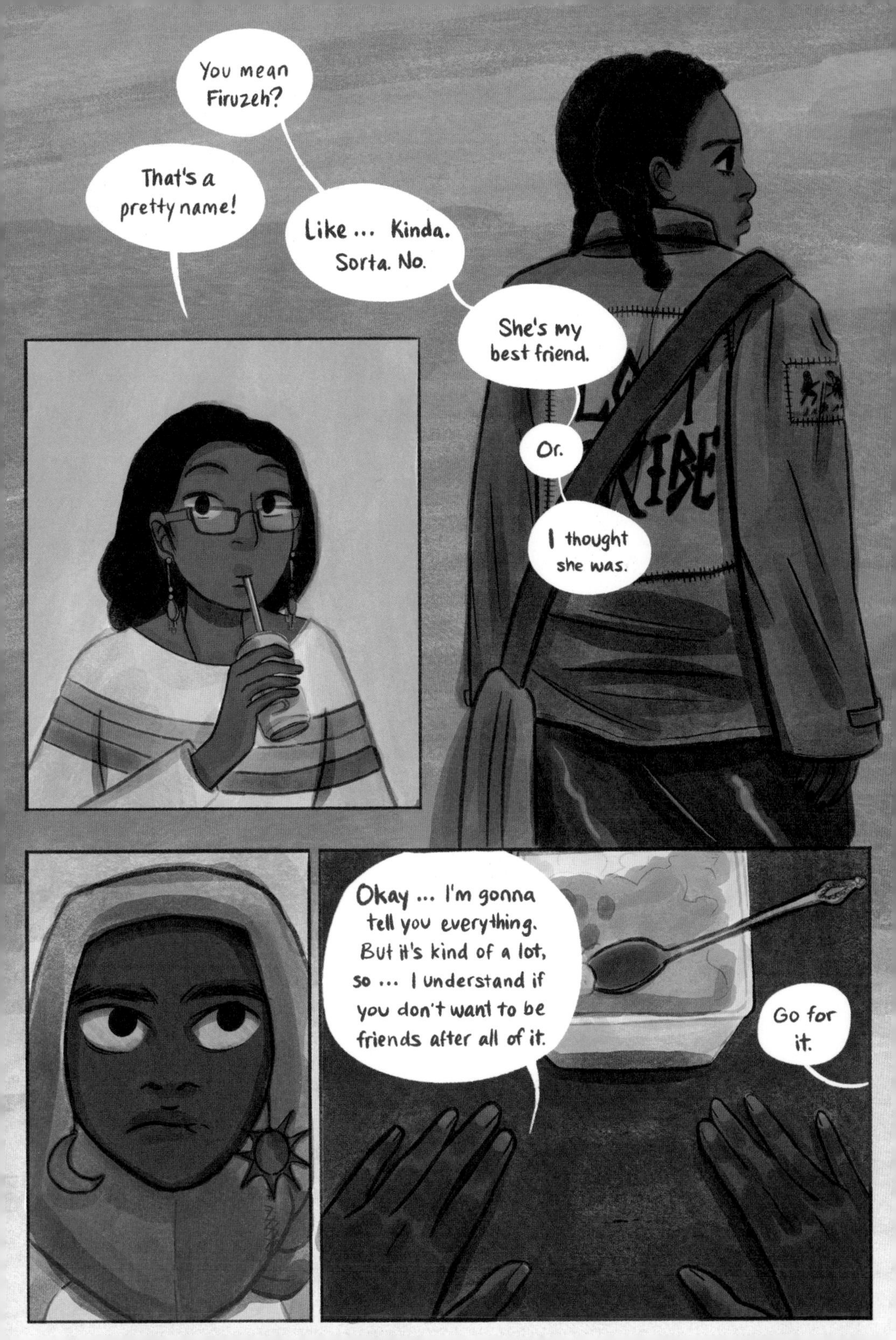
You mean Firuzeh?
That's a pretty name!
Like ... Kinda. Sorta. No.
She's my best friend.
Or.
I thought she was.
Okay ... I'm gonna tell you everything. But it's kind of a lot, so ... I understand if you don't want to be friends after all of it.
Go for it.

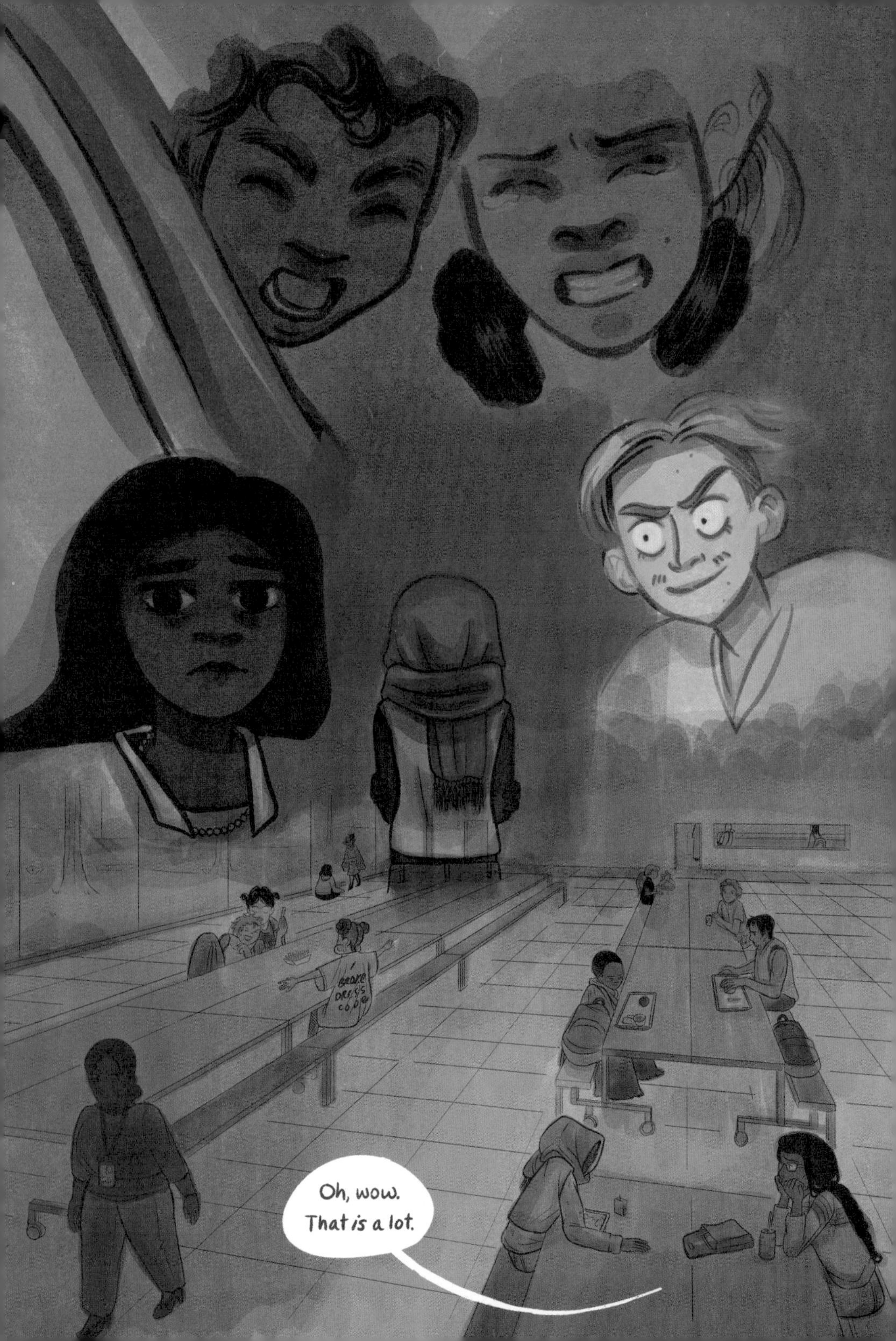
Oh, wow. That is a lot.

I think it's nice you want to be closer to God.

Oh! I'm not ... sure that's ...

Oh gosh, sorry! Never mind.

I just mean, it's nice.

The headscarf is nice.

Thanks.

Maybe you should treat the Islam thing like a school project. Have you done any research into it?

I tried to look stuff up online but it was all horrible.

Yeah, the internet can be pretty terrible.

Have you tried the library?

Oh my god, no, I totally forgot about the library.

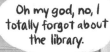

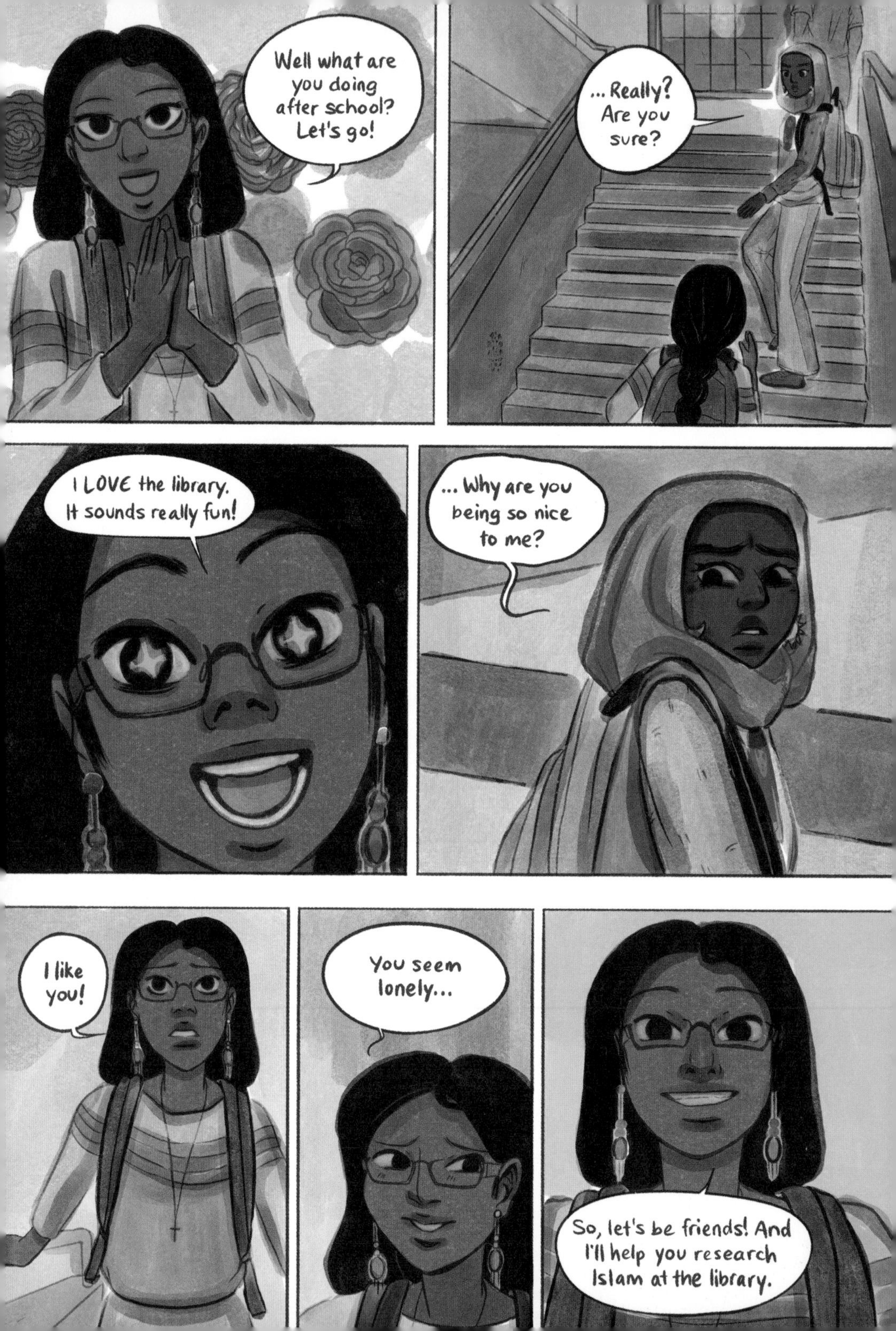
Well what are you doing after school? Let's go!
...Really? Are you sure?
I LOVE the library. It sounds really fun!
...Why are you being so nice to me?
I like you!
You seem lonely...
So, let's be friends! And I'll help you research Islam at the library.

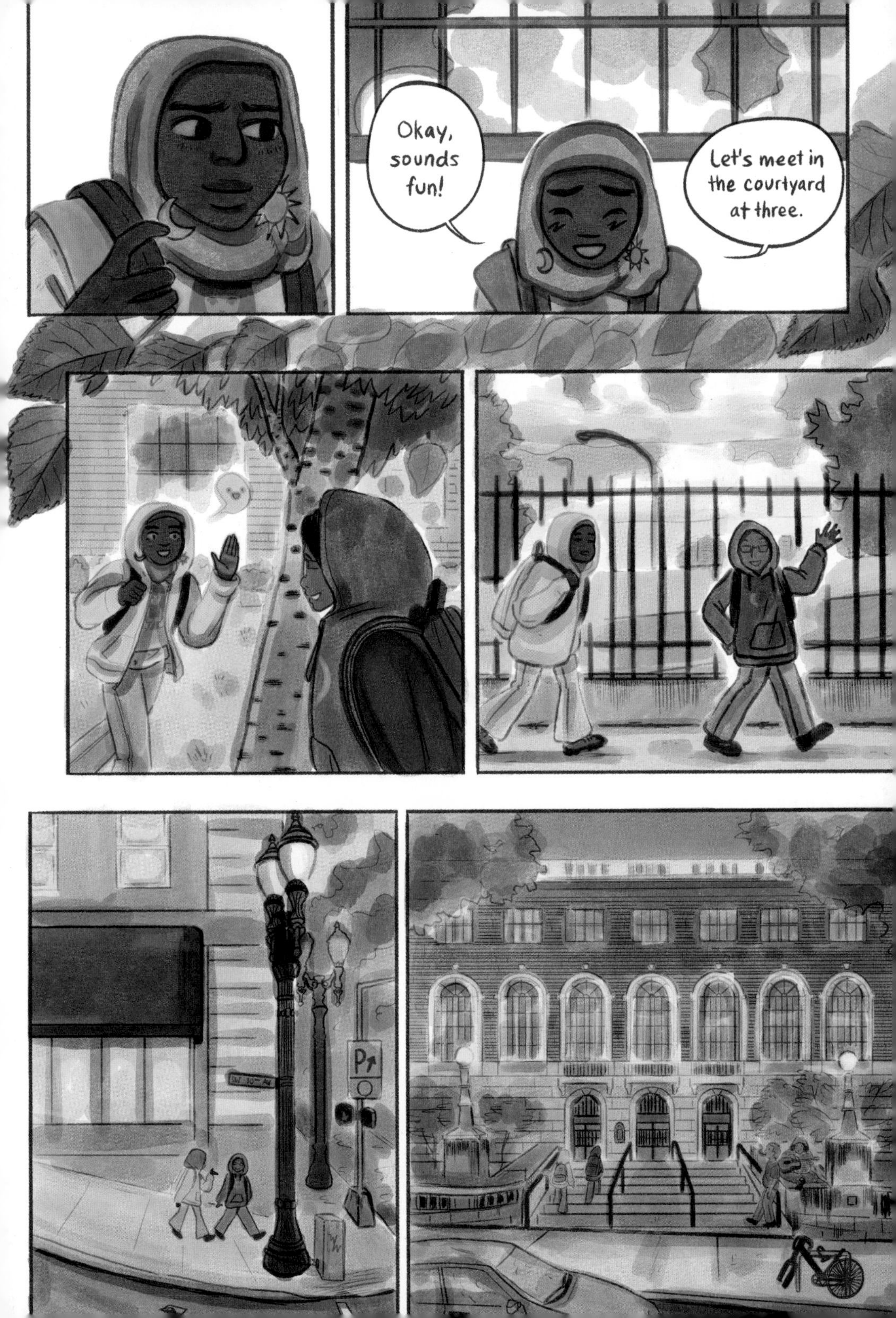
Okay, sounds fun!
Let's meet in the courtyard at three.

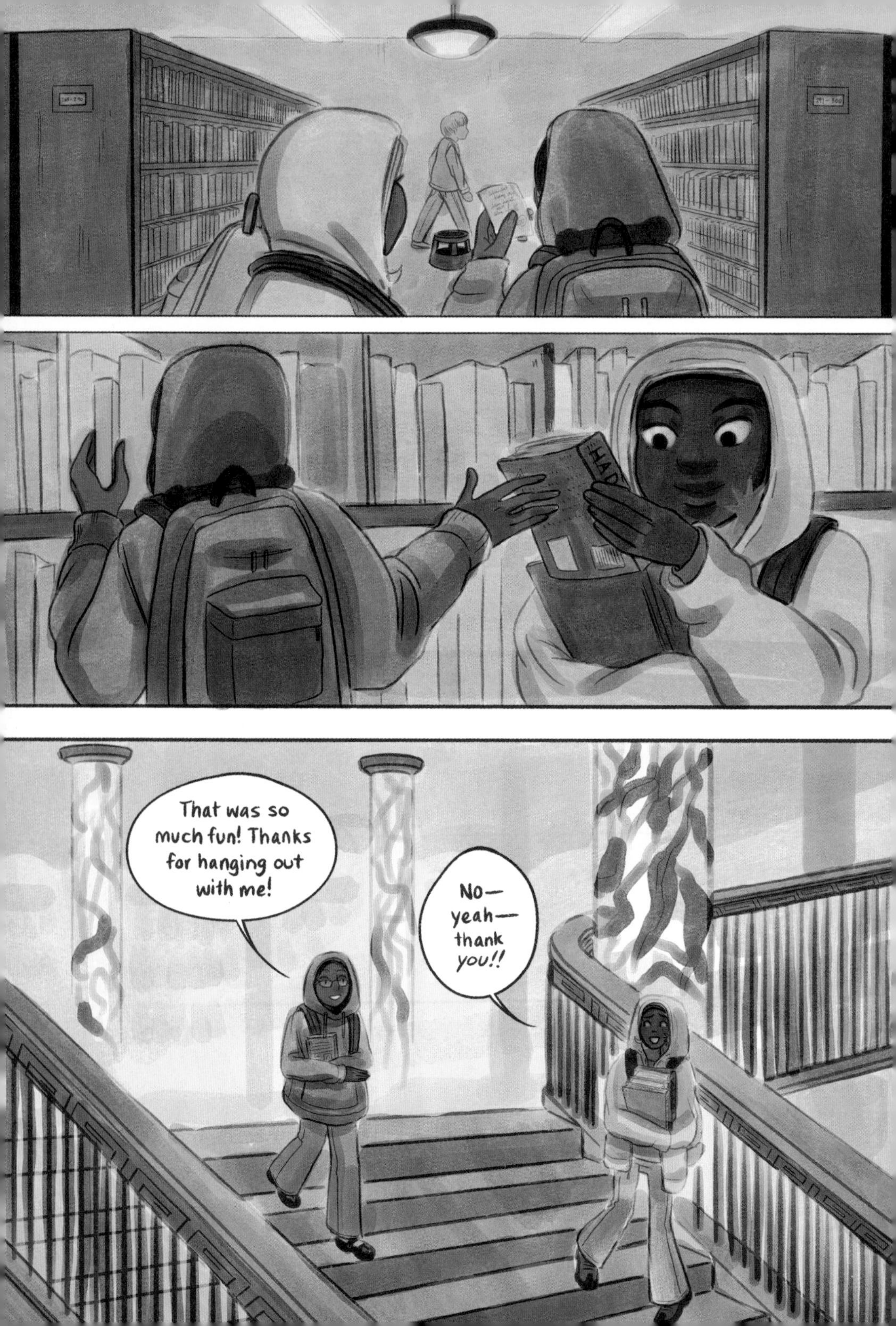
That was so much fun! Thanks for hanging out with me!
No— yeah— thank you!!

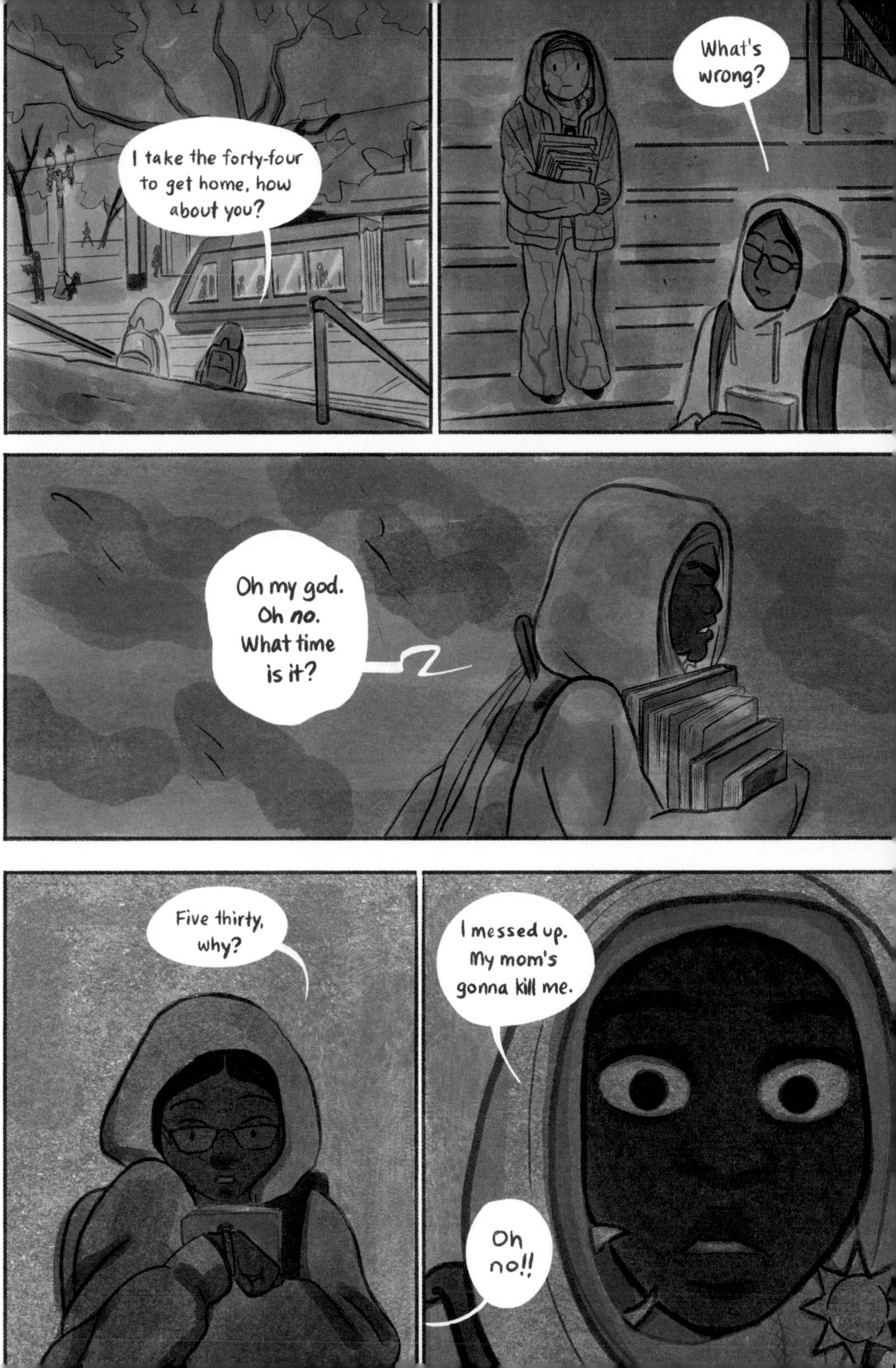
I take the forty-four to get home, how about you?
What's wrong?
Oh my god. Oh *no*. What time is it?
Five thirty, why?
I messed up. My mom's gonna kill me.
Oh no!!

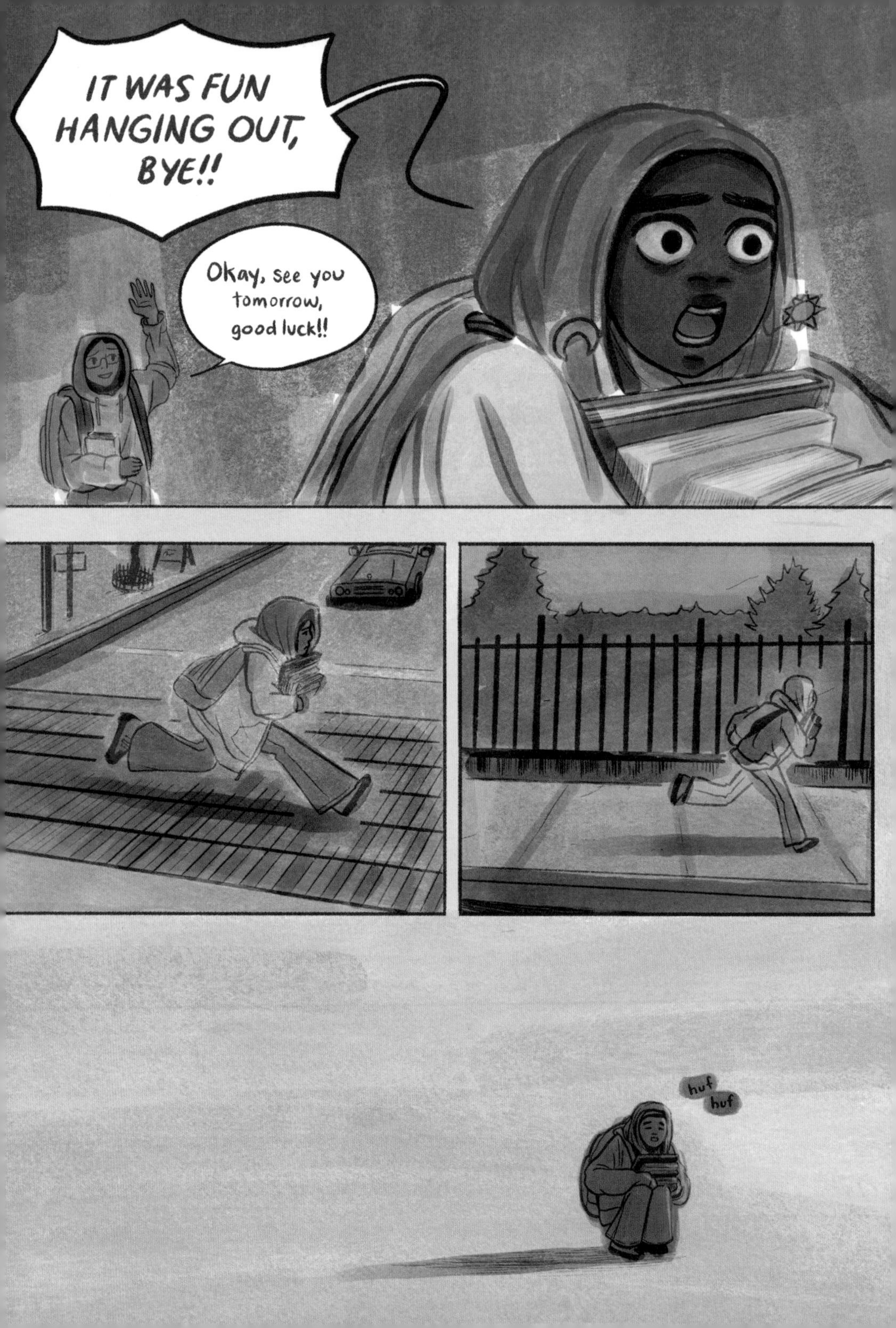
IT WAS FUN HANGING OUT, BYE!!
Okay, see you tomorrow, good luck!!
huf
huf

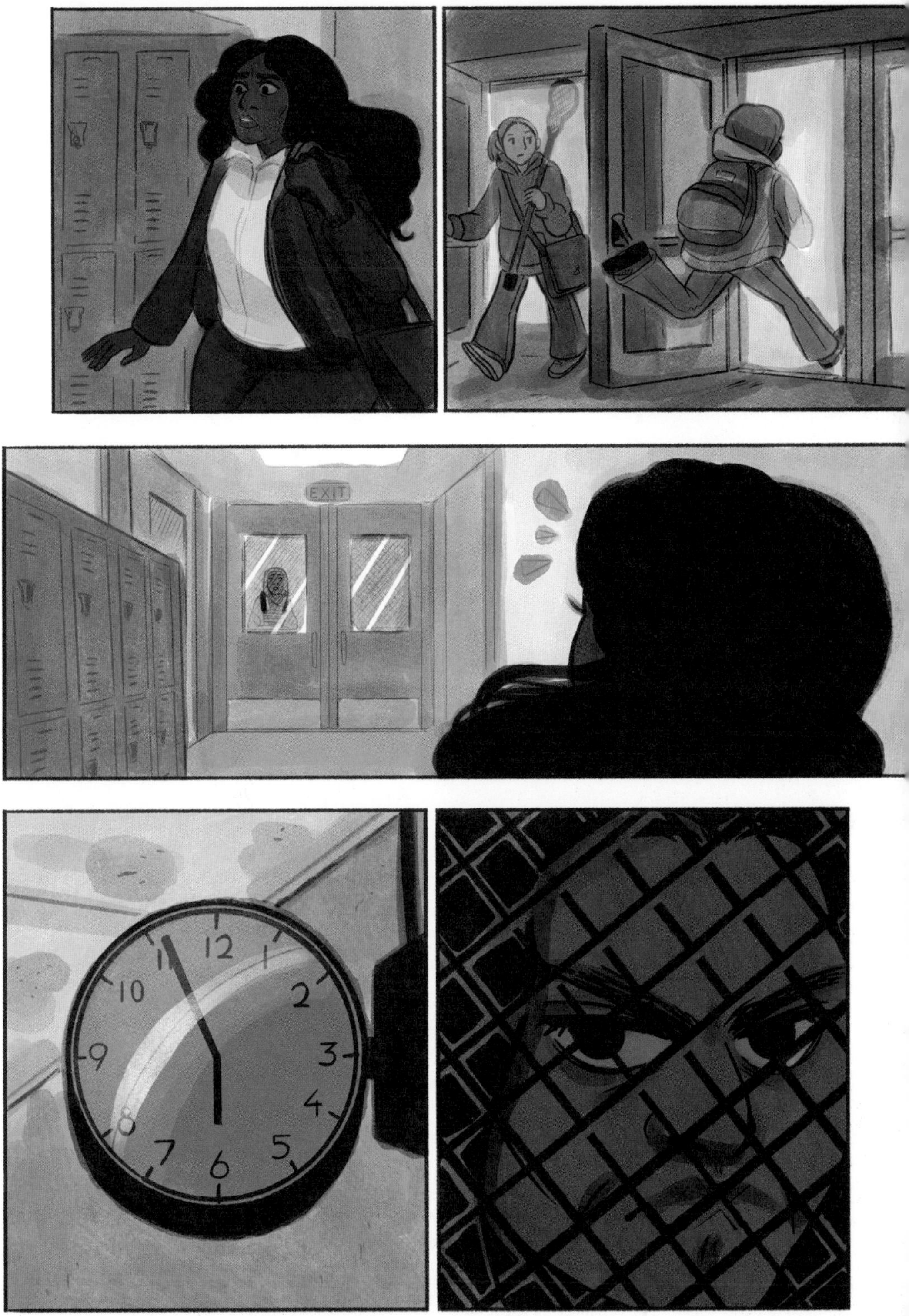
EXIT

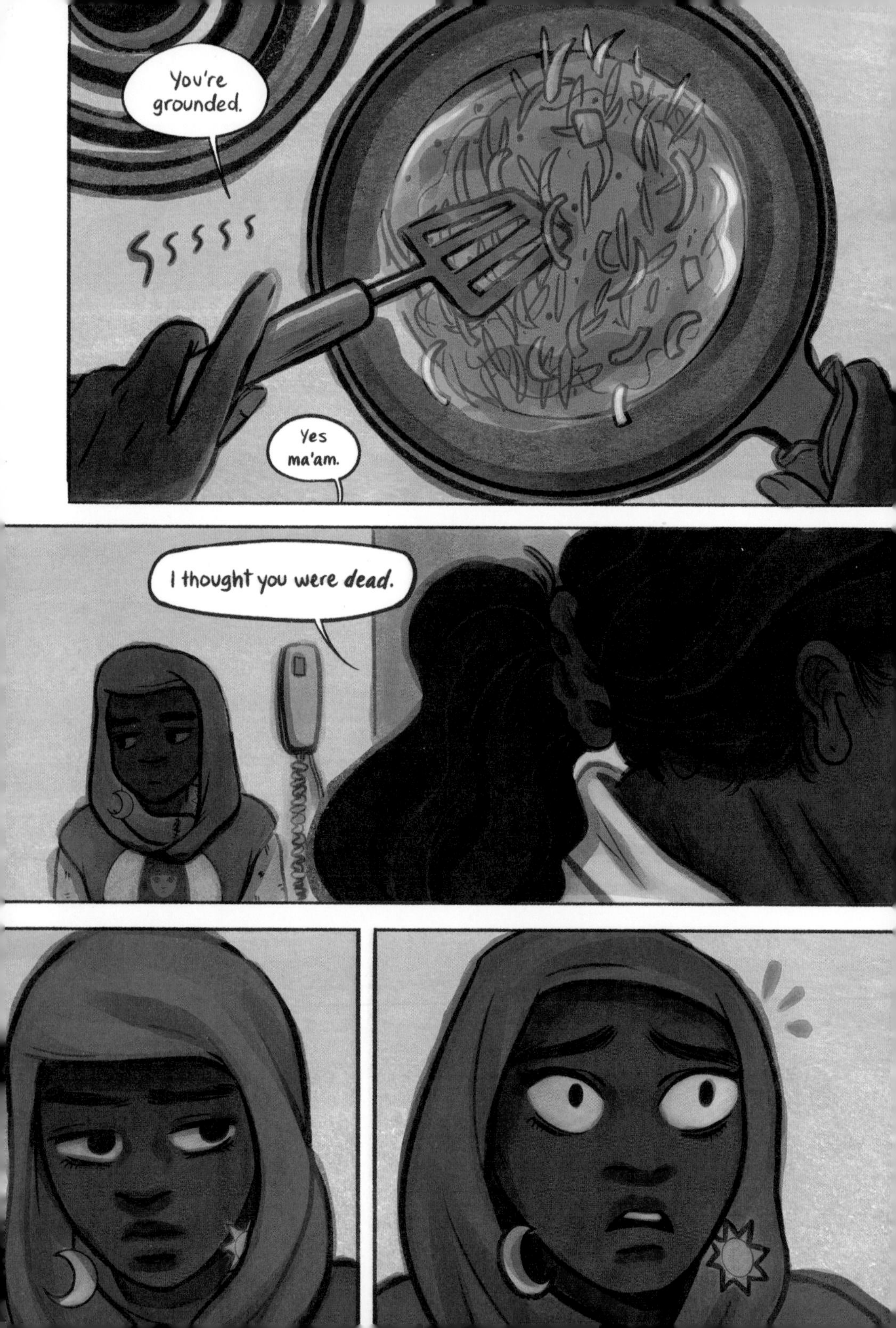
You're grounded.
SSSSS
Yes ma'am.
I thought you were *dead*.

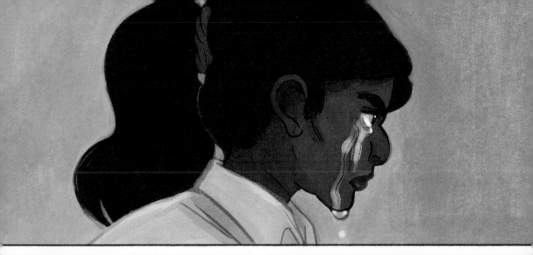

Don't you ever do that to me again.

I won't. I'm sorry.

I'm really sorry, Mommy.

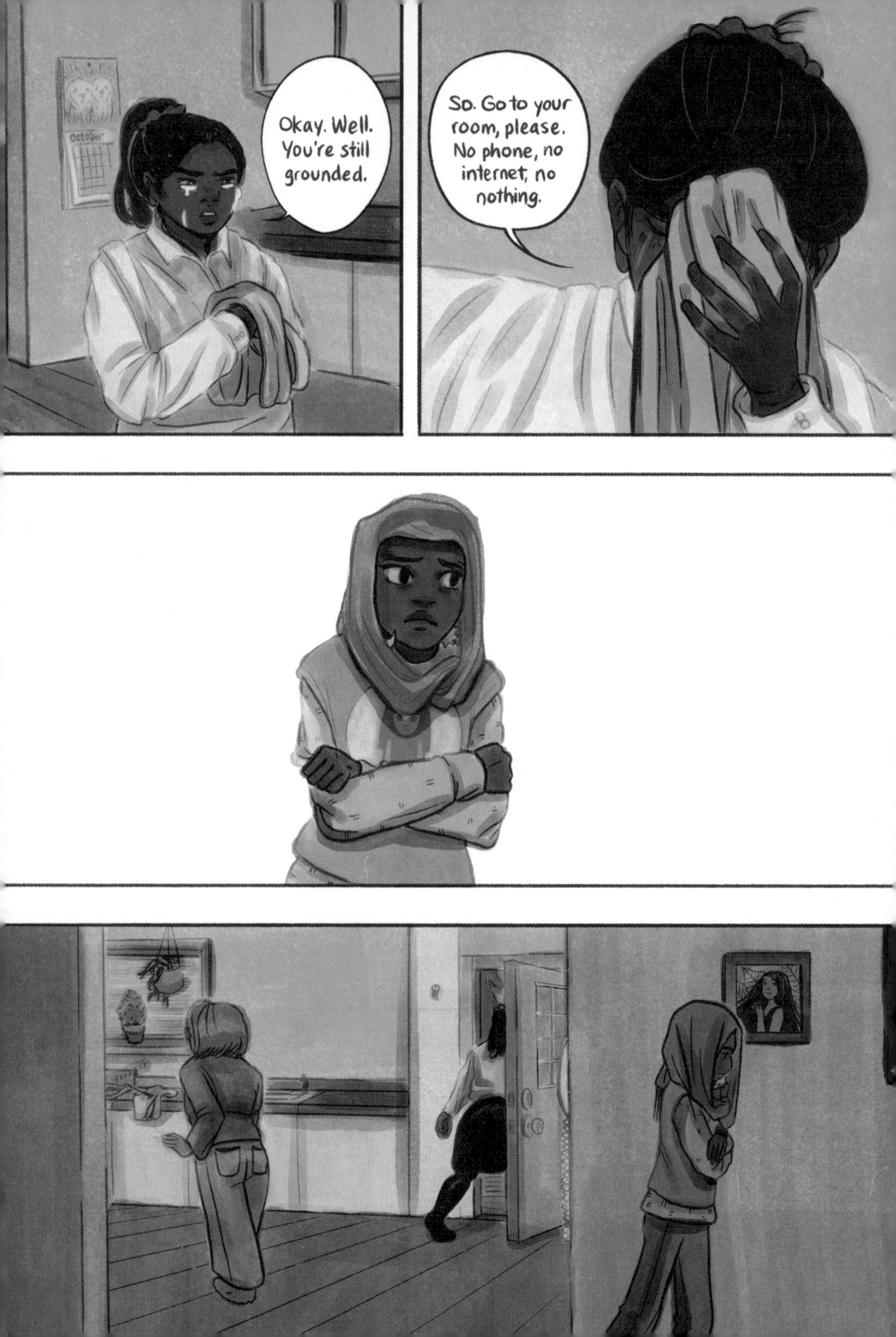
October
Okay. Well. You're still grounded.
So. Go to your room, please. No phone, no internet, no nothing.

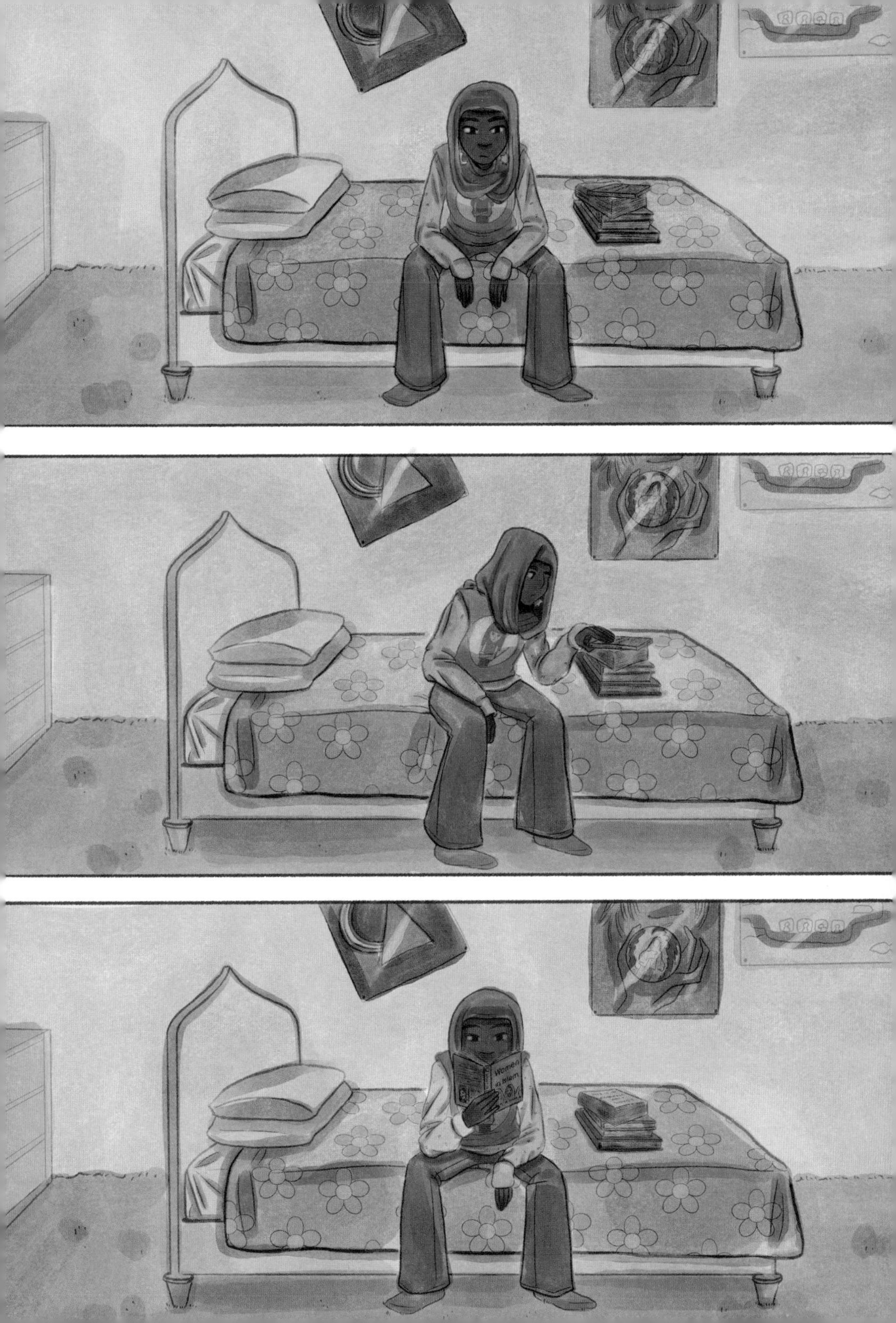
Women in Islam

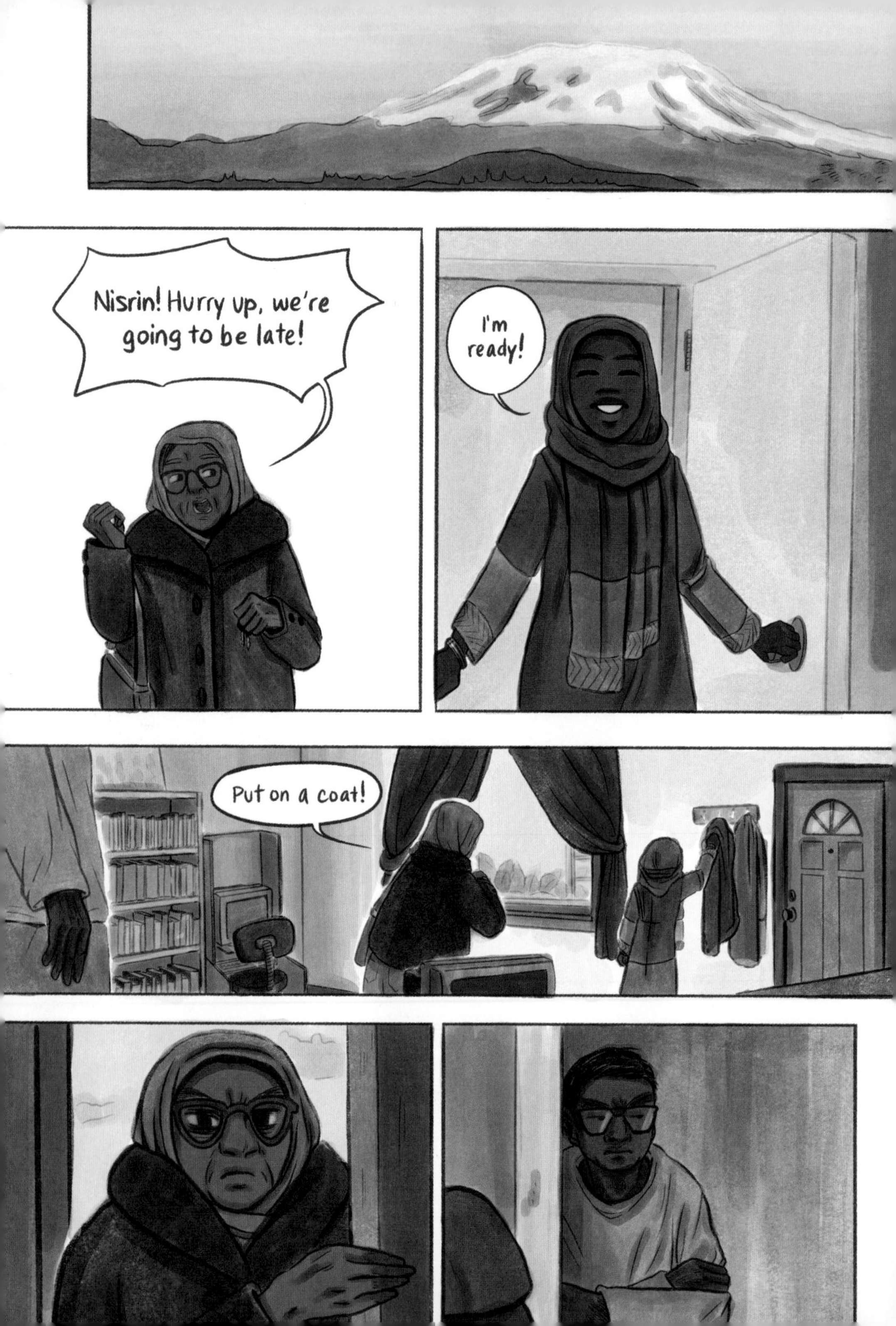
Nisrin! Hurry up, we're going to be late!
I'm ready!
Put on a coat!

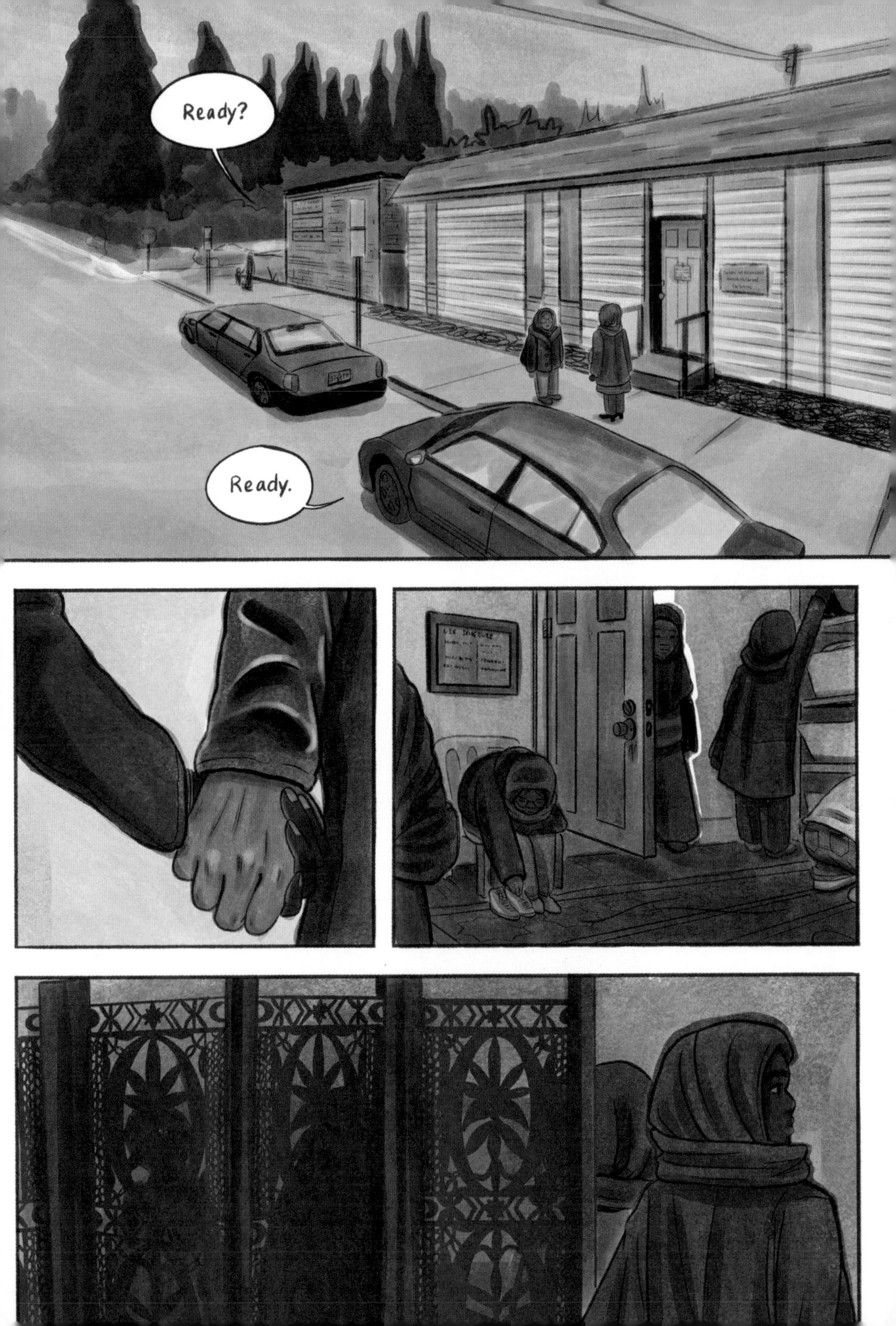

Ready?
Ready.

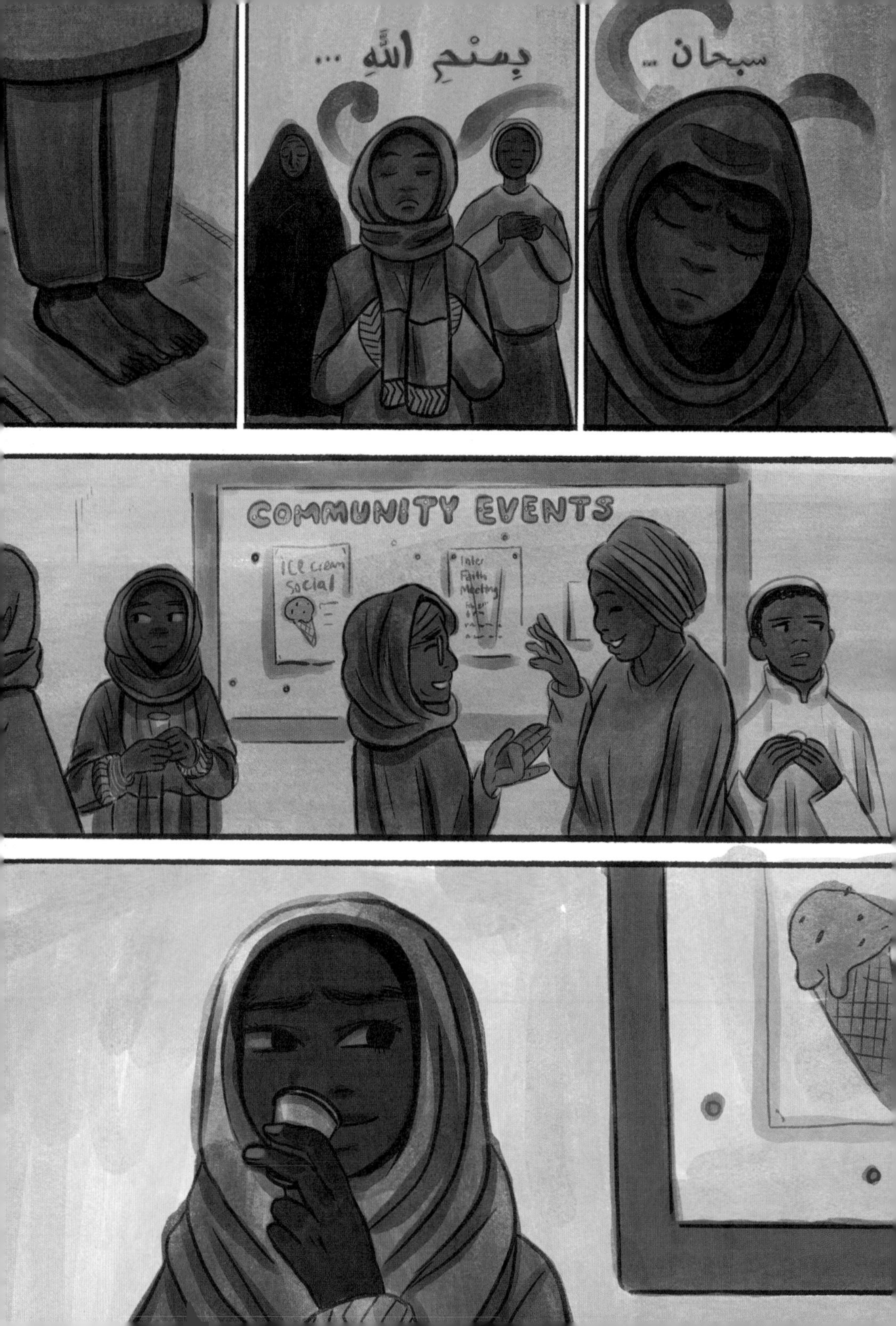
بِسْمِ اللَّهِ ...
سبحان ..
COMMUNITY EVENTS
Ice cream Social
Inter Faith Meeting

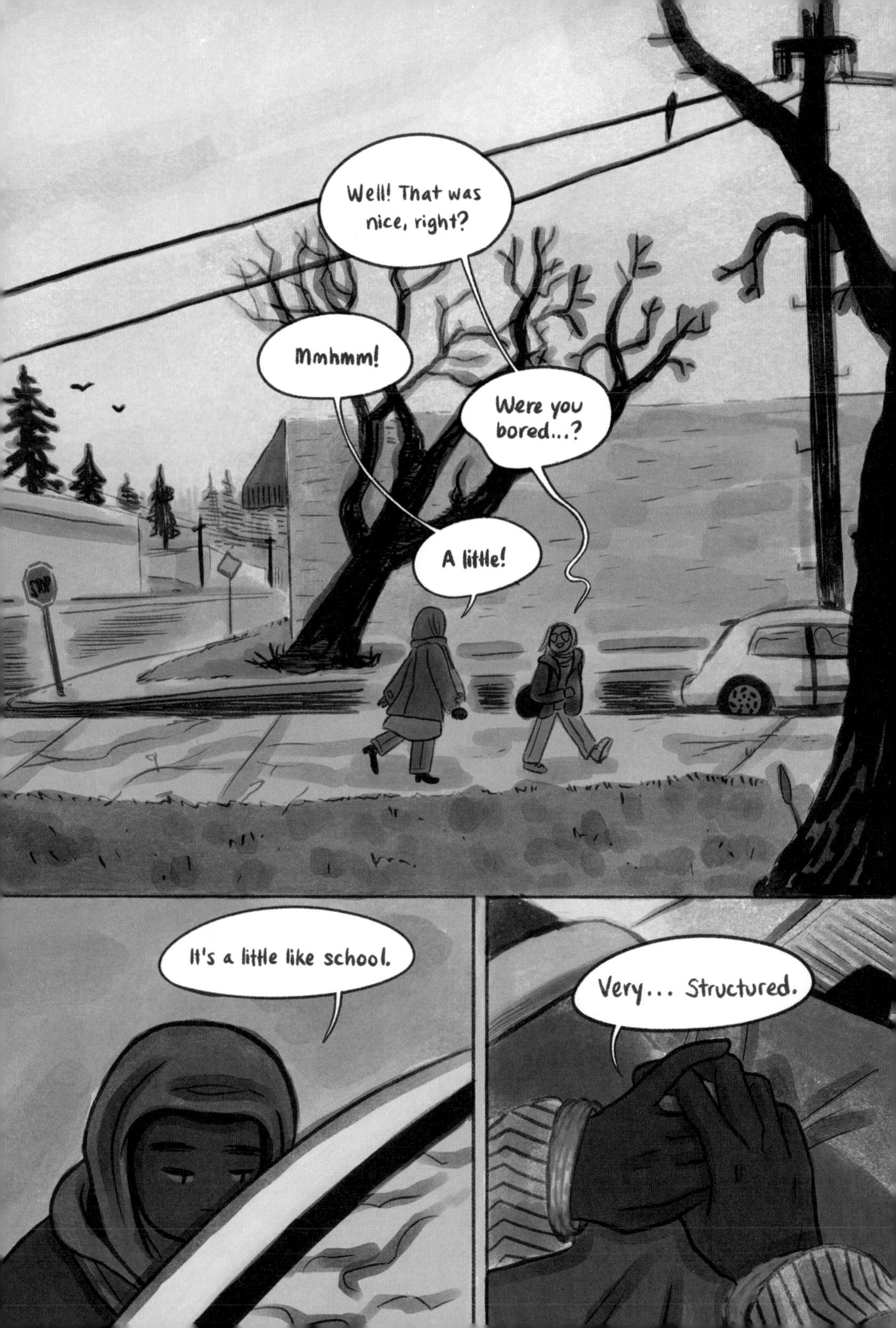
Well! That was nice, right?
Mmhmm!
Were you bored...?
A little!
STOP
It's a little like school.
Very... Structured.

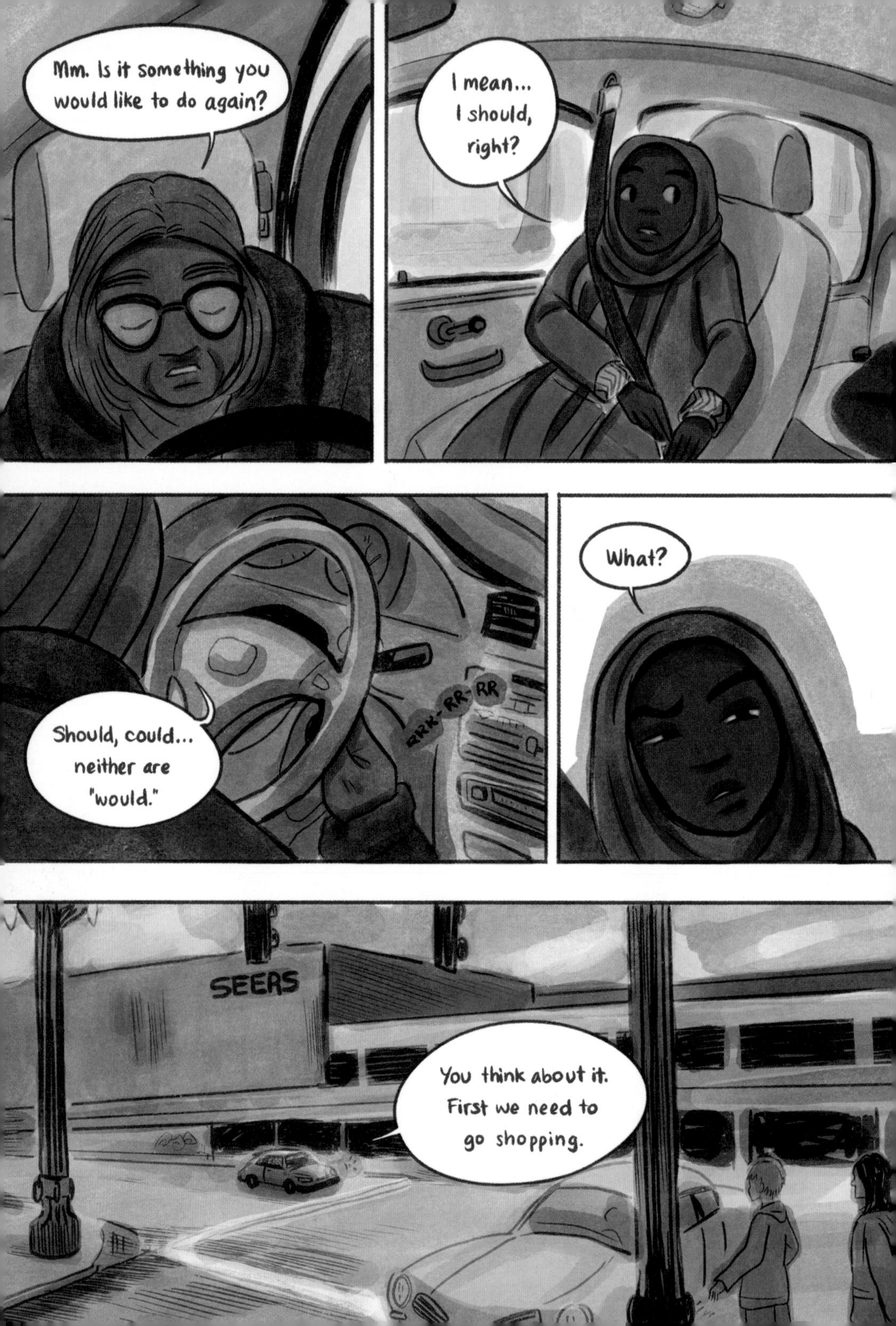
Mm. Is it something you would like to do again?
I mean... I should, right?
Should, could... neither are "would."
RRR-RR-RR
What?
SEERS
You think about it. First we need to go shopping.

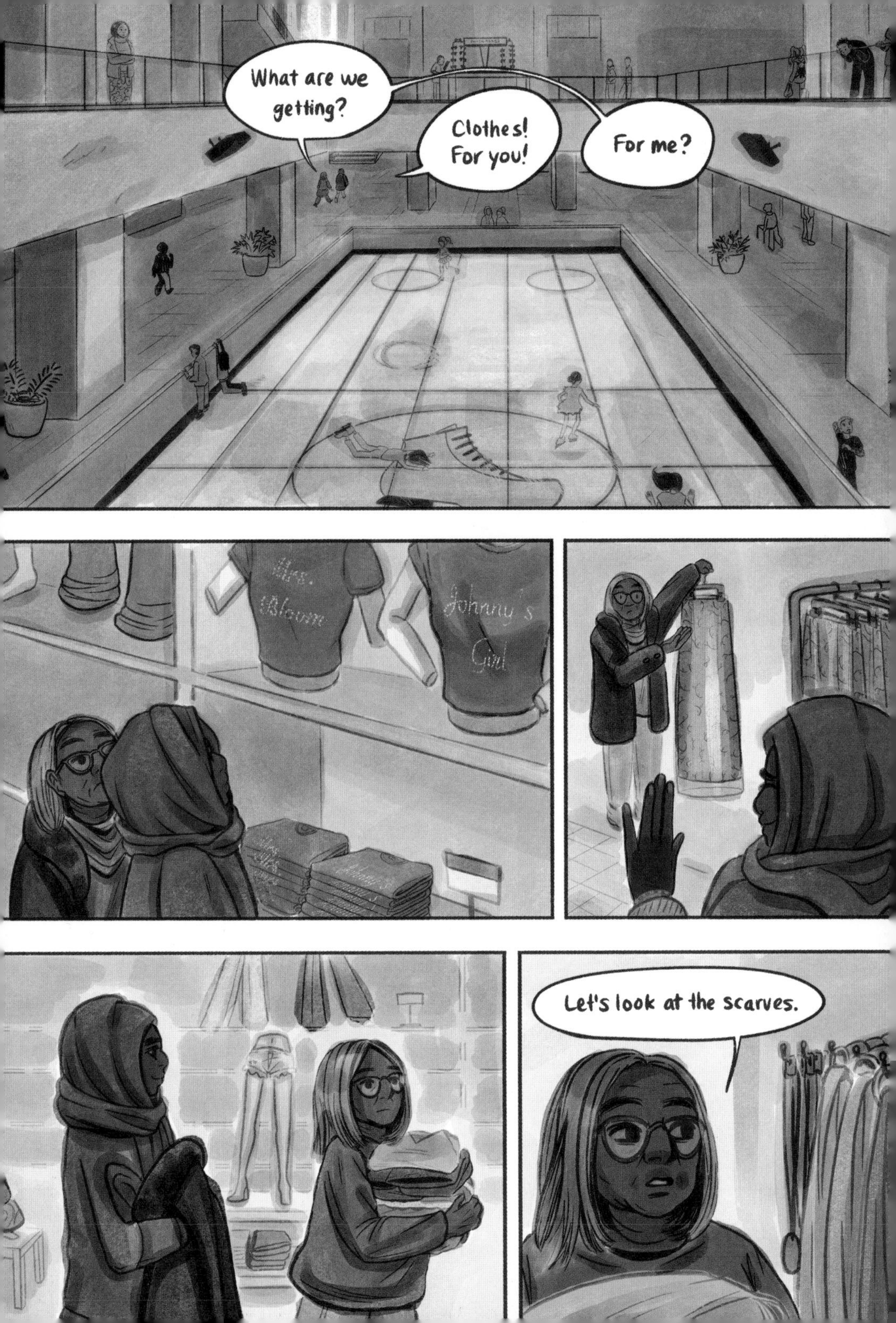
What are we getting?
Clothes! For you!
For me?
Johnny's Girl
Let's look at the scarves.

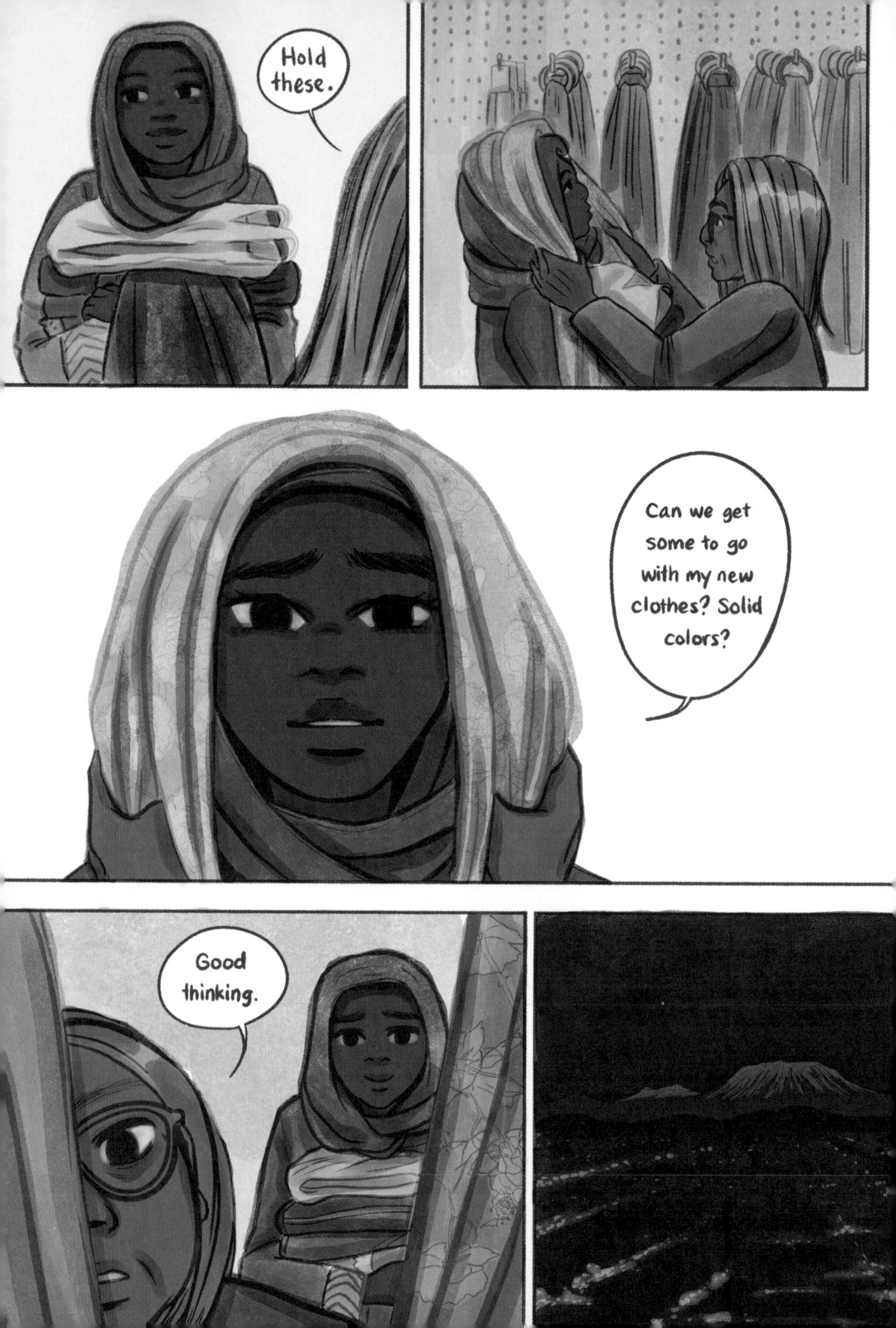
Hold these.
Can we get some to go with my new clothes? Solid colors?
Good thinking.

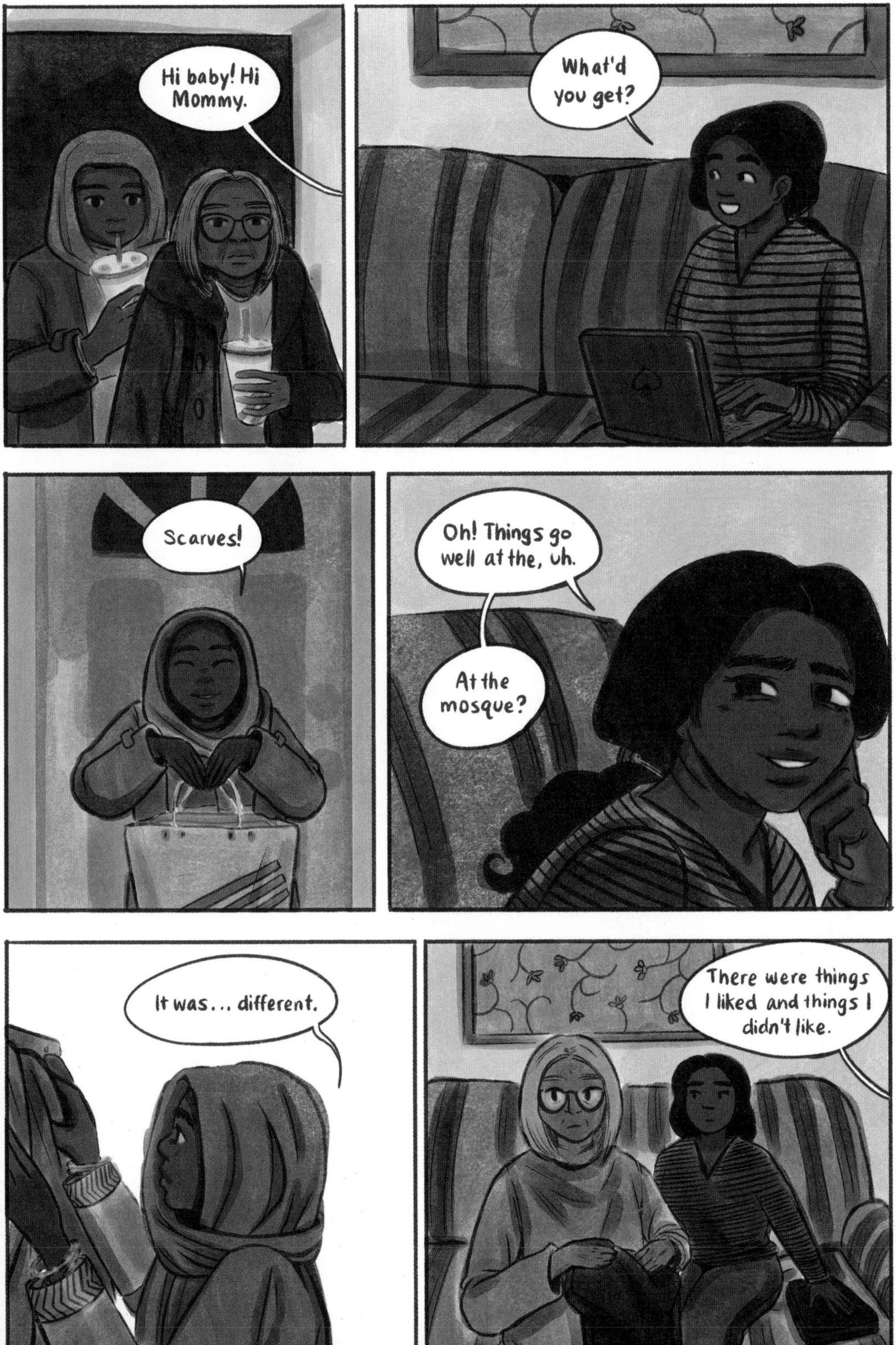
Hi baby! Hi Mommy.
What'd you get?
Scarves!
Oh! Things go well at the, uh.
At the mosque?
It was... different.
There were things I liked and things I didn't like.

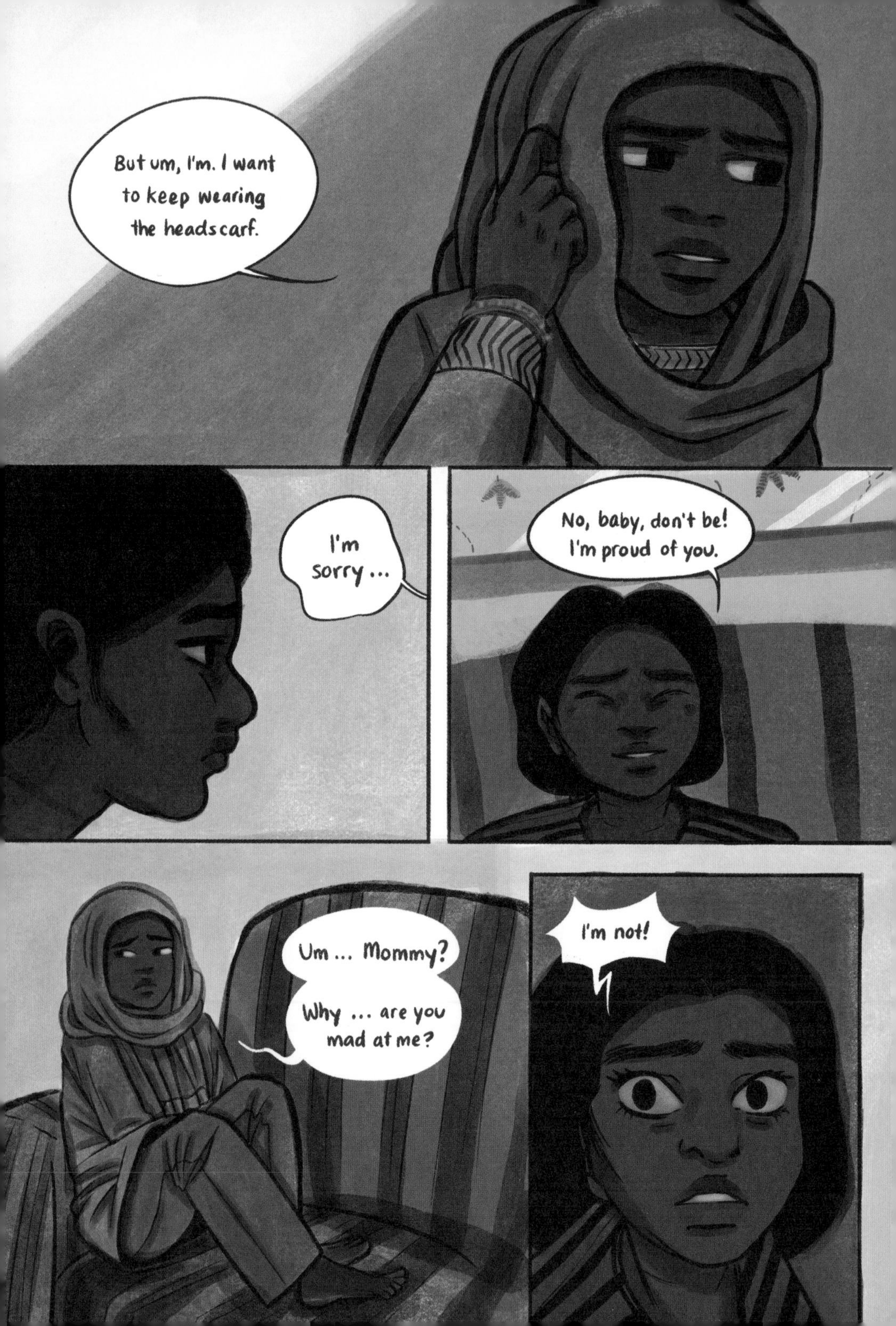
But um, I'm. I want to keep wearing the headscarf.
I'm sorry ...
No, baby, don't be! I'm proud of you.
Um ... Mommy?
Why ... are you mad at me?
I'm not!

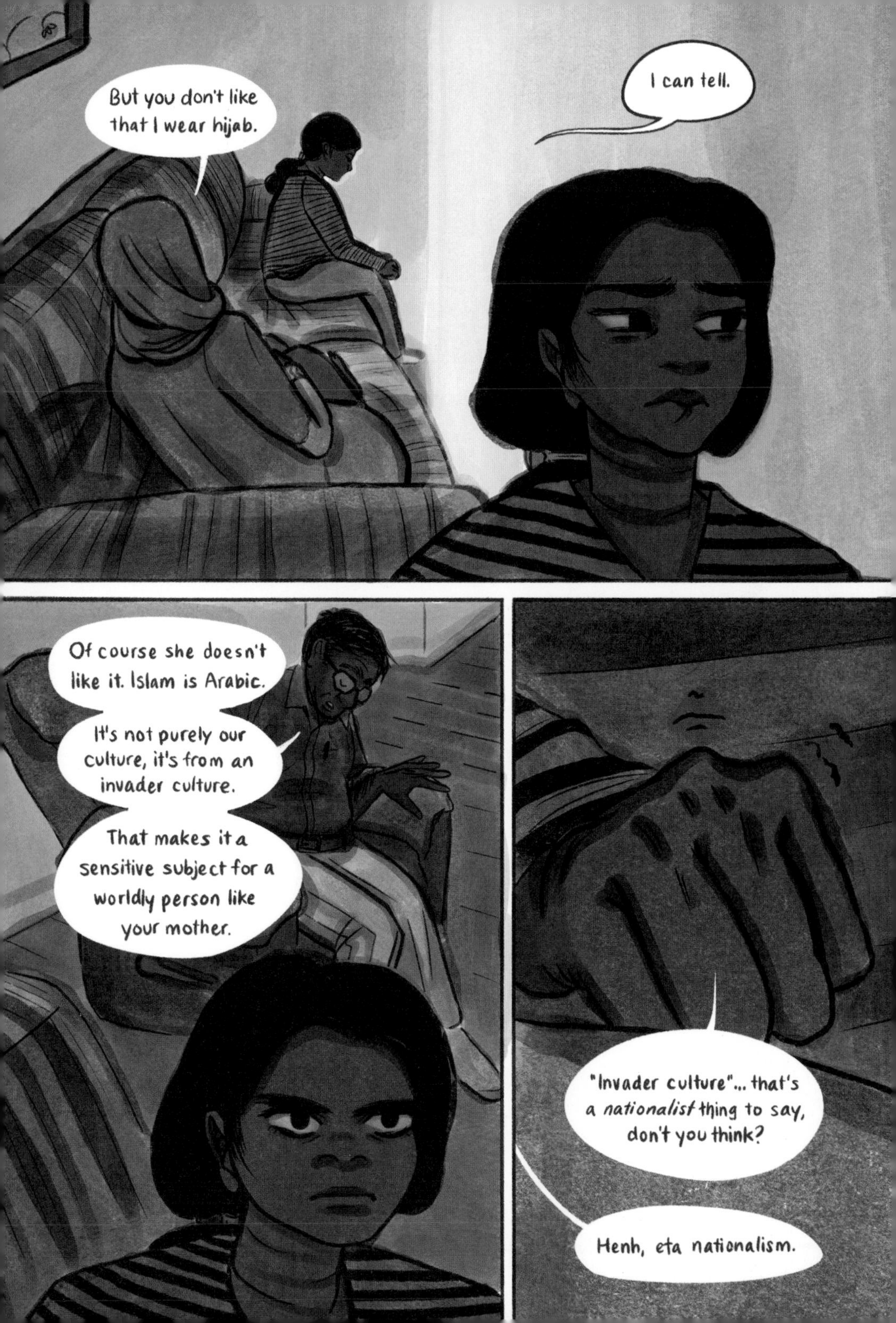
But you don't like that I wear hijab.
I can tell.
Of course she doesn't like it. Islam is Arabic.
It's not purely our culture, it's from an invader culture.
That makes it a sensitive subject for a worldly person like your mother.
"Invader culture"... that's a *nationalist* thing to say, don't you think?
Henh, eta nationalism.

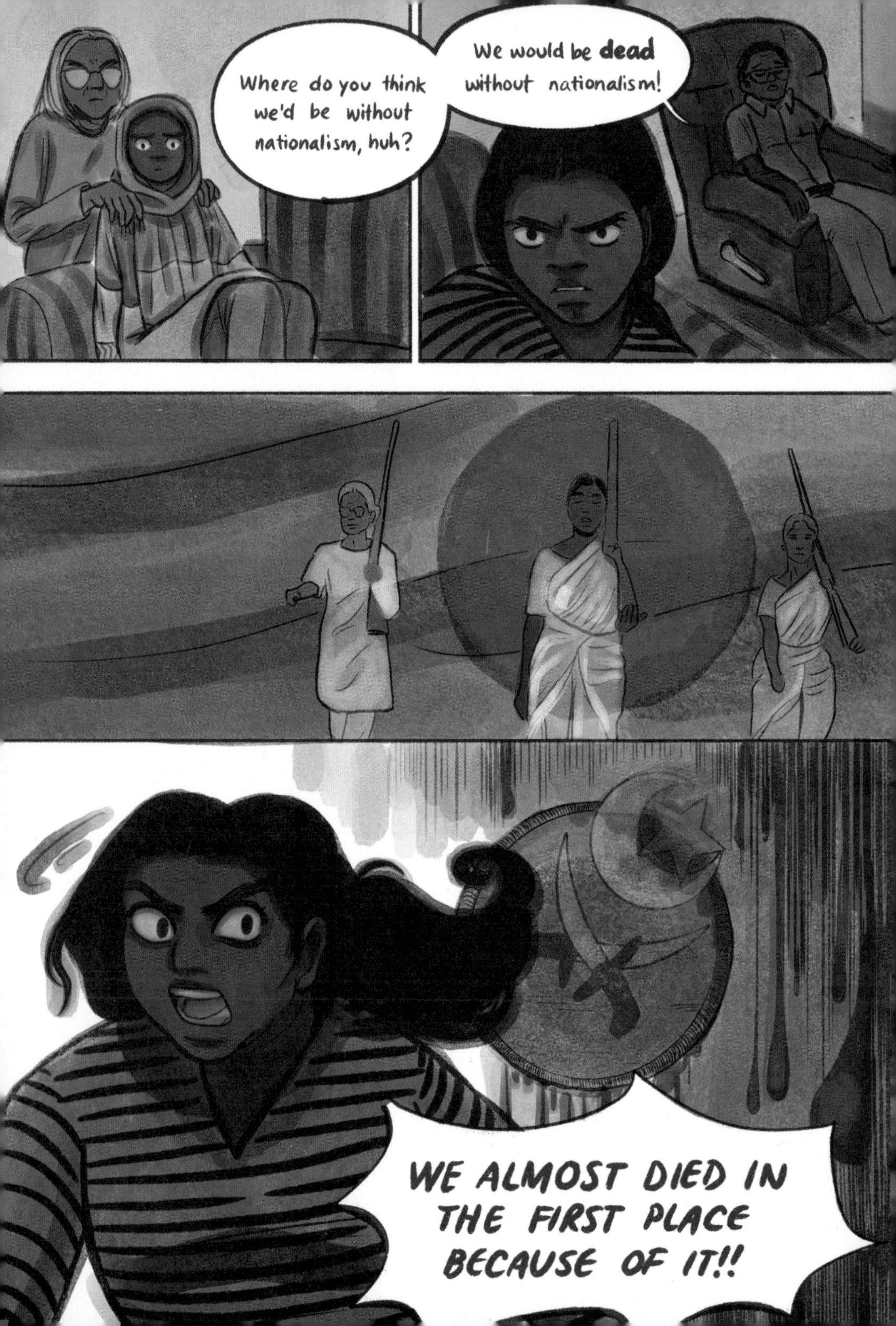
Where do you think we'd be without nationalism, huh?
We would be **dead** without nationalism!
WE ALMOST DIED IN THE FIRST PLACE BECAUSE OF IT!!

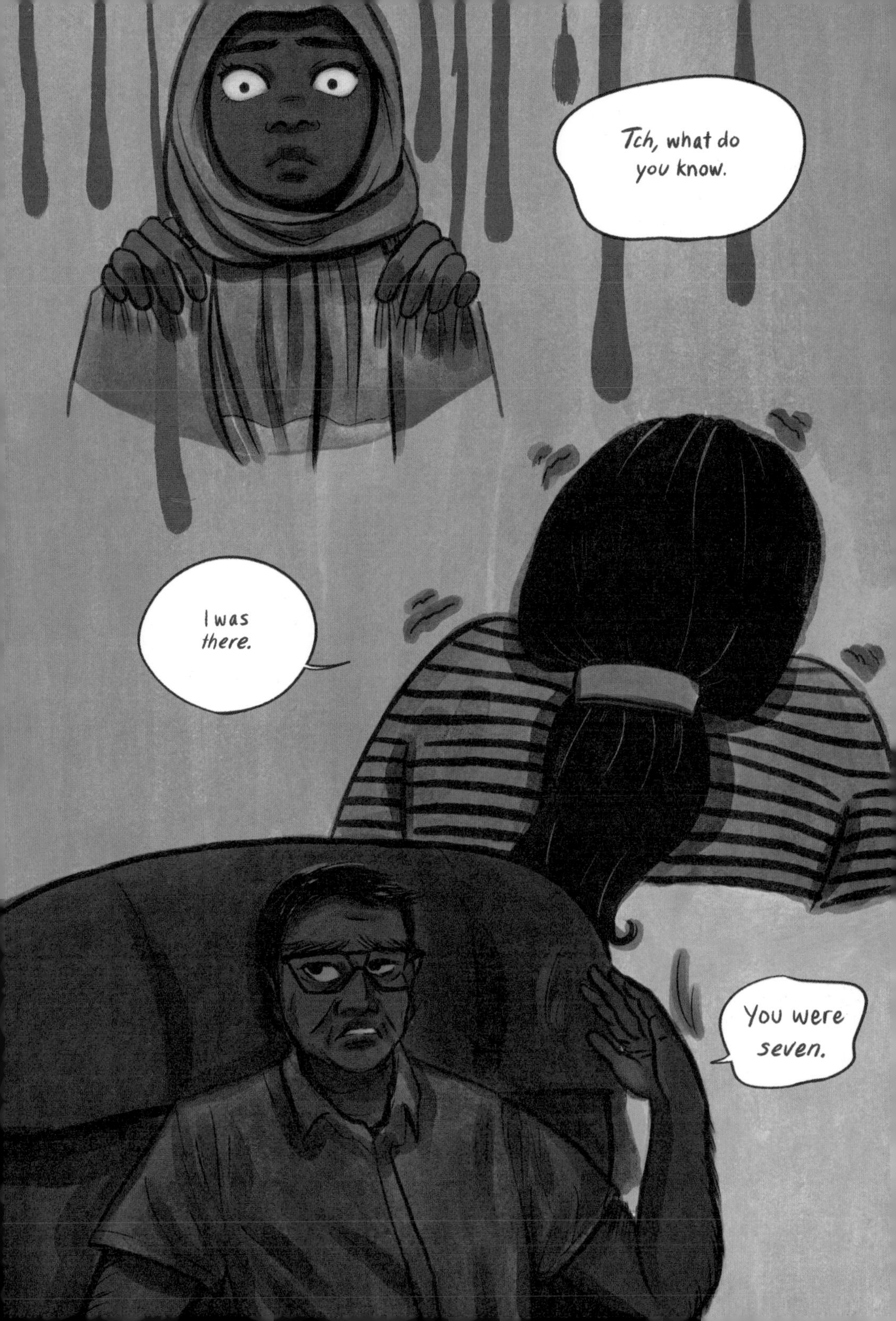
Tch, what do you know.
I was there.
You were seven.

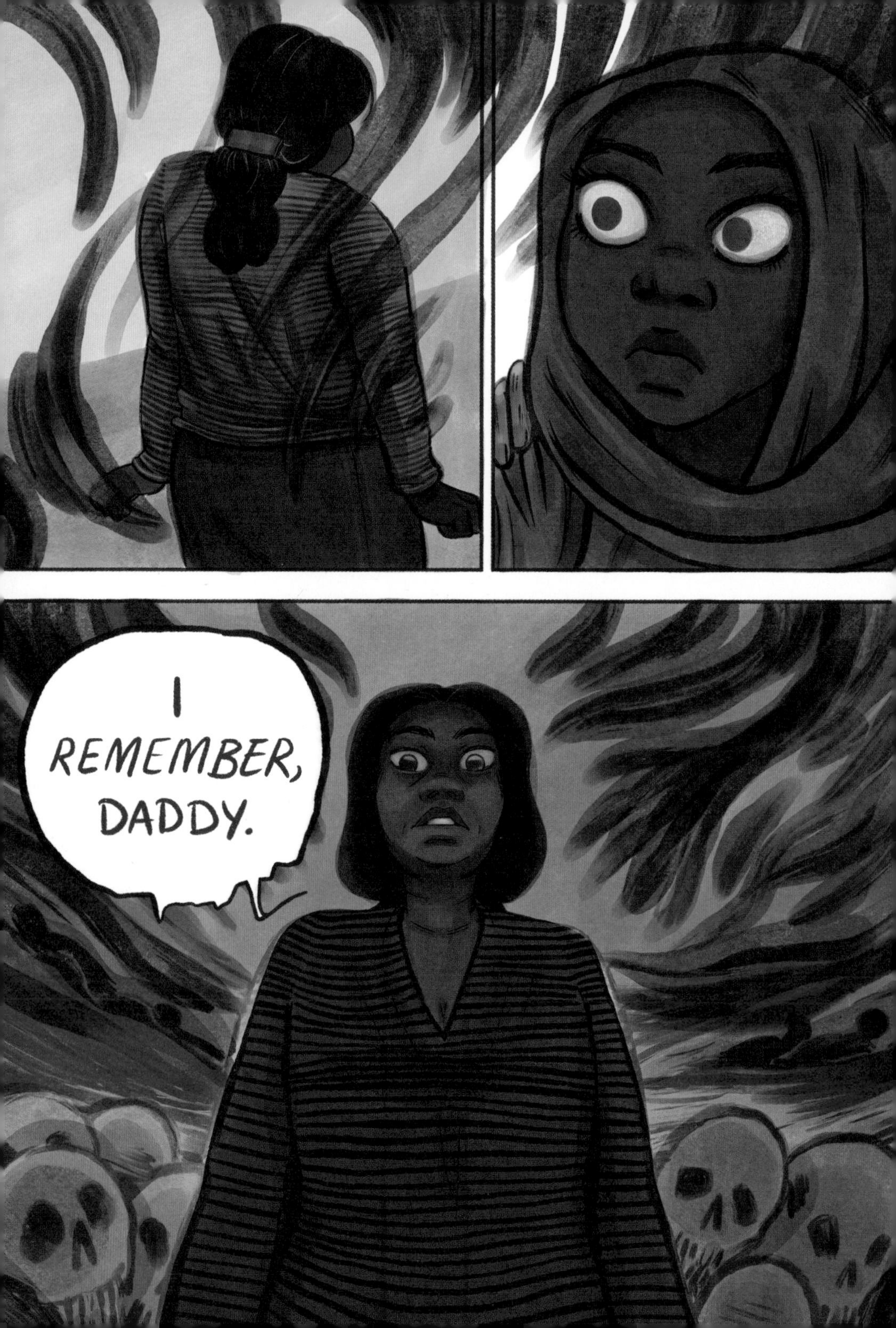
I REMEMBER, DADDY.

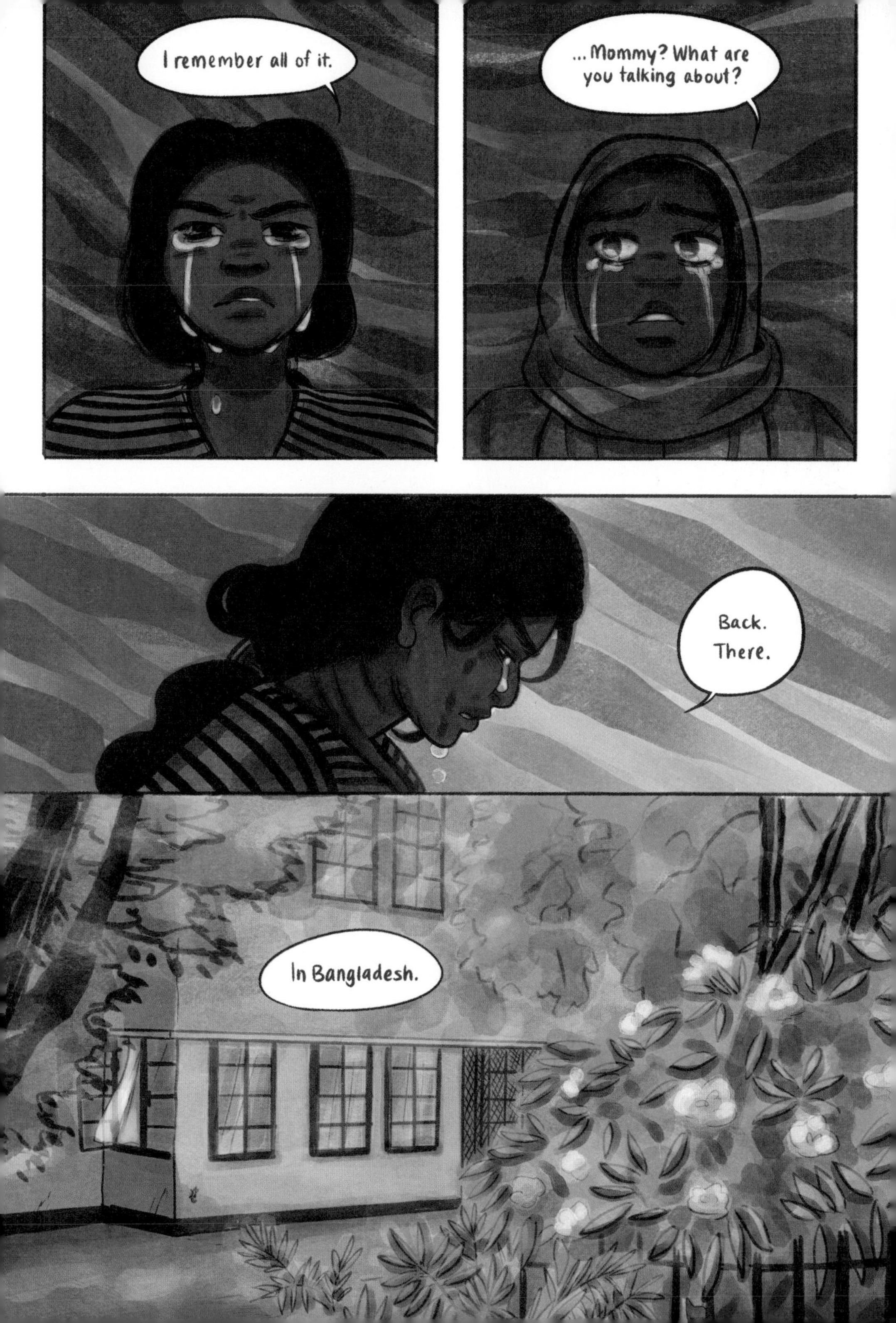
I remember all of it.
...Mommy? What are you talking about?
Back. There.
In Bangladesh.

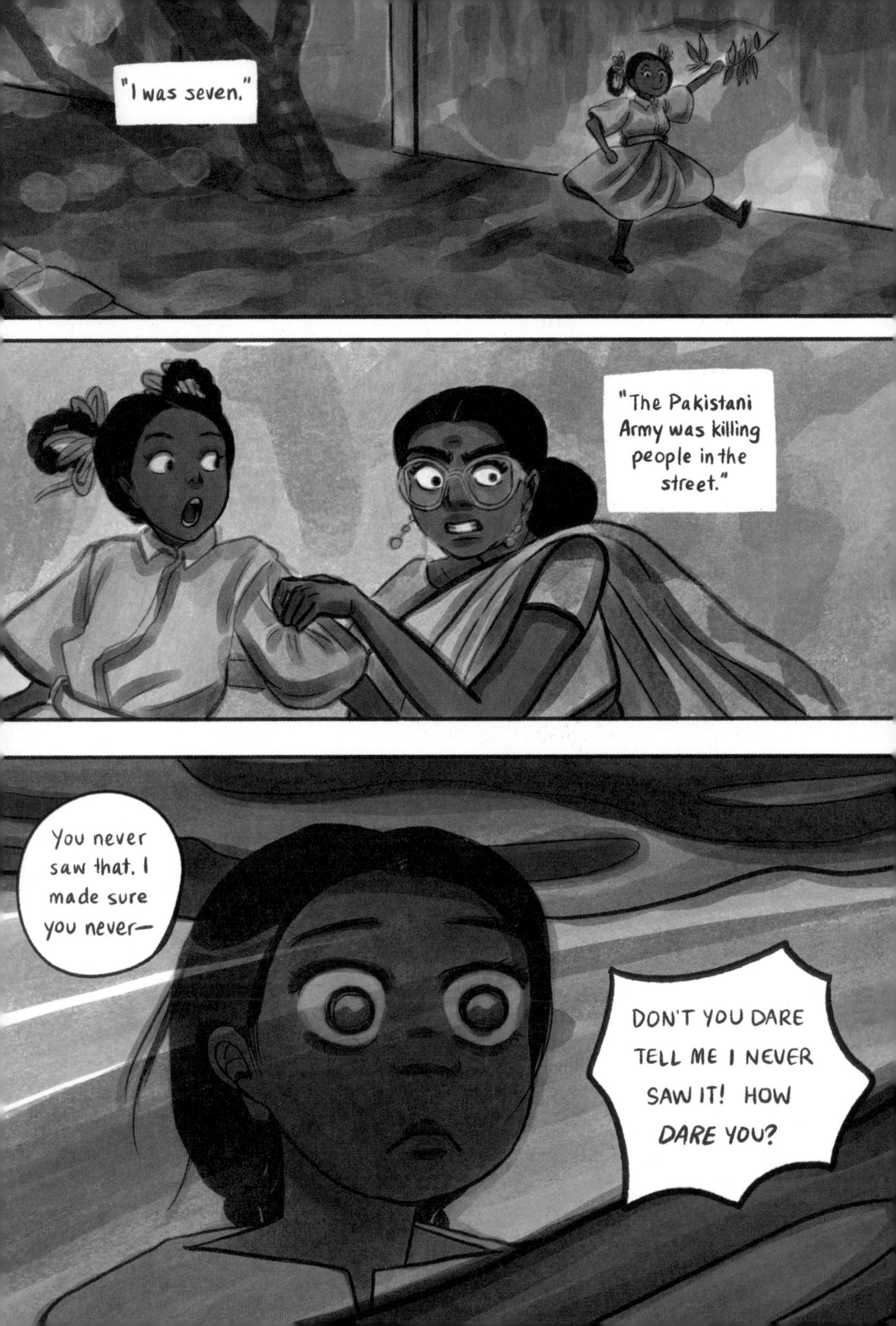
"I was seven."
"The Pakistani Army was killing people in the street."
You never saw that. I made sure you never—
DON'T YOU DARE TELL ME I NEVER SAW IT! HOW *DARE* YOU?

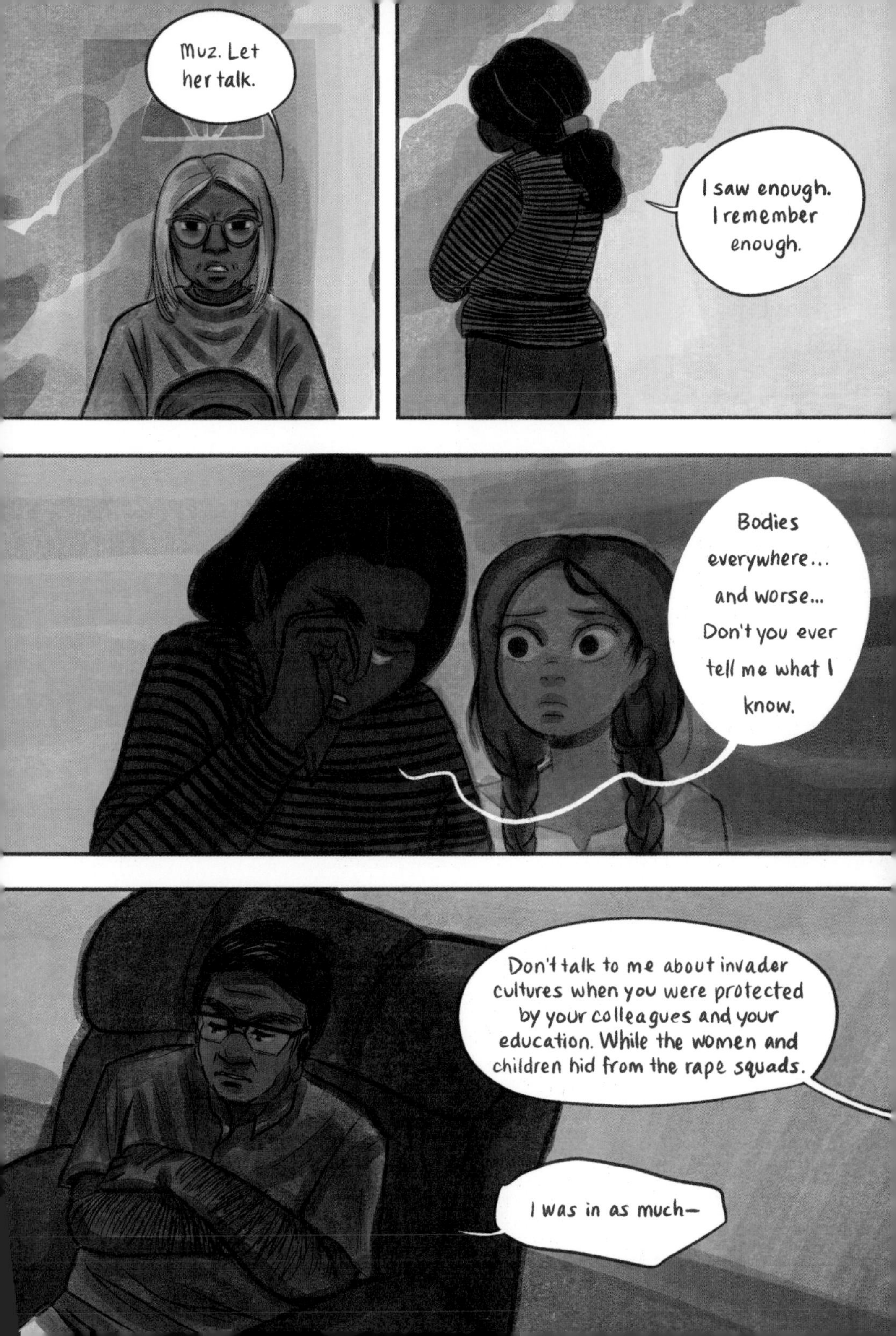
Muz. Let her talk.
I saw enough. I remember enough.
Bodies everywhere... and worse... Don't you ever tell me what I know.
Don't talk to me about invader cultures when you were protected by your colleagues and your education. While the women and children hid from the rape squads.
I was in as much—

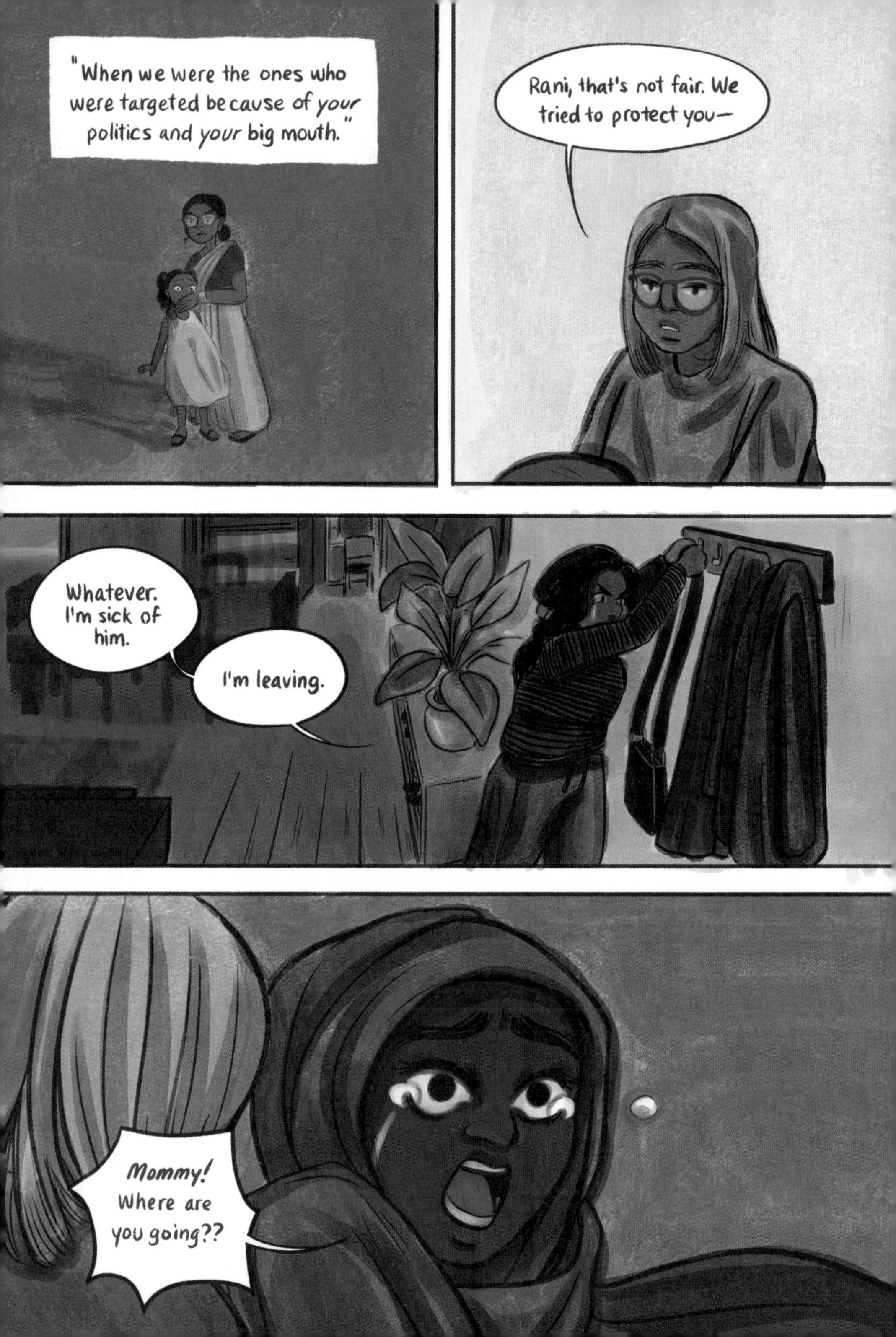
"When we were the ones who were targeted because of *your* politics and *your* big mouth."
Rani, that's not fair. We tried to protect you—
Whatever. I'm sick of him.
I'm leaving.
Mommy! Where are you going??

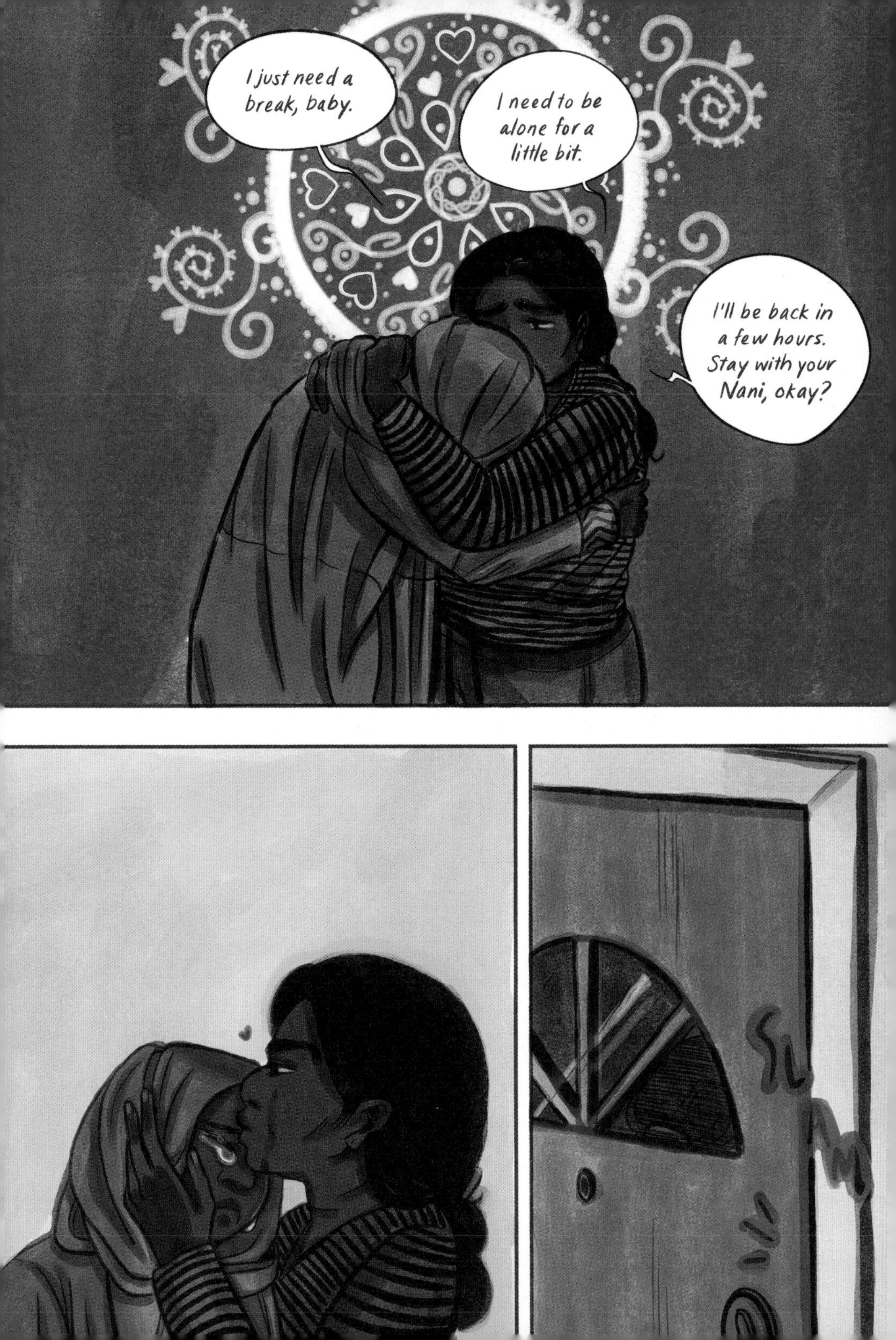
I just need a break, baby.
I need to be alone for a little bit.
I'll be back in a few hours. Stay with your Nani, okay?

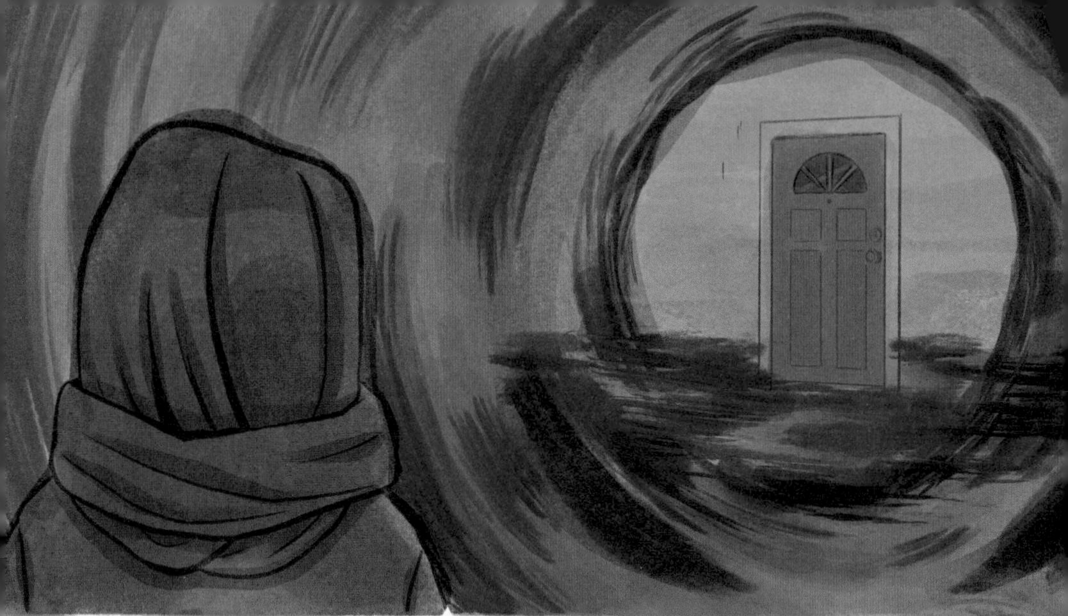

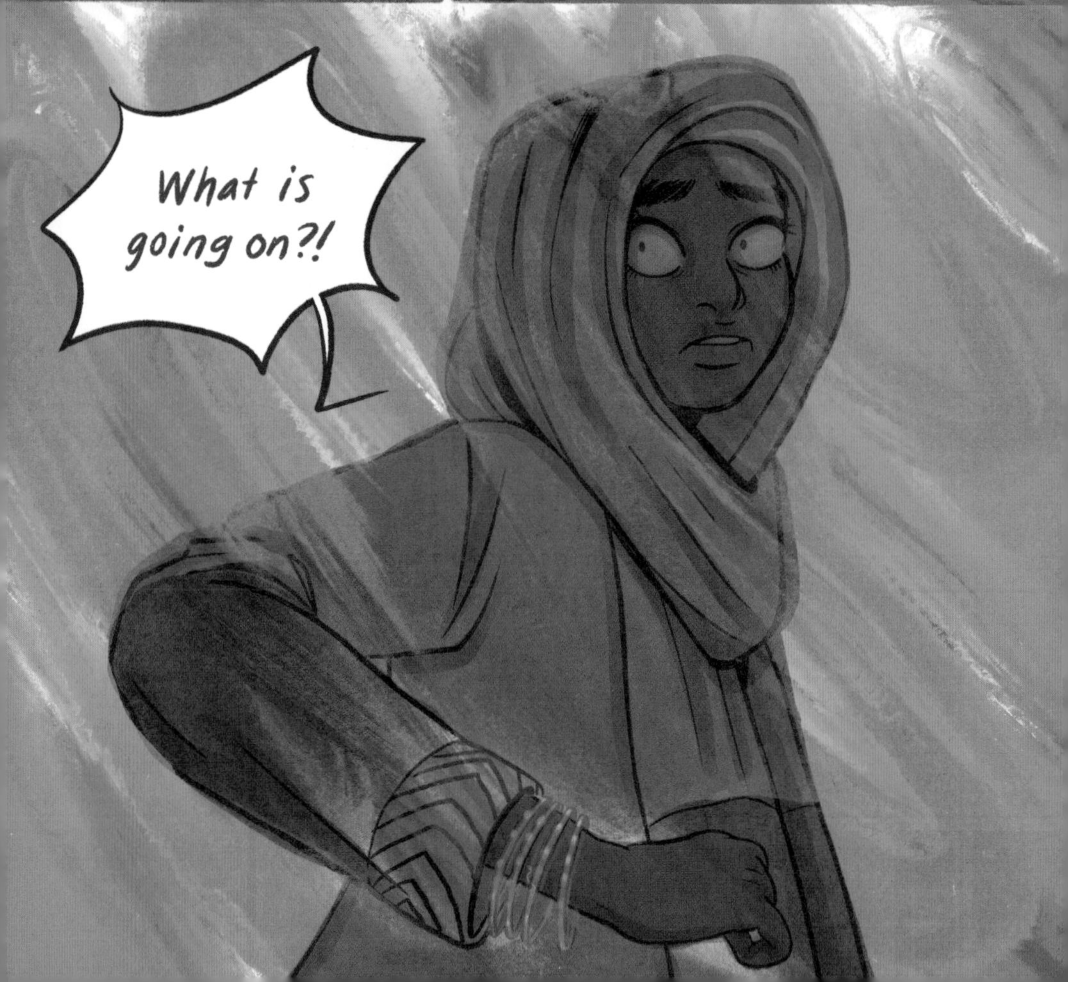
What is going on?!

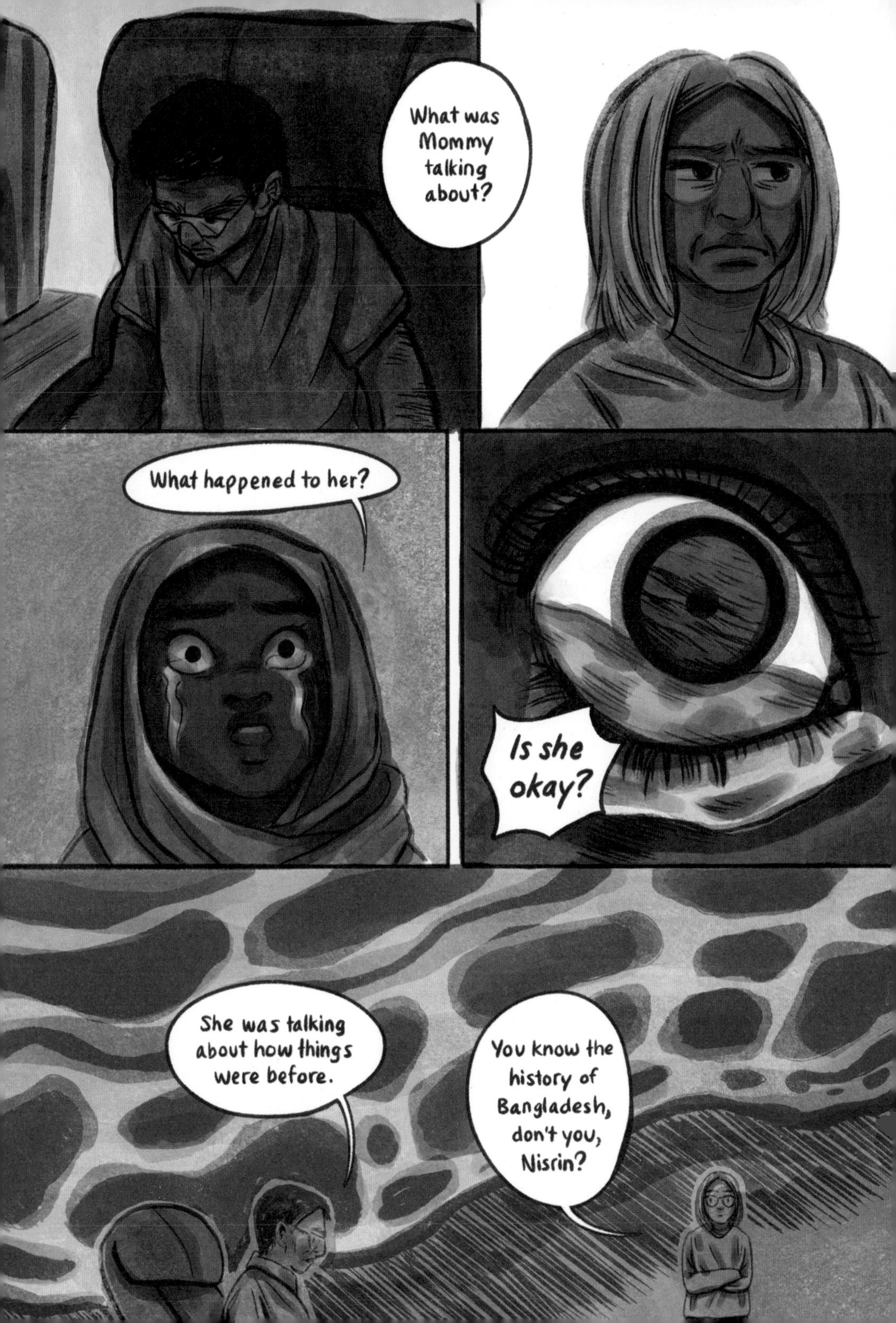
What was Mommy talking about?
What happened to her?
Is she okay?
She was talking about how things were before.
You know the history of Bangladesh, don't you, Nisrin?

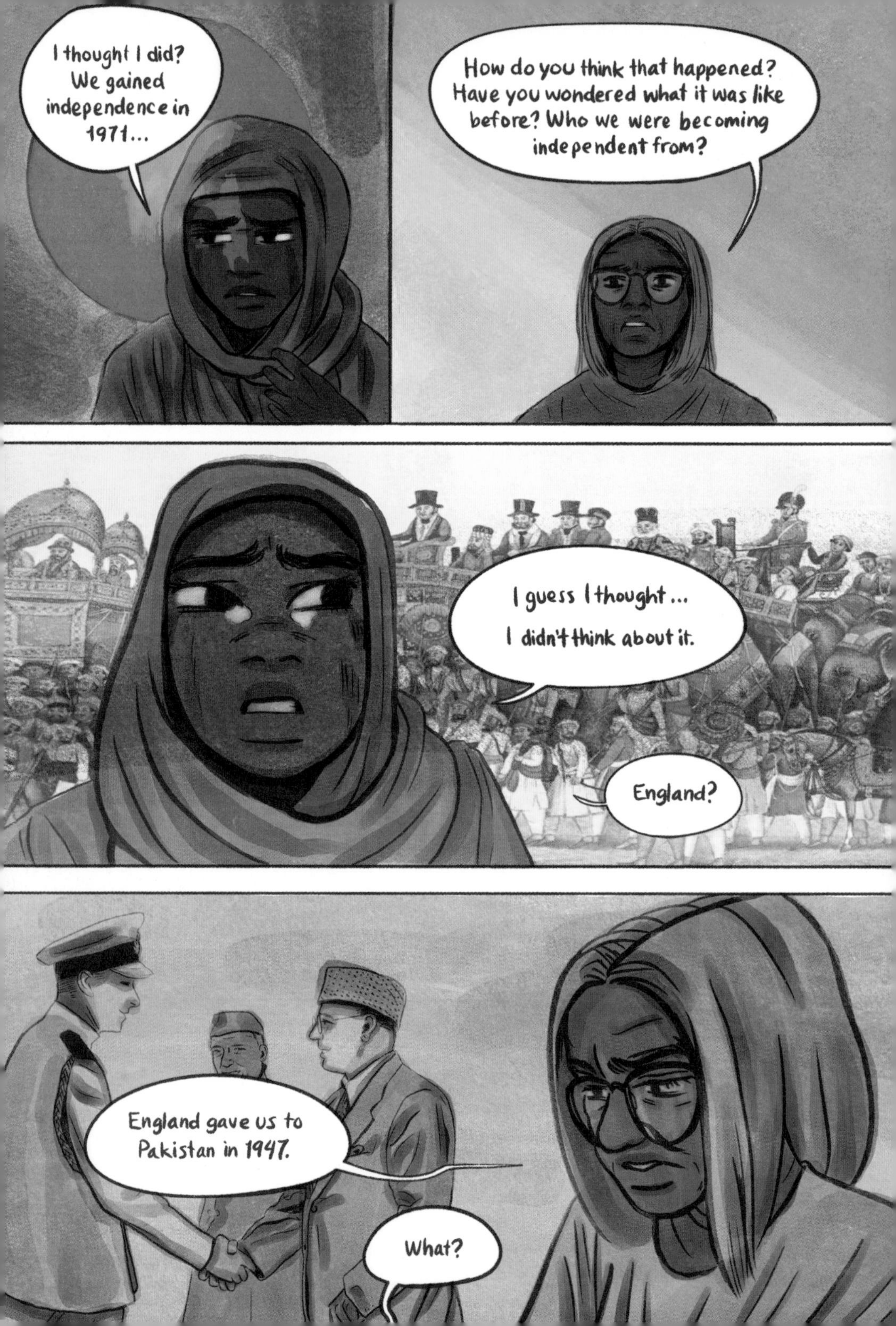
I thought I did? We gained independence in 1971...
How do you think that happened? Have you wondered what it was like before? Who we were becoming independent from?
I guess I thought...
I didn't think about it.
England?
England gave us to Pakistan in 1947.
What?

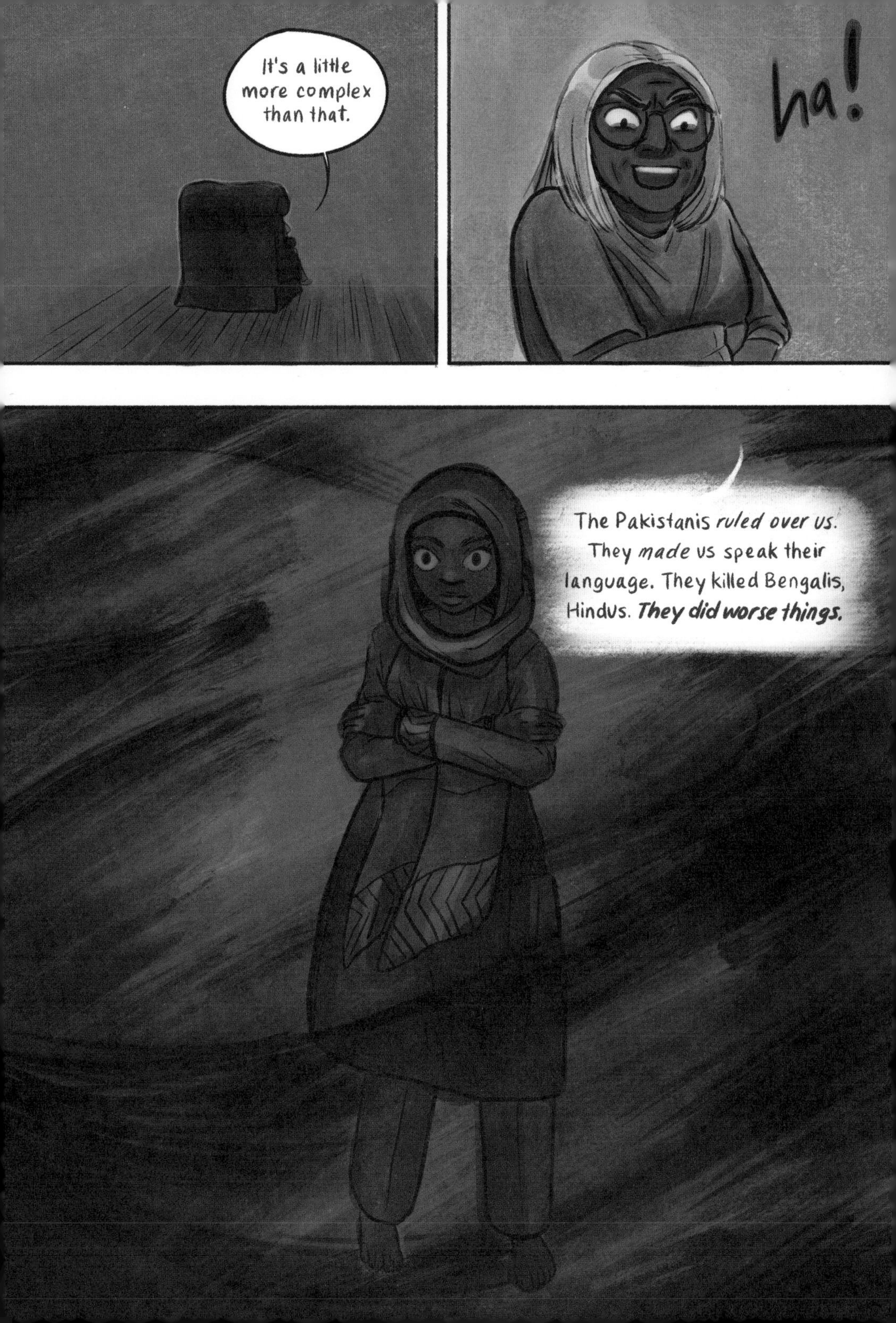

It's a little more complex than that.
ha!
The Pakistanis *ruled over us.* They *made* us speak their language. They killed Bengalis, Hindus. ***They did worse things.***

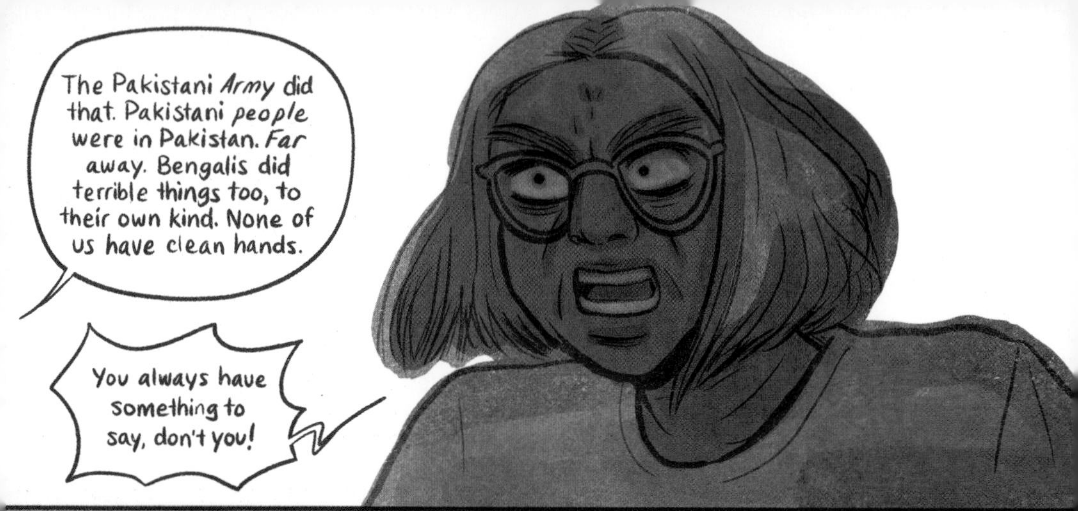
The Pakistani *Army* did that. Pakistani *people* were in Pakistan. *Far* away. Bengalis did terrible things too, to their own kind. None of us have clean hands.
You always have something to say, don't you!

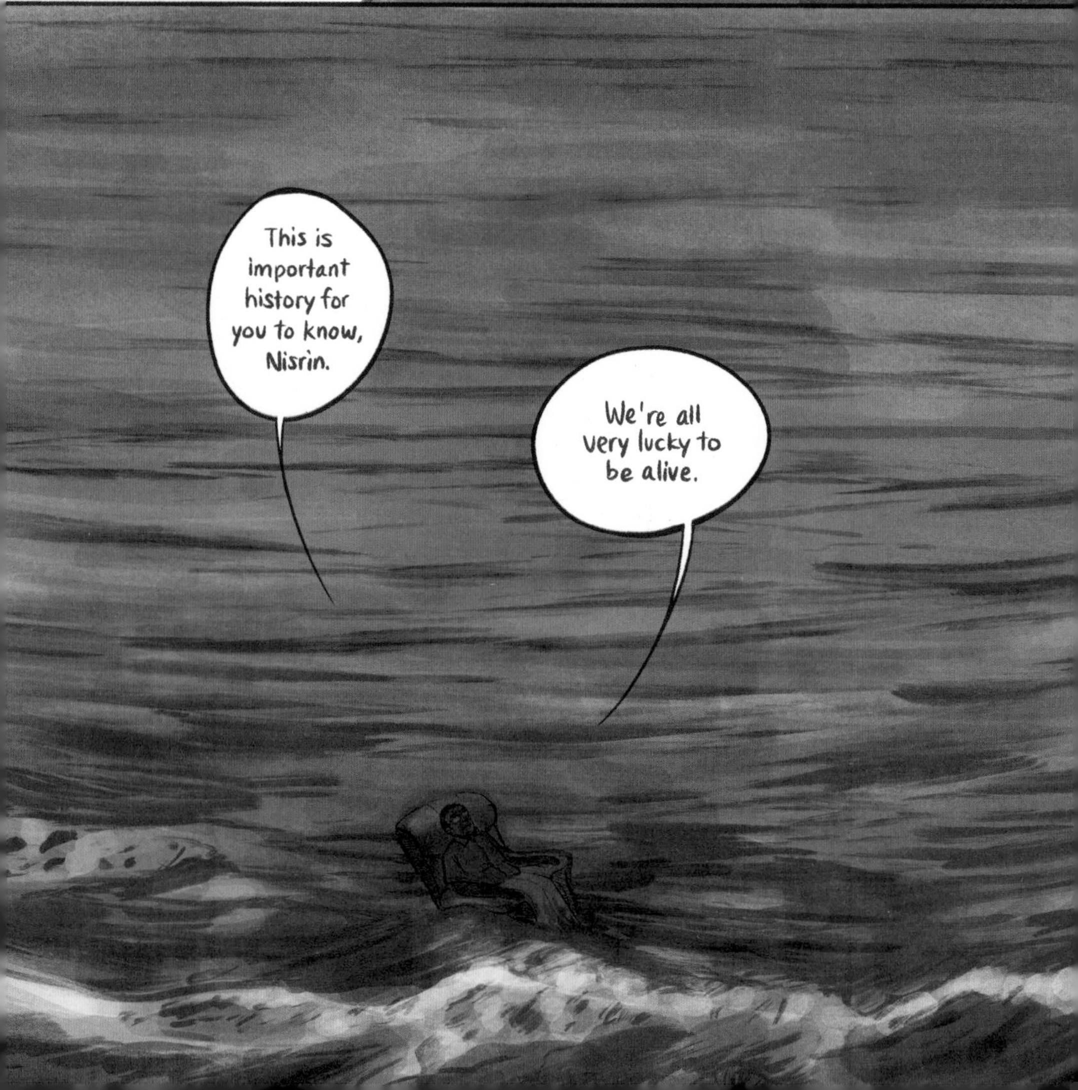
This is important history for you to know, Nisrin.
We're all very lucky to be alive.

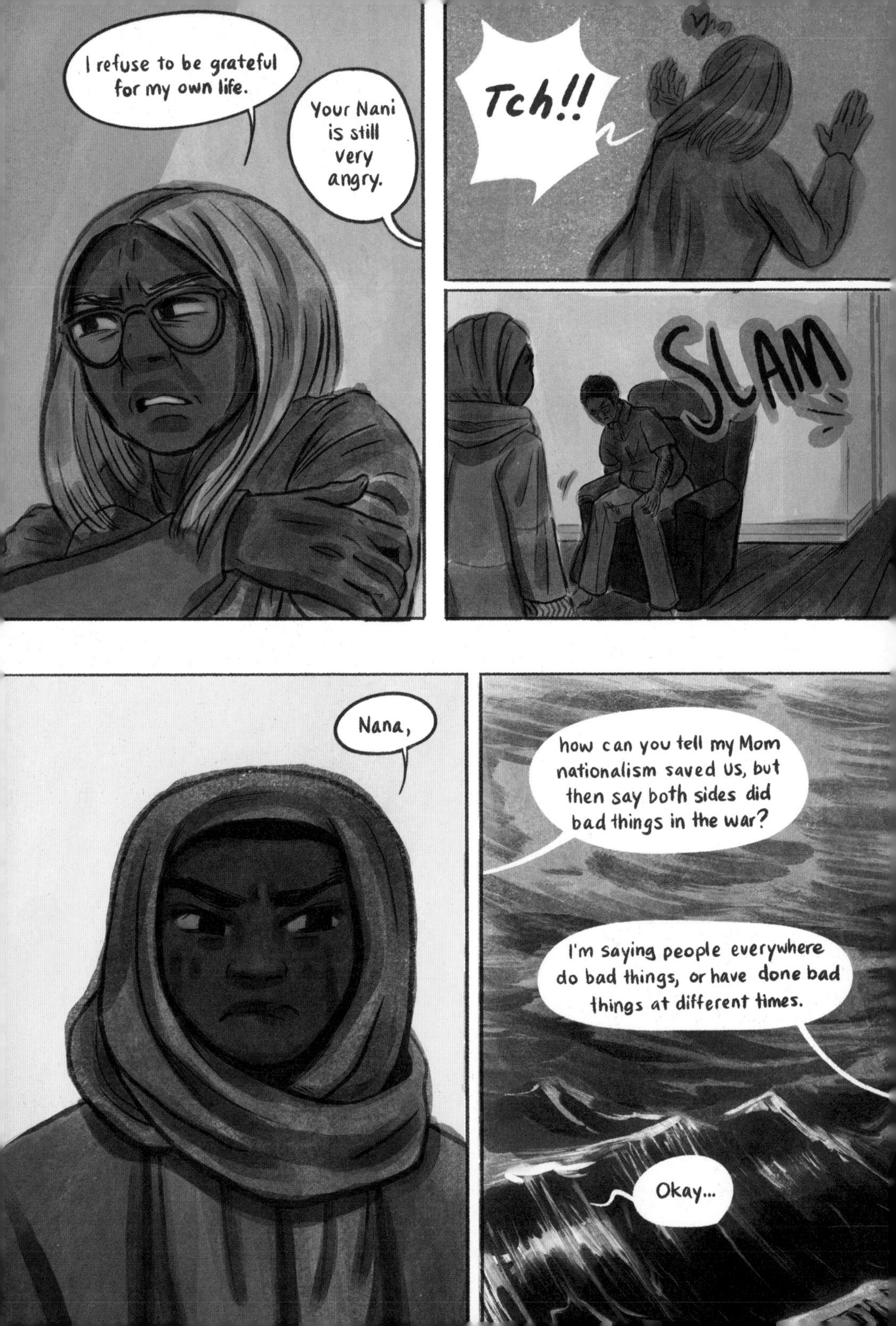
I refuse to be grateful for my own life.
Your Nani is still very angry.
Tch!!
SLAM
Nana,
how can you tell my Mom nationalism saved US, but then say both sides did bad things in the war?
I'm saying people everywhere do bad things, or have done bad things at different times.
Okay...

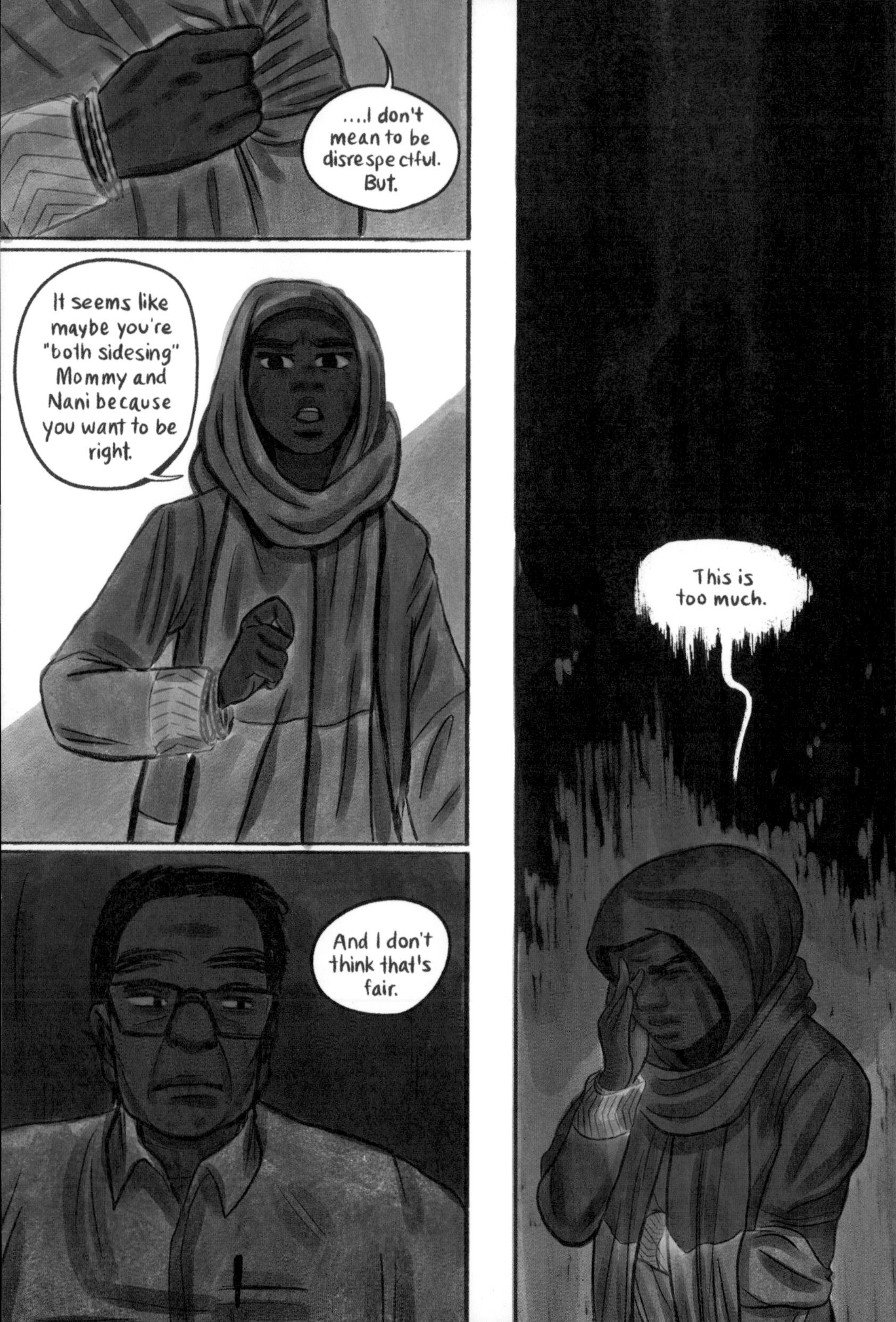

....I don't mean to be disrespectful. But.
It seems like maybe you're "both sidesing" Mommy and Nani because you want to be right.
And I don't think that's fair.
This is too much.

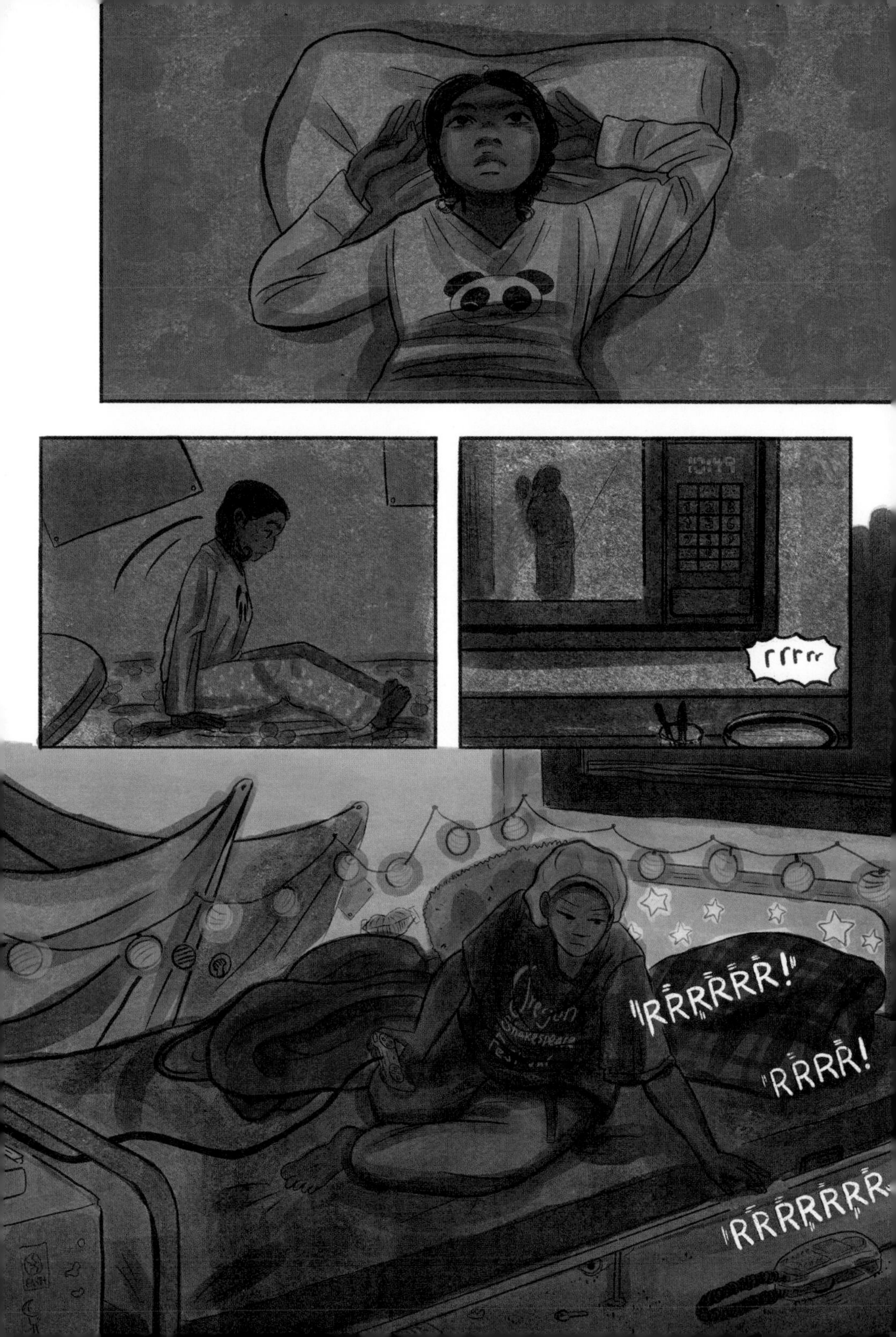
rrrrr
RRRRRR!
RRRR!
RRRRRRR

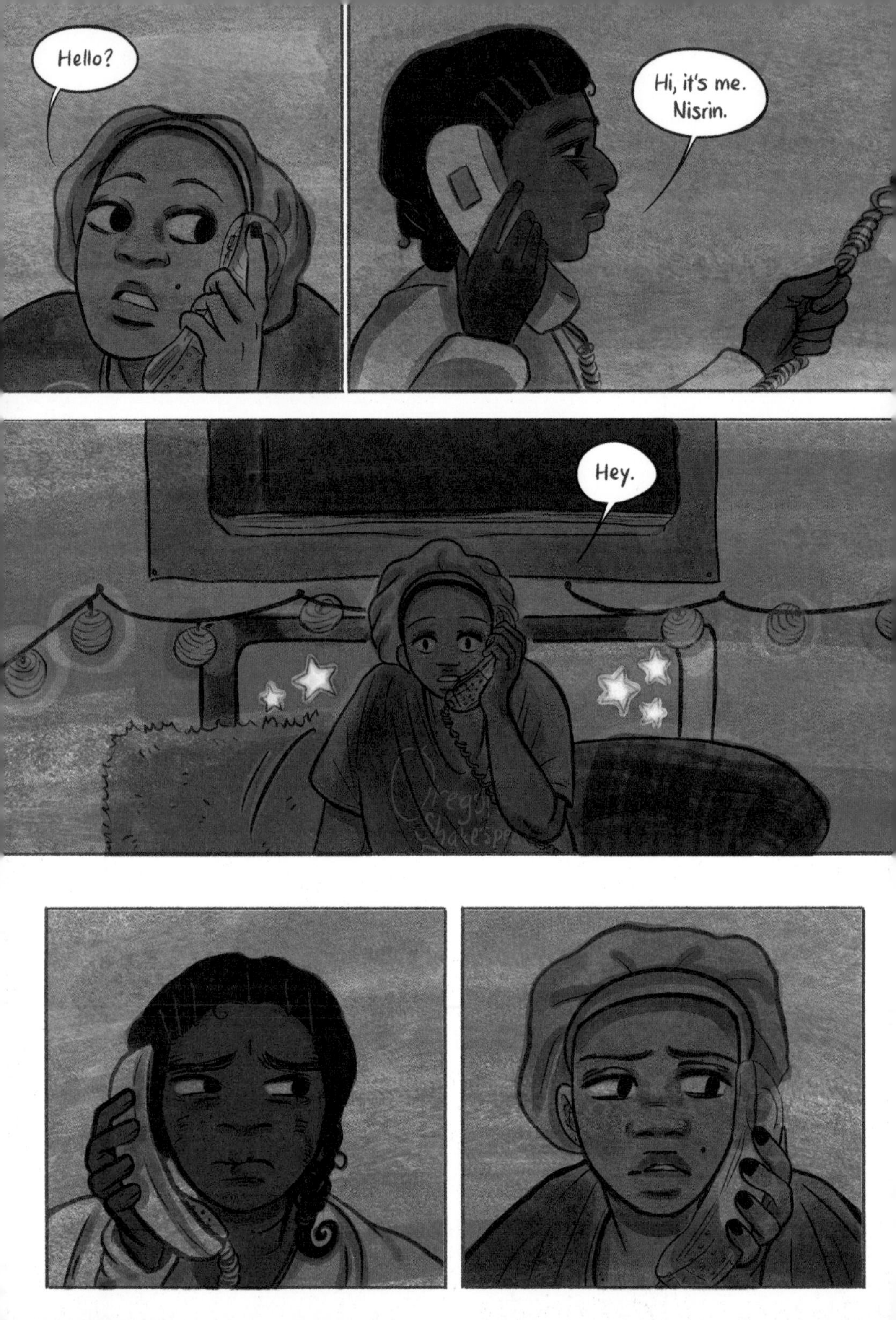
Hello?
Hi, it's me. Nisrin.
Hey.

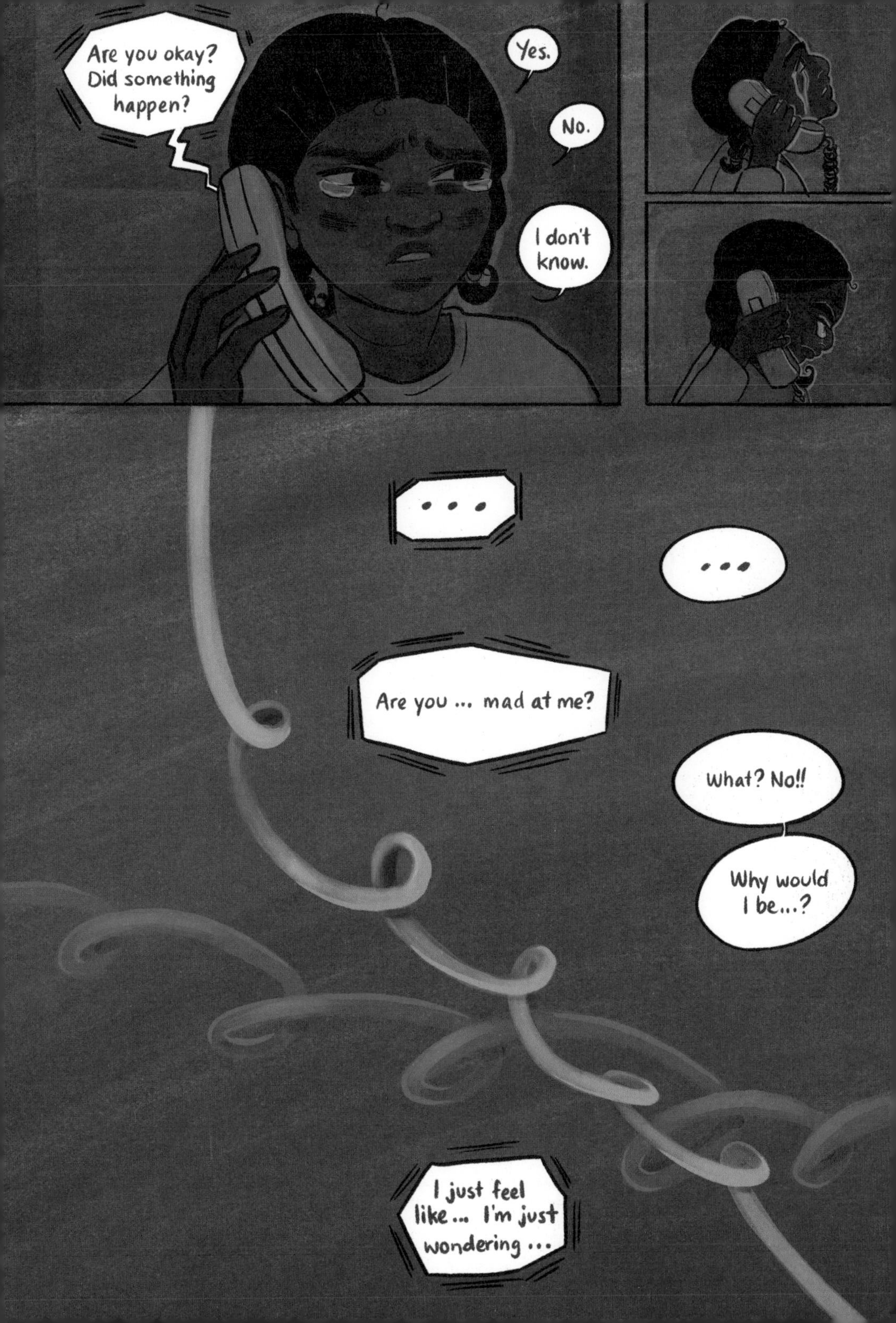
Are you okay? Did something happen?
Yes.
No.
I don't know.
...
...
Are you ... mad at me?
What? No!!
Why would I be...?
I just feel like... I'm just wondering ...

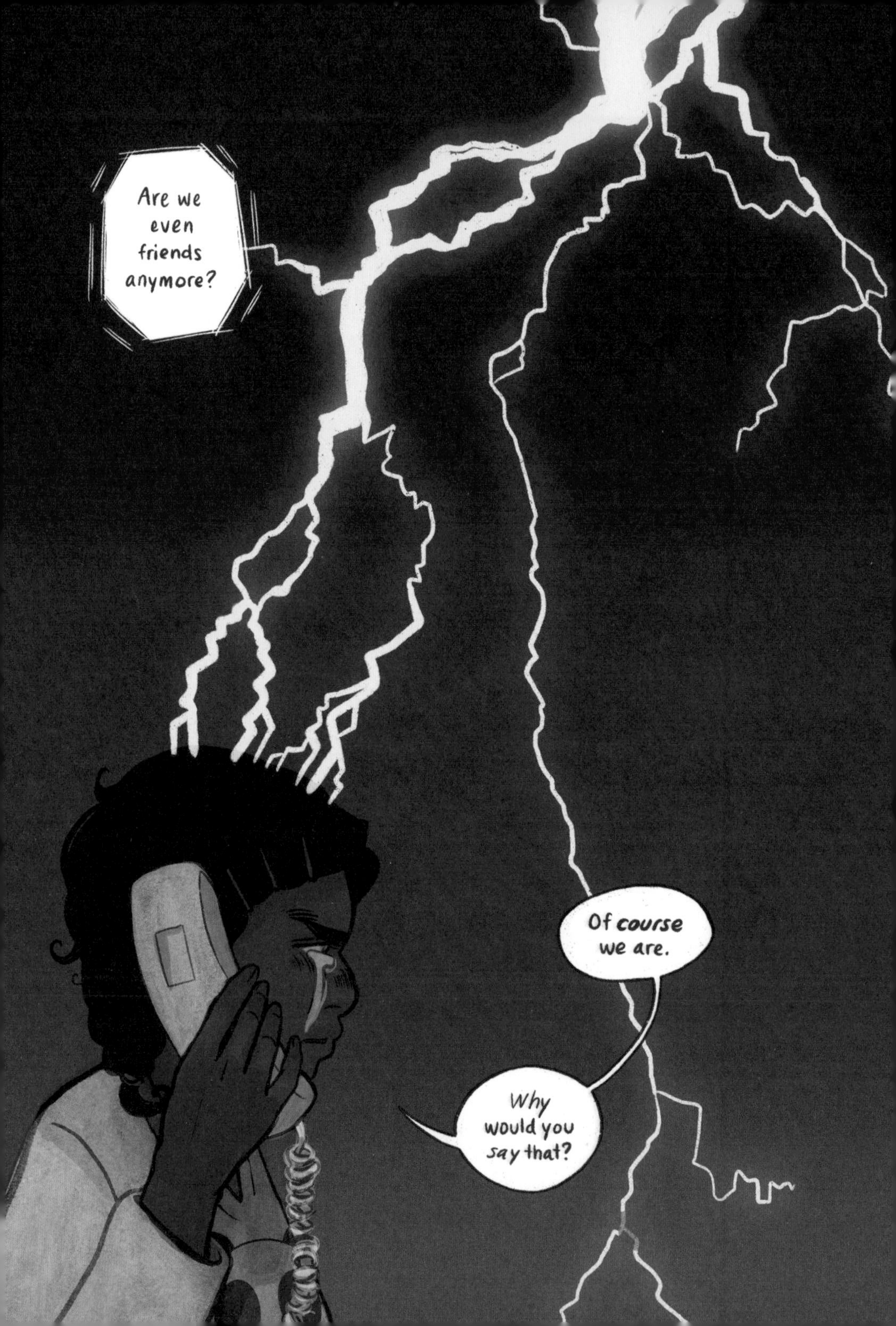
Are we even friends anymore?
Of course we are.
Why would you say that?

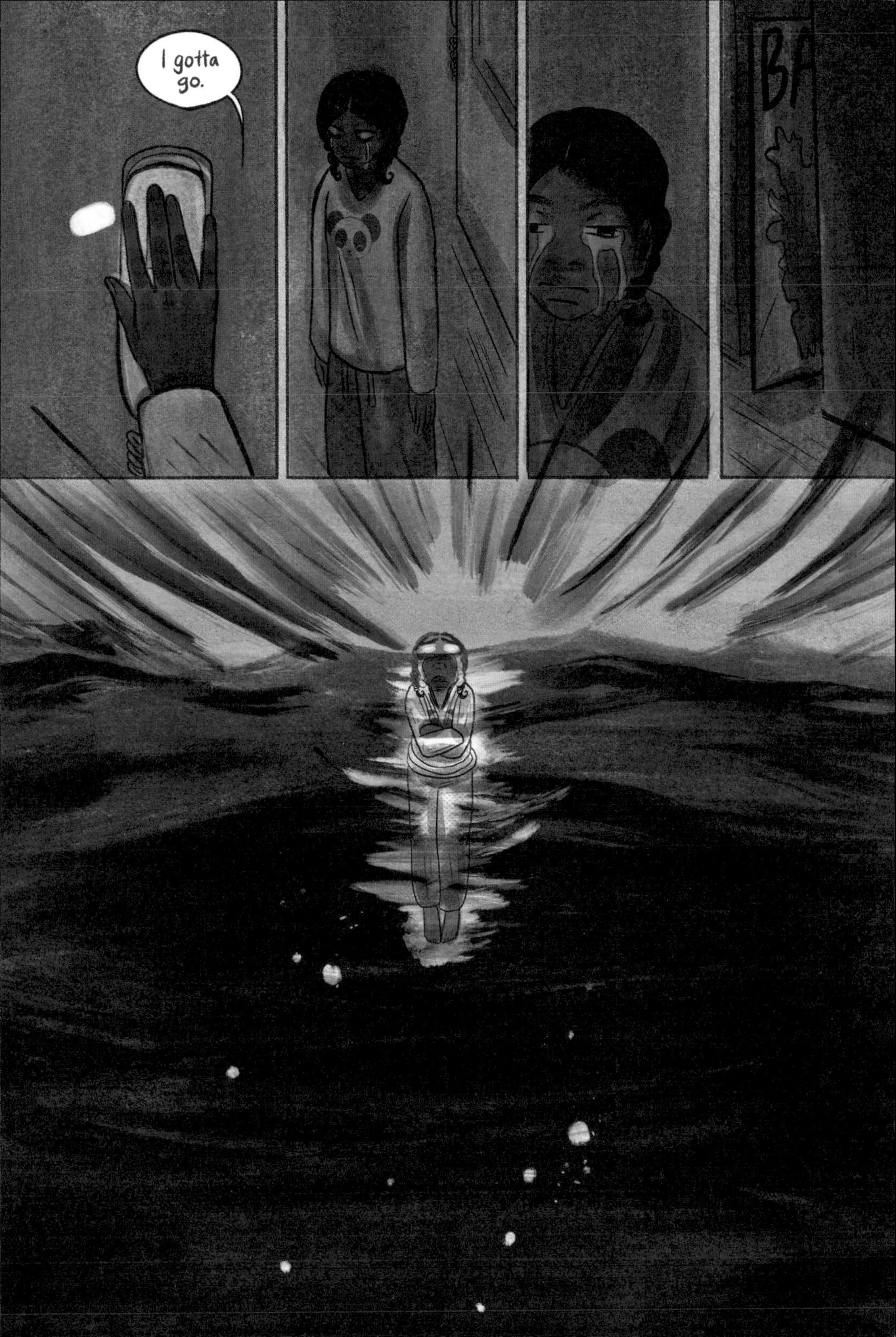
I gotta go.
BA

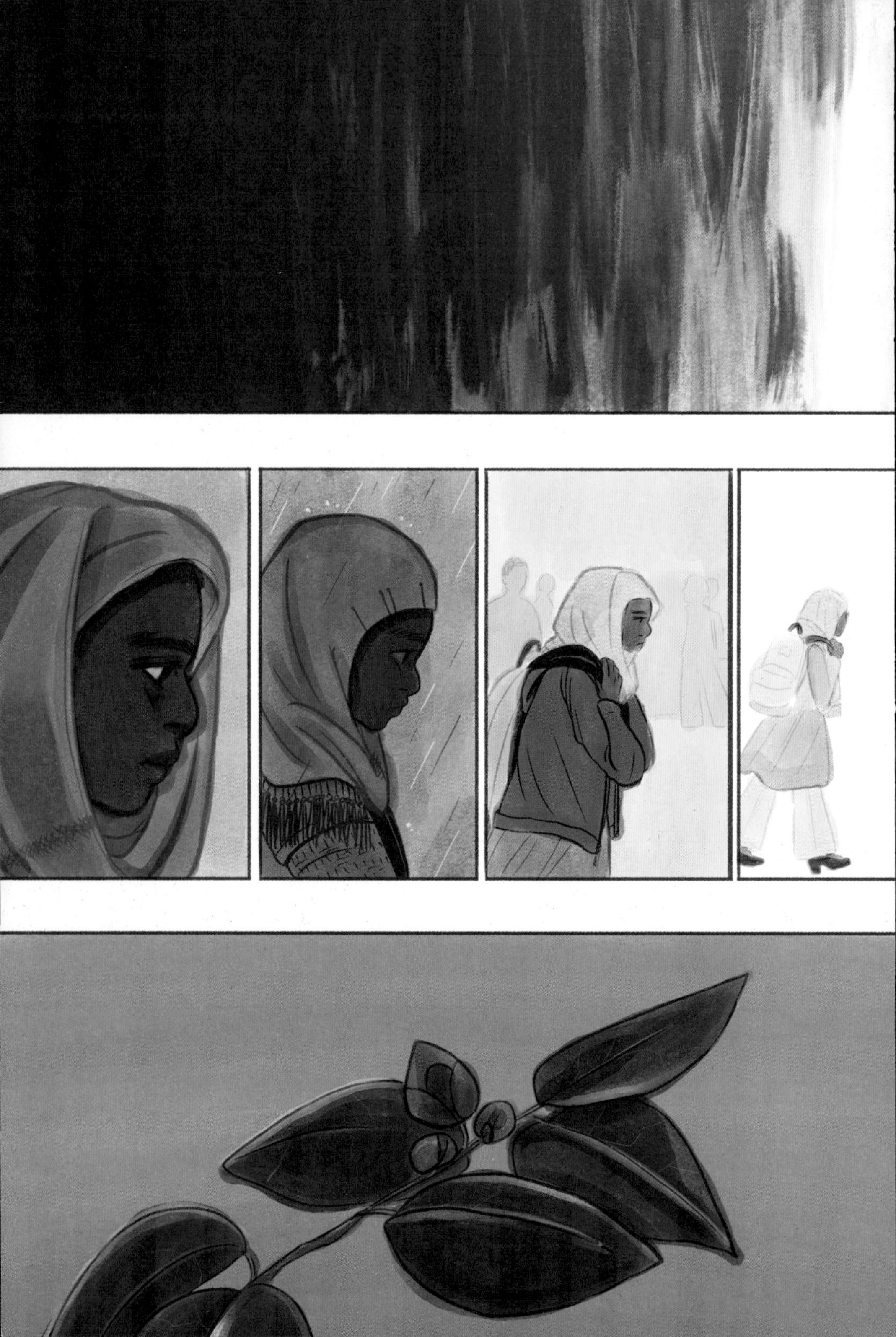

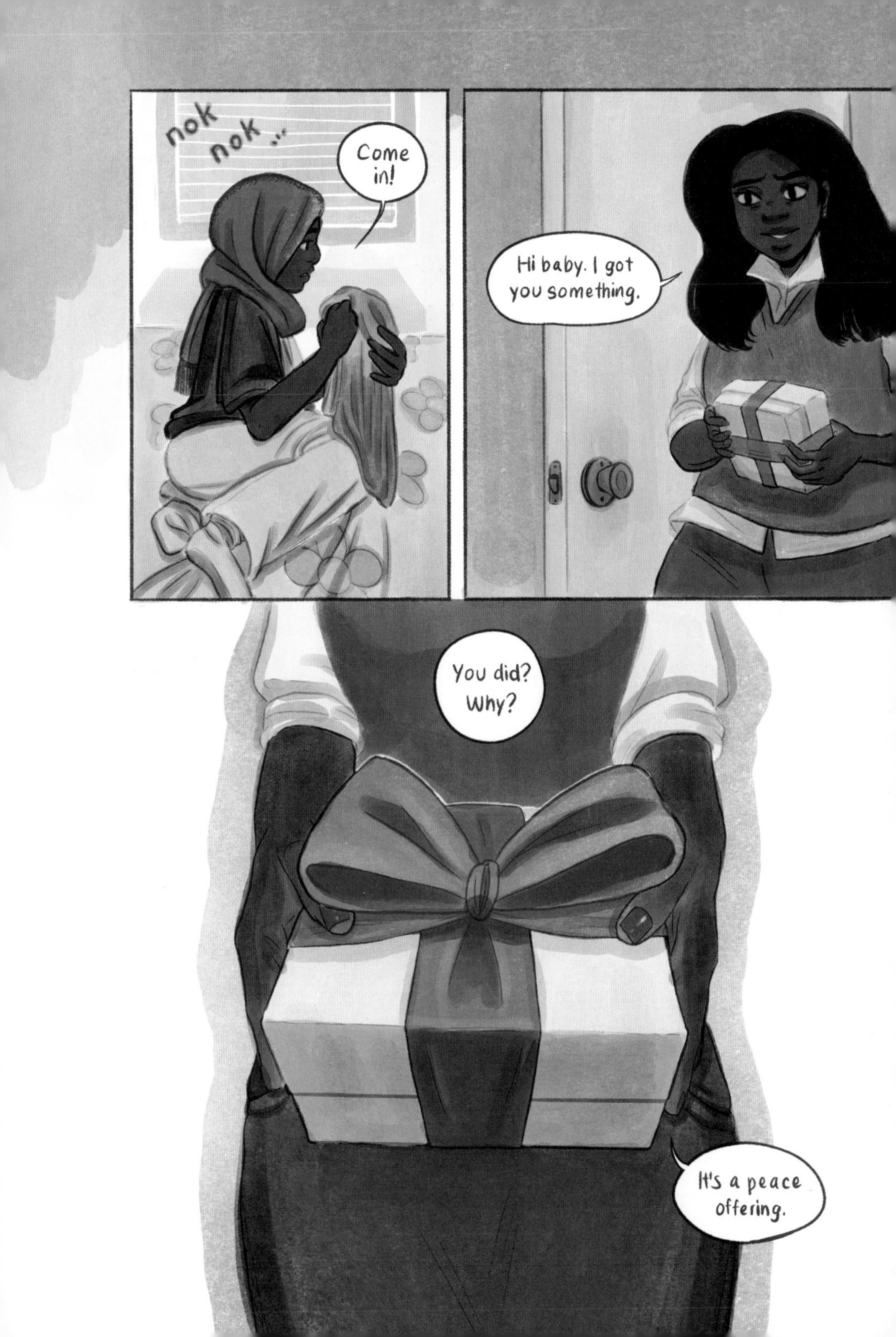
nok nok ..
Come in!
Hi baby. I got you something.
You did? Why?
It's a peace offering.

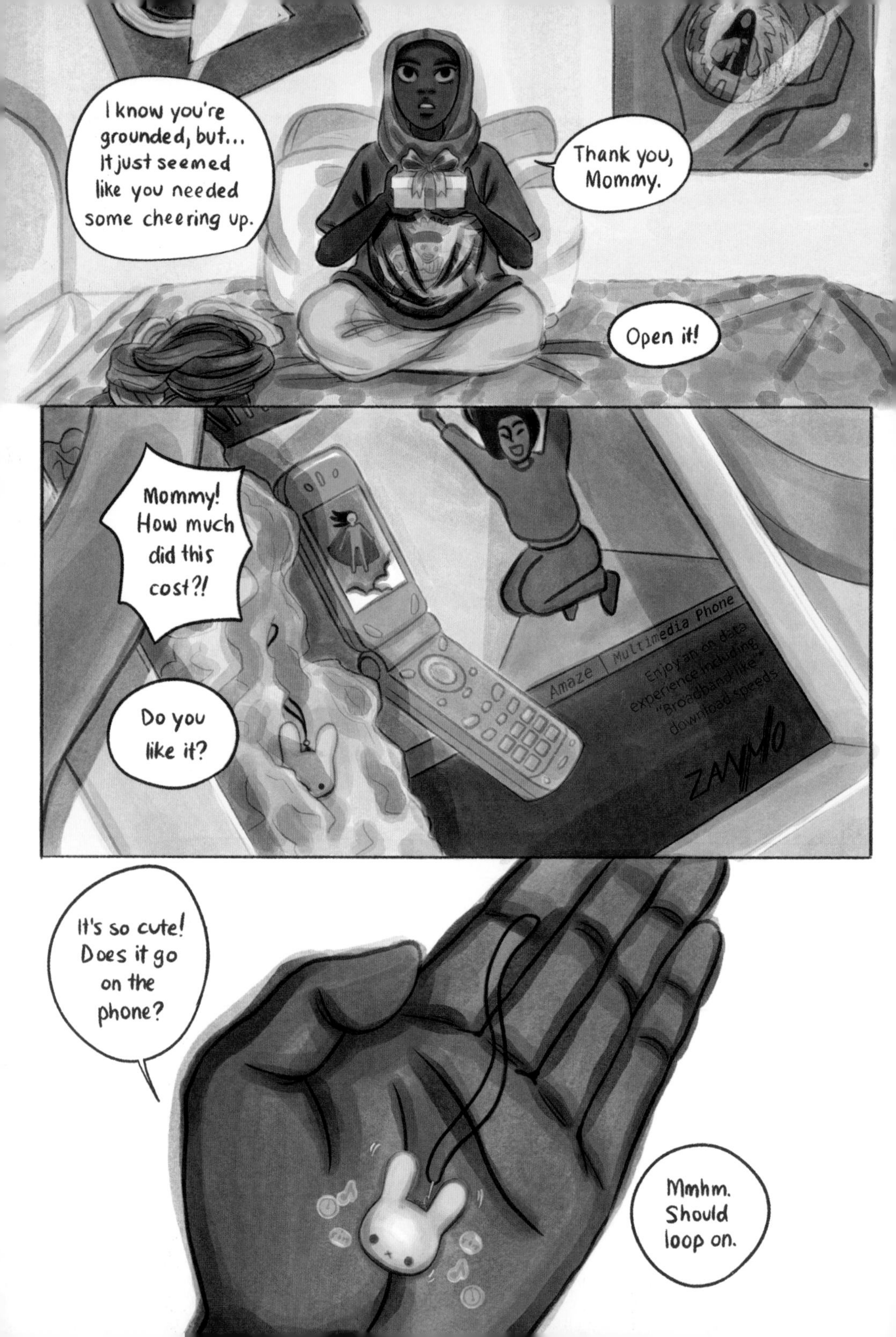
I know you're grounded, but... It just seemed like you needed some cheering up.
Thank you, Mommy.
Open it!
Mommy! How much did this cost?!
Do you like it?
Amaze
Multimedia Phone
It's so cute! Does it go on the phone?
Mmhm. Should loop on.

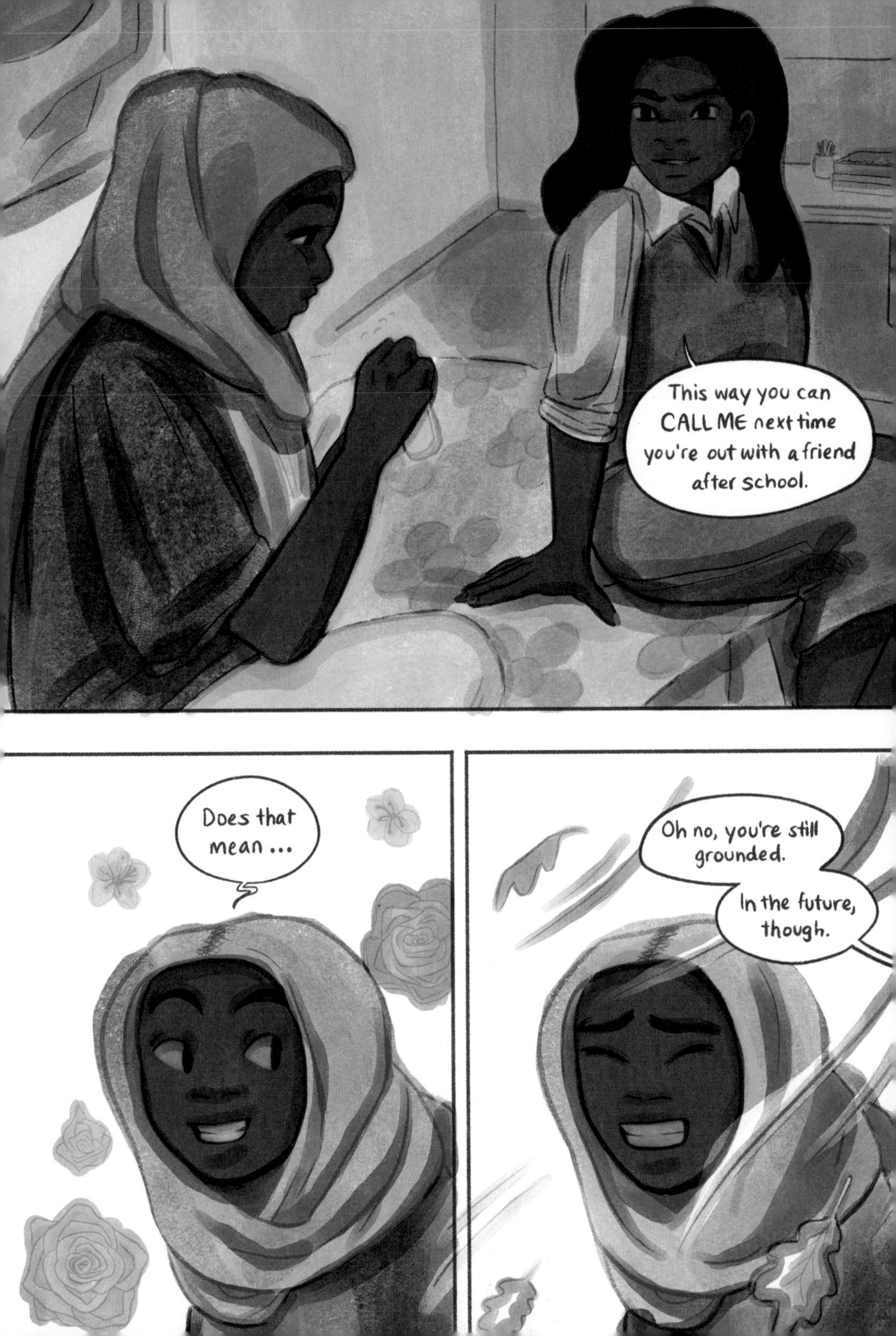
This way you can CALL ME next time you're out with a friend after school.
Does that mean ...
Oh no, you're still grounded.
In the future, though.

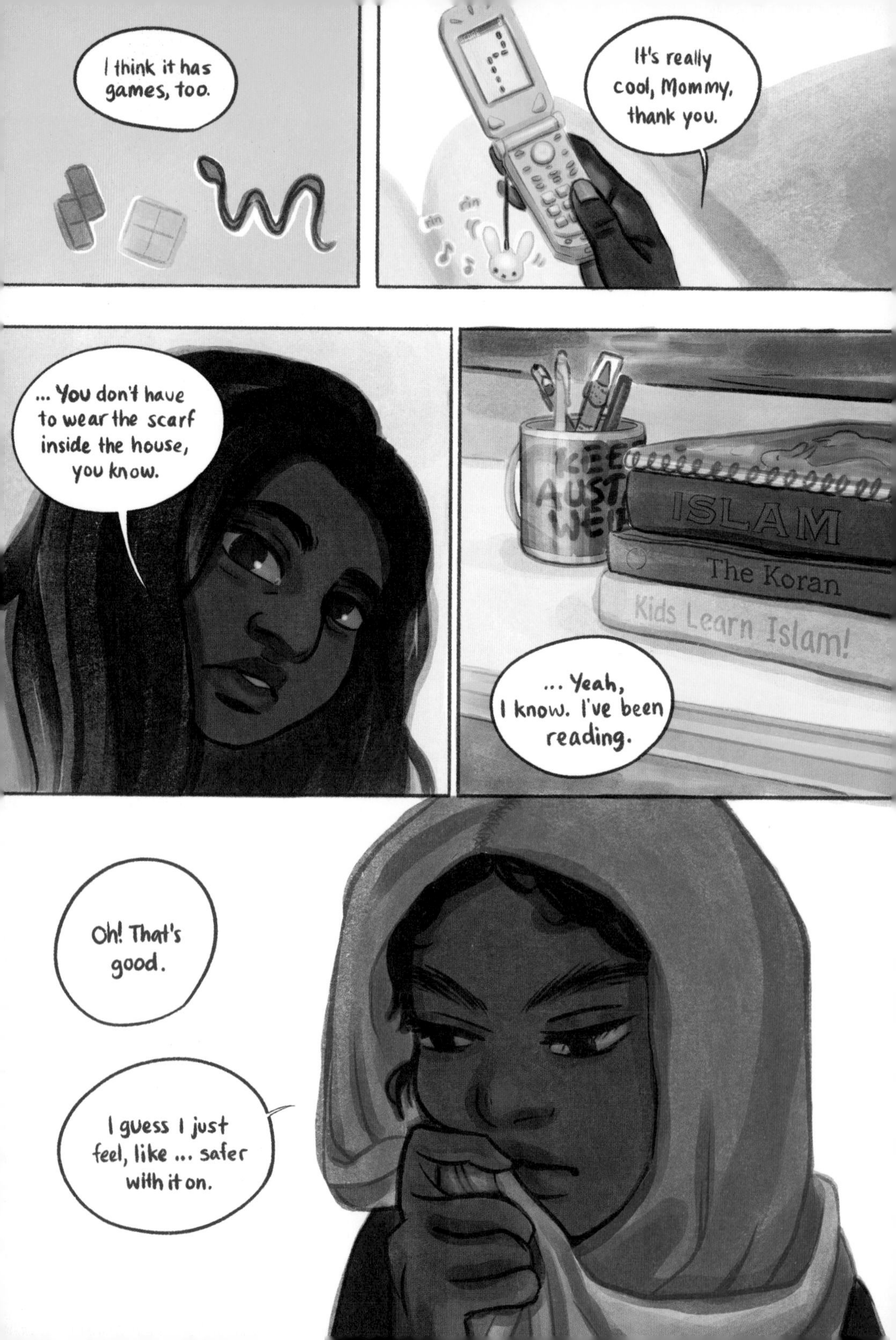
I think it has games, too.
It's really cool, Mommy, thank you.
rin
rin
... You don't have to wear the scarf inside the house, you know.
ISLAM
The Koran
Kids Learn Islam!
... Yeah, I know. I've been reading.
Oh! That's good.
I guess I just feel, like ... safer with it on.

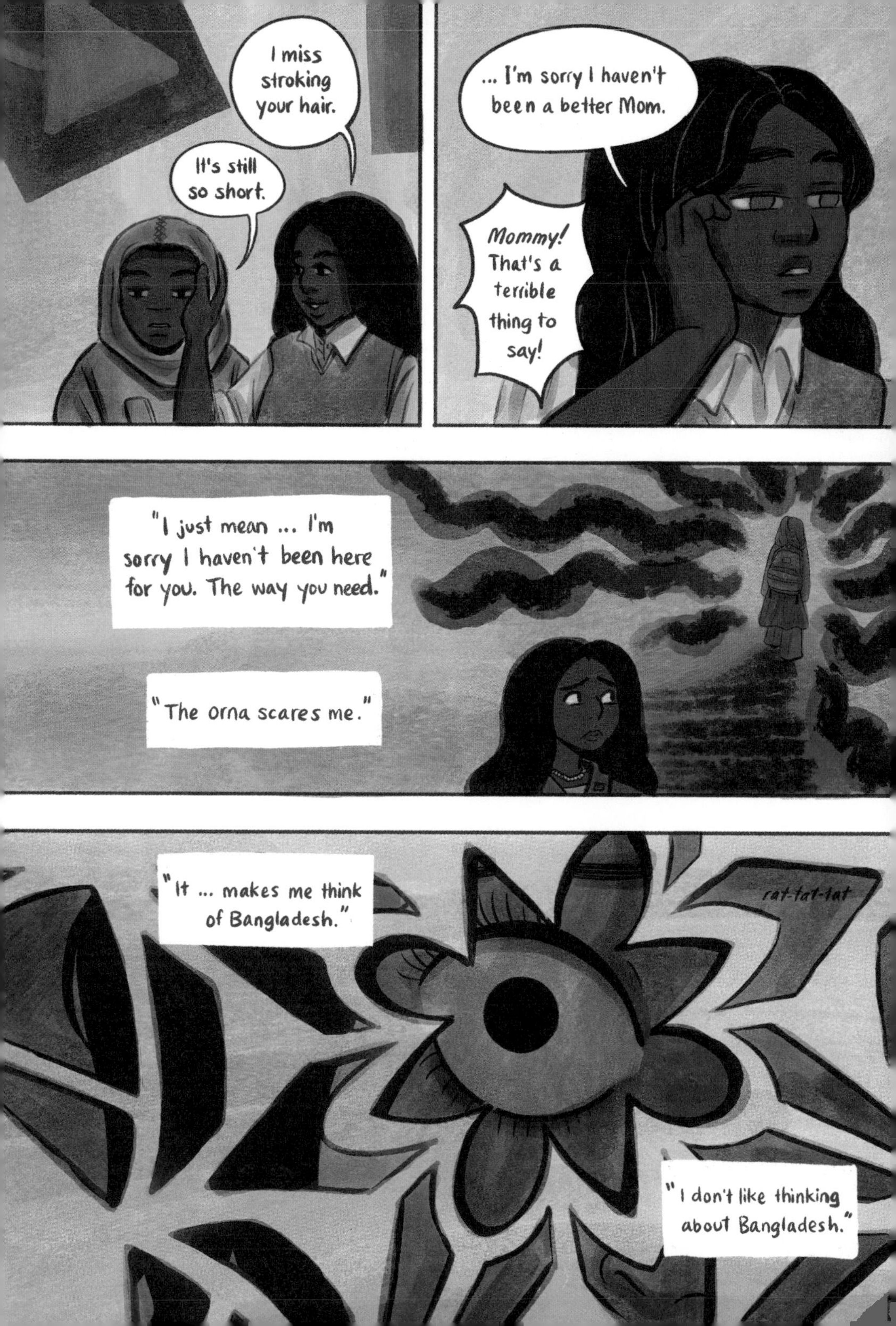
I miss stroking your hair.
It's still so short.
... I'm sorry I haven't been a better Mom.
Mommy! That's a terrible thing to say!
"I just mean ... I'm sorry I haven't been here for you. The way you need."
"The orna scares me."
"It ... makes me think of Bangladesh."
rat-tat-tat
"I don't like thinking about Bangladesh."

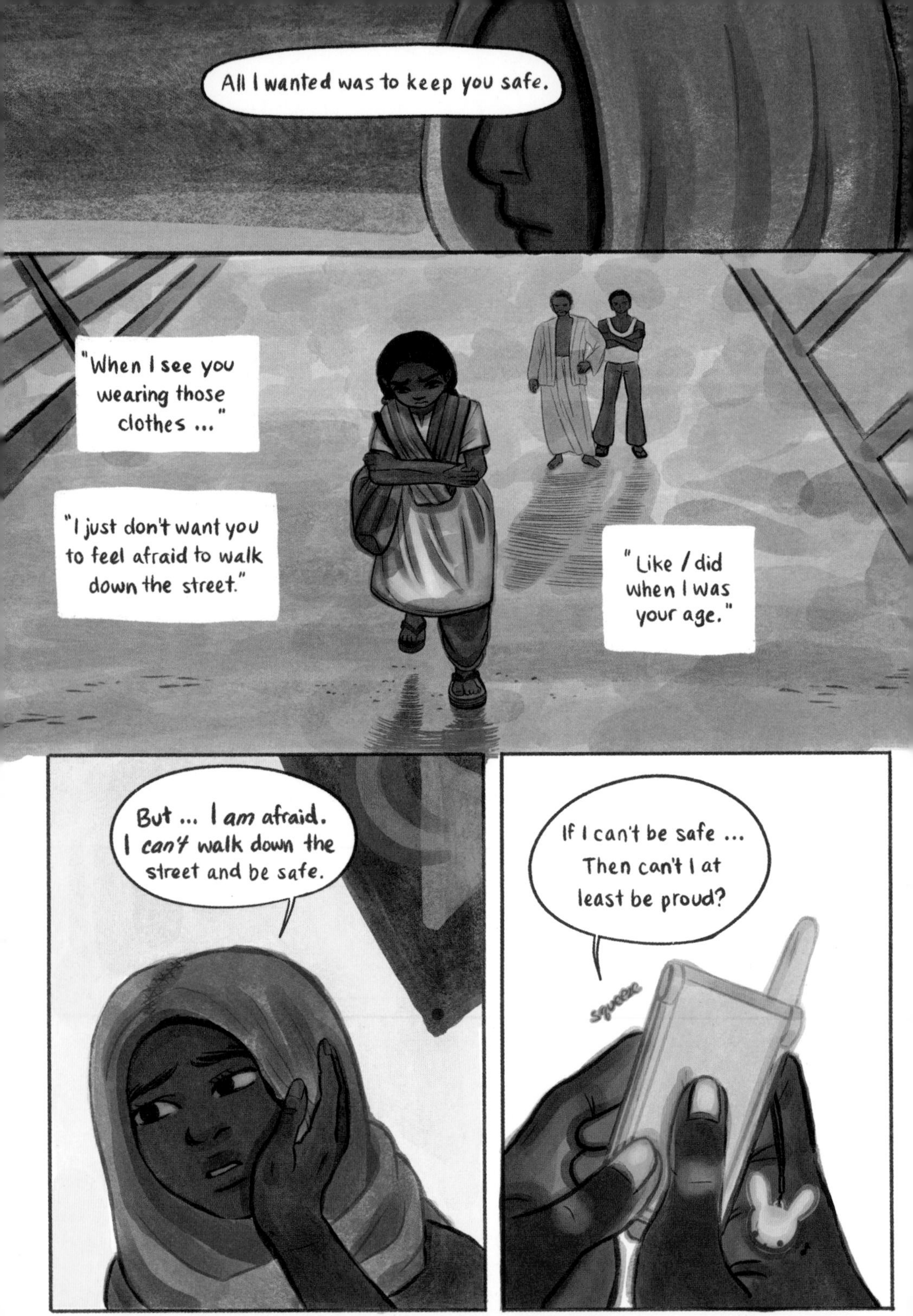
All I wanted was to keep you safe.
"When I see you wearing those clothes ..."
"I just don't want you to feel afraid to walk down the street."
"Like I did when I was your age."
But ... I *am* afraid. I *can't* walk down the street and be safe.
If I can't be safe ... Then can't I at least be proud?
squeeze

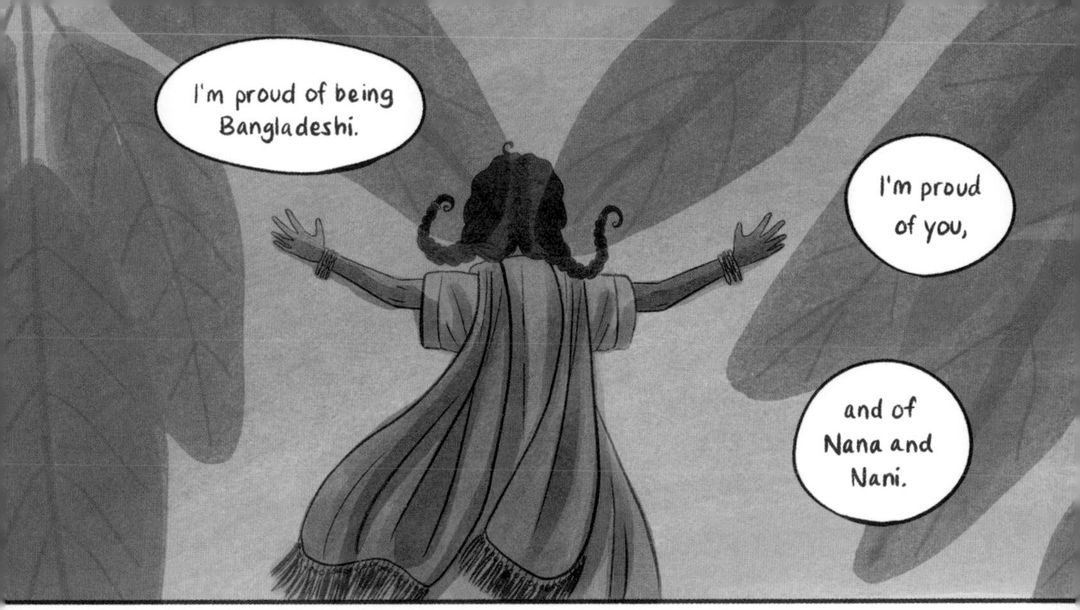
I'm proud of being Bangladeshi.
I'm proud of you,
and of Nana and Nani.

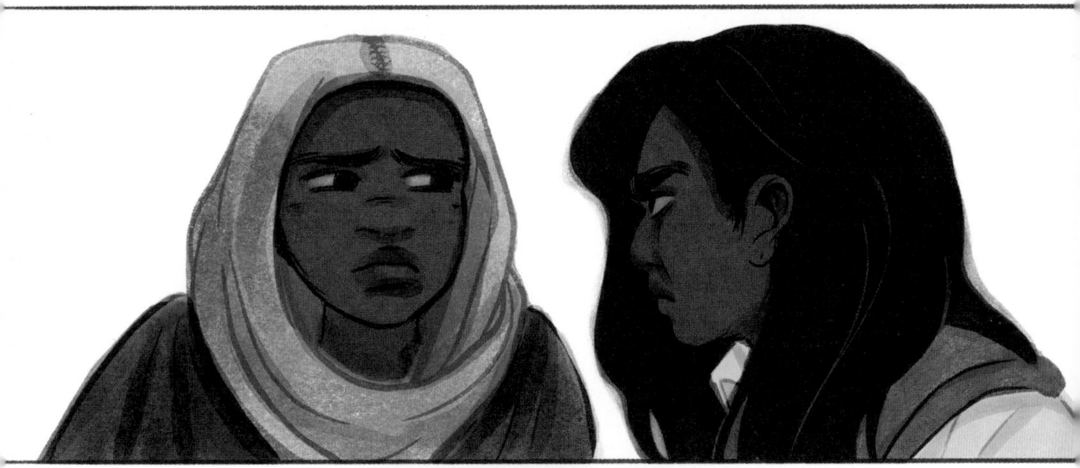

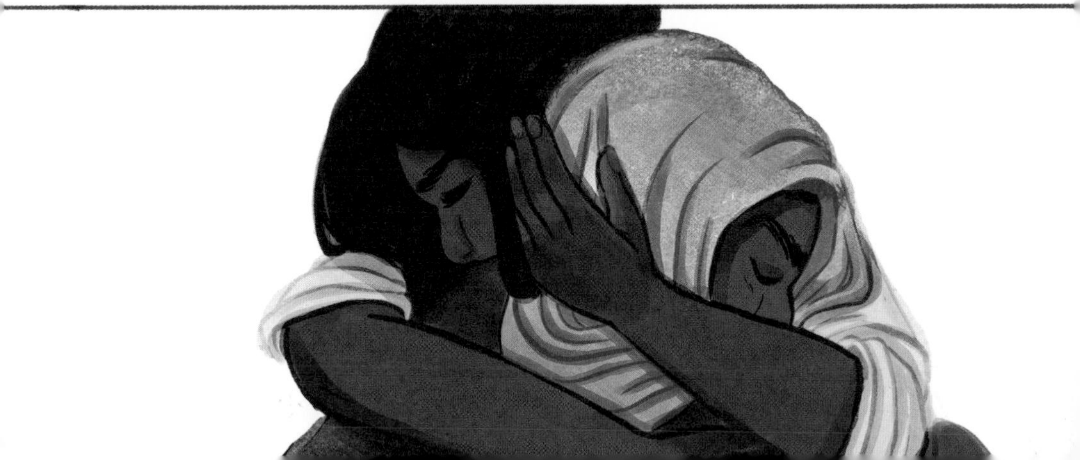

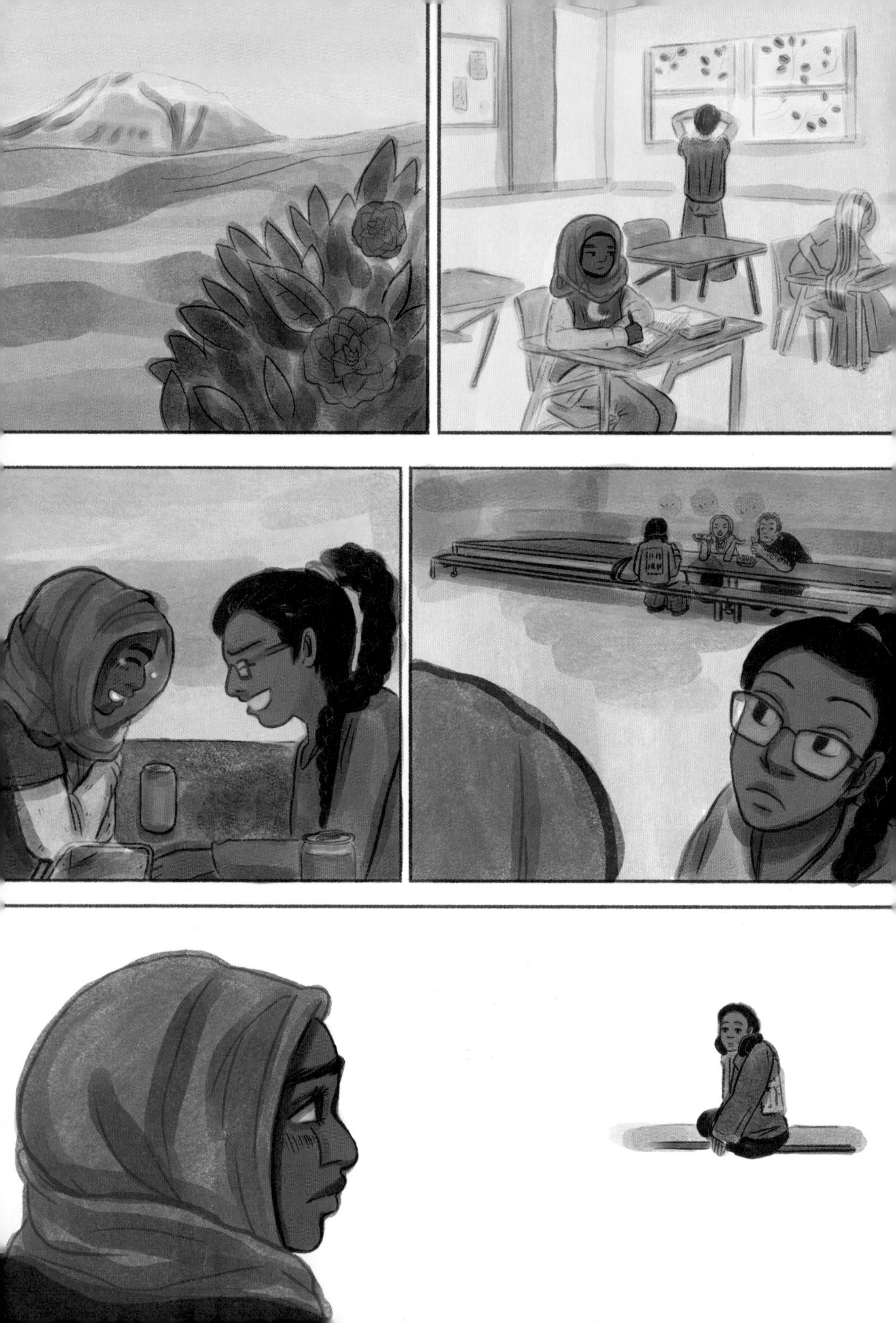

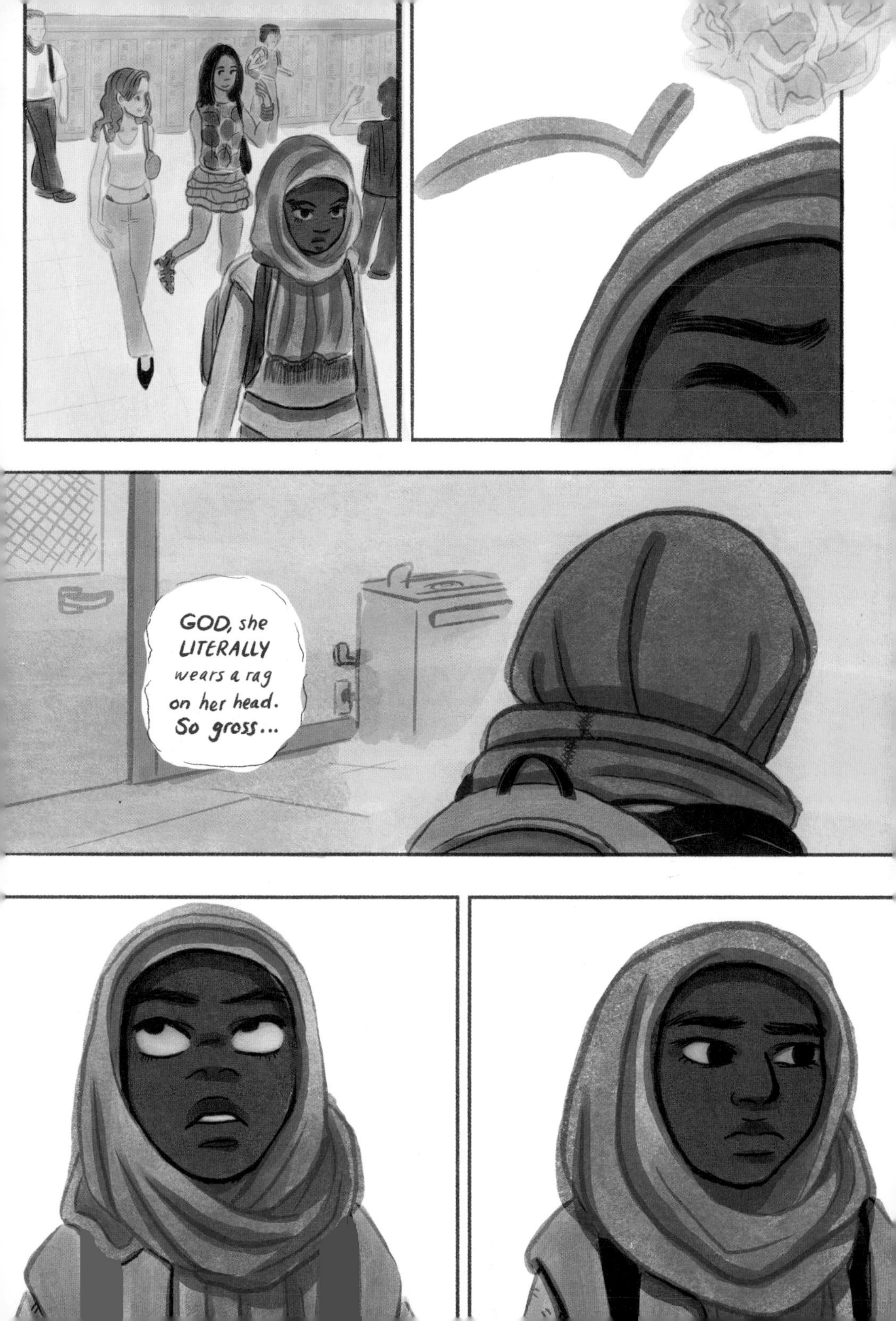
GOD, she LITERALLY wears a rag on her head. So gross...

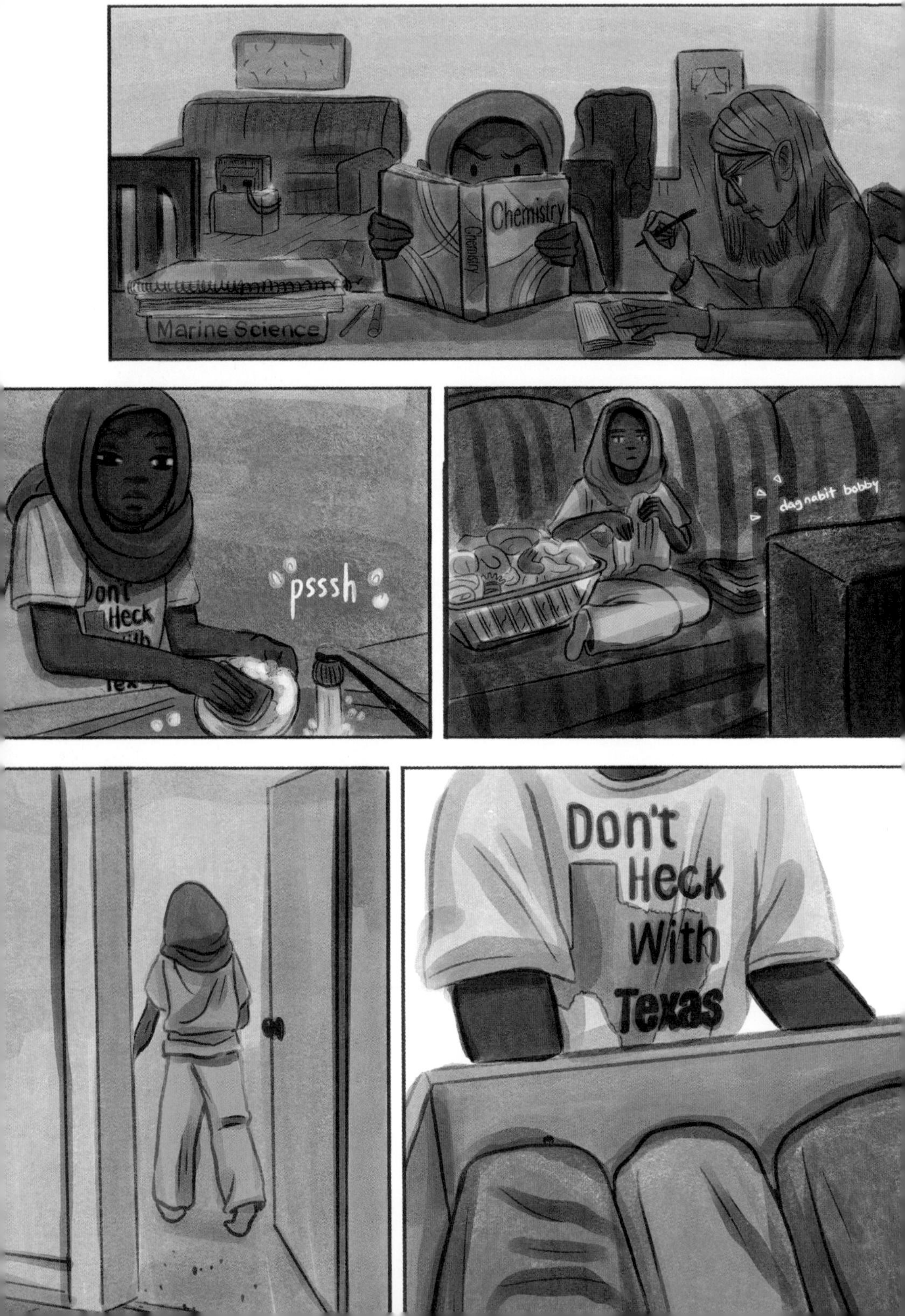
Chemistry
Chemistry
Marine Science
psssh
dagnabit bobby
Don't Heck With Texas

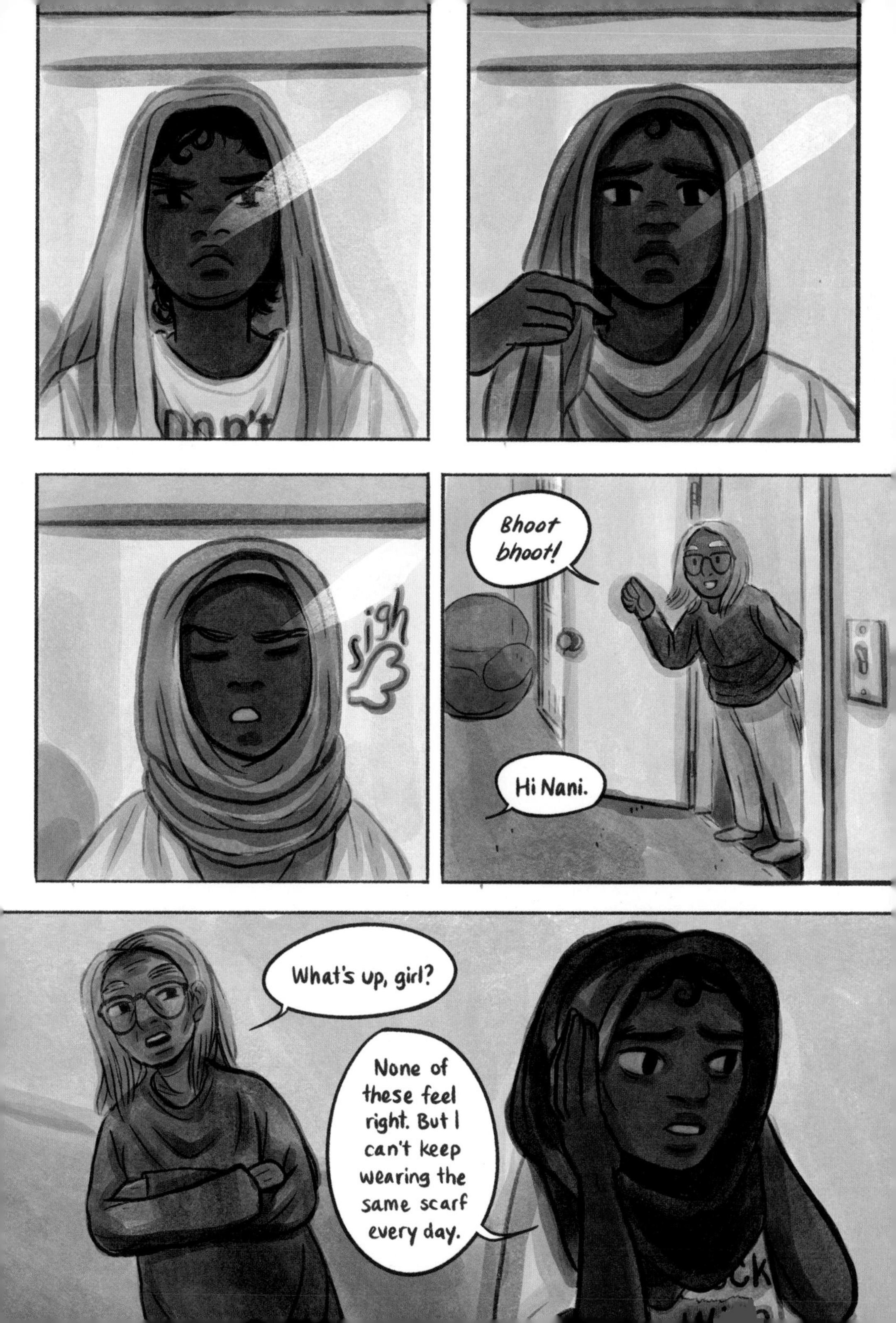
sigh
Bhoot bhoot!
Hi Nani.
What's up, girl?
None of these feel right. But I can't keep wearing the same scarf every day.

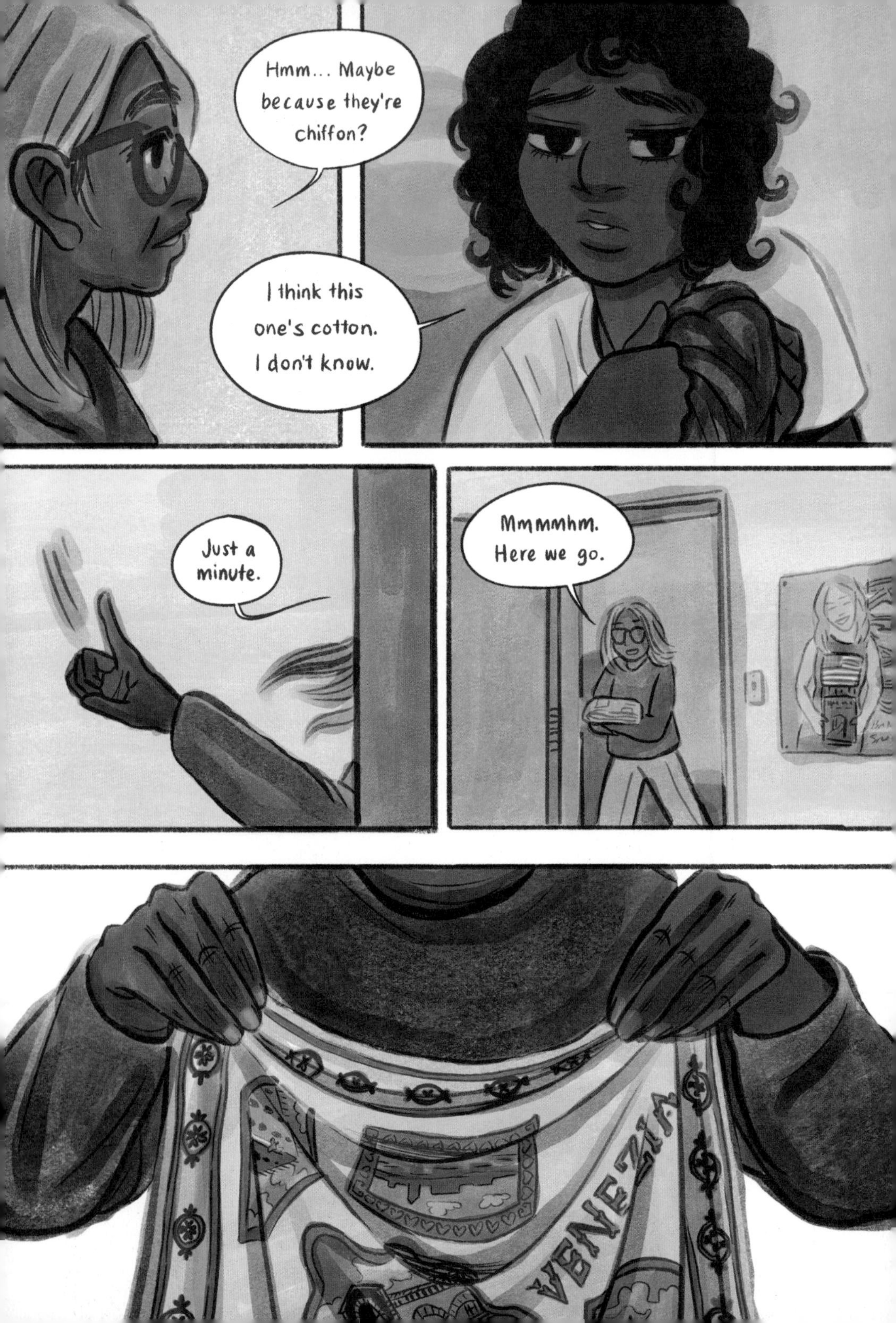
Hmm... Maybe because they're chiffon?
I think this one's cotton. I don't know.
Just a minute.
Mmmmhm. Here we go.
VENEZIA

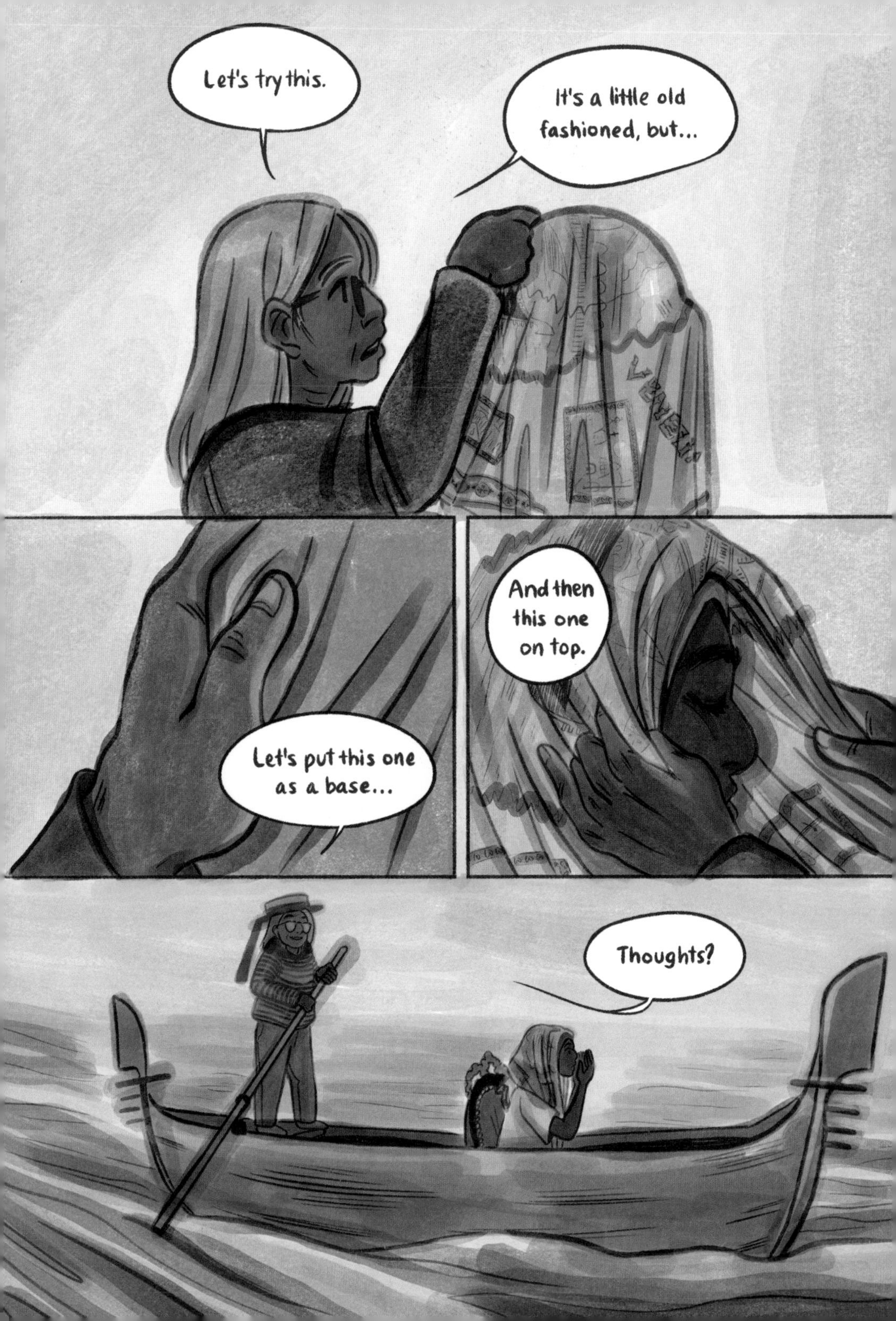
Let's try this.
It's a little old fashioned, but...
Let's put this one as a base...
And then this one on top.
Thoughts?

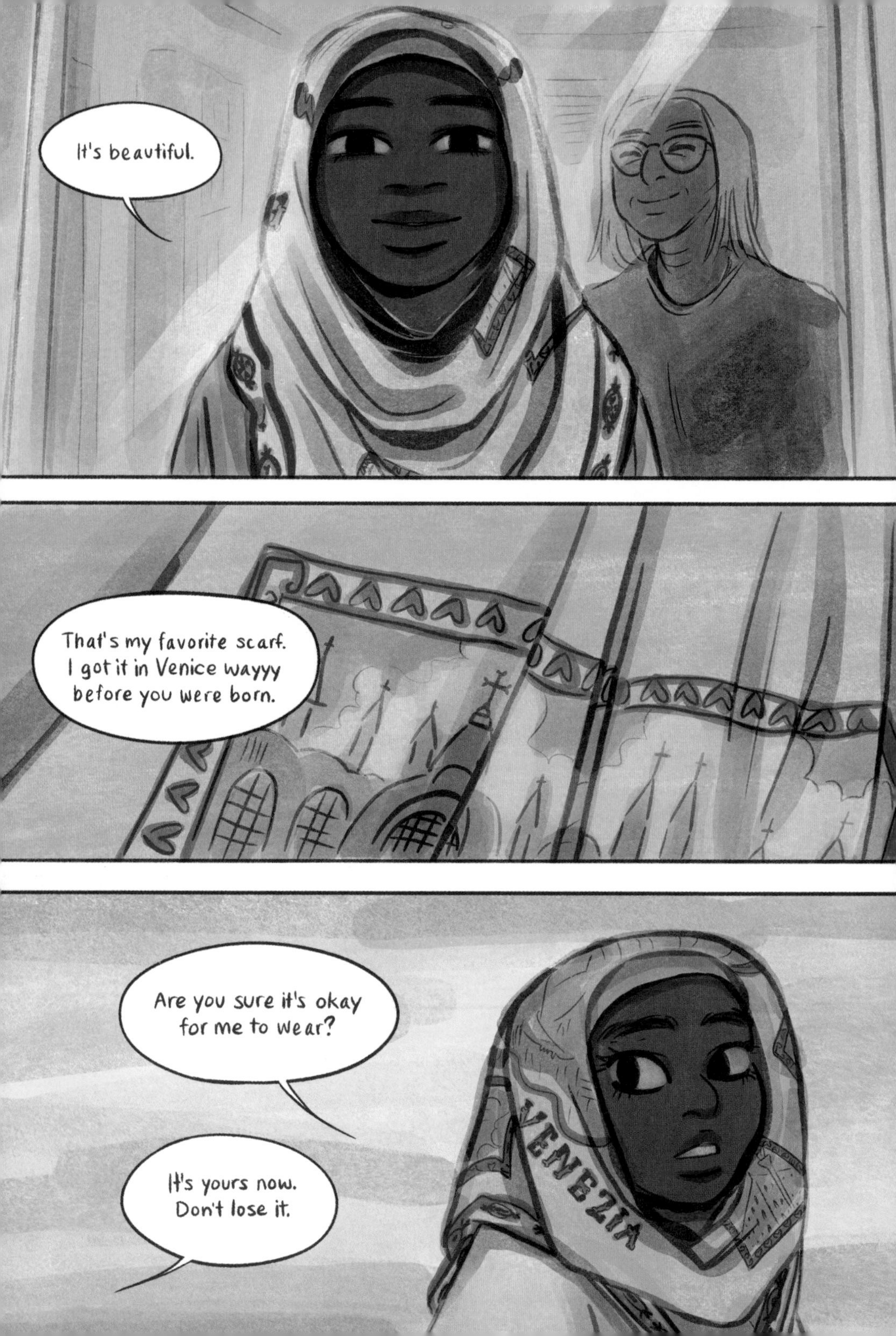
It's beautiful.
That's my favorite scarf. I got it in Venice wayyy before you were born.
Are you sure it's okay for me to wear?
It's yours now. Don't lose it.
VENEZIA

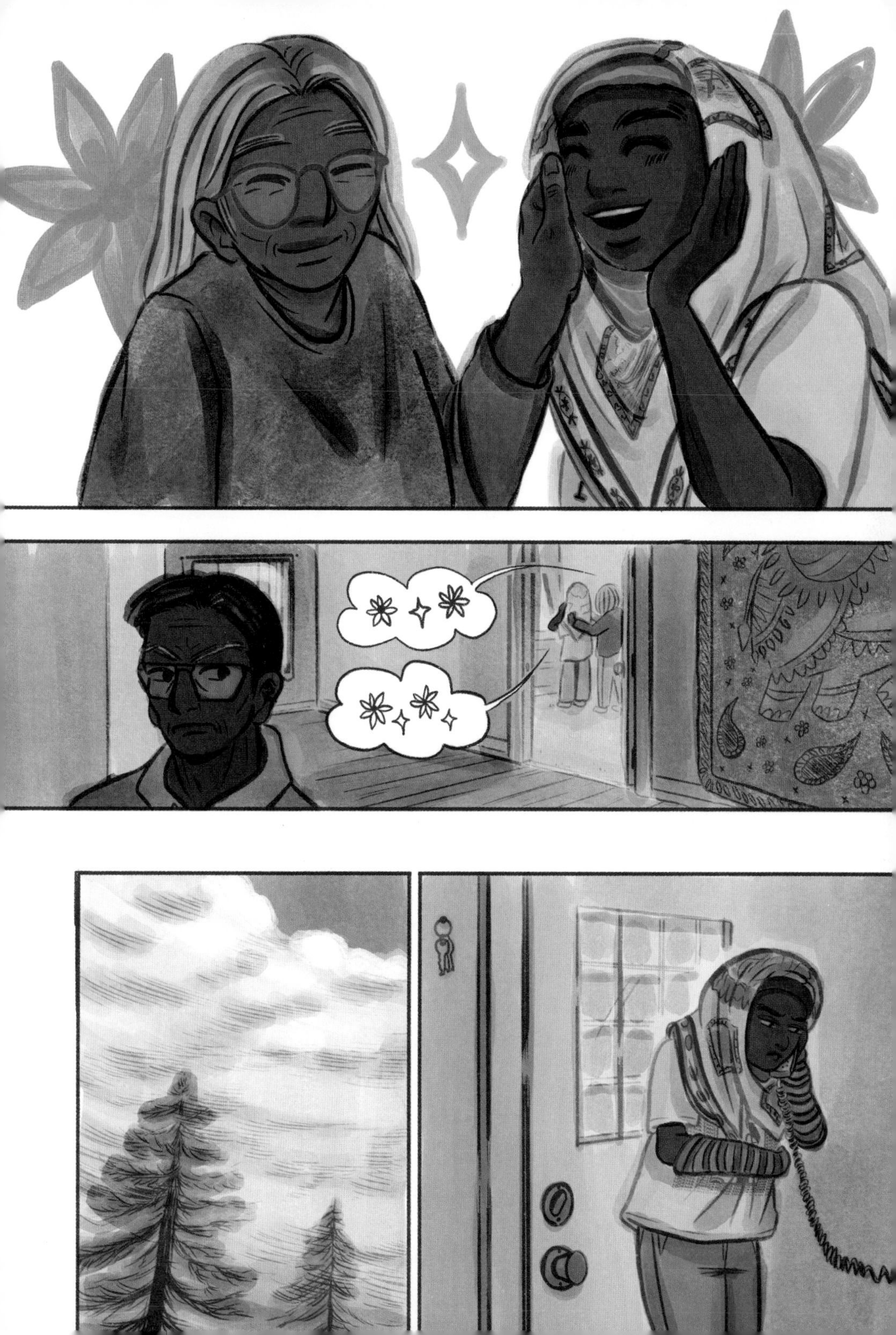

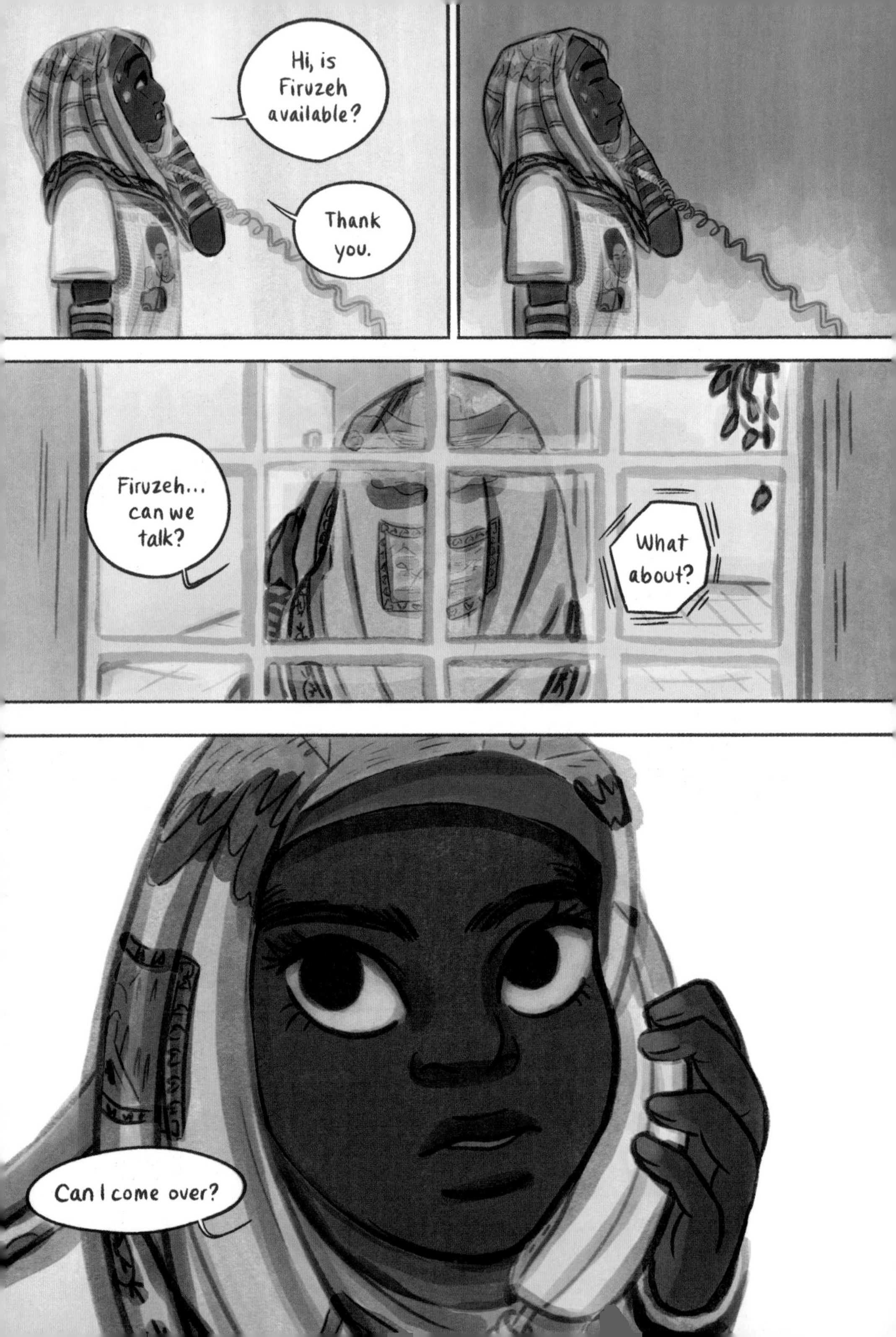
Hi, is Firuzeh available?
Thank you.
Firuzeh... can we talk?
What about?
Can I come over?

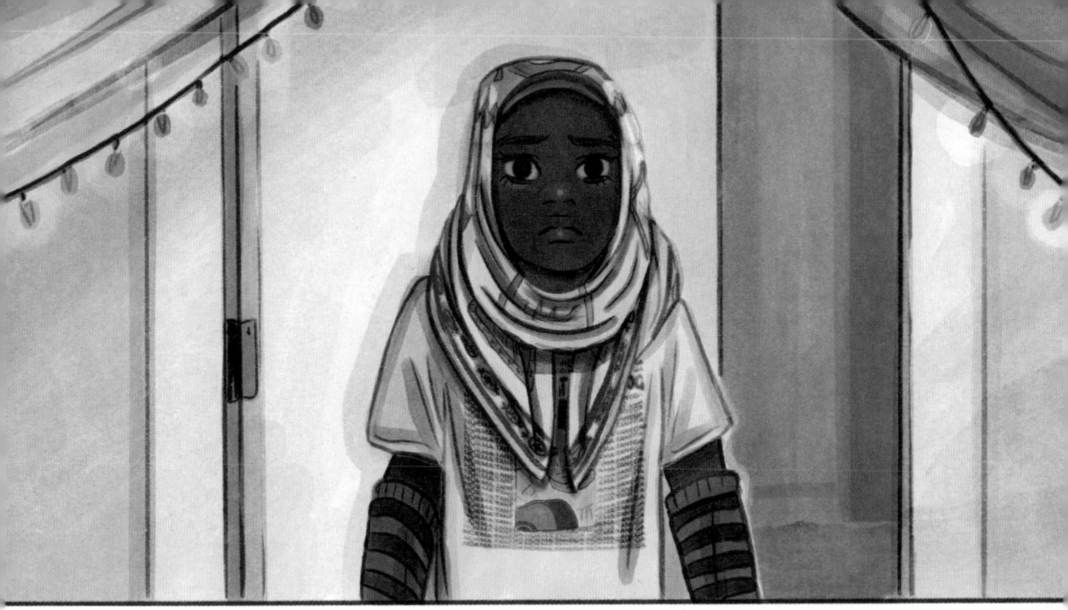

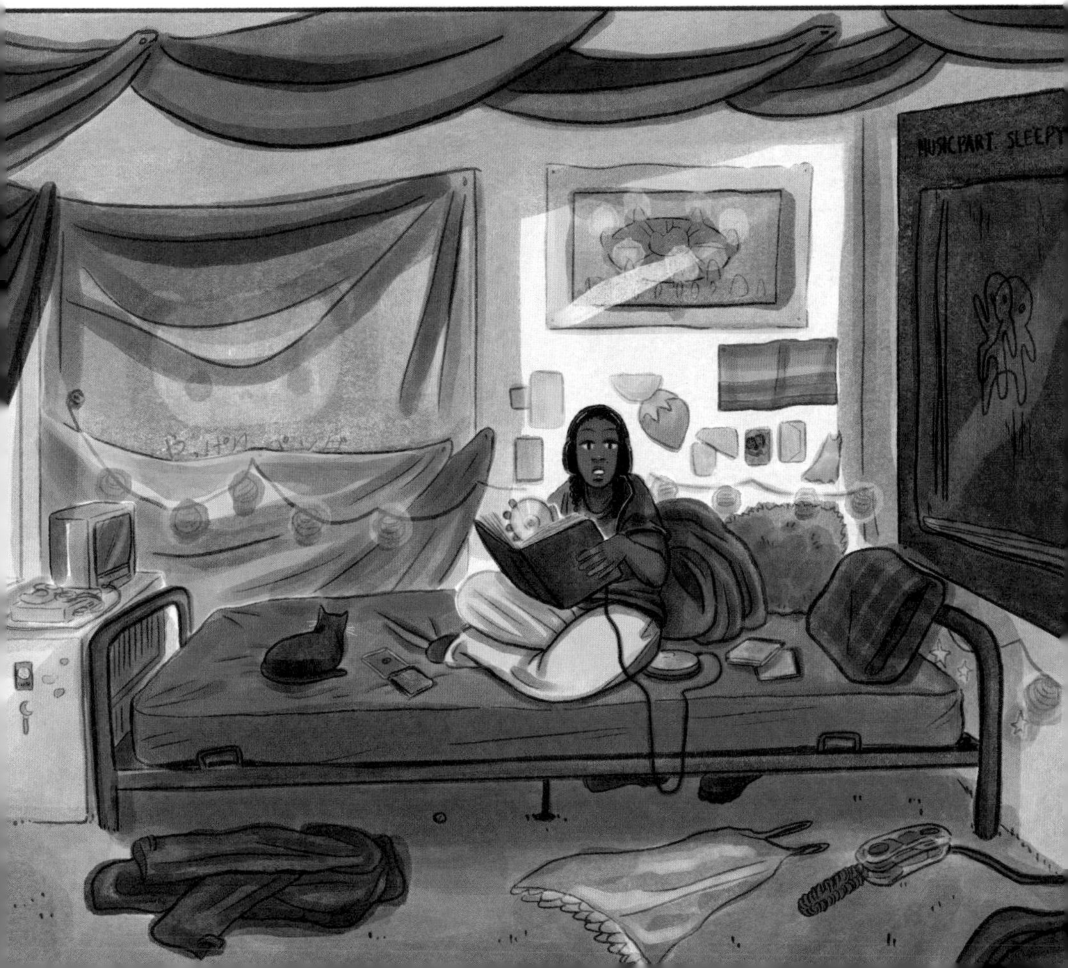
MUSICPART. SLEEPY

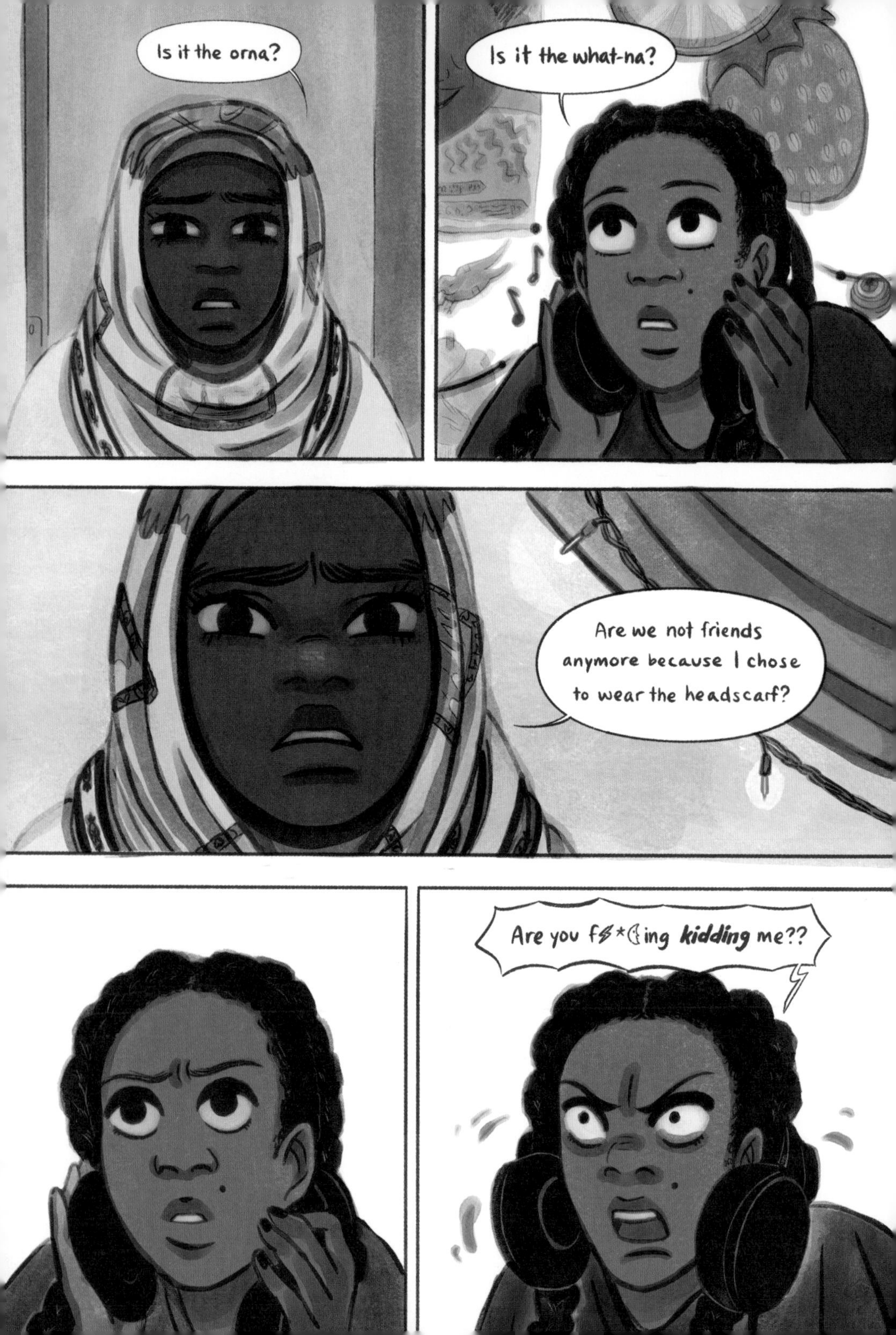
Is it the orna?
Is it the what-na?
Are we not friends anymore because I chose to wear the headscarf?
Are you f$*☾ing **kidding** me??

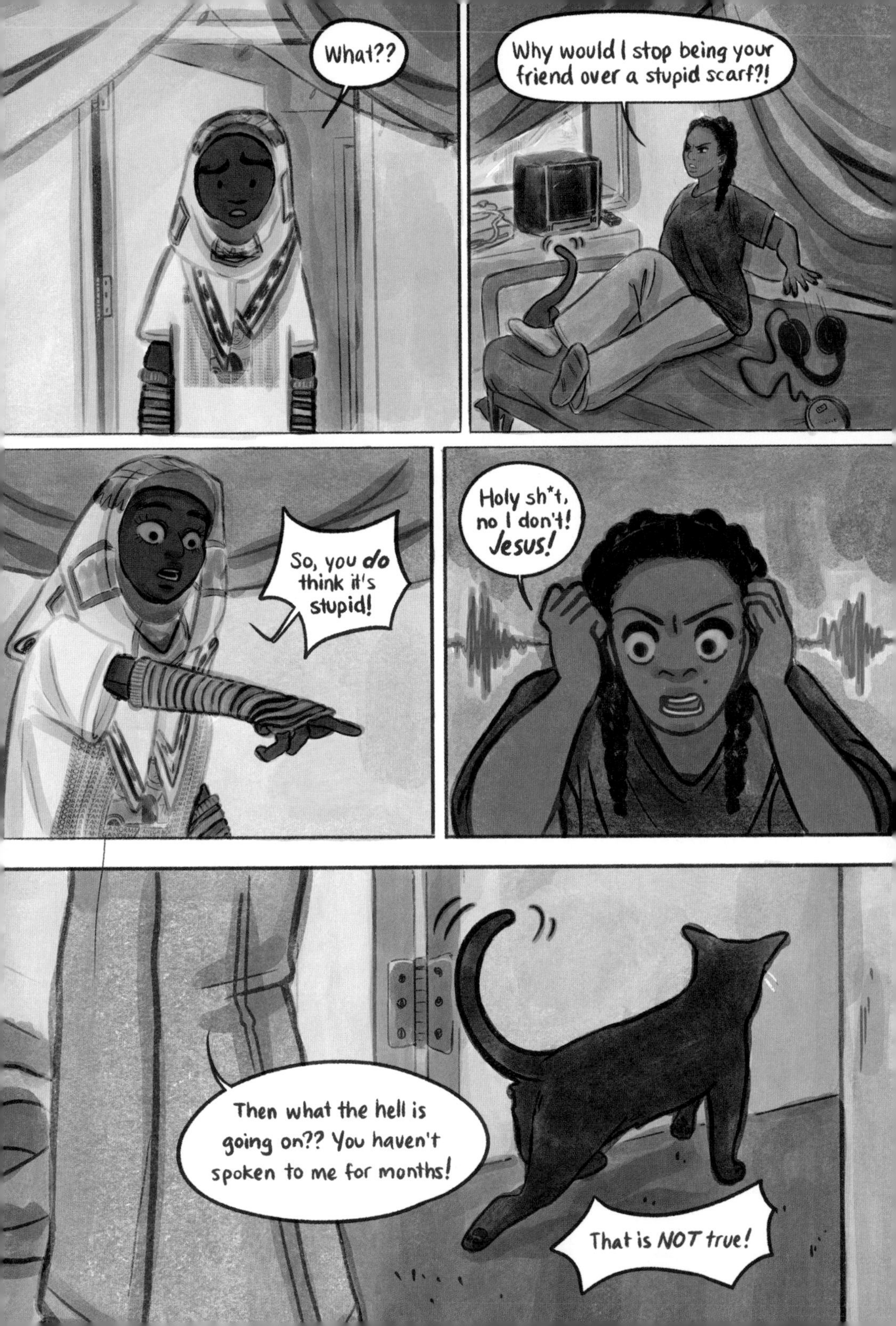
What??
Why would I stop being your friend over a stupid scarf?!
So, you **do** think it's stupid!
Holy sh*t, no I don't! *Jesus!*
Then what the hell is going on?? You haven't spoken to me for months!
That is *NOT* true!

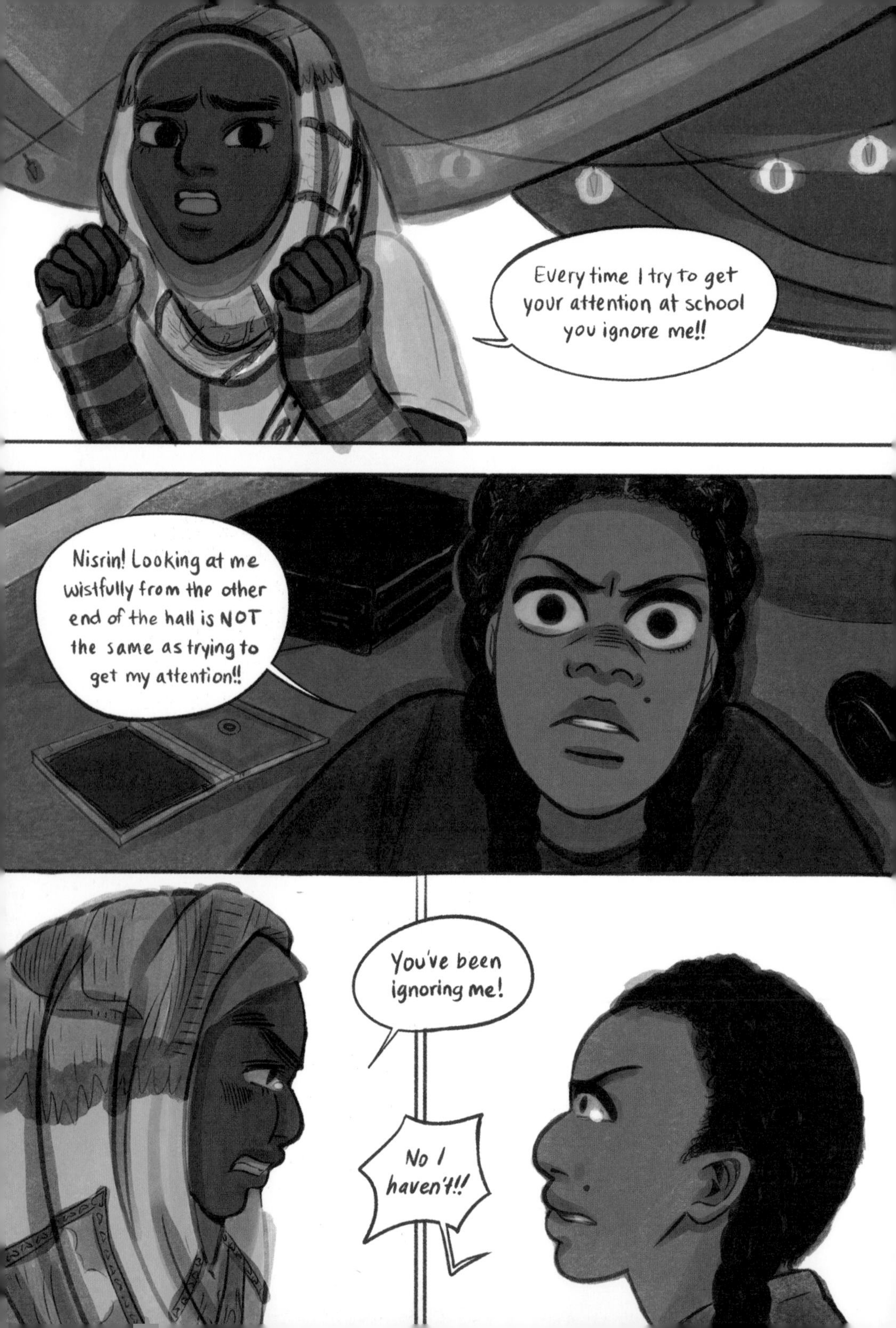
Every time I try to get your attention at school you ignore me!!
Nisrin! Looking at me wistfully from the other end of the hall is NOT the same as trying to get my attention!!
You've been ignoring me!
No I haven't!!

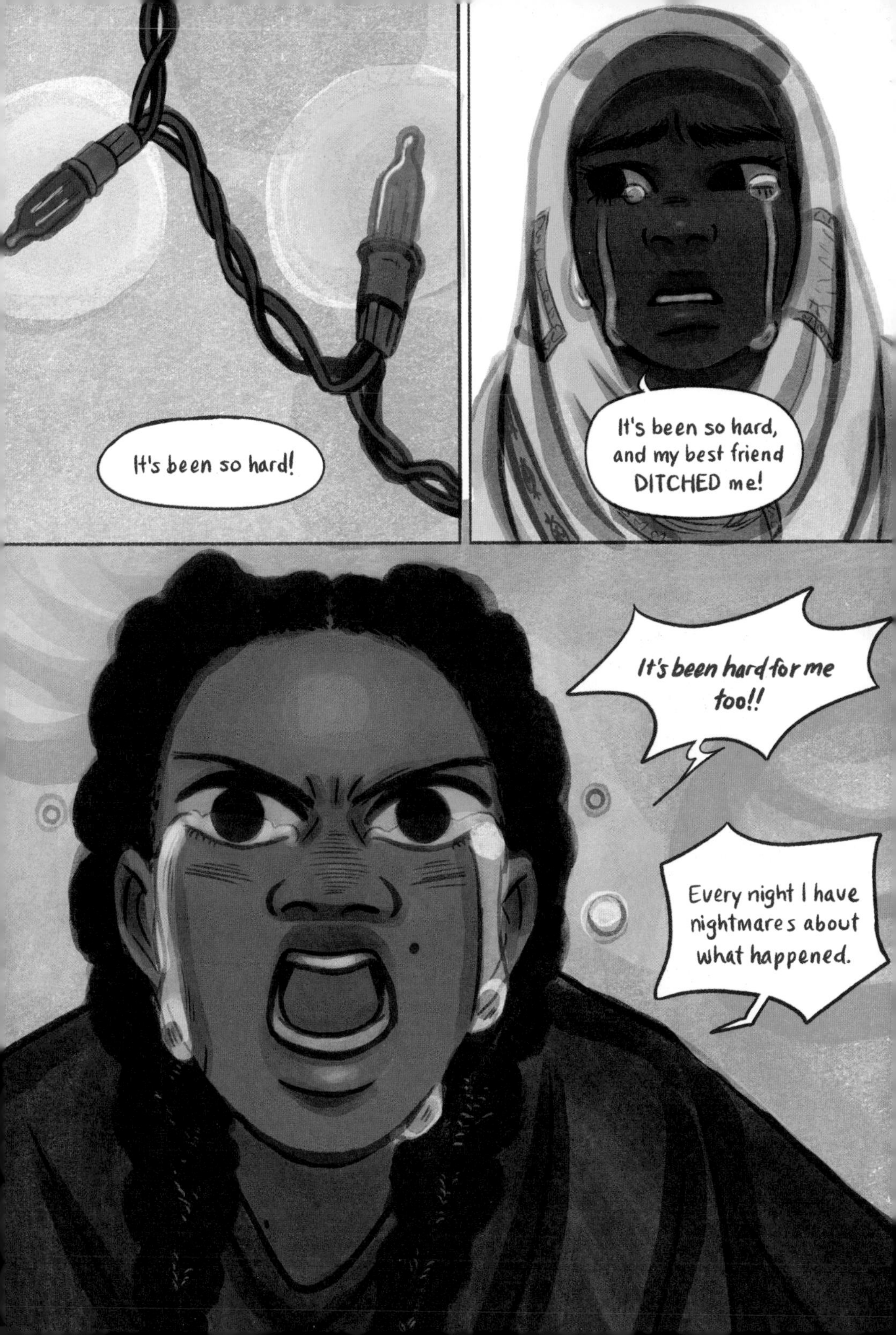
It's been so hard!
It's been so hard, and my best friend DITCHED me!
It's been hard for me too!!
Every night I have nightmares about what happened.

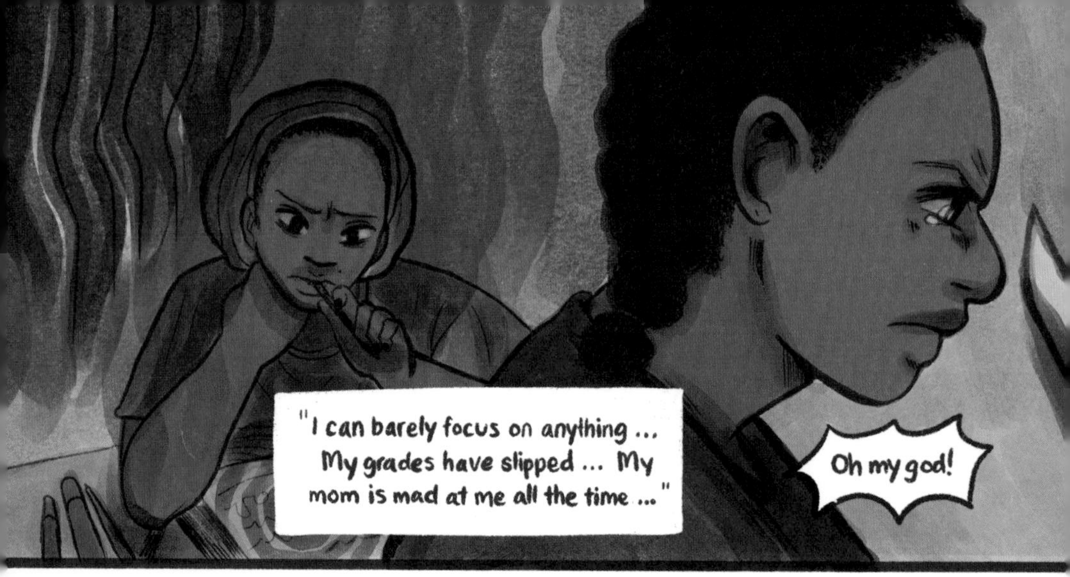
"I can barely focus on anything ... My grades have slipped ... My mom is mad at me all the time ..."
Oh my god!
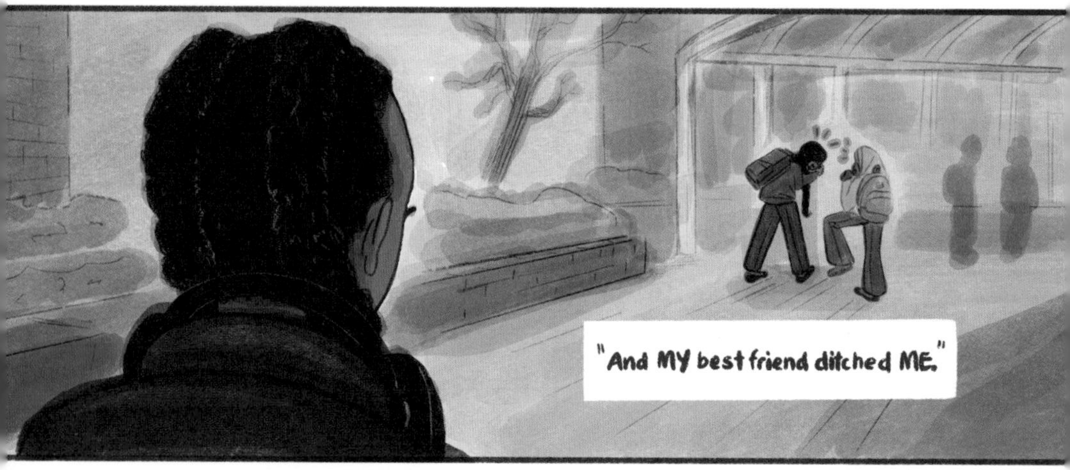
"And MY best friend ditched ME."
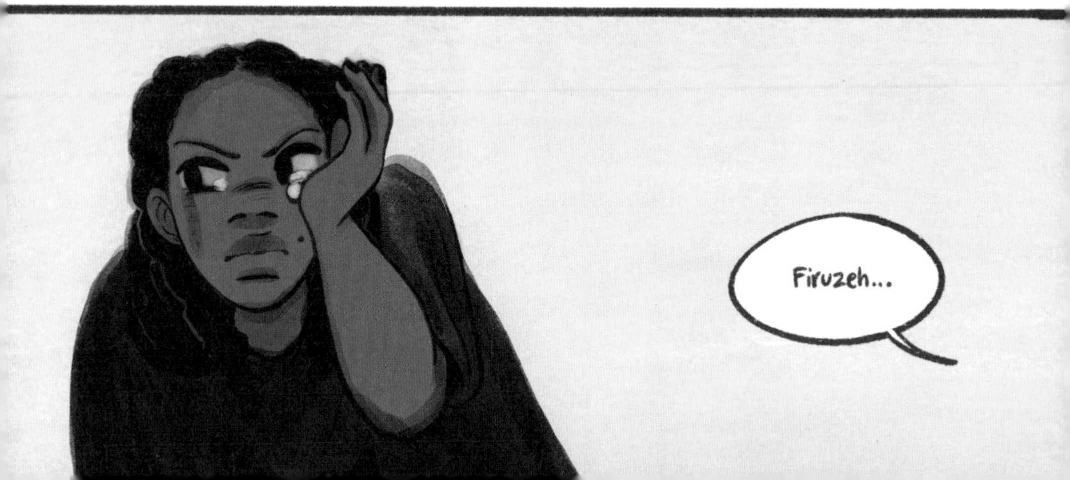
Firuzeh...

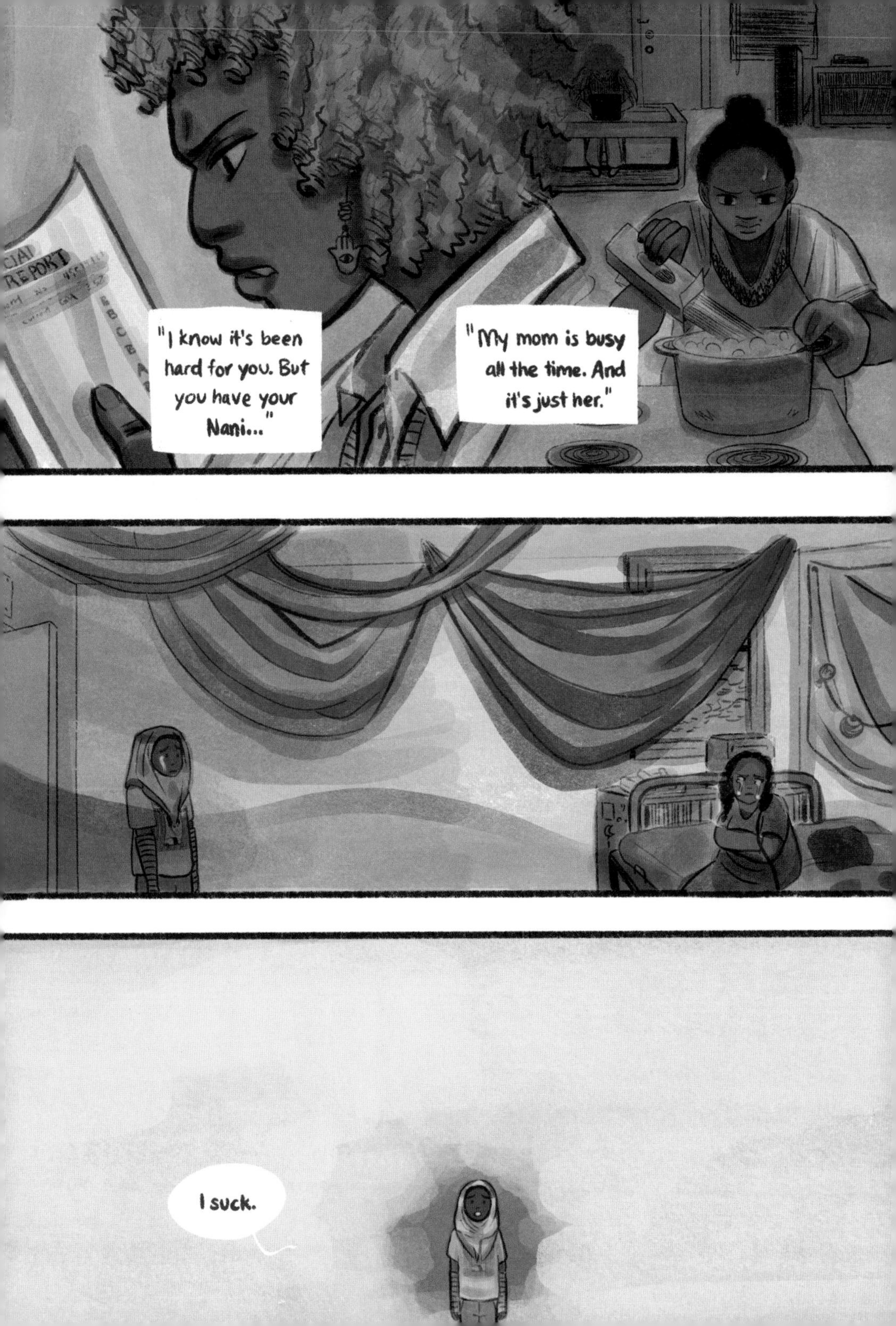
"I know it's been hard for you. But you have your Nani..."
"My mom is busy all the time. And it's just her."
I suck.

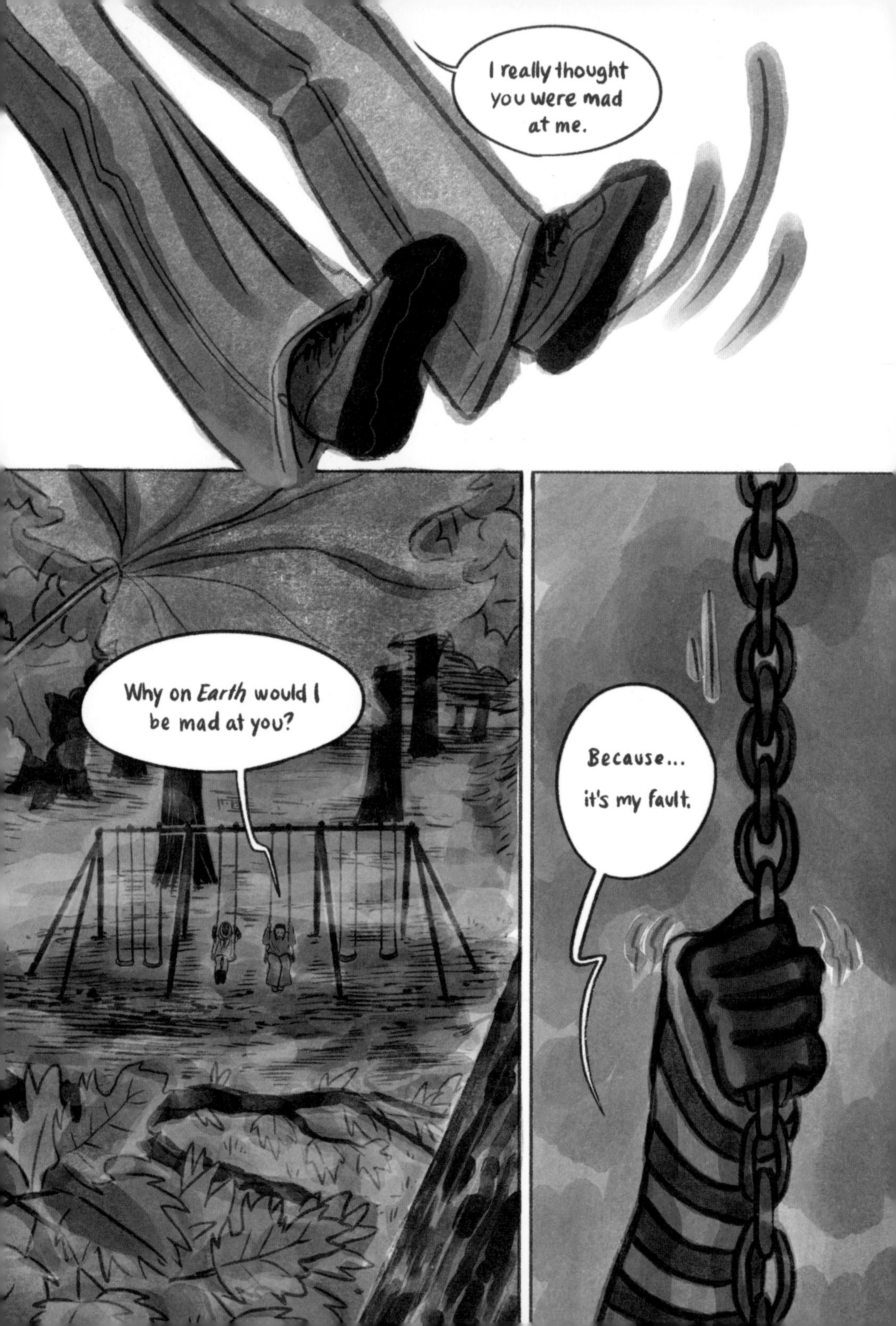
I really thought you were mad at me.
Why on *Earth* would I be mad at you?
Because...
it's my fault.

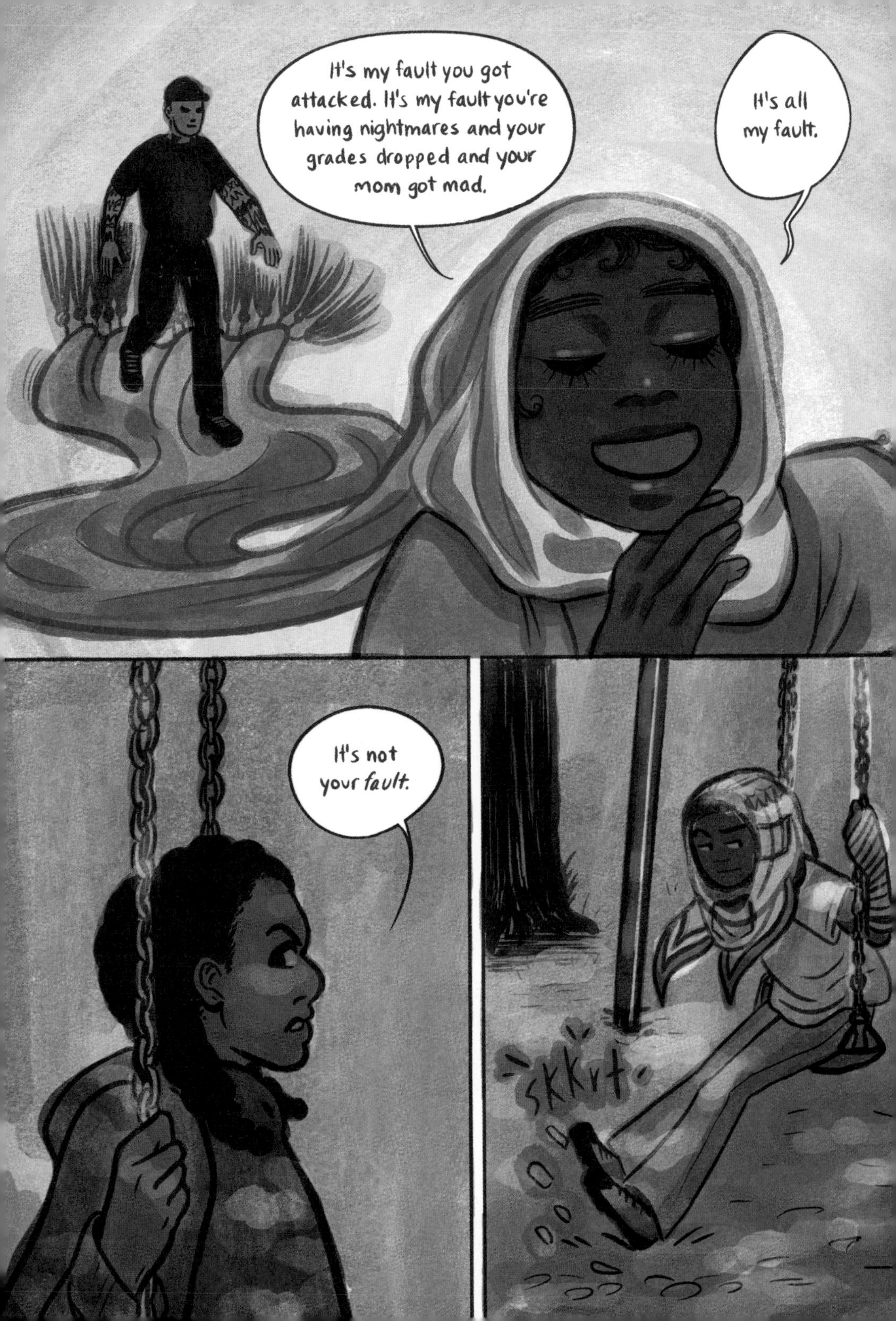
It's my fault you got attacked. It's my fault you're having nightmares and your grades dropped and your mom got mad.
It's all my fault.
It's not your *fault*.
SKKRT

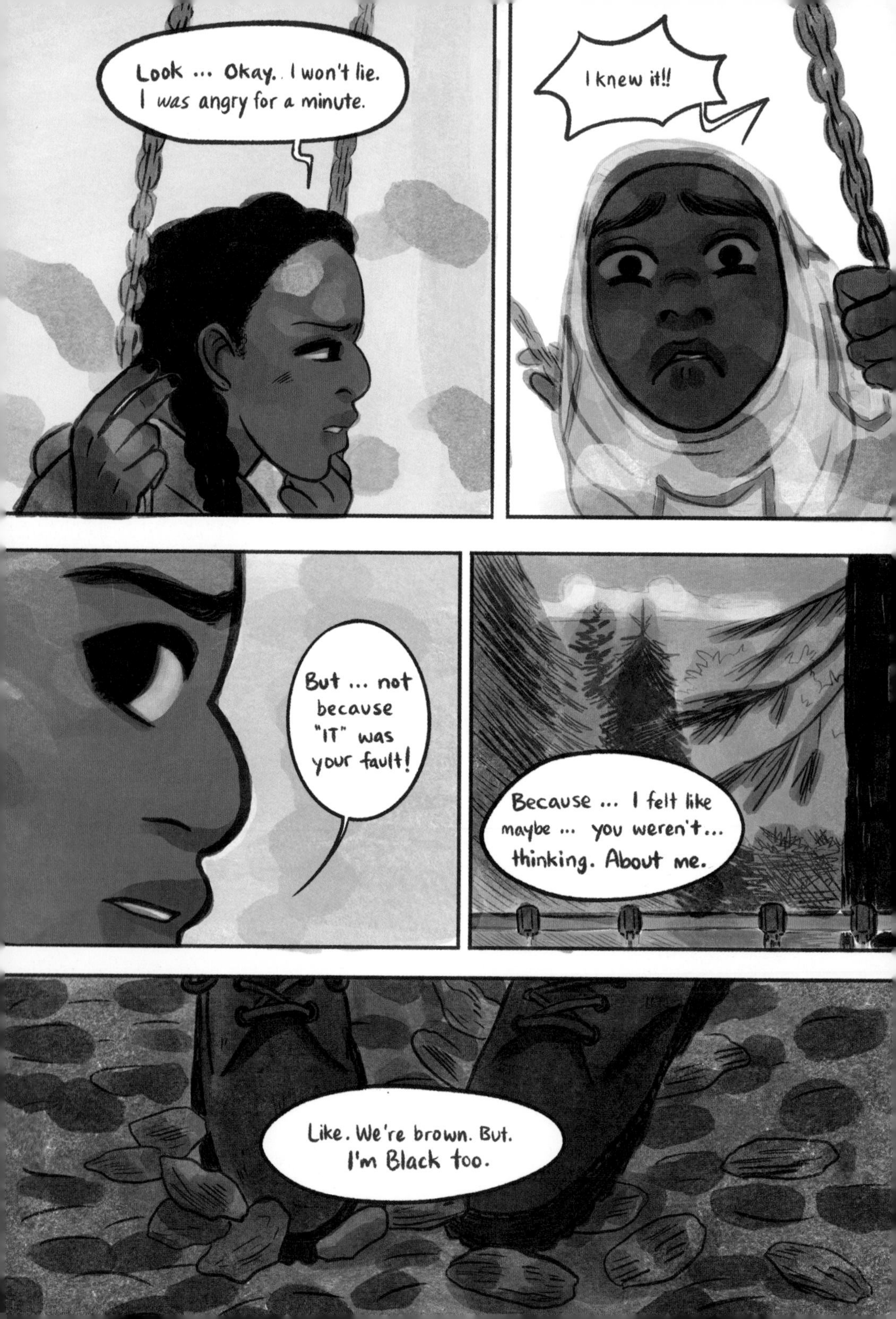
Look ... Okay. I won't lie.
I was angry for a minute.
I knew it!!
But ... not because "IT" was your fault!
Because ... I felt like maybe ... you weren't... thinking. About me.
Like. We're brown. But. I'm Black too.

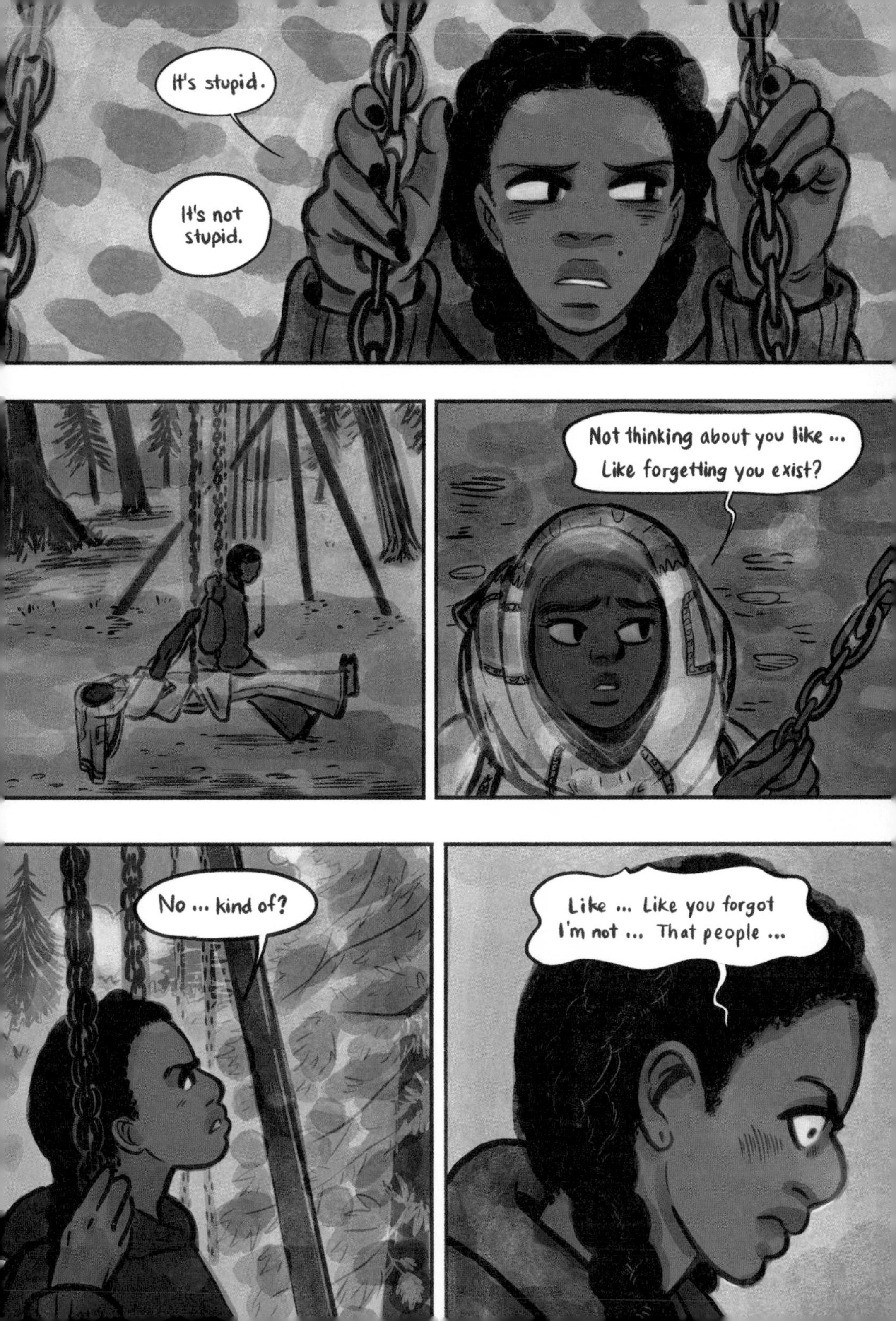
It's stupid.
It's not stupid.
Not thinking about you like ... Like forgetting you exist?
No ... kind of?
Like ... Like you forgot I'm not ... That people ...

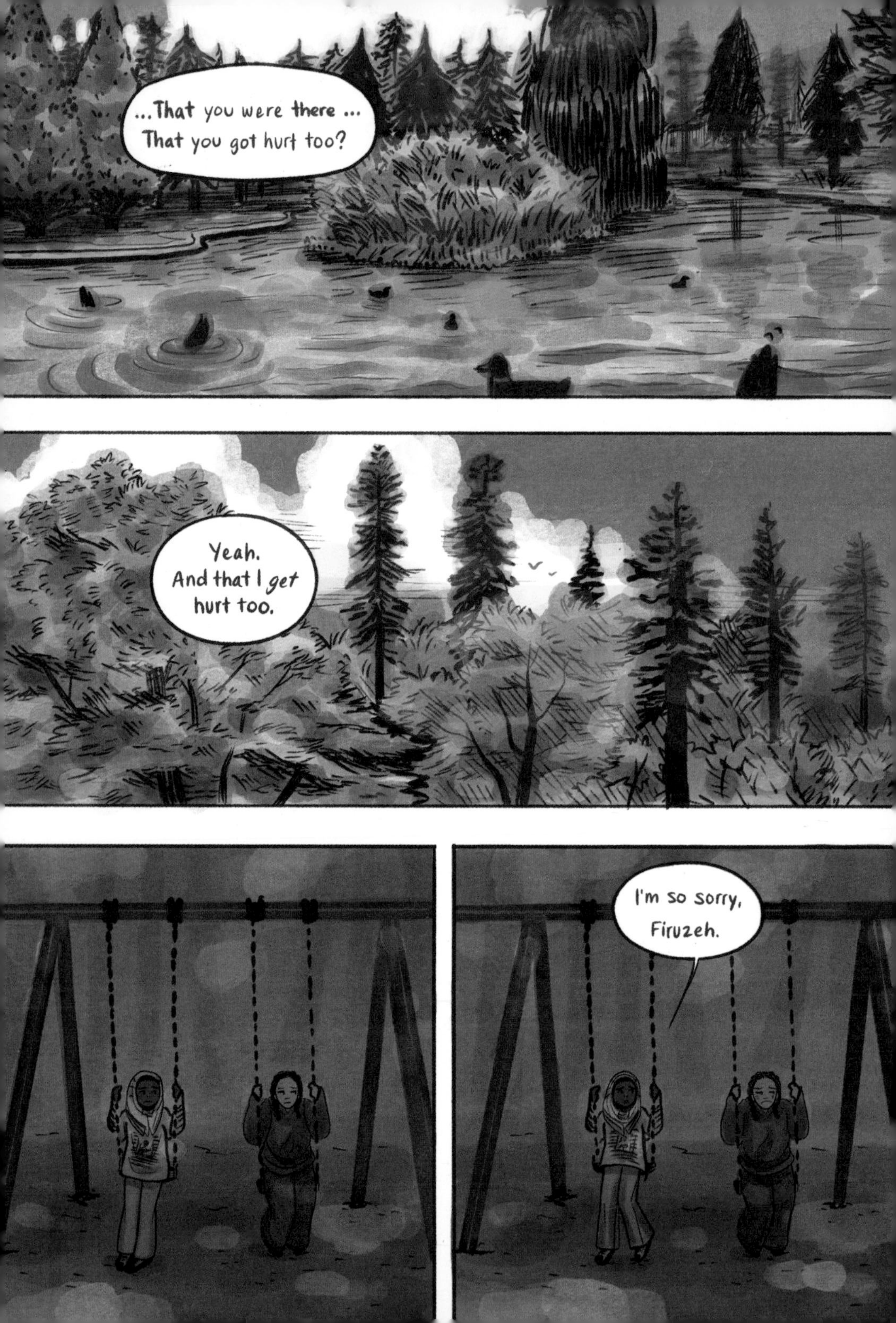
...That you were there ... That you got hurt too?
Yeah. And that I *get* hurt too.
I'm so sorry, Firuzeh.

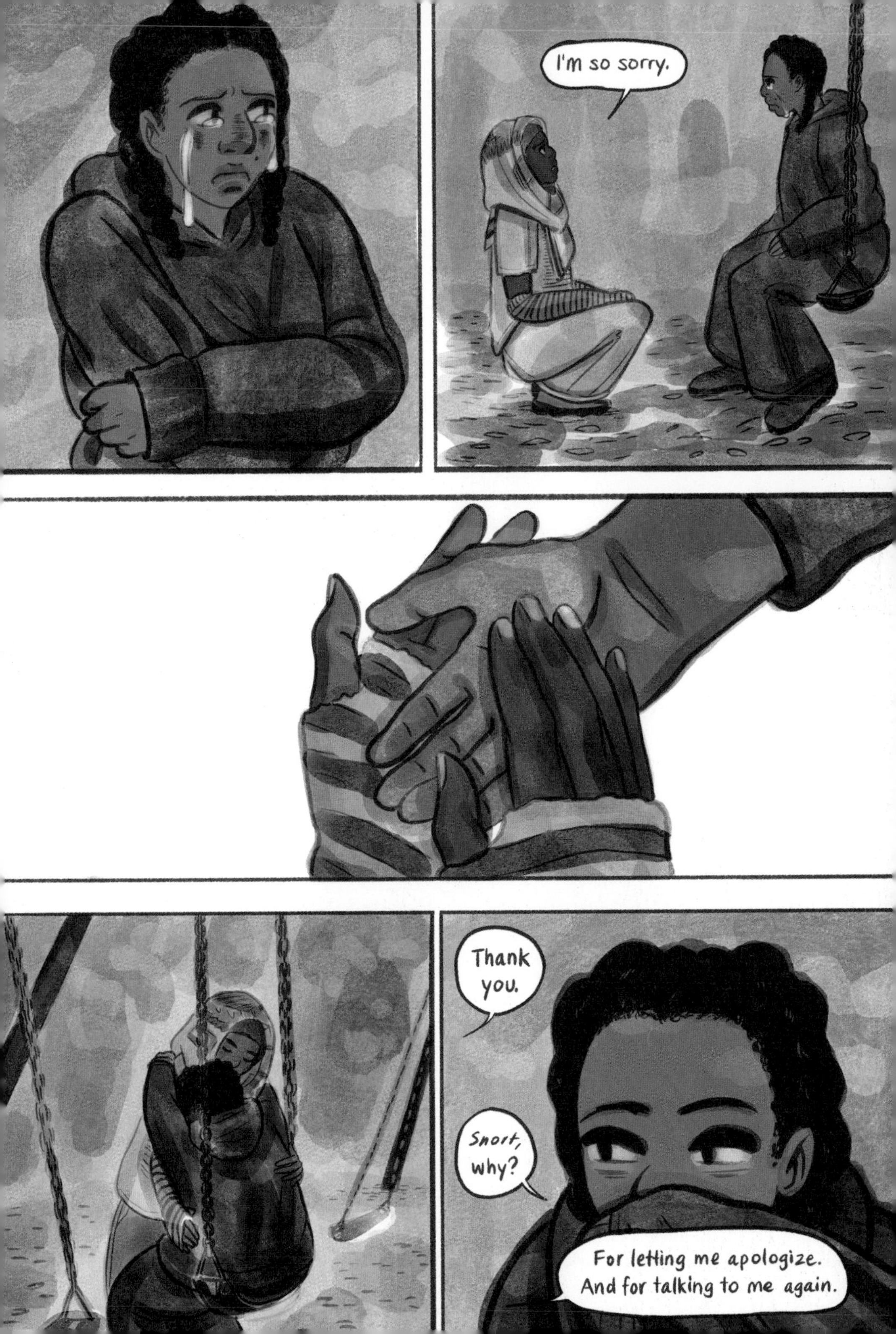
I'm so sorry.
Thank you.
Snort, why?
For letting me apologize. And for talking to me again.

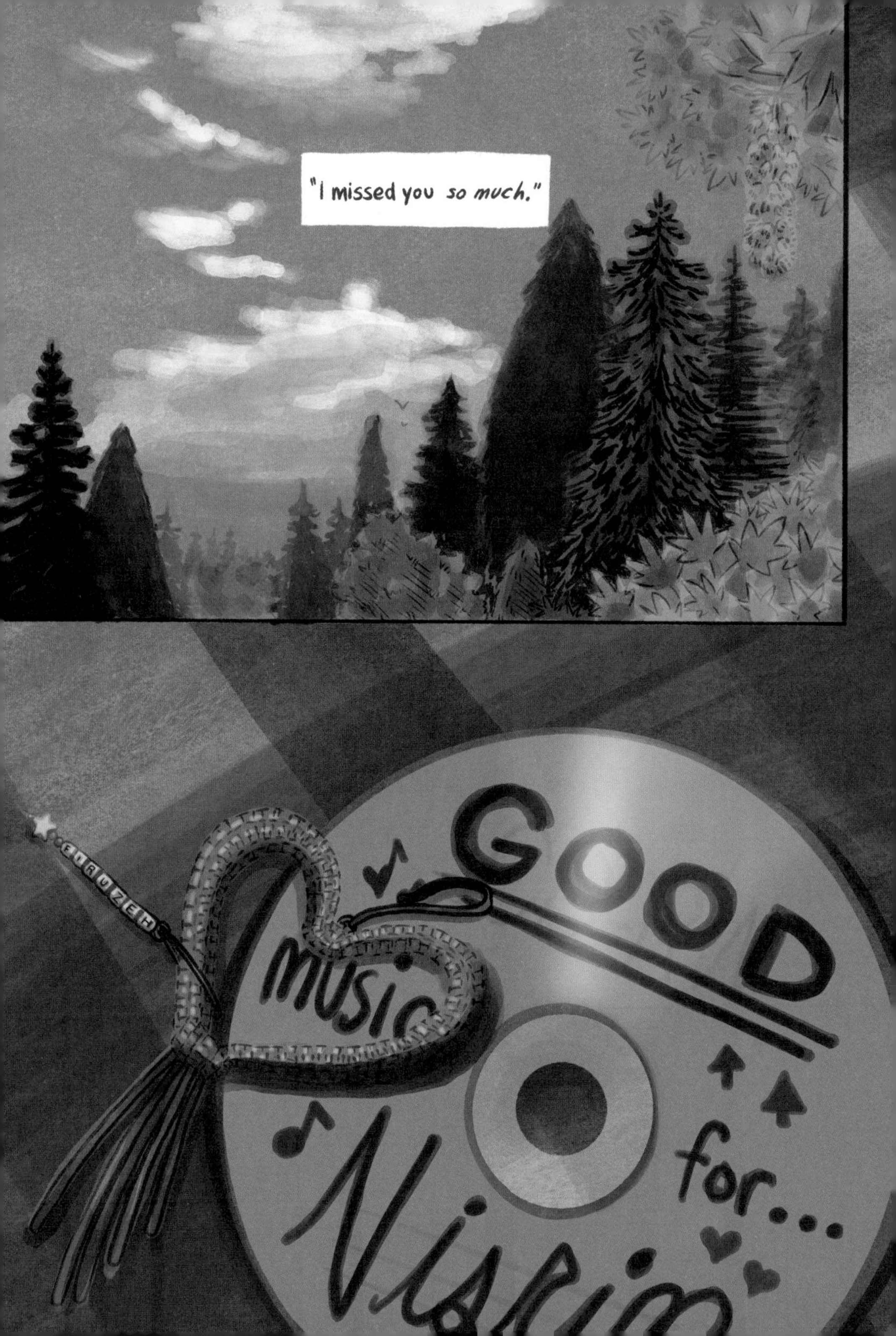
"I missed you so much."
GOOD
MUSIC
for...

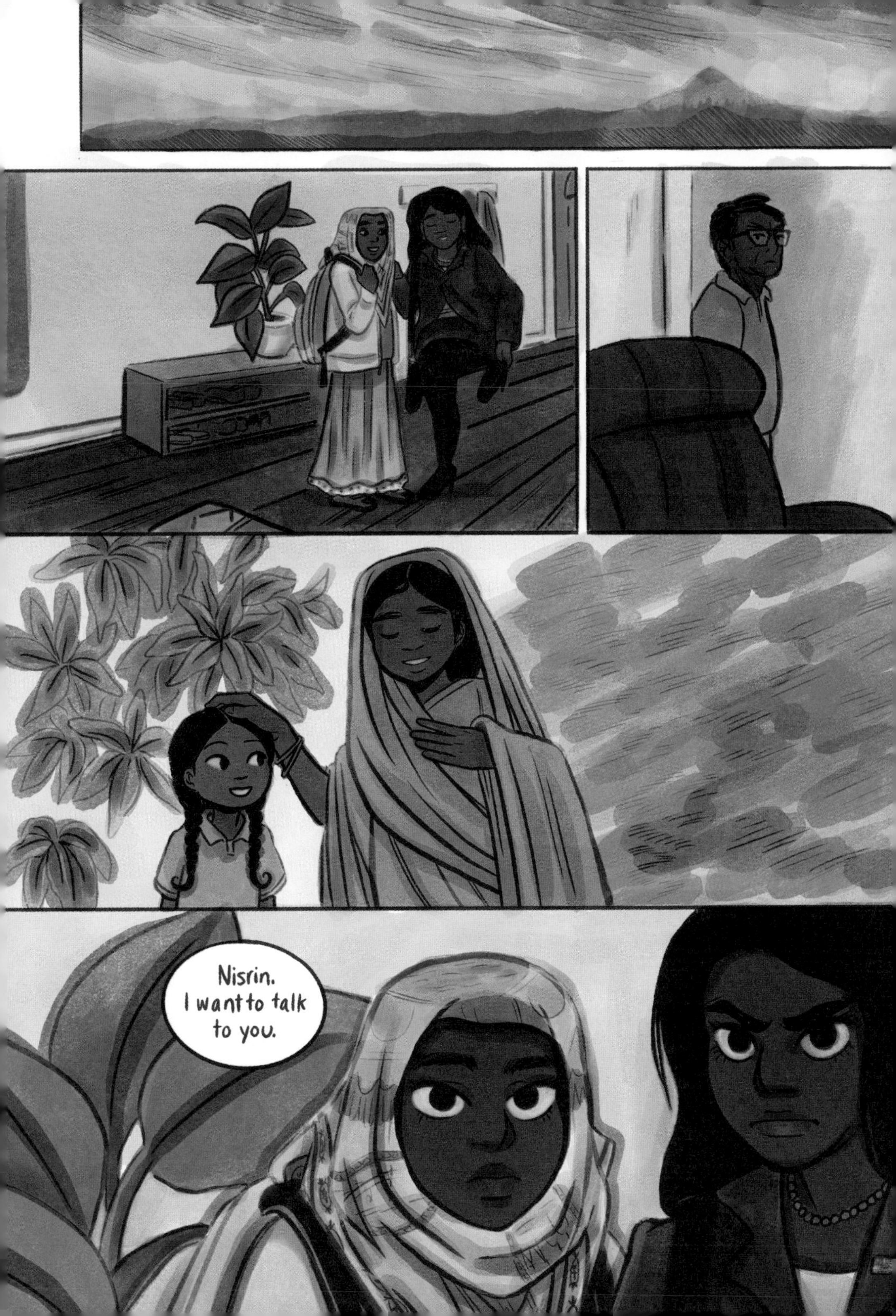
Nisrin. I want to talk to you.

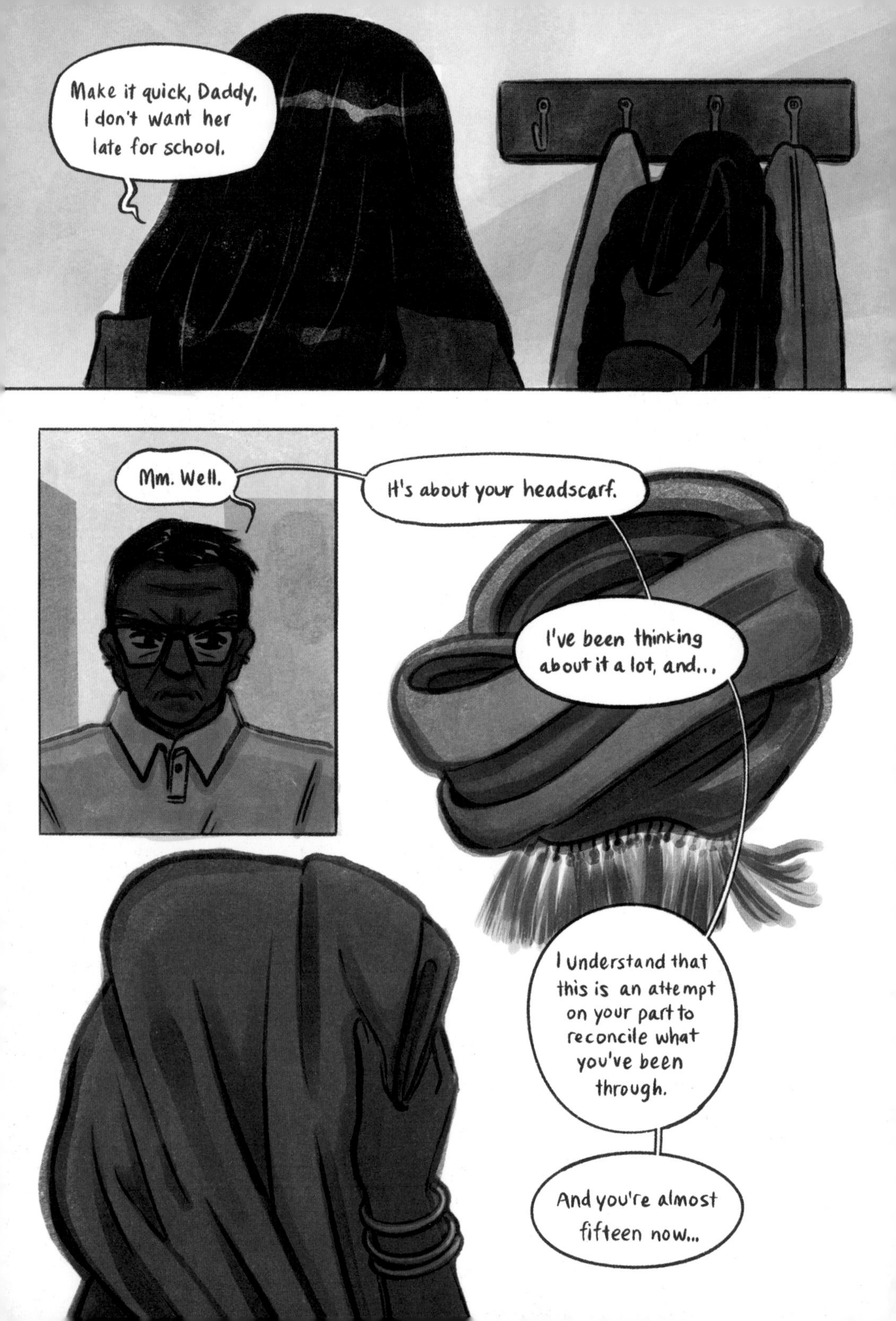
Make it quick, Daddy, I don't want her late for school.
Mm. Well.
It's about your headscarf.
I've been thinking about it a lot, and...
I understand that this is an attempt on your part to reconcile what you've been through.
And you're almost fifteen now...

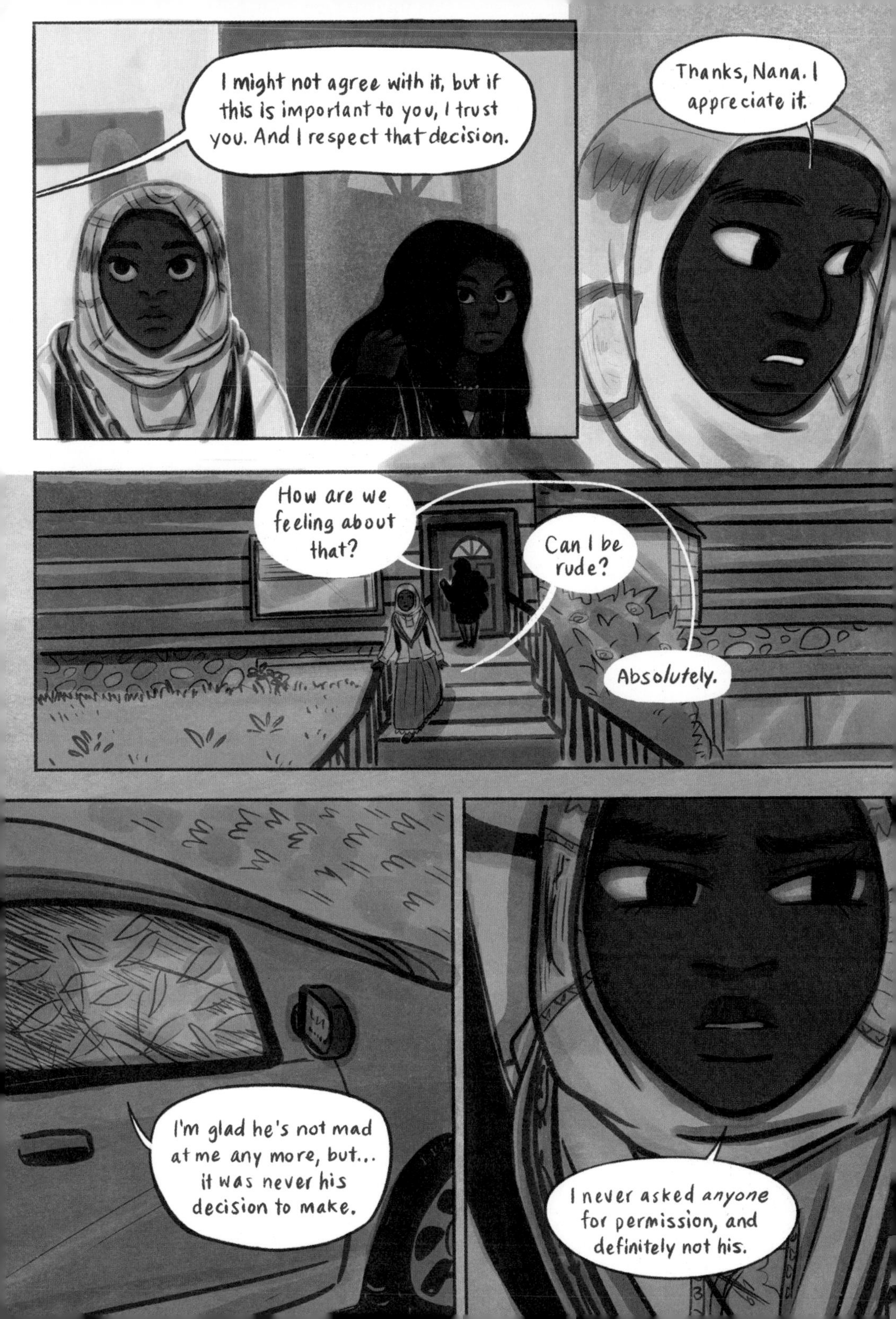

I might not agree with it, but if this is important to you, I trust you. And I respect that decision.
Thanks, Nana. I appreciate it.
How are we feeling about that?
Can I be rude?
Absolutely.
I'm glad he's not mad at me any more, but... it was never his decision to make.
I never asked *anyone* for permission, and definitely not his.

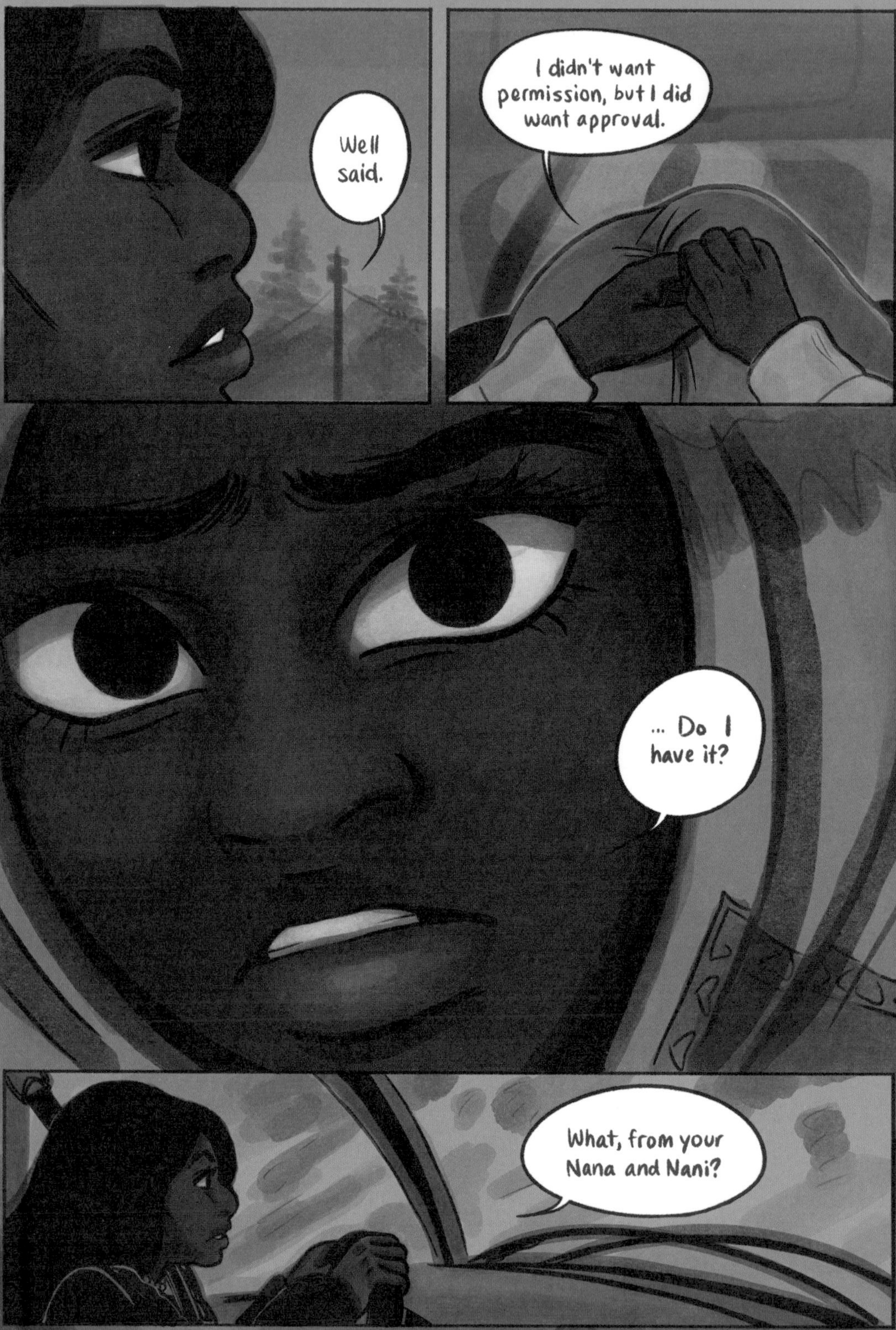
Well said.
I didn't want permission, but I did want approval.
... Do I have it?
What, from your Nana and Nani?

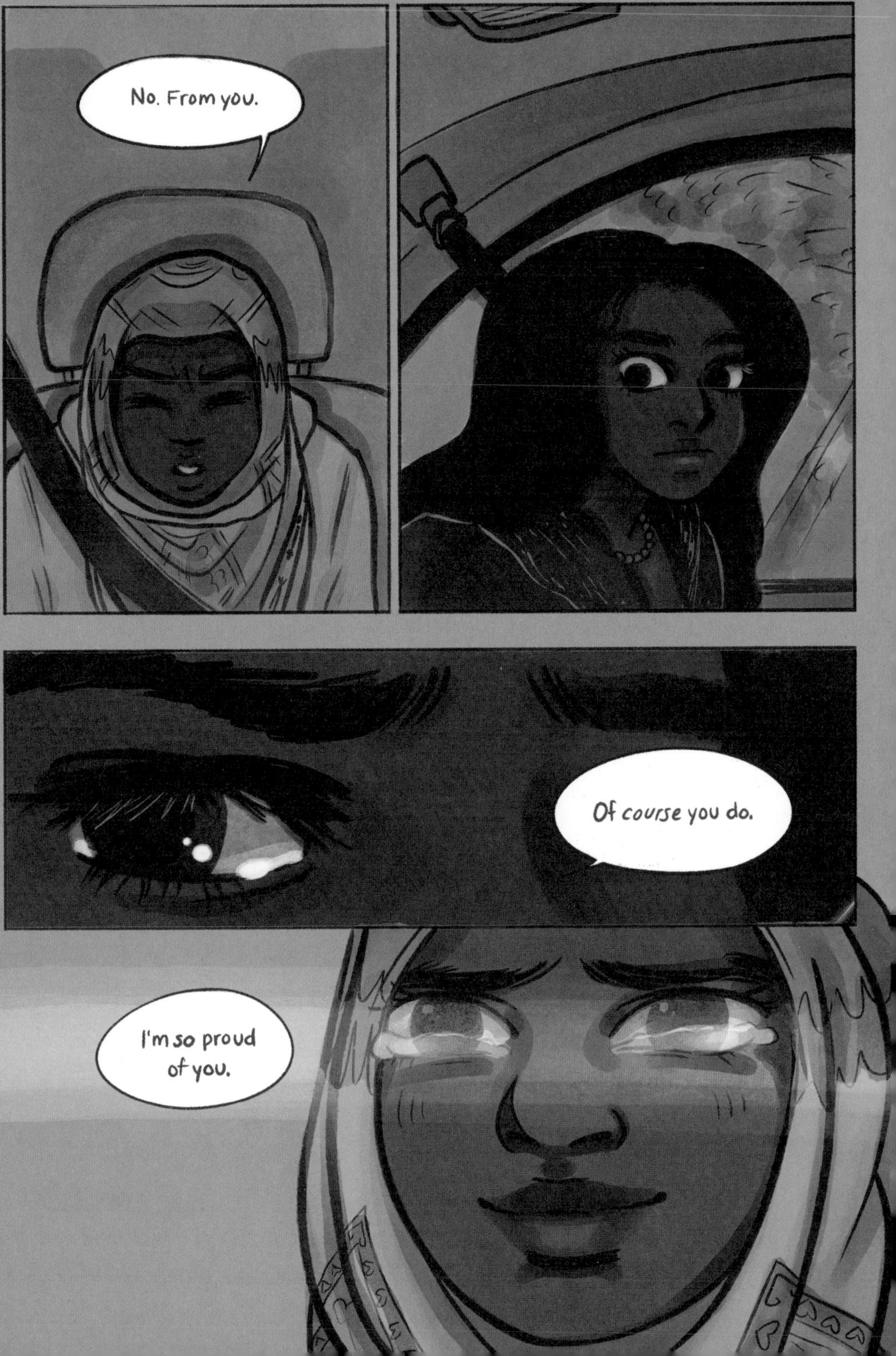
No. From you.
Of course you do.
I'm so proud of you.

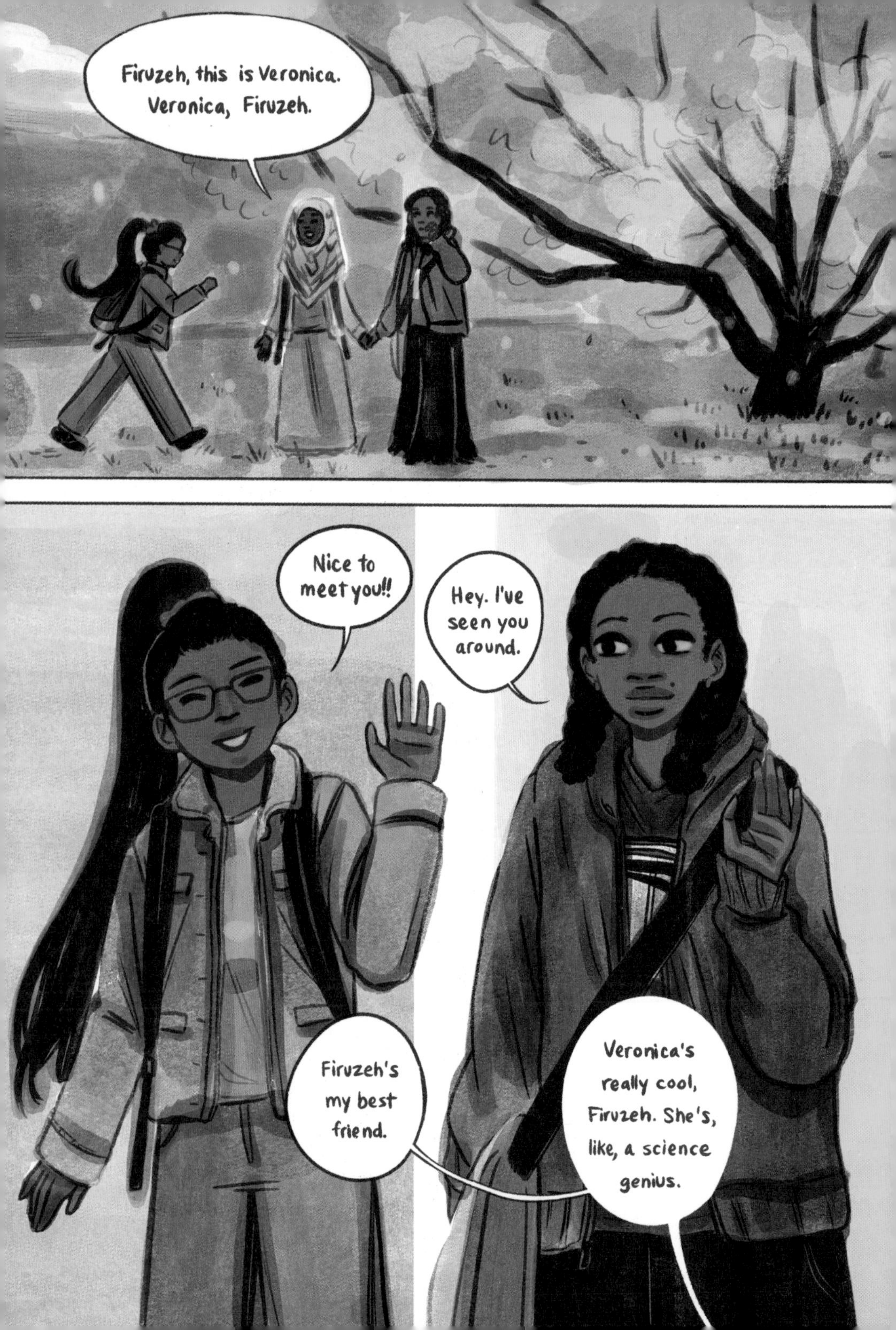
Firuzeh, this is Veronica. Veronica, Firuzeh.
Nice to meet you!!
Hey. I've seen you around.
Firuzeh's my best friend.
Veronica's really cool, Firuzeh. She's, like, a science genius.

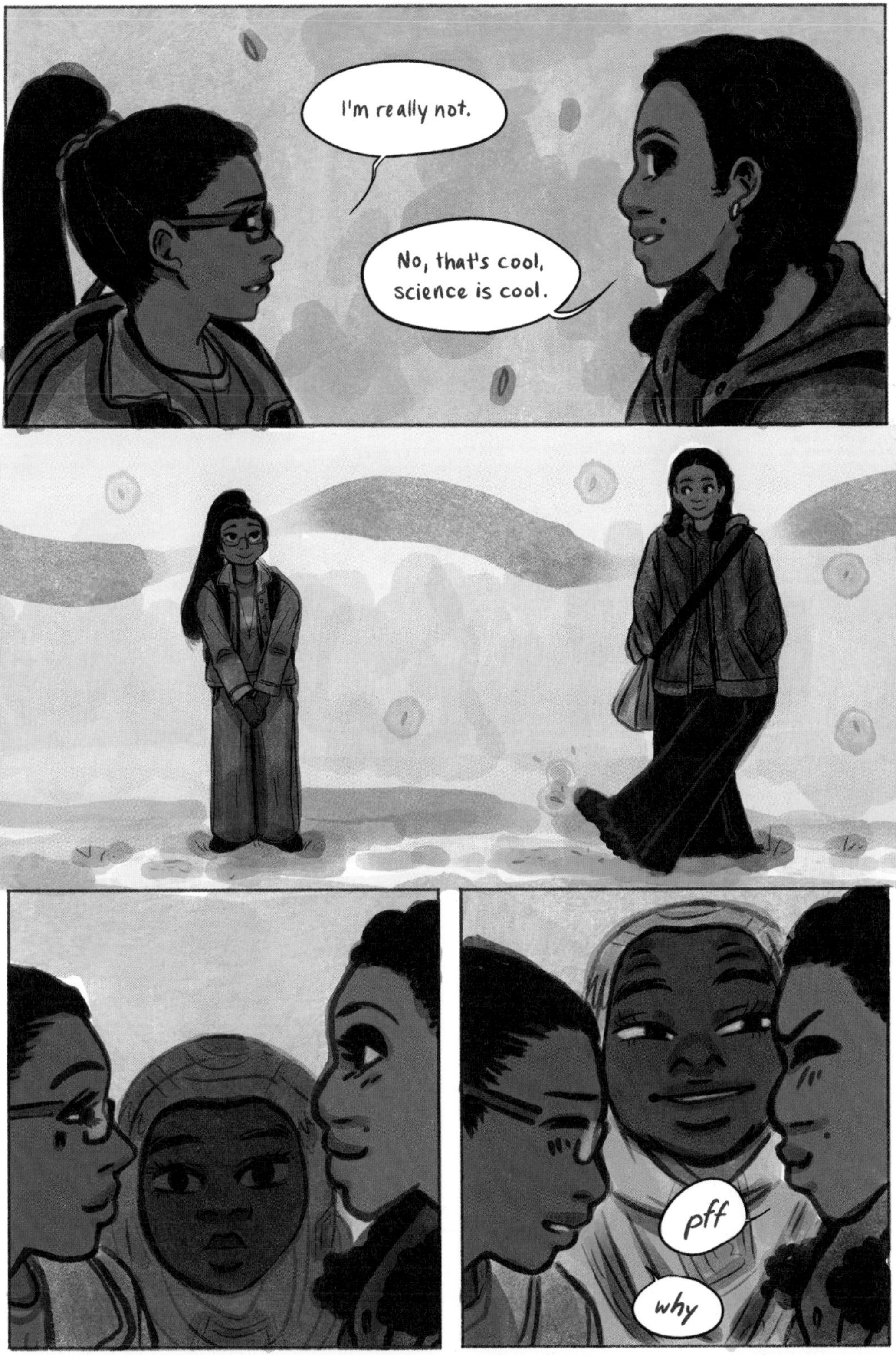
I'm really not.
No, that's cool, science is cool.
pff
why

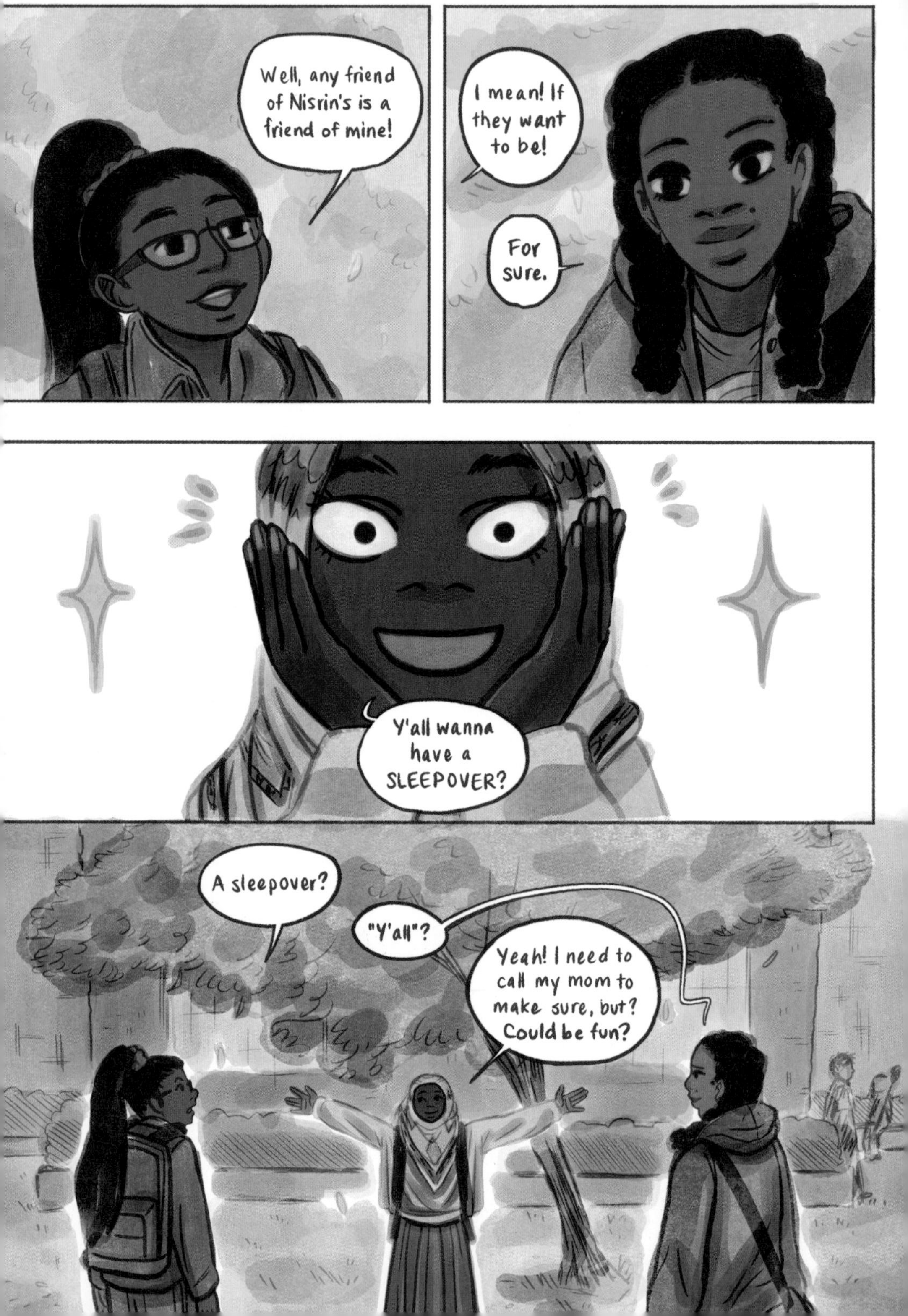

Well, any friend of Nisrin's is a friend of mine!
I mean! If they want to be!
For sure.
Y'all wanna have a SLEEPOVER?
A sleepover?
"Y'all"?
Yeah! I need to call my mom to make sure, but? Could be fun?

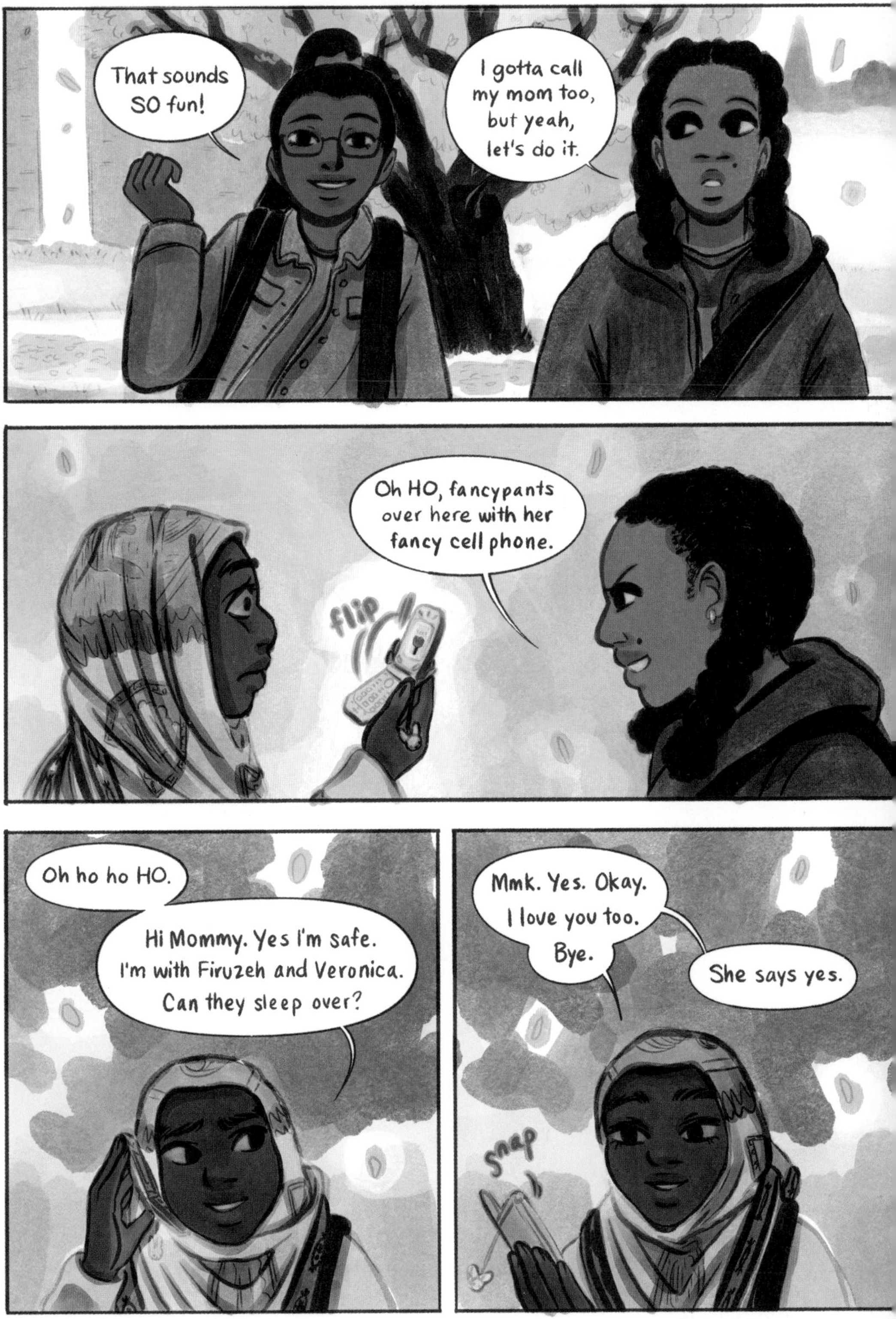
That sounds SO fun!
I gotta call my mom too, but yeah, let's do it.
Oh HO, fancypants over here with her fancy cell phone.
flip
Oh ho ho HO.
Hi Mommy. Yes I'm safe. I'm with Firuzeh and Veronica. Can they sleep over?
Mmk. Yes. Okay. I love you too. Bye.
snap
She says yes.

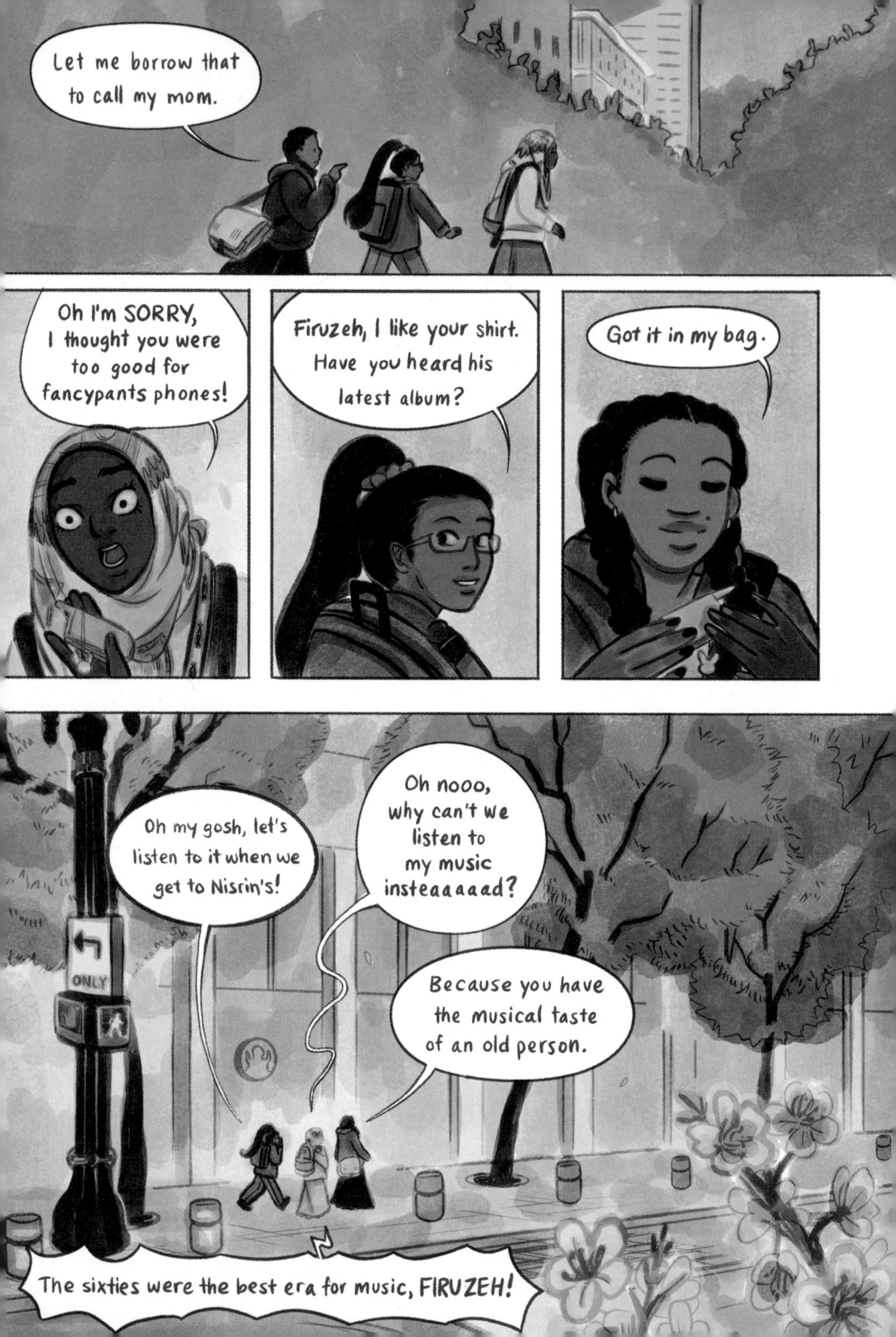
Let me borrow that to call my mom.
Oh I'm SORRY, I thought you were too good for fancypants phones!
Firuzeh, I like your shirt. Have you heard his latest album?
Got it in my bag.
Oh my gosh, let's listen to it when we get to Nisrin's!
Oh nooo, why can't we listen to my music insteaaaaad?
Because you have the musical taste of an old person.
The sixties were the best era for music, FIRUZEH!
ONLY

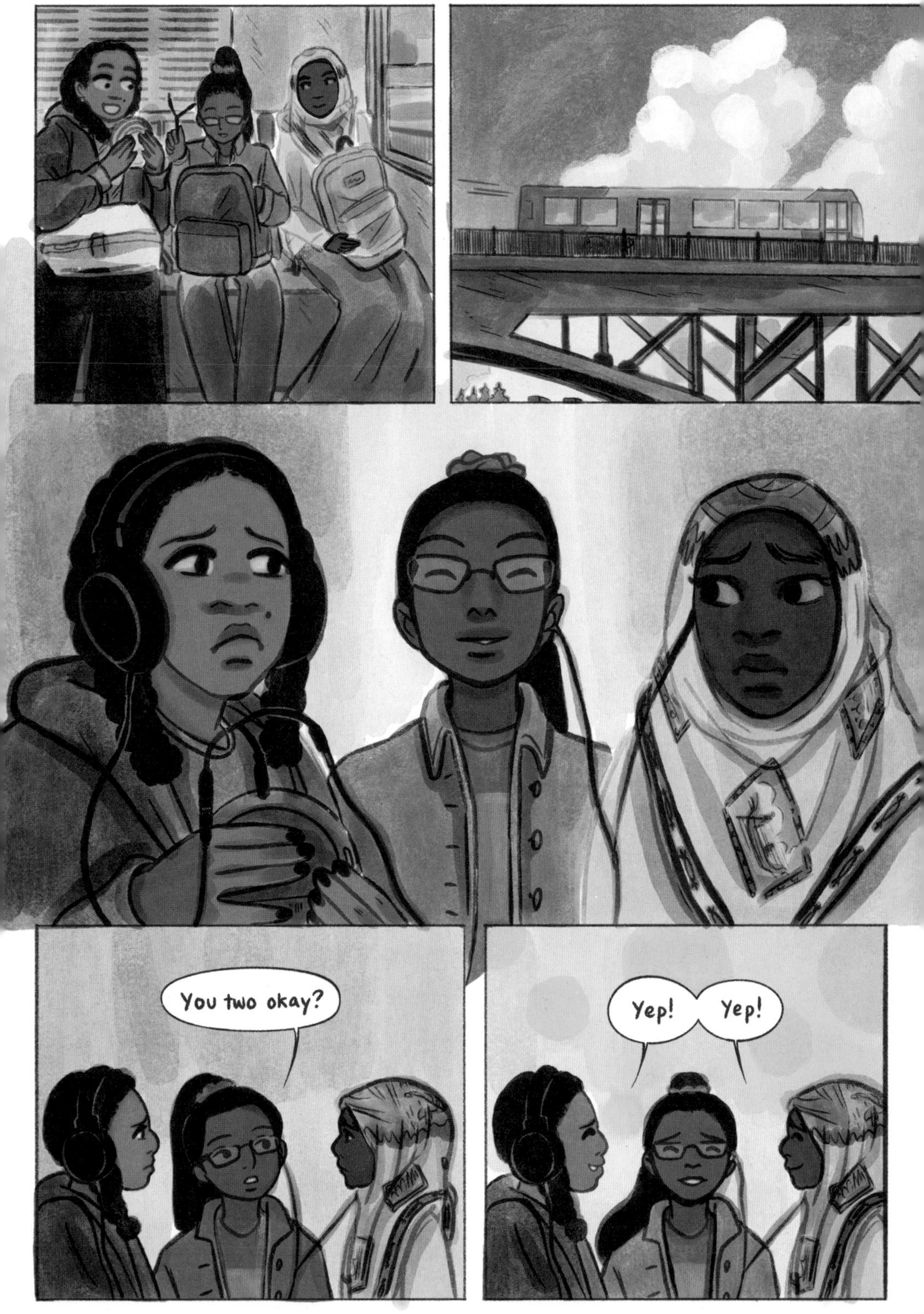
You two okay?
Yep!
Yep!

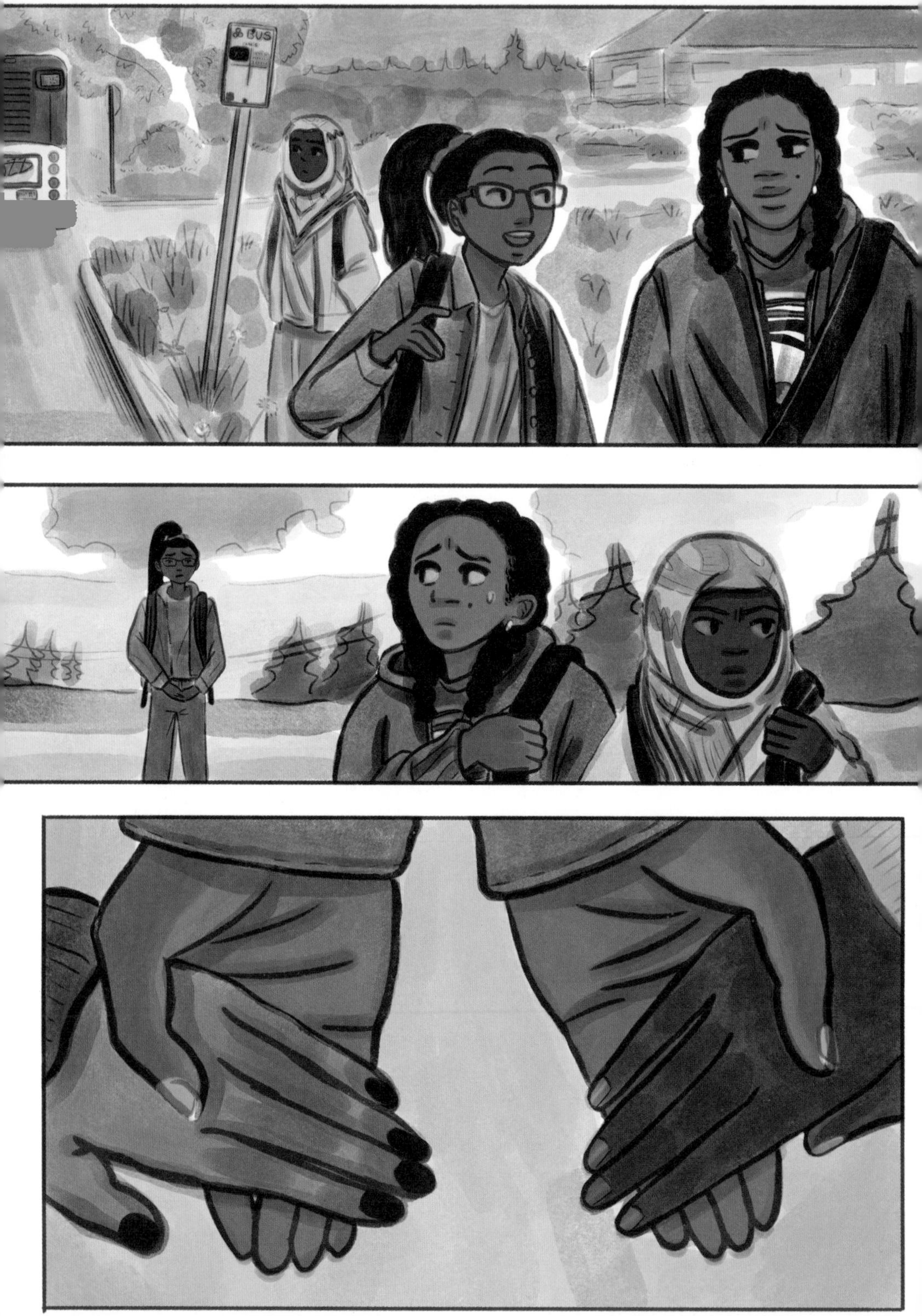
BUS

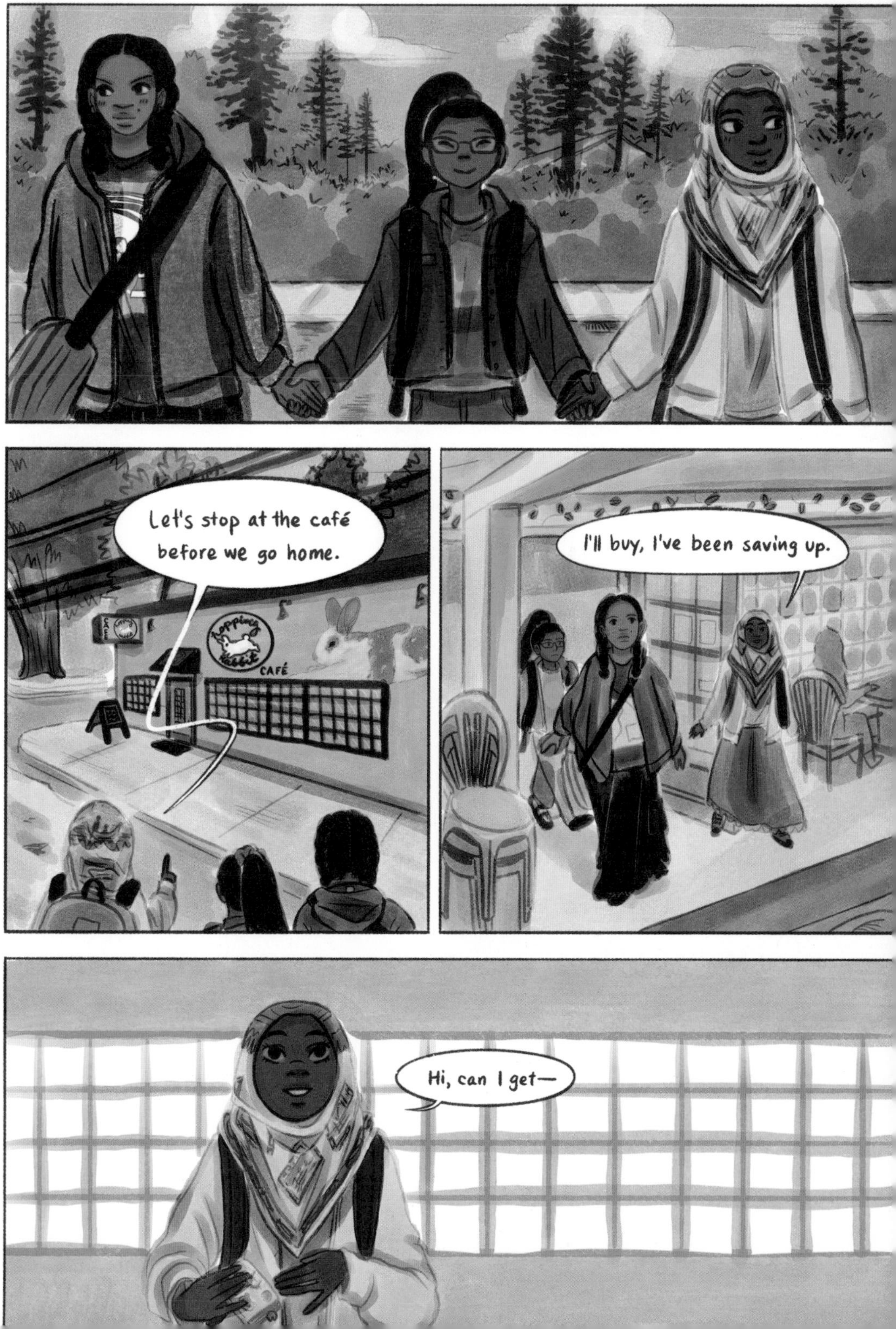
Let's stop at the café before we go home.
Hopping Rabbit CAFÉ
I'll buy, I've been saving up.
Hi, can I get—

...

Do you need a minute to decide?

No. Sorry. I like your scarf.

$3.25 $1.15   whipp
$4.25   bacon le   nato.. $4.75   roran
$6.00   croissant $3.75

Aww, thank you!

I like yours!

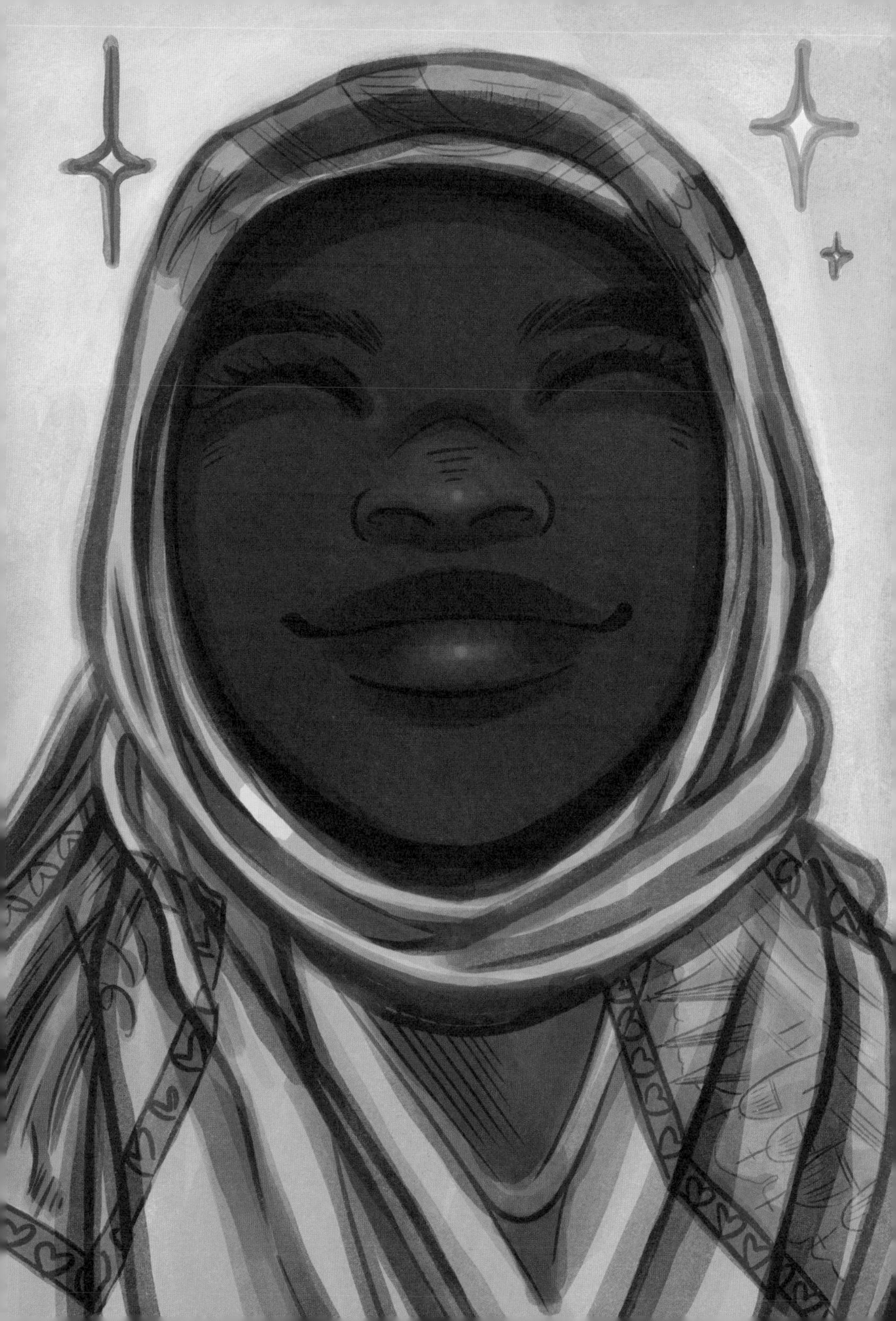

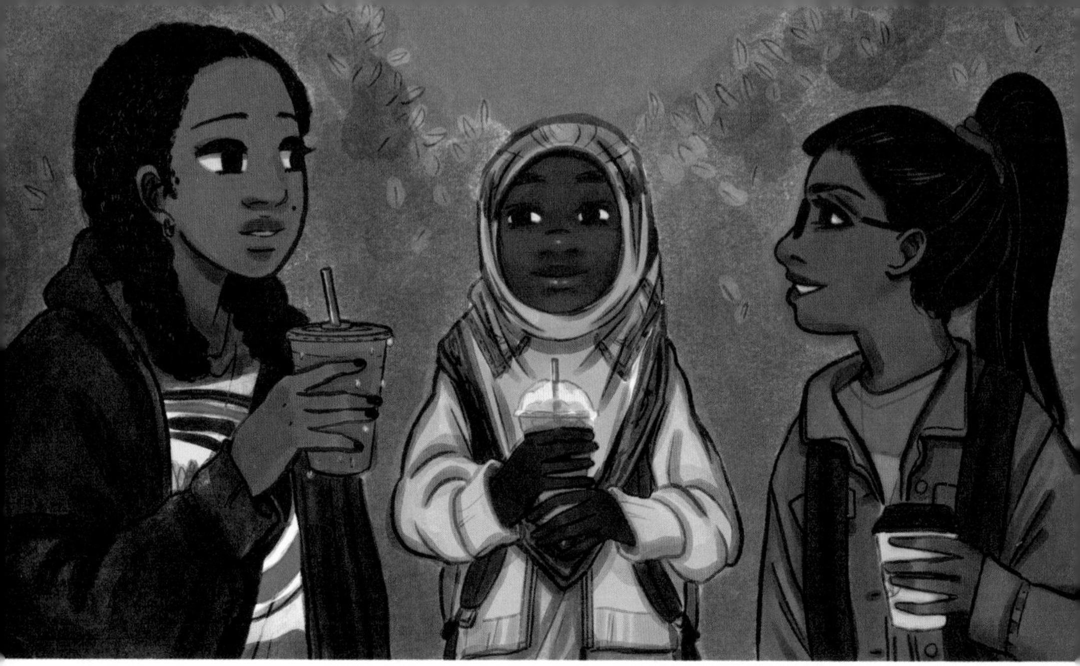

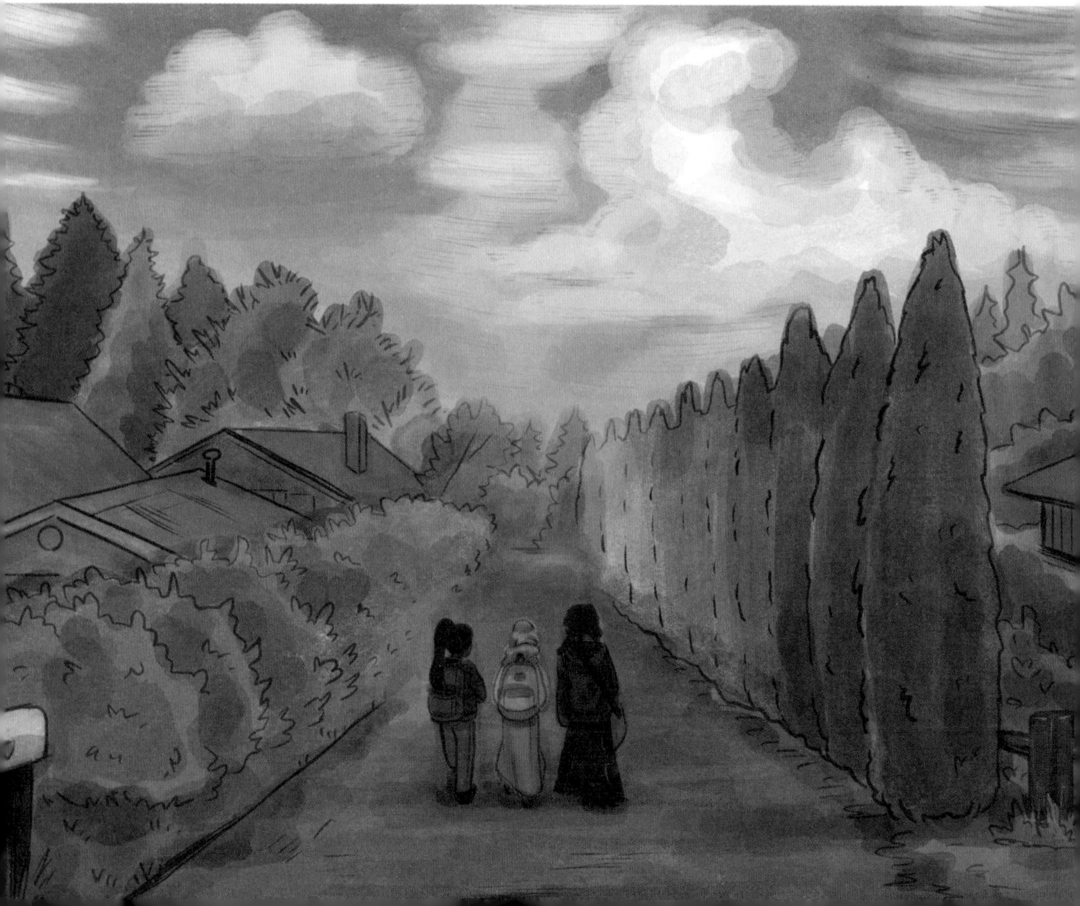

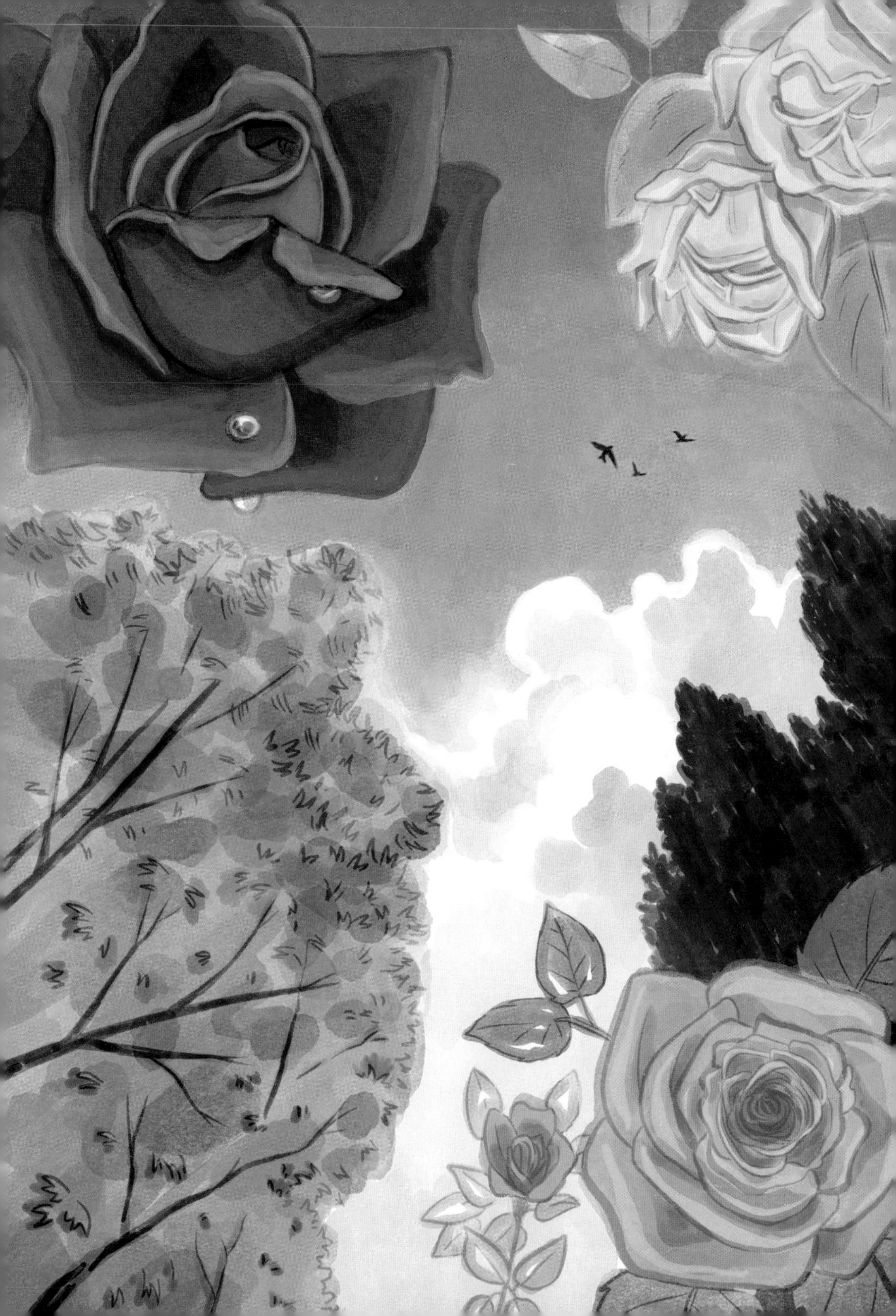

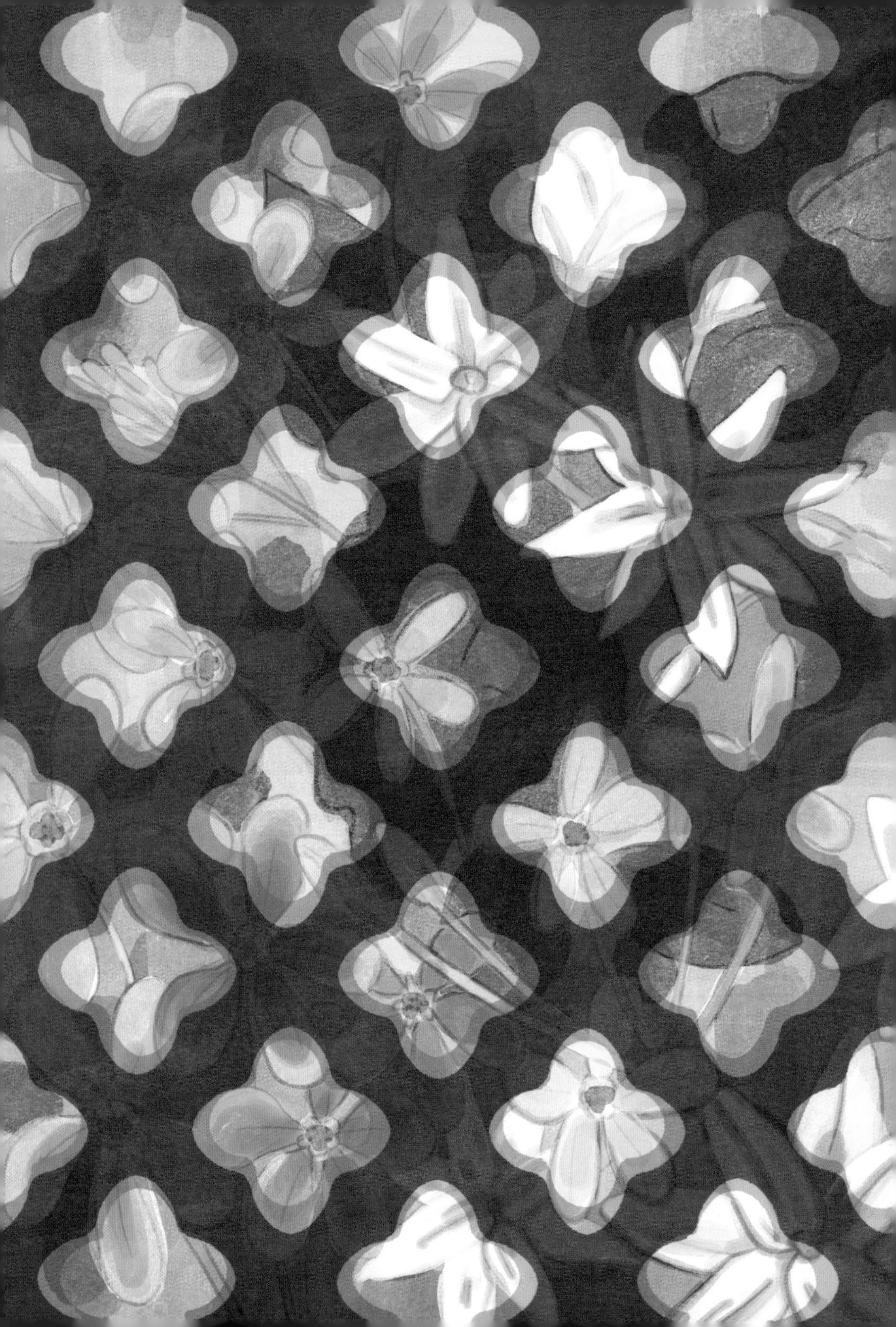

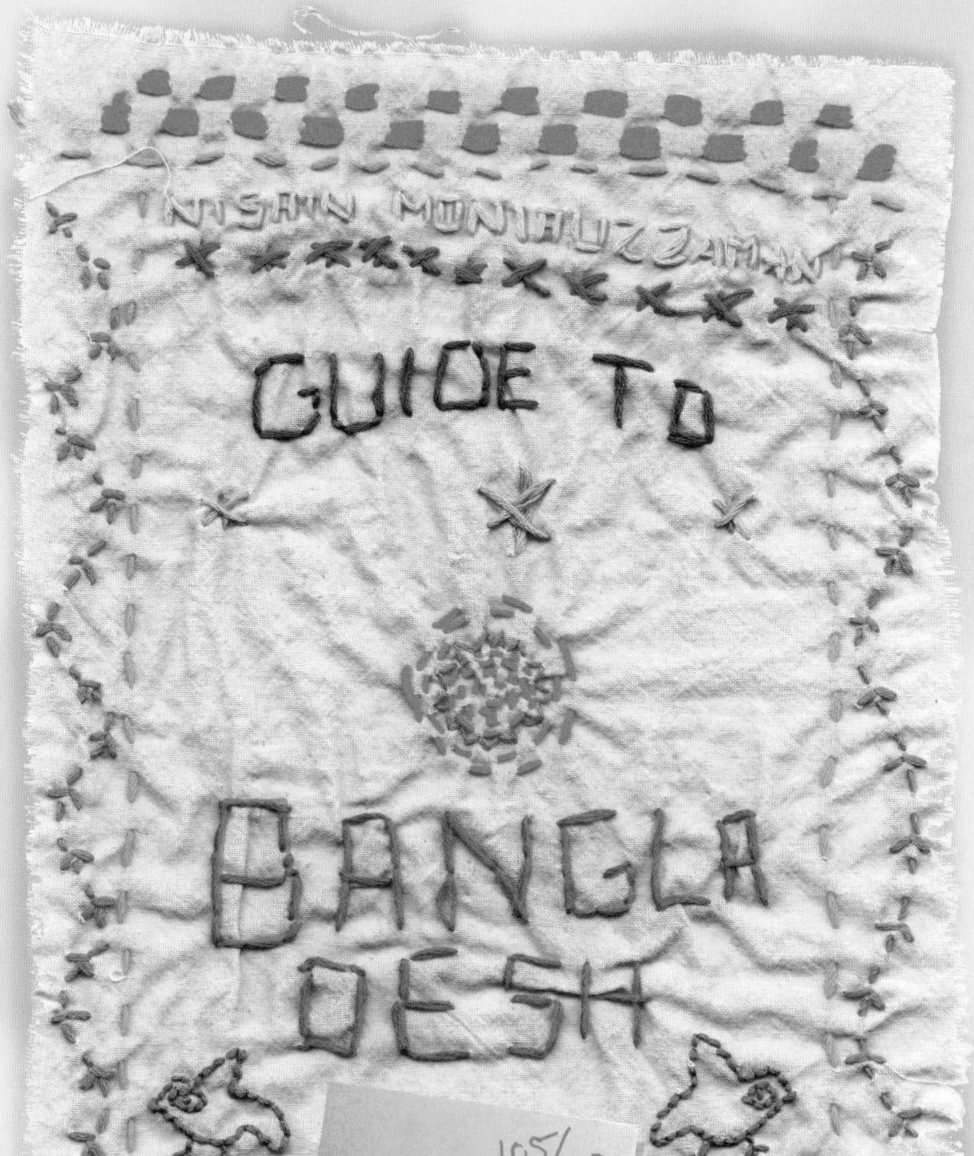
GUIDE TO
BANGLA
DESH
105/100
Nisrin-
excellent work
& esp love the
"kantha" work —
I hope to visit
someday!
Ms. M

Nisrin Moniruzzaman
Language Arts 8
Ms Mayorena
May 21st, 2002

BANGLADESH

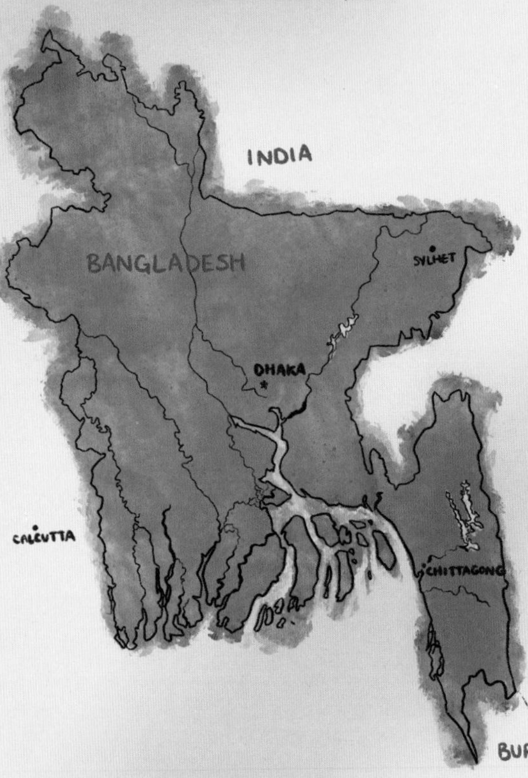
INDIA
BANGLADESH
SYLHET
DHAKA
CALCUTTA
CHITTAGONG
BURMA
Fig.1

My family is from the People's Republic of Bangladesh. Bangladesh was established in 1971 and is nestled between the countries of India and Burma (Myanmar, Fig.1). The national language of Bangladesh is Bangla (Bengali).[1]

Bangladesh's currency is the *taka* (Fig. 2) and their GDP in 2001 was 2.9 trillion Bangladeshi Taka ($54 billion).[2] Bangladesh's main export has traditionally been jute fiber. However, in 2001 clothing accounted for 53% of Bangladeshi exported goods.[3]

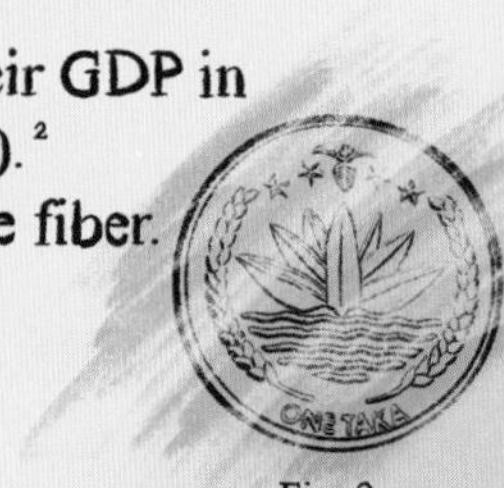
ONE TAKA
Fig. 2

GOVERNMENT

The People's Republic of Bangladesh is a parliamentary democracy with an elected Parliament, President (elected by Parliament), and Prime Minister (appointed by the President).' The Constitution was ratified in 1972, but because of several military coups, has not always been historically enforced. In 1991, parliamentary democracy was reestablished and elections have been held since then.'

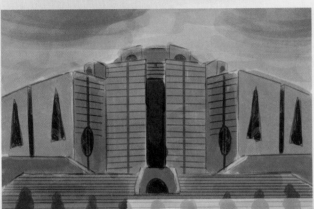

Bangladesh's National Parliament House (Jatiya Sangsad Bhaban, Fig. 3), located in the capital, Dhaka, is one of the biggest parliament buildings in the world. It was conceived while Bangladesh was still East Pakistan by Louis Khan and finished in 1982.'

Fig. 3

A note from Priya:

The Bangladesh Liberation War and 1971 Genocide

When I was growing up in the 90s, we did not talk about the war. I overheard my mom recording a speech for class in which she described experiencing it as a seven year old. I was around the same age when I eavesdropped on this and it stayed with me forever. She described hiding under a bed with her mom and baby brother, and how one of the Pakistan Army's rape squads tried to break down the door. They couldn't and eventually gave up. She considered this a miracle, because the door was not very strong. Later, when they escaped in secret, her mom (my nani) told her not to go above decks of the boat. My mom did anyway and the river was so clogged with corpses, she couldn't see the water.

Operation Searchlight

Later, I learned that my family had survived something called Operation Searchlight. In order to curb Bengali resistance against their rule, the Pakistan Army planned Operation Searchlight for March 25–April 10 of 1971. The President of Pakistan, Yahya Khan, said, "Kill three million of them and the rest will eat out of our hands." They especially targeted intellectuals and Dhaka University, where my nana worked.

More and more people have come forward with their stories and history, and there is much more information in English than when I (and Nisrin) was a kid. We will learn more as time goes on. To the genocide deniers: Your lies will never silence the survivors.

ENVIRONMENT

Ganges
Brahmaputra
Gangetic Plain
Meghna
Padma
Bay of Bengal

*Now known as climate change-p

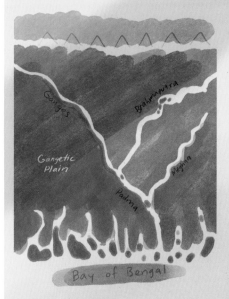

Bandgladesh is a country of rivers in a tropical climate. It is a delta made up of the Ganges, Brahmaputra, and Meghna rivers and is part of the Gangetic Plain, which flows from Pakistan, across India, and into the Bay of Bengal. Flooding is common during and after the Monsoon season.[6]

Global warming*is threatening much of the Bangladeshi environment, not only through sea level rise but also through rising salinity, which kills crops and freshwater fish.[7]

Farming is very important in Bangladesh, and rice is grown throughout the country. Tea is traditionally grown in the hills of Sylhet.[8] While urban areas are growing, there are thousands of small villages, and the biggest city is Dhaka. Bangladesh's population in 2001 was 129.3 million.[9]

SEASONS

গ্রীষ্ম	Grissho Summer	mid-April to mid-June	
বর্ষা	Borsha Monsoon Season	mid-June to mid-August	
শরৎ	Shorud Fall	mid-August to mid-October	
হেমন্ত	Hemont Dry Season	mid-October to mid-December	
শীত	Sheet Winter	mid-December to mid February	
বসন্ত	Boshount Spring	mid-February to mid-April	

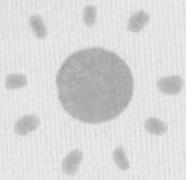

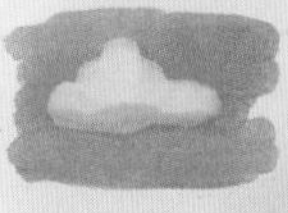

Bangladesh is the eastern part of the region of Bengal and shares many cultural characteristics, such as language and folk traditions. One of these folk traditions is the embroidery I used for the cover of this report. This embroidery is called kantha work and traditionally is used to decorate and even mend clothes!

PLANTS AND ANIMALS

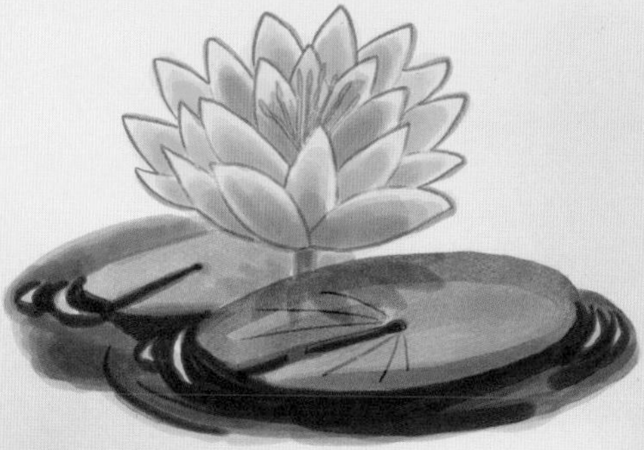

The national flower of Bangladesh is the water lily. The jackfruit is the national fruit, and the mango is the national tree. The national animal is the Bengal tiger.[9] Sadly, Bengal tigers are endangered![10]

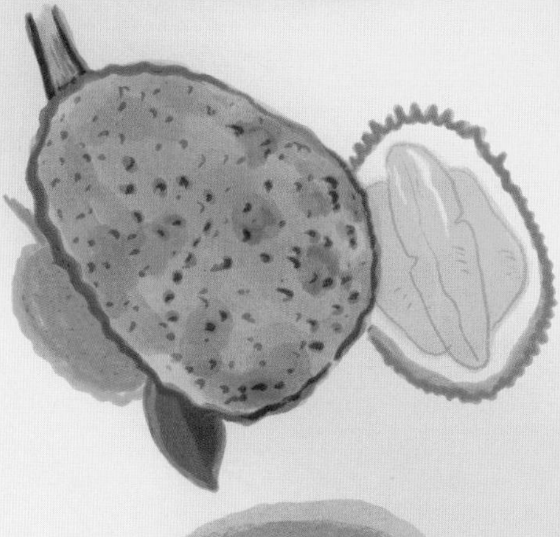

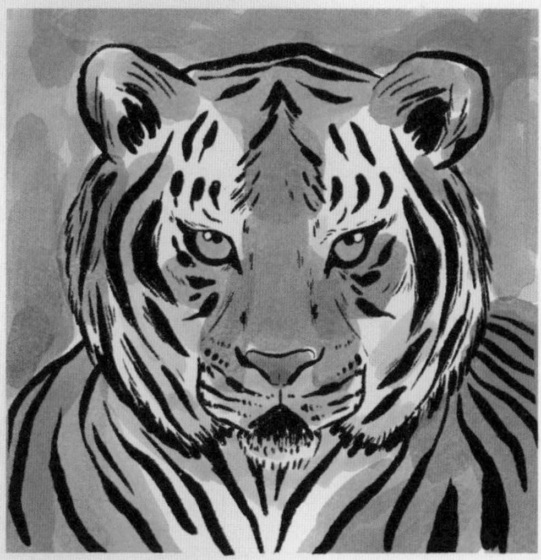

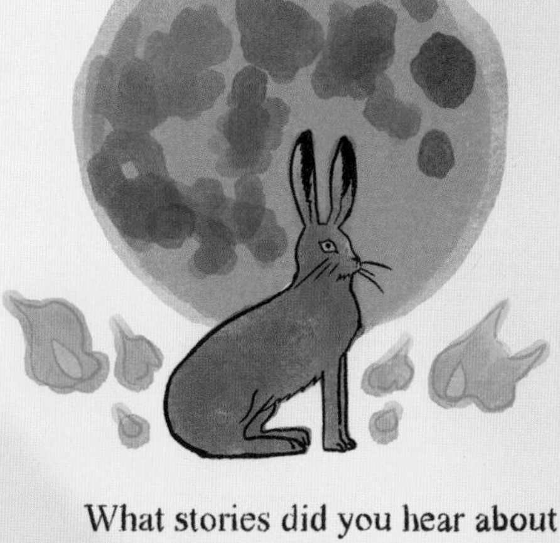

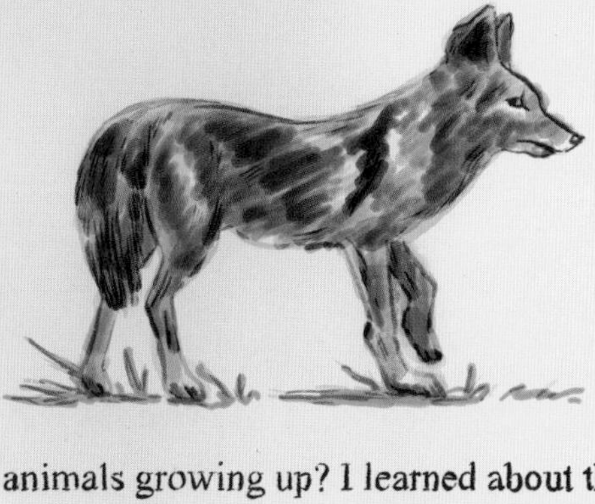

What stories did you hear about animals growing up? I learned about the noble hare in the moon, mischievious monkeys, and very stupid tigers. Tigers can be very scary in real life, but in Bengali folk tales they get into lots of trouble, tricked by other animals (usually a jackal).

BANGLA

The Bengali Language is known as **Bangla** and is the fifth most popular language in the world. Bangla is spoken by Bengali people all over the world, most commonly in Bangladesh and India.[11]

Some common Bangla phrases and words are:

Hello! (Hindu)
Nomoshkar

Hello! (Muslim)
Slamaleykum

How are you?	Apni kemon acho?
I'm good.	Ami bhalo ache.
What is your name?	Apnar nam ki?
My name is ____.	Amar nam ____.

Yes
Henh

No
Na

Mango
Aam

Me
Ami

You (regular)
Apni

You (intimate)
Tumi

MOTHER LANGUAGE DAY

Ekushey February (21 February) is Mother Language Day, celebrating the Bengali Language Movement (along with the preservation of all mother languages). On February 21st, 1952, several students were killed at Dhaka University. They were protesting the suppression of Bangla by the government. International Mother Language Day was offically adopted by the UN this year (2002). [12]

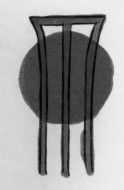

POETRY IN BANGLADESH

Poetry is incredibly important to the Bengali people. Rabindranath Tagore (pronounced "Takoor") is our most famous poet, and the first ten lines of his poem *Amar Shonar Bangla* is the national anthem of Bangladesh. [13] Poetry does not translate well from Bangla to English, so if you want to properly read Bengali poetry, my grandfather says you should learn Bangla first.

AMAR SHONAR BANGLA
(Partial)

Amar shonar Bangla, ami
tomay bhalobhashi,
Chirodin tomar akash, tomar
batash, amar prane bajay bashi.
O Ma, phagune tor amer bone
gharane pagol kore,
Mori hay, hay re— O Ma,
Oghrane tor bhora khete ami ki
dekhechhi modhur hashi.

MY GOLDEN BENGAL
(Partial)

My golden Bengal, I love you.
Forever your skies, your air set my
heart in tune as if it were a flute.
Oh Ma, the smell of the mango
orchard in Spring drives me crazy,
What a thrill— Oh Ma,
In the dry autumn, time sees sweet
smiles all through the ripe paddy
fields.

FOOD

Bangladesh's main crop is rice. Rice is harvested in all seasons and grows in paddies. People in Bangladesh eat lots of rice, lentils (dal), bread (parathas), fish, and vegetables like eggplant and okra.[15]

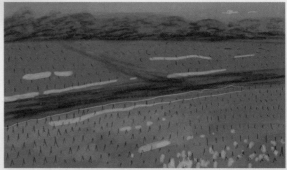

Rice paddy in Bangladesh

I love Bengali food! Here's a recipe for my mom's beef curry.

1 tsp cumin seeds
chop up onion
chop 2 potatoes
ground beef
ORGANIC
1 tbsp turmeric
TURM ERIC
1 tsp cumin
CUMIN
salt
6 cloves garlic
(chop)
1 tsp ginger
1 fry seeds
med-hi heat
2 add onions and fry
med-hi heat
3 add ginger, garlic, and spices (don't burn!)
med heat
4 add beef
high heat
5 stir til beef is browned!
med-hi heat
6 add potatoes and water, cover
low heat

7 Cook until potatoes are soft

Thanks Mom!

8 Serve with rice

CLOTHING

shari

Bangladesh has produced textiles for the West since the late 1970s.[1] Our own style of clothing involves wrapping long pieces of cloth around the body in various ways. Many women all over South Asia wear the shari (sometimes anglicized shadi in Bangla)[2], a dress made by wrapping a long piece of cotton, silk, or nylon around the waist and draping it over the shoulder. Men wear a piece of clothing called a dhoti, which wraps around the legs and tucks into the waist. There are many ways to wrap these items, and sometimes women will wrap the shari like pants to make working outside easier.[3]

shalwar kameez

People also wear shalwar kameez, which was introduced to Bengal (possibly) by the Mughals in the sixteenth century and have become more popular since. Girls like me wear them to school as a uniform. "Shalwar" comes from the word for pants in Farsi.[4] "Kameez" means shirt. Girls and women wear a scarf called an "orna" ("dupatta" in India)[5] with shalwar kameez. It's both fashionable and modest.

orna   hijab

HEAD COVERINGS

Some women cover their head with the pallu (train) of their shari or with their orna, to be modest or respectful. An orna (or any scarf) can also be used for hijab (the religious head covering). The women in my family do not wear hijab, but I have cousins and aunts who do.

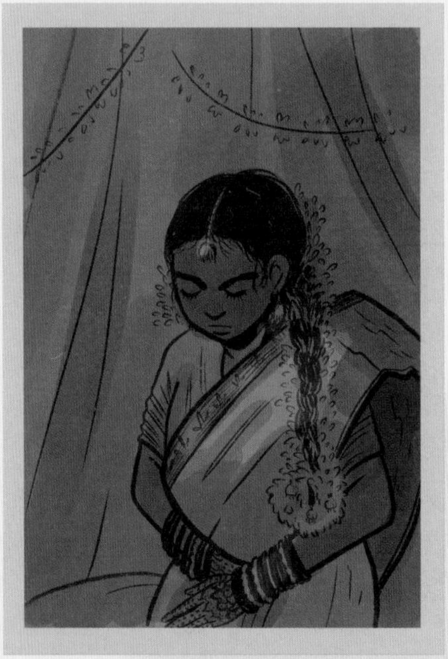

My nani at her wedding in 1962.

MY FAMILY

My mom's name is Rani Khan. She was born in Bangladesh in 1963 to Amira and Muzzammil Moniruzzaman. My mom moved to the United States for college in the 1980s and her parents followed when I was born in 1988.

Families in Bangladesh are traditionally patriarchal, but not the way Western European families are. A man controls the house but his mother runs it. If you are a girl, you marry into your husband's family and your mother-in-law has the final say in everything. Then if you have a son, you become the head of *his* household when *he* marries.

My family is not like this. For one thing, my mom is not married. For another, my grandfather (Nana) is a feminist. My grandmother (Nani) runs the household and my mom and Nana make the money. My nana is a sociologist and my mom is a financial specialist. Sometimes my nani works part-time at a department store.

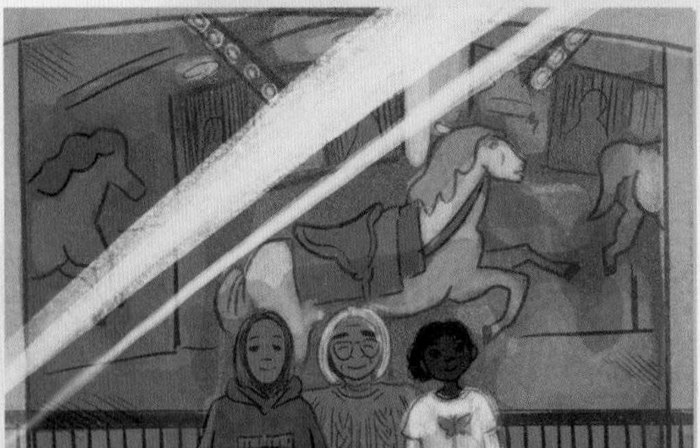

My best friend Firuzeh Brown, my nani, and me at Oaks Park over spring break.

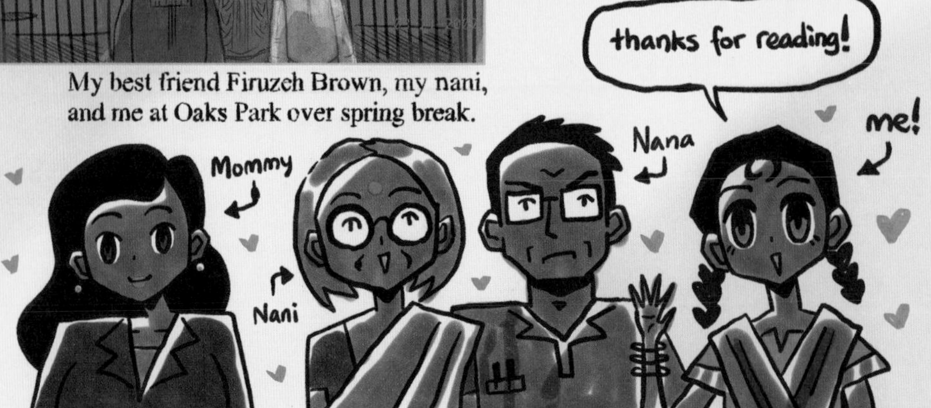
thanks for reading!
me!
Nana
Mommy
Nani

ACKNOWLEDGMENTS

Thank you Steenz, for knowing I could do this and believing in the project. Thank you Anjali, for your encouragement, enthusiasm, knowledge, and help. Thank you Charlotte, for fighting for this book and holding me to your highest standard. Thank you Wendy Xu, for insisting I get an agent. Thank you Shivana Sookdeo, for insisting I'm legit. Thank you Ashanti, Autumn, Bianca, Lin, Jade, Jem, Jo, Marian, Mikhaila, Olive, Shannon, Shing, and Sunmi, for your friendship and inspiration. Thank you Carrie McClain, Claire Folkman, and Kelly Phillips for giving me my first shots. Thank you Claire Napier, for doing the first edits and giving me the confidence to move forward. Thank you Morgan, for your invaluable hard work. Thank you Niki Smith, for making the "Literary agents who represent graphic novels" list. Thank you to every person who worked to get this book published, whether we met or not. Thank you Eri and Mary. Thank you E, e, M, and M for supporting me when no one else would and for keeping me fed, sheltered, and loved in my worst moments. ♥

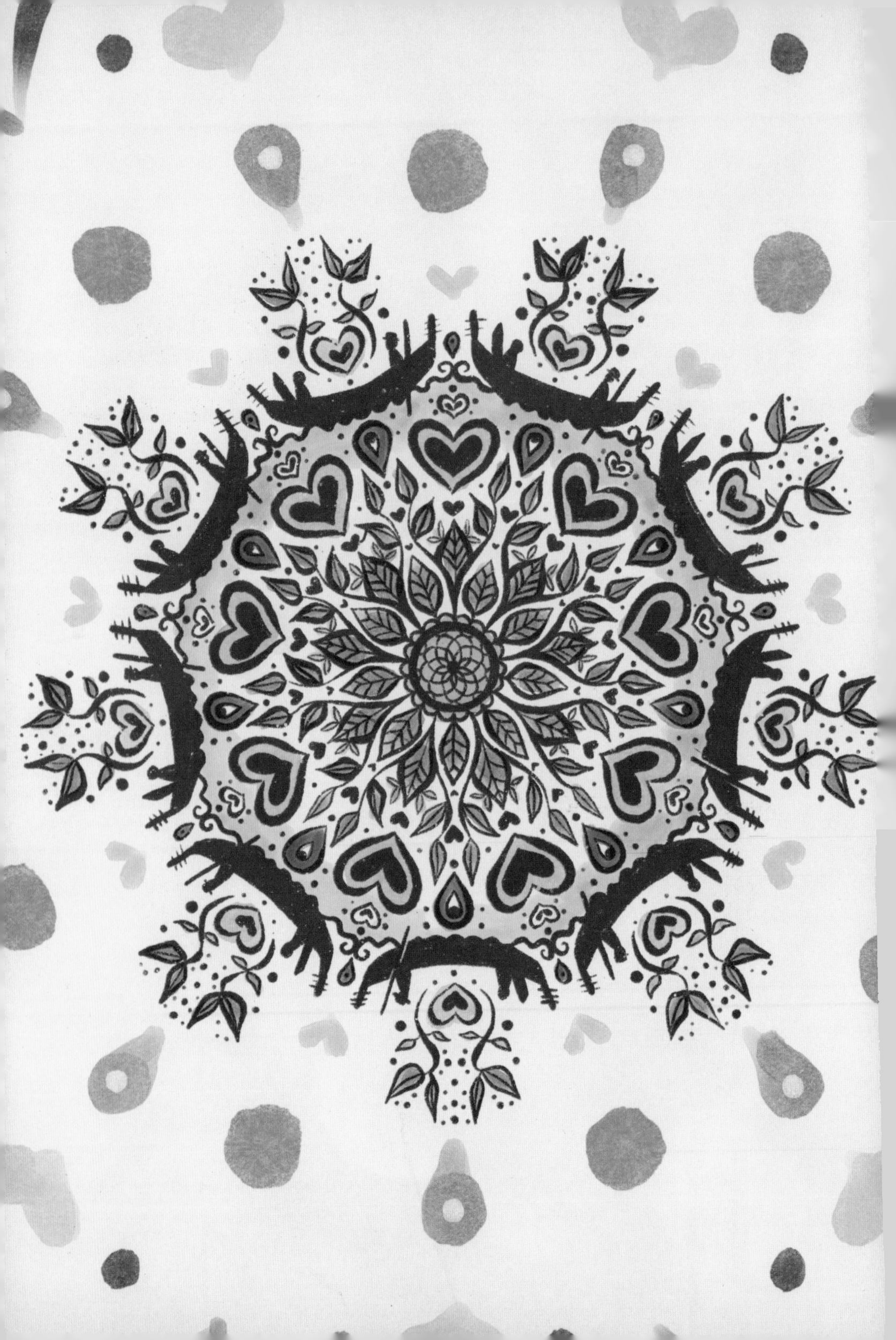